# THE SINS OF THEIR FATHERS

## Gilda O'Neill

PARAGON

CHIVERS PRESS
BATH

First published 2002
by
William Heinemann
This Large Print edition published 2002 by
Chivers Press
by arrangement with
Random House UK Group Ltd

ISBN 0 7540 9225 9

British Library Cataloguing in Publication Data available

Printed and bound in Great Britain by
BOOKCRAFT, Midsomer Norton, Somerset

For Ali Gunn

# ACKNOWLEDGEMENTS

And with my special thanks to Kate Parkin
and Kirsty Fowkes

*She knew Gabriel O'Donnell was no angel, but this time it was different. No matter what lies he tried to tell her, or how he tried to twist it, Eileen was sure that it was Luke who was telling the truth. That was how it all started: with Pete Mac making the biggest mistake of his whole stupid life, because Gabriel had asked—no, he had* insisted—*that the boys take the gun.*

# November 1960

# CHAPTER ONE

Commercial Street, the broad thoroughfare linking Whitechapel to Shoreditch, had been built in a grand moment of Victorian moralising, optimism and innovation. Designed to slice its way through one of the East End's most notorious rookeries, the idealistic intention behind its creation was the sweeping away of overcrowding, disease and corruption, in the foul and crime-ridden slums that were so uncomfortably close to the City of London—the fabulously wealthy hub of the greatest Empire ever seen. The road would literally open up the area to the light, making it available for inspection by authorities and worthies alike, allowing them to check on the feckless underclasses, who lived on their very doorstep.

Just thirty years after its completion the world's gaze would again be focused on the area. Not to admire the social and environmental improvements, but to be appalled and stunned by the brutal acts of the proto-serial killer known as Jack the Ripper, and consequently on the shameful, persistent presence of such grotesque poverty and depravity.

The bold new road had proved itself embarrassingly worthy of its name, as a shocked public realised that commerce of many different kinds took place in its shadowy environs, and, despite the best intentions and interventions of the Establishment, they would long continue to do so.

\* \* \*

3

The racing green Jaguar inched along Commercial Street in the dense fog, passing between the elegantly looming hulk of Hawksmoor's Christ Church and the squat, practical form of the Spitalfields wholesale fruit and vegetable market, at little more than a brisk walking pace.

'Still nothing?' The driver was hunched over the wheel, squinting through the windscreen, the swishing wipers doing little to aid his view.

The man in the passenger seat rubbed the heels of his thumbs into his eyes, feeling the strain of staring out into the silvery blanket of heavy, wet air.

'Not a thing.' He dropped his hands and sat up, suddenly alert. 'Hang on. Over there. Corner of Fleur-de-Lis Street.'

Brendan O'Donnell eased the motor to a halt.

A tall, plump teenager—acid yellow blouse, tight crimson skirt, and bare, corned beef legs—said something to the two girls she was standing with, then wiggled her way over to the car. She didn't seem bothered by the cold.

She rested one hand on the roof of the Jag and, with the other, released one of her breasts from her top and pressed it against the passenger window. Puckering up her fuchsia painted lips, she blew them a kiss.

'Hello, boys,' she mouthed, rubbing her breast from side to side across the window, flattening the dark brown nipple, and leaving greasy smears on the glass. 'Fancy doing business?'

Brendan signalled, with swift, angry hand movements, for his brother to wind down the

4

window.

'Who the fuck are you?' he demanded, leaning across Luke, and ducking his head to get a better look at her.

'Any one you want me to be, darling. But it'll have to be double if you want me to take on the two of you.'

Brendan looked about him as if someone had just released a bad smell. 'If you don't stick that tit away, and get off this motor—*now*—even *you* won't know who you are. So, just do up that blouse, and go and tell your mates you're all pissing off back where you came from. Got it?'

'Charming,' she said, flipping them tipsy and tottering back to her post.

Brendan watched the girls in disbelief. They obviously had no intention of moving. He looked at his watch. Half eleven. Nearly bloody dinner time. 'Where the fuck's that idiot Pete Mac?'

The whereabouts of Peter MacRiordan, Luke and Brendan's brother-in-law, were, as they so often were, a mystery.

Luke glanced at his brother. 'I wouldn't put it past the daft bastard sending them home cos of the fog.'

Brendan flung open his door. 'Wait here.' Basic rule: never leave a smart motor unattended in an unknown situation.

Luke sank down in his seat. Content to get no more involved in this than he had to.

Fists clenched in anger and ready to attack, Brendan looked about him, his actions sharp and agitated, trying to figure out what was going on. For birds to have such bottle, there had to be someone looking after them. Someone who really scared them.

And there he was. Over there, on the corner of Wheler Street.

A bull-necked, muscled up, black man in a heavy navy overcoat and suede porkpie hat, standing under the streetlight on the junction with Commercial Street. Like he had every right. Across from him stood another huddle of ropey looking toms—cheap, bottom of the market brasses, just like the one who had propositioned him and Luke. Toms that Brendan had never seen before.

Was this bloke taking the piss or what?

Brendan weighed up the situation. He wasn't scared. He'd been involved in plenty of physical stuff in his time. Bad stuff. A few years ago, when he was still in his teens, he had beaten a man to death, single-handed, on a bombsite in Stepney, and walked away without so much as a backward glance. But he wasn't stupid either. This was one very big bloke. He had to get it right. Or lose.

He took a deep breath and started to move. Fast.

'Here, you,' he hollered, jabbing his finger, steaming in. 'What the fuck do you think you're doing?'

The man frowned, and lifted his chin to one side as if in thought, then pushed his ear really close to Brendan's mouth, the shock making Brendan back off. 'Would you say that again?' His voice had the singsong lilt of the Caribbean. 'I don't think I heard you right the first time.'

Brendan recovered quickly. His finger was in the man's face. 'What, don't understand English, moosh?'

The man took off his hat, ran his hand over his head, flattening his cap of shiny, oiled curls even closer to his skull. 'Are you being impolite to me, man? Unneighbourly?'

'*Me* being impolite? You're having a grin, right?' Brendan took a moment to look him up and down. 'This, pal, is our patch. Ours. The O'Donnells. We run things round here. All of it.'

The man replaced his hat, turned down the corners of his mouth and shook his head. 'Sorry, I ain't never heard of no O'Donnells.'

Brendan didn't like this. The bloke was too confident. Maybe he wasn't alone. Time to put on a show. Let the bloke know they were team handed.

'Luke!' he shouted across the road to his brother, who was now standing by the car, smoking, watching the giggling girls. 'Luke!' he hollered again, putting on the hard man bit for the stranger and the toms. 'What's MacRiordan got to say about this *gentleman* being here?'

'Dunno.' Then, as an afterthought, 'Still no sign of him.'

Brendan could feel the situation slipping away from him. How could Luke show such weakness in front of this big, flash slag? Always have your team look tough, in control. That was the only way to play this game. He wondered about Luke sometimes, he really did.

He flashed a menacing look at the now smirking black man, and turned on his heel, determined to collar Pete Mac and find out what the hell he thought he was up to. Brendan had specifically told him to collect the first of the takings before noon. Before they got busy with the dinner time trade. You never knew who might be on the creep in this fog.

And the pub on the corner of Hanbury Street

7

seemed a reasonable place to start looking for him.

As he strode off, Brendan could feel the man's eyes watching him every step of the way.

*　　　*　　　*

The Heart was packed, just as it always was late on a Friday morning. The Spitalfields wholesale fruit and vegetable market on the other side of Commercial Street had shut up shop for the day, and, after grafting since the early hours, the porters and wholesalers were enjoying the beginning of their weekend by downing rows of pints and eating massive fry ups. And, after stoking up, many of them would be keen and ready to share some of their hard-earned wages with the toms across the street. But the O'Donnells' toms were nowhere to be seen. And neither was Pete Mac. Not in the pub, anyway. His lardy bulk and ginger hair would show up even in a boozer as crowded as this one.

But then again, there was no sign of anybody who looked like he might have anything to do with the big black bloke either. These were market people to a man, not the sort to earn a living doing anything more dodgy than letting the odd box of carrots or tomatoes fall off the back of their barrows.

Brendan allowed himself a brief smile. Nobody in here? Nobody out there in the street with him? It was beginning to look like the stranger might be all on his Jack after all. Now why waste an opportunity like that?

Leaving the fug and bustle of the pub, Brendan stepped back out into the cold, damp air. He whistled and showed out for Luke to follow him.

8

Then, with Luke on his heels, he sprinted back to where the man was standing on the corner, and yelled 'Oi! You!' from right behind him.

As the man turned, Brendan landed him one—smack! —an uppercut right on the chin.

'Jesus Christ!' Brendan waved his hand up and down. The bloke's jaw was like iron.

One of the girls, who was standing on the corner of Fleur-de-Lis Street started squealing. 'Millie, here quick, look. They're only thumping Joshua.'

In case one of the girls decided to run off to a phone box and call for reinforcements, Brendan acted fast. 'Grab him, Luke.'

Before Joshua could work out what direction he was coming from, Luke had grabbed Joshua's arms, and dragged them behind his back. Brendan got stuck in, punching with all his force, one fist after the other, straight into the man's guts.

Tough and impressive as he was, the surprise had given Brendan and Luke the advantage, and the succession of blows to Joshua's solar plexus soon winded him. He flopped forward from his waist, gasping, trying to catch his breath. 'All right,' he wheezed. 'That's enough.'

Brendan, panting from the effort of pummelling the man's massive bulk, stepped away from him as though giving him a chance. But before Joshua could straighten up again, Brendan drew back his arm, and then threw his whole body weight forward, whipping his upper body round in a tight quarter circle. He landed a sickening, crunch of a blow to Joshua's nose, spraying blood in a high, scatter-gun arc. Joshua's brain hadn't even had a chance to register the pain, when Brendan pivoted round, and landed a direct kick to the man's balls.

9

A bellow came roaring from somewhere deep in Joshua's chest.

It was over. For now.

'Let that be a lesson about what happens when you mess with the O'Donnells.' Brendan snatched up Joshua's hat from the pavement and stuffed it in the man's hand. 'You keep off our patch. Right?'

Joshua crumpled his hat in one single, pan-sized palm, raised his bloodied head and looked at Brendan through rapidly swelling eyes that could still show their anger. 'You'll wish you hadn't done that,' he said flatly, then limped off along Wheler Street towards the fog-shrouded railway arches.

Before he disappeared from view, he turned and pointed at Brendan and Luke in turn.

'I'm telling you. And you. Mr Kessler's not going to like this.'

*Kessler.* Brendan registered the name with no more than a flicker of a frown.

Joshua paused to spit a bloody gob of phlegm into the gutter then, suddenly, he started staggering back towards them.

Brendan and Luke stood ready—hearts thumping, fists alert—but he lurched straight past as if they didn't exist, and shouted at the now gawping girls. 'And you lot had better still be here when I get back. You got that?'

He didn't wait for a reply. He was gone.

Brendan and Luke started to cross Commercial Street, ready to explain to the girls that, if they knew what was good for them, they'd sling their hook and take their chance at upsetting the big black bloke rather than get on the wrong side of the O'Donnells, when a familiar voice stopped them in their tracks.

'All right, lads. What's the story here then?'

They turned round.

Peter MacRiordan.

'Hurt your hand, have you, mate?' he asked Brendan. 'Them knuckles of your'n look right sore. You don't wanna get an infection. They can be nasty. Get yourself down the London for a bandage and a dab of iodine.'

Brendan sucked at his fist, clearing the blood, then shoved Pete Mac hard in the chest, rocking him back on his heels. 'Where the fuck have you been, you lazy arsehole? And where's our fucking toms got to?'

'They not here, Brendan?'

Across the street, the girls were watching the three men.

'Looks like another ruck's starting,' bawled one of them, to the group on the opposite corner. 'But don't reckon this one's gonna be very exciting. The ginger bloke's not exactly got Joshua's muscles on him, has he?'

'But you should see the size of me willy, darling,' Pete Mac shouted back, treating the girls to a grin and a friendly wave.

Brendan slapped Pete Mac's arm down to his side. 'This ain't a joke, Pete. There's you standing there like Billy fucking Big Bollocks, while we've had to clean up your mess. Again.'

'What you on about now?'

'Give me fucking strength.' Brendan lifted his fist, only just stopping himself from smashing it into Pete Mac's face. 'Who do you think they are?' He jerked a thumb over his shoulder at the girls. 'They're Kessler's. And if we don't stop him, he's gonna think he can put them wherever he feels like

11

it. That's what I'm talking about you stupid, brainless prick.'

'Who d'you think you're talking to?' Pete Mac considered grabbing hold of his brother-in-law's lapels, show he wasn't scared, but thought better of it when he saw the look on Brendan's face. He stepped back, shooting his cuffs and adjusting his tie instead. 'Keep your hair on, eh, mate?' he said. 'And how about you and Luke getting yourselves out of that road? Don't want you getting knocked over, now do we? How would I explain that to Gabe? *Sorry, and all that, but your boys went under a bus.* That don't sound very nice, now does it?'

Brendan stepped up on to the pavement. His face now so close to Pete Mac's he could feel his breath on his face. 'Buses?' he said, his voice low, more threatening than a shout. 'You wanna worry about more than fucking buses. I give you one simple job and what do you do, you useless, streak of piss? Now, *where are our girls?*'

On the other side of the street, the toms, with the instinct for self-protection of women who had been on the wrong end of too many men's fists, began to melt away into the fog.

'Don't waste your time on him, Brendan.' Luke placed a hand on his brother's shoulder. 'Let's get back to the yard. Dad'll be expecting us.'

'Yeah,' snarled Brendan. 'With the fucking takings. The takings we ain't got cos of this idiot.'

'Well, I ain't coming back to the yard,' said Pete Mac, his face and neck flushing red. 'I need a drink to calm me down. Brendan's showed me right up. Going on at me like I was a little kid in front of all them tarts.'

'I showed you up?' Brendan was poking Pete

12

Mac again, backing him towards the road. 'If you'd been doing what you were told, there wouldn't be no strange tarts, now would there? And we'd have some takings, wouldn't we? Eh?'

'I overslept,' said Pete Mac, staring down at his feet. 'I was out late last night.'

'What, round your bit of stray's again?' Brendan spat the words through his teeth, slapping Pete Mac around the side of the head. 'You piece of shit.'

Luke grabbed his brother's sleeve. 'Brendan, leave it.'

Brendan shook off his hand. 'Don't you start.'

'Come on. This ain't the place. And we've all got some figuring out to do about what happens next.'

Brendan made as if to swipe the back of his hand round Pete Mac's face. 'You don't know how lucky you are Luke's here, MacRiordan. Now get in that motor. I ain't letting you out of my sight.'

*     *     *

As he bent forward to put the key in the driver's door, Brendan caught Pete Mac's reflection in the window. He was standing behind him with his mouth all scrunched up like a cat's arsehole, acting like he was the one who'd been wronged. The bloke was a complete moron.

Brendan turned to say something to him, when a small, skinny boy, who'd been collecting spoiled fruit and vegetables from the gutters round the market, slunk past them at just the wrong moment. Without warning, Pete Mac's hand flicked out and caught the shabbily dressed child with a whack right across the narrow of his back.

13

The boy gasped with shock and pain. 'Oi! I never done nothing.'

'Bugger off or you'll get another one,' he growled.

Luke and Brendan looked at him in disgust. If he wasn't their brother-in-law . . . But he was, although neither of them had ever been able to understand how a useless, lazy, bullying toe rag like Pete Mac had ever managed to get a girl like their sister Pat to even look at him, let alone let him get near enough to knock her up.

It was one of life's fucking mysteries.

*     *     *

'This is a really gorgeous colour, Pat.' Catherine, who was stretched out on the sofa, flat on her back, held her hand high above her head, admiring her freshly painted nails. 'Coral Moon. Really dreamy.'

'If you can manage to keep still for five minutes instead of fannying around, I can finish your other hand for you. But if you'd rather do it yourself then that's fine by me. You can just see what sort of a mess you can make of it.'

Eileen O'Donnell stopped knitting and frowned at her elder daughter, who was kneeling on the rug beside the sofa, with the nail varnish brush poised in midair. She had a face on her like she was having her arse grated.

'Patricia,' Eileen said, in her soft Irish brogue. 'Please, don't snap at your sister like that. There's no need for it.'

Catherine, keeping her wet nails well away from the upholstery, dug her elbows into the cushions and hoisted her shoulders off the sofa and smiled broadly. Her whole face lit up as her cheeks folded into childlike dimples. 'She didn't mean anything, did you, Pat?'

'No. Course I didn't.' She closed her eyes and sighed wearily. 'But Mum's right. I'm sorry, Cath. I'm feeling a bit tired, that's all. Come on, let's get this finished or they won't be dry before you go out.'

Eileen's frown deepened as she looked at her girls. From behind, you could barely tell them apart. They had the same slim but curvy build, and their glossy black hair styled in the latest urchin cut, and both of them dressed in all the latest up-to-the-minute gear. Although, it had to be admitted, Pat had stopped showing much interest in buying her own things, and seemed content just to benefit from Catherine's many castoffs. Today, she was wearing bronze, clam-digger slacks and a black gypsy blouse that had hardly been on her sister's back, while Catherine, despite it being gone noon, was still in her pink baby dolls. Eileen could only wonder how she didn't catch her death in this weather, and thanked goodness for the four bar fire they'd had installed when they ripped out the old cast-iron fireplace.

She nibbled at her lip. Looking at them, anyone else would simply see two young women who knew what was what, and, what's more, what they liked. It's certainly what the salesmen saw after the pair of them had finally persuaded her to get rid of nearly all of the perfectly good furniture from the front room, and to replace it with the 'contemporary' things that the girls had been raving on and on about. At first, Eileen hadn't been at all sure about the bright, swirly-patterned hearth rug,

15

the shiny blue laminate wall units, the grey and red three-piece suite with its splayed, spindly legs that looked as though they were about to break; and as for the matching poodle lamps they'd made her buy to go on the strange, triangular shaped occasional tables . . . Poodle lamps! It was like living in some smart shop window in the West End instead of in a terrace on the Mile End Road. And it had certainly cost enough. More than most families in Stepney could even dream of. But the girls had been right. It all looked, as Catherine would say, 'gorgeous'. And they could afford it. Even Gabriel had said he liked it. After she'd asked him.

As she always did, Eileen hurriedly pushed aside any thoughts about her husband's lack of interest in anything more domestic than the food on his plate and the whiskey in his glass, and allowed herself a smile as she remembered the bustle and excitement of those shopping expeditions. And the pleas and promises from the pair of them that she'd *just love it all* when she got it home.

Her smile faded. It was a pity Patricia's excitement wasn't so much in evidence these days. When the girls turned round and she saw their faces, they told their mother very different stories.

Catherine, a dead spit for the young Audrey Hepburn, was, as Patricia had once been, a real live wire, always jigging about and singing along to the latest rock and roll records and making them all laugh with her daft antics. While Patricia looked as if she had the worries of the world on her shoulders.

It was so hard being a mother. Wondering what was best for your children. Getting the balance right. With Catherine, Eileen worried that she

16

might have a bit too much of the free spirit about her, and she couldn't stand the thought of her youngest child getting caught out as Patricia had been.

The girls nowadays seemed to think they could get themselves done up in whatever clothes and make-up they felt like, and act as if they had the same freedom as the boys—to Eileen that was all wrong. But, then again, if she had a choice, she would have loved to see the old sparky Patricia again, acting up and gadding about the way she used to. It was as if a light had gone out and no one had bothered to replace the bulb.

It was no mystery what had happened. Eileen, like the rest of the family, knew what was wrong with her. It was being married to Pete Mac. If only she hadn't let the great oaf get anywhere near her. But it was too late for regrets. She might have lost the baby, but, before the eyes of God, she had made her vows. Till death her do part.

She could only hope that Catherine had learned from her big sister's mistakes and that she would carry on having plenty of fun going out and about with her friends before she tied herself down to some man.

\*     \*     \*

Gabriel O'Donnell ran his fingers through his hair, and then tugged distractedly at his tie, staring unseeingly at the electric fan as it vibrated and edged its way across the scratched and battered surface of the desk. Being winter, it wasn't intended to cool the air, rather to clear it. But it made little impact on the heaviness of the smoke-thickened atmosphere in the harshly lit lean-to, barely disturbing the stacks of scruffy papers that supposedly legitimised the business dealings of the chaotic scrap yard outside.

'No, Jimmy,' he said—again—his jaw aching from the effort of keeping his temper under control. 'Just listen will you? There are definitely no changes to the arrangements. You pay the boys as usual and—'

He stopped, shocked, in mid-sentence.

*Jimmy had interrupted him.*

Gabriel stared at the telephone as if it were smeared with something he'd just scraped off the bottom of his shoe.

It was a long moment before he took charge again. 'I said, Jimmy, there're no changes to the arrangements. Brendan'll be round later.' He raised his eyes and looked at his two sons and his son-in-law as they came in through the scuffed metal door. '*And you fucking remember it, right?*'

He slammed down the phone. 'That,' he said to the three young men, 'was Jimmy the Stump. He's not a happy man.'

'What's up with him this time?' It was Pete Mac talking. 'Miserable bastard's always bleating on about something or other.'

Brendan O'Donnell exchanged a look with his father, and then glared at his brother-in-law. 'Do us all a favour and shut up for once, will you, Pete?'

Gabriel continued. 'What's up with him is, he's paying us good money, and now two of Kessler's goons have gone in his boozer and threatened to smash it up. In front of all the customers. One of Jimmy's barmen said something, and, do you know what happened? They glassed him. In a boozer

18

we're meant to be looking after. How does that look? Eh? I'll tell you, it looks like a right show up. And I'm not having it.' He turned to his eldest son. 'I want this sorted out, Brendan. Today. I want you to get yourself round that yard of theirs and—'

'But Dad—' It was Luke.

'Jimmy the Stump, Pete Mac, and now you getting mouthy with me, Luke?' Gabriel rubbed his hand over his chin, clearly bewildered by this new turn of events. 'Can I ask who you think you are, interrupting me?'

'I was only going to say, Dad; shouldn't we calm down, figure out if the Kesslers can really do us any harm?'

Brendan shoved his brother in the side. 'Luke!' he hissed at him under his breath.

Gabriel rose slowly to his feet. The only sound in the room apart from the furious snorting of his breath, the whirring of the fan on his desk in front of him.

He spoke slowly, his voice deceptively quiet, the words' sharp edges softened by traces of an Irish burr beneath his rough cockney. 'Any harm? Have you gone raving mad?'

Luke shifted around uncomfortably. He knew it wasn't done, questioning his dad, but he had to do something. Play for a bit of time. 'No, it's just—'

Gabriel thumped his fist on the table, silencing his son. 'I'll explain to you, shall I, Luke? If he didn't want to do *any harm* he wouldn't have fucking come back here, would he? He'd have moved out to Essex. Like other people.'

'Or Kent,' suggested Pete Mac.

They ignored him.

'But, no, he came right back here to shit on my

19

fucking doorstep. Moving in on businesses in *my* toby. Don't you think that's harm enough? The bastard moves out of here twenty years ago, talking some old shit about saving his family from the blitz, when everyone knows it was him what swallowed, the fucking coward. And now he's giving everyone some old toffee about coming back here to get his family away from the riots. Riots that were over *two years ago*. Turning up here like he's never been away. Like he's just nipped out for a packet of fags, and found himself a bit waylaid on the way home.'

'Maybe you'd have done the same, Dad.'

'You *what*?'

Luke's mouth was so dry, he could hardly speak. 'Moved us out if you thought there were gonna be riots.'

'Luke. Son. The O'Donnells don't run away from anything.'

'Well, his haulage firm's not treading on our toes.'

Gabriel looked at Luke with genuine puzzlement. What the hell had got into the boy? 'But going round Jimmy the Stump's fucking is. That *is* pissing on my patch.' He smacked his hand on the table again. 'For fuck's sake, Luke, this is a business we're running here, not some two bob bit of spivvery. A business I've worked my nuts off to build. A business I've had to fight every step of the way to put together. And if this business is gonna thrive, we don't need them fuckers moving in mob-handed from West London. What do they think? We're gonna just hold up our hands and surrender? Let 'em take whatever they fancy. I'm not having it. Understand?'

Gabriel's head ached and his heart was sore. He

hadn't slogged his guts out dragging himself out of the Galway mire to be rolled over and shat on by a fucking Russian or Pole or whatever the cunt was.

He dropped down heavily on to his chair, leaned back, and loosened his tie.

'Barry and Kevin were just here.' The words came out as a weary sigh. 'Someone's offering better odds opposite every single one of our street pitches. And Anthony phoned in earlier.' Gabriel directed a look at Pete Mac. 'Reckons one of the girls told him they all went out as usual this morning, but one of Kessler's heavies turned up and they were too scared to stay. So scared they'd rather face a big fucker like Anthony. And now Jimmy the Stump's bending my ear'ole about protection. What is this—a Sisters of Charity set up I'm running here? I supply the gambling, protection and whoring pitches for them cunts to work?'

Pete Mac silently cursed Anthony. Fuck him. Now Gabe knew the girls hadn't worked today. He'd have to smooth things over. 'Look, Gabe,' he said, all cajoling smiles and tipped-to-one-side head. 'Before we get carried away here, Luke might be right. Maybe we shouldn't be worrying ourselves.'

'What?' Gabriel mouthed at his idiot son-in-law.

'I mean, little bits of protection? Street betting? Everyone knows that's gonna disappear when the new shops are up and running. And as for the toms . . . Who needs all that agg? Let the Kesslers have it. We've got better things to think about. Proper business.'

'Brendan, will you get this stupid cowson out of my sight?'

21

Pete Mac didn't speak until he'd backed away, well out of Brendan's reach. 'Stupid cowson am I? You didn't say that when I got that demolition contract last week. And all that lovely copper piping laying about on the building site next door.'

'How do you think you got that contract, Pete? And how do you think we—you—have such a good life? Shifting a few second-hand bricks? Choring a few lengths of copper pipe when the night watchman's not looking?'

Out of his depth, Pete Mac's face contorted into a moue of confusion.

'No, Pete, it's because I'm not a mug, that's how. And don't you *ever* think you can treat me like one. I know every move you make, you bollock-brained moron. You're only tolerated here because of our Patricia. You remember that. And you remember *no one* mugs me off. No one. And that's why I'm not having the Kesslers coming around here, thinking they can do what they fucking well like.'

Hard as he tried, Pete Mac couldn't keep quiet. 'But you haven't seen the big black feller he's fetched with him, Gabe. Built like a brick shithouse.'

Brendan flashed him a look of pure contempt. That was the reason he hadn't been around to mind the girls: he'd seen the bloke minding Kessler's girls and bottled out.

Gabriel snatched a cigarette from the packet of Players on the desk, lit one, and took a long draw, pulling the smoke deep into his lungs. 'I'm sick of all this. There's Poles running the protection up in Leeds. Scotsmen making a move on the firms in Liverpool. Maltese and Italians all over the poxy West End. Well, I'm telling you, I'm not having

22

Kessler thinking he can move the League of fucking Nations in round here. Got any problems with that, any of you?'

No one answered him.

'Good. So, perhaps now you'll do as you're told and get yourselves round that haulage yard and put the fear of fucking Christ up the bastards.' He studied the red glow of the tobacco. 'Burn their fucking lorries out. Frighten the shit out of 'em. Do whatever you have to do, but just fucking do it.'

Brendan and Pete Mac walked towards the door, but Luke hesitated. 'Dad, I—'

Gabriel shook his head. 'Forget it, son, just do as you're told.'

As Luke reluctantly joined the others, Gabriel spoke again. 'Hang on. Not you, Pete.'

The three of them turned to face him, Brendan with his hand on the door.

'In case there's any trouble. Go round yours and get Patricia. Drop her round home.'

'She's already there. Went earlier.'

'Good. So you can go with Brendan and Luke. I'll call Eileen. Tell her to make sure Patricia stays indoors with her and Catherine.'

If Pete Mac wasn't in such a bad mood he'd have laughed out loud. The old fool thought he was so clever, but he had no idea that whenever she had the chance, his precious little Catherine was off out, here, there and everywhere with her mates. And all with Eileen's blessing.

Gabriel stubbed out the barely smoked cigarette, pushed back his chair, and reached down by his feet. He pulled out a heavy canvas bag, and heaved it up onto the desk. 'And you'd better take these with you. You'll be needing something a bit more serious than blades and brass knuckles.'

'Dad, shouldn't we think about this?' Luke was looking really concerned. 'Pete Mac's right. There's all sorts of rumours about the lunatics they've got on that firm.'

'Are there now?' Gabriel got up and went over to a dull-grey metal stationery cupboard stuck in the corner behind a wonky-legged coat stand. He unlocked it, and took something wrapped in oily sacking off the top shelf. It was the size of a table leg, but obviously a lot heavier. He carried it back to his desk, set it down carefully, and opened it up. 'Then you'd better take this with you, hadn't you?' He picked up the sawn-off shotgun and held it out to them. 'Silence them rumours once and for all.'

\*　　　\*　　　\*

Gabriel stood at the single, grimy window, watching the three young men slope off across the scrap yard.

Brendan: a mirror image of his own dark Irish looks, but with twenty-two years less wear on his face. Then, Luke: a year younger, but just as tall and as immaculately turned out his brother—sharp, three-button, navy blue suit, pure white shirt, well-polished shoes—but somehow less of a presence than Brendan. Maybe that's what being the younger brother did to you. But they were two handsome men all right: dark-haired and powerfully built, just like him, but with eyes of deep, violet blue—like Eileen's—instead of green like his.

And then there was Peter-bloody-Mac-fucking-Riordan.

24

His son-in-law, with his pale freckled face, his wiry, carrot red hair, and his wide, countryman's body that was already threatening to run to fat just as his father's had done. His suit had, no doubt, cost as much as his sons' had done, but it certainly didn't look it, not on him.

He was a stupid fuck, but, apparently, he made Patricia a happy woman. And even if he didn't, it was too late now. The good Lord forgive him, it was only a pity she hadn't had the miscarriage before the idiot had got her walking up the aisle.

Gabriel turned from the window and closed his eyes as if in pain.

Before he knew it, Catherine would be bringing home some useless, spotty Herbert, who they'd all have to make welcome, and smile at, and shake his hand like he was God's bloody gift. But Gabriel wouldn't make the same mistake again. Catherine would stay safely at home with her mother. At nearly eighteen years old, she was his and Eileen's baby, the surprise who'd completed the family he'd always dreamed of having, and no man was going to get his dirty hands on her for a good few years yet.

He walked back to the desk and flopped down in his chair, ripped his tie from his neck, and lit another cigarette. He'd had plenty of dreams over the years and a whole lot of them had come true, but he never forgot what his mother had said to him when he was still a raggedy-arsed kid back in Ireland. He'd sworn to her that one day his dream of having a good life would come true, that he'd have money in his pocket, food in his belly and be beholden to no one. He would be someone. He'd be Mr Gabriel O'Donnell.

*Now you just remember,* she'd said to him, pointing a work-calloused finger at him across the rough deal table in their dirt-floored hovel, *when dreams do come true, boy, they have a nasty habit of turning into nightmares.*

And this was a nightmare all right. Having the Kesslers turning up on his fucking doorstep, and then having to argue not only with Pete Mac, but with his own bloody son into the bargain. Christ alone knew what had got into Luke.

Gabriel put his hands over his eyes, feeling the headache tightening like a steel band round his forehead. Eileen had always been too soft on the kids; ever since they were babies she'd spoiled the lot of them.

One of the phones on his desk began ringing, the phone that no one but Gabriel was allowed to touch.

He dropped his hand from his eyes, picked up the receiver, and breathed softly, lovingly into the mouthpiece, 'Rosie, my own darling angel . . .'

# CHAPTER TWO

'Is it going to be a big wedding, Sammy?' the girl asked, her voice at once shy but with a discernibly wheedling edge to it.

'Big?' Sammy paused, concentrating on shifting down to third. He was driving as cautiously as if he were taking his test, extra careful not to crunch the gears of the car he had borrowed from his older brother Daniel—the brother who was out on business with their father, and who would kill him

26

stone dead if he knew he'd even touched his motor.

'Are you kidding?' he went on. 'If my mother thought Daniel wanted the Chief Rabbi to be there, Dad'd make sure he turned up. They wouldn't deny our Danny anything.'

'And I bet Rachel's dress is gonna be really pretty.'

As she spoke, the girl stared out of the car window into the fog. Why was it that when you were born that's what you were for the rest of your life? It didn't matter if you were a dog in a kennel or a princess in a palace, that's what you'd always be. It wasn't fair.

Take Rachel, she'd been born into a nice, Jewish family, and what did that make her? A nice Jewish girl, just right to marry Sammy's big brother, Daniel.

Jewish. Exactly what she wasn't.

Her attention was snatched back by Sammy's laughter. 'Don't know whether it's pretty or not,' he said, slowing the car to a halt by the offside kerb. 'But I know her mother's as bad as mine. I'm telling you, whatever it comes to, Rachel'll have exactly what she wants. And I guarantee it won't be no schmutter. And the knees up afterwards? That's going to make that Princess Margaret's do look like a shotgun job at Gretna Green.'

The girl stared down into her lap as visions of virginal white net, sparkling crystals, and creamy, teardrop pearls, danced around in her head like will o' the wisps—there, but just out of her grasp.

'Sammy . . .'

'Yeah?'

'Do you think I'd look nice in white?'

He didn't hesitate. 'No.'

27

His bluntness stunned her. She pulled the fur collar of her astrakhan coat tightly up about her face. 'I'm cold. I want to go home.'

He rolled his eyes. 'Will you let me finish? What I meant was: I think you look best . . .' He turned off the engine, leaned over, and whispered something in her ear.

'Sammy Kessler!' she squealed, all shoves and mock offence. 'You are so rude.'

'Course I am. That's why you love me. Now come here.'

'Don't, everyone'll see.'

'In this fog?' He slipped a hand inside her coat, cupping her breast, and nuzzling into her ear. 'They'd need flipping good eyesight.'

She lifted her chin, luxuriating in the damp warmth of his breath on her neck. 'Where are we anyway?' The words came out as a soft moan.

'Sclater Street.'

She pulled away from him, ducking her head and squinting up at the high brick wall, trying to make out the lettering on the street sign. 'What the hell are you up to, Sammy? We're practically outside your dad's yard.'

'So?' He ran his fingers through his springy fair hair. 'You are such a panicker.'

'Say someone recognises me?'

'You can hardly see a hand in front of your face out there. And even if you could, who'd recognise you in that new coat? Makes you look just like a film star.'

'It is lovely,' she said, stroking the high fur collar that she knew framed her pretty, heart shaped face perfectly.

'Nothing but the best for my girl.'

*My girl* . . . She smiled up at him.

'Is it nice and cosy?'

She wrinkled her nose with pleasure. 'Really lovely.'

'Good, it'll keep you warm while I'm gone. I'll be two minutes. Tops.'

'Sammy!'

He took hold of the door handle. 'I've just gotta nip in the yard and make sure the lazy so-and-so's have got all the lorries back.'

But he didn't get out right away; he sat there looking at her, as she returned her gaze to her lap, resigned to waiting for him.

She knew Sammy's father insisted that his transport business was all shut up before sunset on Fridays. His mother liked the family to do things properly, religiously. Her own mother was the same. And it seemed it wasn't only their mothers who had things in common. His dad sounded a lot like hers as well. Both men didn't actually care much about their 'official' means of making a living—a haulage business in Sammy's dad's case, a scrap metal yard in hers—other than the fact that they acted as useful fronts for their other activities. Activities the women were kept well away from. But both men kept their wives happy by paying lip service to their religions. And in turn, their wives ran well-kept, comfortable homes, and turned a wifely blind eye to the reality of what was going on right under their noses: the businesses which kept their families in such style. She and Sammy wouldn't be like their parents. They'd tell each other everything.

Sammy pushed her fringe of heavy dark hair away from her face, physically moved by her almost childlike beauty. 'Just think,' he whispered, 'if we hadn't moved back to the East End, I'd never have met you.' He could hardly believe it was just two short months since he'd gone with his brother Daniel to that club in Ilford.

Danny had promised him a good night: a few drinks, the chance to pick up a couple of shiksas, and the guarantee of having some right laughs. They'd both had the drinks, all right, plenty of them, and they'd both met the shiksas, but only Daniel had had the laughs.

Sammy had gone and fallen in love.

He had known from their very first meeting that he'd make his life with her. The fact that she wasn't the good Jewish girl his mother had always presumed he would marry, didn't matter. He would set up something of his own, get away from the family, make himself independent. He loved her. No discussion. He just needed to work out how he was going to do it. How hard could it be?

Sammy touched her cheek, and felt himself harden as the soft, peachy skin of her cheeks folded into the dimples he couldn't resist.

'You gonna be okay?' he asked, his voice low, full of desire.

She nodded again, her violet-blue eyes wide and round.

'Remember what I told you? You're my bashert. The one meant for me. What are you?'

'Your bashert.' She paused, dropping her chin shyly. 'Can I have a kiss before you go?'

'Do you really have to ask?'

\*     \*     \*

30

Eileen stuck the end of her knitting needles in the ball of wool, got up from her chair and went to answer the telephone. She still moved with the quiet grace and dignity that had first attracted Gabriel O'Donnell when they had been little more than children back in Galway.

'2314,' she said, her accent retaining far more of the Irish than her husband's.

'Is that you, Eileen?'

'Yes, Gabe.'

'Where are the girls?'

She hesitated for a split second. 'They're here. With me. Listening to the wireless.'

'Let me talk to them.'

Again, Eileen paused for the briefest of moments, looking across at Patricia, signalling with a raised finger to her lips for her to be quiet. 'You can't, love, not really. Pat's painting Catherine's nails. Primping and preening as usual. You know what the pair of them are like.'

Patricia made a big show of widening her eyes and dropping her jaw, but Eileen rejected the admonishment with a flap of her hand. 'I'll give them a message, if that's all right with you.'

'Fair enough. Tell them I don't want them going out in this fog, and I'll send someone to drive Pat home later.'

'Don't worry yourself, Gabriel, they'll be grand. We're sitting here snug as bugs.'

'Mum,' gawped Patricia, as soon as the receiver was safely back in its cradle. 'If I'd have done that . . .'

'Done what?'

'Pretended Catherine was still here.'

Eileen bent forward and patted Scrap, a now

31

Labrador-sized bundle of tan fur that she'd rescued from an abandoned litter of tiny, trembling puppies dumped outside her husband's yard in an old cardboard box. 'A little white lie never hurt anybody.'

Patricia picked up her almost cold cup of tea from the occasional table, went to take a sip, but then put it down again. 'D'you reckon?'

*       *       *

Brendan O'Donnell steered the dark grey car through the fog-bound back doubles of Bethnal Green. He'd forgone the pleasures of driving his Jaguar, opting instead for the staid anonymity of a Standard saloon borrowed from one the men who worked in the scrap yard.

Pete Mac, still furious as a hornet about the way he'd been treated, sat in the back next to Luke, the front passenger seat being occupied by a heavy canvas bag. The bag that contained several lengths of tape-wrapped lead piping, four pickaxe handles, four lump hammers, and the cloth-wrapped sawn-off shotgun.

He rapped his knuckles agitatedly against his top teeth. 'I'm not kidding, Brendan. I mean it,' he snarled in his flat, Romford growl. 'What does your old man expect us to do? Blow their brains out for 'em? I can see the headlines now: *The O'Donnell Gang Goes Barmy. Ten Fucking Dead.* Including two O'Donnells and one sodding MacRiordan. No, better, we get fucking hung for murder. I mean, striping a bloke's face or arse is one thing, or using knuckle-dusters, that's all right with me. I've got no problem with any of that. But guns? We're not fucking cowboys and Indians.'

Brendan flashed a look at his brother in the rear-view mirror. 'Will you shut him up, Luke?'

Luke said nothing; he just stared down at his feet, and gnawed distractedly at his cuticles.

'I'd like to see him try,' sneered Pete Mac. 'I'd knock his block right off his shoulders.'

Brendan snorted scornfully 'You sure, Pete? You couldn't knock the skin off a rice pudden.'

He sniffed angrily. 'All I'm saying is, I don't like the idea of going over there tooled up. Not when we ain't got a clue how many geezers they're gonna have on parade. And if the size of that one on Commercial Street's anything to go by then we're gonna be right in the shit. Right up to our fucking necks.'

Brendan shook his head. 'So you did turn up then? And saw the size of him—'

Pete Mac shifted in his seat. 'Not properly, like.'

'I knew it.'

'And you thought you'd just leave us to it,' chipped in Luke.

'That's why you went amongst the missing when you should have been keeping an eye on the girls.'

'I was just being careful. It was all right for you, there was two of you.'

Brendan's lip curled in disgust. 'You should be ashamed of yourself. If—'

Brendan never finished the sentence. He braked so suddenly that the mini-armoury on the front seat shot onto the floor and rolled under the seat, and Pete Mac bashed his head, with a dull thud, on the side window.

'Oi, Brendan. That bloody hurt.'

'Serves you right for staring out of the window

33

like a fucking spaniel,' muttered Brendan. 'Now give your eyes a chance. There's a brand new Jag parked over by the Kesslers's yard.'

'Anyone in it?' asked Luke, suddenly interested.

'Yeah. And it's got to be one of the Kesslers,' replied Brendan. 'Can't see it belonging to one of their drivers, or anyone else round here.'

'Is he alone?'

'What is this, Luke?' snapped Brendan. *Take Your Pick*? How the fuck do I know if he's alone? I don't even know what the Kesslers bloody look like, let alone whether they've got sodding company or not.'

'I know what Sammy Kessler looks like.' Luke rested his elbows on the front seat and stared hard through the windscreen. Praying silently that what he'd dreaded wasn't about to come true.

Brendan twisted round. 'How?'

Flustered, Luke sat back in his seat. 'Some bloke pointed him out to me. In a pub.'

'What pub?' asked Pete Mac, gormless as a sack of spuds.

Brendan and Luke both stared at him.

'What pub?' Brendan screwed up his face in wonder at his brother-in-law, threw open the door and got out.

'Pete,' he said, sticking his head back in the car, 'just get out here and give us them tools. We're gonna surprise him, whatever boozer he uses and whoever he's with. Right? Luke, you jump in the driving seat. Get the engine running, in case we need to shoot off a bit sharpish.'

As he took the bag, Brendan grinned. 'Here, let's see what you're made of, Pete. Cop hold of this.'

Brendan held out the sawn-off to his now grim-faced brother-in-law, who had shoved his hands deep into his pockets.

'Aw, sorry, I forgot. There might be a nasty big man to scare you.'

'Scare me?' Pete Mac's lips twisted with anger. 'Give it here.'

'All right, but mind you don't aim it at your bollocks, eh, Pete. We don't want no accidents, now do we?'

\*       \*       \*

Reluctantly, Sammy pulled away from her, running his finger gently down her cheek. God, she was a good-looking girl. He was going to work out a way to be with her if it was the last thing he did.

'I'll be two minutes, okay?' he said, getting out of the car.

He had one foot on the pavement, with his body half twisted away from the steering wheel, and his gaze angled down at the ground, when he realised something was wrong. A hand—a big hand—had clamped over his shoulder. But he didn't look up to see who was standing over him, he was too busy concentrating on the truncated barrels of the sawn-off shotgun that someone was pointing in his face.

'Hello,' said Brendan, talking to the top of Sammy's head over Pete Mac's shoulder. 'It's Kessler innit? And who's your little friend? Bit shy is she?'

The girl had pulled her coat right up to her ears and was trying to crawl out of the passenger door onto the road.

Brendan groaned as if he were disappointed by

such a pathetic escape attempt. 'Pete, get round there and stop that bitch getting away, will you?'

Pete Mac, sawn-off in hand, his determination to prove himself to Brendan making him act flash, did as he was told with a lip-curling smirk. 'My pleasure, Brendan, old son.'

Sammy Kessler had no chance to think things through. He just knew it couldn't get out that he was seeing a shiksa. He flung himself sideways to cover her with his body.

The violence of his sudden movement, combined with his weight, threw her right out of the car, and she went sprawling, face down onto the roadway.

Making a wild grab for the sawn-off, Sammy tumbled out of the car on top of her, muffling her screams in an arm-waving, leg-flailing confusion of body parts.

He scrambled to his feet, planting them firmly on the ground, and tried to wrestle the gun from a now wild-eyed and cursing Pete Mac.

For a moment, Sammy thought he had a hold of it, but the barrels were slick with oil and it slipped from his grasp.

Pete Mac jerked it high in the air out of Sammy's reach. But he hadn't reckoned with Sammy's speed.

With his head down, Sammy barged him in the gut.

Pete Mac doubled over. And the gun went off.

Luke jumped out of the car and raced over to them.

Sammy had straightened up and was staggering backwards. The front of his overcoat was covered with blood, but it wasn't him who'd been hurt. It was the girl.

She lay there, face down in the road, with bright red blood puddling around her head and shoulders.

'What the fuck have you done, Pete?' Luke stood over the girl, his arms hanging loosely by his side.

'It wasn't me. *He* did it.' Pete Mac waved the shotgun at Sammy Kessler, who was backing away from them towards the haulage yard, his gaze fixed on the girl sprawled out on the roadway.

'He threw himself at me. You saw him, Brendan. I lost my balance. It wasn't my fault.'

Brendan snatched the gun off him. 'Get back in the motor, you moron, before he calls the law.'

'A Kessler call the law?' Pete Mac did his best to sound bold, contemptuous.

'All right then, before he calls an ambulance. *Just get in that fucking motor.*'

'Brendan, wait.' It was Luke. 'It's Catherine.'

*'What?'*

'Catherine.' Luke swiped his hand across his forehead, pushing back his hair. 'Pete Mac's gone and fucking shot her.'

\*  \*  \*

Why was she bothering? Eileen looked down at the half completed sweater. Conker brown. For one or other of the boys. Not that they'd been seen dead in it. Forty-two years of age and finding ways to pass the time. She might as well be sitting there by the fire like her mother, with her face pinched, her shoulders hunched, and a shawl draped round them. And just like her grandmother before that. Women old before their time. Not like their men, who, except for a few grey hairs and slightly thicker

37

waistlines, seemed to look the same in their forties as they did in their twenties.

Eileen smoothed down her smart navy skirt, and checked the sheen of her stockings as they stretched over her ankles, proving to herself that she was still an attractive woman, a woman who took care of herself.

A woman who might as well have been invisible for all the attention her husband paid her.

'Not happy with the jumper, Mum?'

'If I'm honest, Patricia, not really love. But it keeps me busy.' Eileen smiled, gathering up her pride. 'You know how it is.'

'Yeah, I know.' Patricia nodded, then added casually, 'Fancy coming shopping tomorrow?'

'Don't we always on a Saturday?' What else was there to do when she'd already cleaned the house from top to bottom, and done all the chores during the week, when the men were out and she wouldn't be a bother to them?

'I just thought we might go up West for a change. Selfridges, or Marshall & Snelgrove. Somewhere like that.'

Eileen flashed her eyebrows with interest. This sounded promising. More like her old Pat. 'The Roman Road or East Ham not good enough for you all of a sudden?'

'I never said that. I feel like going somewhere a bit, you know . . .' She cast around trying to find the right word. 'Special.'

'Why not? Let's treat ourselves. Catherine'll be raring to go.' Eileen tipped her head and looked sideways at her daughter. 'Here, you're not getting the old shopping bug back like your little sister, are you? She's more shoes than a shoe shop that one.'

Patricia shrugged. 'I want to get away for a few hours, that's all. Go somewhere different.'

'I know how you feel.' Eileen shifted forward in her seat as she saw the dejected look on her daughter's face. 'All right, love, I didn't mean to upset you. I was only teasing.'

Patricia looked away, unable to face her mother.

'There's nothing's wrong is there? You're not feeling unwell?'

Patricia nibbled at the inside of her cheek. Here goes, saying it made it real, made her have to deal with it. 'Mum, I'm expecting.' There, she'd said it. 'About twelve weeks gone, I reckon.'

'My little Patsy!' Eileen rushed over to her daughter, arms stretched wide.

Patricia accepted her hugs, but Eileen could feel the stiffness, the wariness in her child.

'Don't tell Pete will you, Mum. Not yet. If it goes wrong again I don't want to . . .' She considered her words. '. . . disappoint him.'

'It won't go wrong, love, not this time. I promise. With all my heart. You weren't well before. All that fuss when your dad found out. Then rushing the wedding through so no one knew. And then . . .' She hesitated, tipping her daughter under the chin and looking into her eyes. 'Look, everything's going to be wonderful. And Dad'll be so happy for you this time.'

'I still want to make sure nothing goes wrong before I say anything to him, Mum. Please. Promise me.'

'Okay, but it'll be fine, I just know it will.'

Patricia blew her nose noisily. 'I do love Pete, you know.'

'Yeah, I know, sweetheart. Just like I love your

father.'

Patricia's chin dropped. She stared down at the cosy familiarity of the brown and green patterns in the carpet, the carpet she had grown up with, that she'd played on, sat on, stretched out on to listen to all her mum's stories about living 'back home' in Ireland—the carpet that meant home and safety, even during the noise and clamour of the war. The carpet her mum had stubbornly refused to replace. She loved it for all those reasons, but most of all she loved it because it had nothing whatsoever to do with her life with Peter MacRiordan.

Yes, Patricia loved him all right, just as much as she had said she still loved him when she found out before they were even engaged that she wasn't only carrying his child, but also the pubic lice—and the subsequent lies and humiliation—he had given her into the bargain.

If only it wouldn't have hurt her parents so badly she'd have told the selfish, fat-headed pig what to do with their marriage. But, good Catholic girl that she was, she had to get used to the fact: she was married to him. And it was a life sentence.

Patricia sniffed back the tears. It was no good thinking about what might have been, she was pregnant again, carrying a new life inside her. She'd just have to lump it. Especially now she'd told her mother.

And that was that.

*　　　*　　　*

Brendan was really having trouble taking in what had happened. It felt as if time had somehow lost its power to move forward, that everything had

40

been cranked down to agonisingly slow motion, making things hyperreal yet dream-like at the same time.

He turned and watched Sammy, who was now running towards the entrance to the Kesslers's haulage yard. His movements were those of a silent film being shown at the wrong speed. His arms pumped up and down—thwack! thwack!—but so slowly that they were useless, ineffectual pistons. His head moved from side to side in great wagging nods, and his legs described ridiculous looping strides that were getting him nowhere.

Then Brendan turned back, dragging against an invisible force, and saw his brother kneeling on the ground by Catherine.

Pete Mac was standing over them both—his face distorted, his mouth opening and closing. He might have been shouting or even screaming, but Brendan could hear nothing.

Not until his brother broke the spell.

Luke reared up from his knees, grabbed Pete Mac by the lapels and smacked his forehead full into his brother-in-law's face with a sickening, skin-splitting crunch.

The force threw Pete Mac backwards off his feet.

When he hit the ground, Brendan could hear him crying like a baby.

Brendan shook his head like a swimmer emerging from the waves. He had to help Catherine.

\*       \*       \*

'Here, I'm talking to you, Kessler,' a man called to

Sammy over the loudly revving engine of a blue Bedford truck. 'Are you listening to me? I said, this lorry needs two new tyres and it could do with something or other to stop this bleed'n' whining. It's gotta be the gearbox. Hark at it, how can I be expected to . . .'

The man continued speaking, but Sammy ignored him.

Without a word, and with his blood-splattered topcoat bundled in his arms, he raced up the wooden steps into the old caravan his father used as an office. He slammed the door shut behind him and paced wildly up and down the grubby strip of carpet.

He had to think.

How on earth was he going to explain what he was doing with Catherine O'Donnell? His old man would kill him.

He could feel his chest rising and falling like he'd just run the four-minute mile.

Or why he'd left her there in the road.

*What a bastard.*

It was all too much. There were too many complications.

Like what he was doing driving Daniel's new Jag.

And then there was the new coat that he'd bought on his mother's account. How could he return it to the shop now it was all stained? He laughed slightly hysterically. It had been such a good plan: he was going to make it sound as if he really didn't want to take it back off her, but would, as a favour when Catherine realised she wouldn't be able to take it home.

Coats? Why was he thinking about fucking coats? It was Catherine he should be worrying

42

about. And the law.

Shit! As soon as the ambulance crew saw what had happened, they'd be sure to start sniffing about. Danny would go raving mad, his mother would go crazy, and as for his father . . . No, that didn't even bear thinking about.

How was he going to get out of this little lot?

He couldn't help it. He hadn't known when he'd first met her that Catherine was one of the O'Donnells. But at least he knew she'd understand why he'd had to leave her out in the road like that. She knew how families like theirs worked.

And he'd make it up to her. Show her he loved her. Find those crap hounds who'd hurt her, and kill them. Or maybe let the bastards know who she was. That'd do the trick all right—finding out the O'Donnells were after you.

And when he finally sorted everything out they'd have the best life together. He'd get them a beautiful house, they'd have lovely kids, and Catherine would be the best-looking wife a bloke could ever dream of.

His hand hovered over the telephone. He should call an ambulance. No. Let them animals out there do it. Let them explain what they'd done, and why they had a sawn-off shotgun in a London street in the middle of the afternoon.

He swallowed hard. He'd better have a quick look round the watchman's door in the yard gates, make sure they'd sorted her out. That they hadn't driven off and left her there.

Then he'd get himself back home.

He had no choice. If he didn't get back in time for the Shabbas meal his mother would kill him before his father had the chance. And God alone knew what Danny would do to him if he realised his car had been missing all afternoon.

What a fucking mess.

## CHAPTER THREE

As Brendan screeched out of Brick Lane and onto the Bethnal Green Road, Pete Mac lurched across the back seat.

'Get off her, you stupid bastard,' yelled Luke. 'I'm trying to bring her round and you're fucking suffocating her.'

'That's nice language in front of your sister.' Pete Mac was doing his best to sound casual, but he was very close to losing control of his bowels. Gabe was gonna kill him for this.

'Anyway, it ain't my fault. It's him. He's driving like a bloody maniac.' Pete Mac squeezed himself into the corner, putting as much distance between him and Catherine as the back seat of a Standard saloon allowed. 'And maybe I could see what I was doing if you hadn't smashed me nose open for me, Luke. You've made all me eyes puff up. Patricia's gonna have the right hump when I go home looking like this.'

Luke lifted a blood-stiffened strand of hair away from Catherine's drawn and pallid face, speaking to Pete Mac as he stroked her cheek with the side of his thumb. 'You're lucky that's all I did to you. You couldn't even help me grab that pigeon you dozy, useless bit of crap. If I hadn't chucked me coat over it in time, how would it have looked?'

The soreness in his hands from the beating he

had given Joshua long forgotten, Brendan whacked them down on the steering wheel, making the car swerve towards the middle of the road. *'Will you two keep quiet?* I'm trying to get us back to the yard without drawing attention to the fact that my sister is on the back seat with a fucking gunshot wound, and you two just . . .'

*A shotgun wound.*

*Jesus Christ.*

Brendan felt the vomit rise in his throat. The bitter taste making him close his eyes and grimace. He had to pull himself together. It wasn't quite dark yet, and now the bloody fog was starting to lift. He should get off the main drag and onto the back doubles before anyone got a look in the car.

Again he pulled the wheel hard to the right, and stuck his foot down on the floor, swerving off the Bethnal Green Road and round into Chilton Street.

Luke cradled Catherine closer, protecting her as the car raced across the busy junction. 'Come on, Cath. Wake up,' he whispered into her ear. 'Give us one of your smiles.'

*'What the hell now?'* Brendan stamped on the brake.

'What's the matter with you? It's only a removal van.' Pete Mac was peering over Brendan's shoulder. 'You could get a bus past that, easy. And this girl needs a doctor, mate.'

'What d'you think I'm trying to do?' Brendan spat the words through gritted teeth as he stuck the car in reverse, and twisted round to see where he was going. Batting Pete Mac out of the way, he roared the car back onto the Bethnal Green Road.

He'd finally urged the complaining engine back

into top when he had to hit the brakes yet again. A kamikaze copper had jumped out in the road, right in front of them, his hand stuck in the air, palm outward, in a command to stop. Not exactly what they needed. Not now. Not with his sister bleeding all over the back seat, and with Pete Mac looking like he'd been in the ring with Rocky Marciano.

'What's going on?' Luke tugged at Catherine's coat, doing his best to hide the blood behind the high fur collar, and motioned for Pete Mac to help him kick the pile of weapons under the front seat. 'You don't think they're after us already, do you, Brendan?'

'Dunno.'

Brendan fumbled around, lighting a cigarette. The car had to reek of blood. He puffed on it furiously, creating his own, personal, indoor fog, and then slowly wound down the window. 'Yeah?' he said, exhaling smoke out of the side of his mouth.

The policeman smiled. 'Congratulations, sonny.' He spoke in an agonisingly slow Welsh accent. 'You're my first of the day.'

'Do what?'

The officer held up a gadget that looked like a cross between a Pifco hair dryer and a Martian ray gun. 'Another weapon in the armoury of the crime fighter.' His voice was full of proud admiration for the thing. 'A weapon to stop toe rags like you from making the streets dangerous for law abiding folk—' he jerked his thumb over his shoulder '— like those little old ladies over there, innocently buying their potatoes and greens from the fruit and vegetable stall.'

He sighed contentedly, all shiny uniform buttons

46

and self-congratulation. 'Been brought in specially, I have, to train the locals on the equipment.'

Brendan flicked the barely smoked cigarette out of the window. '*Toerags* like me?' The dangerousness of the situation forgotten, Brendan was frowning hard, as if he were concentrating on trying to understand what the man could possibly mean. 'Do you know who I am?'

'Well, let's see, shall we?' The policeman rested one hand on the roof of the car and lowered his head to get a better look at Brendan's face.

Hurriedly, Luke wound down the rear window to get some fresh air circulating, folded his arm around his sister as if she were a sleeping lover, and told her quietly, 'It's okay, Cath, I'll look after you.'

'With that quiff, you do bear more than a passing resemblance to Mr Presley. But you can't be Elvis, now can you? He's away in the army, isn't he? But there is something a bit greasy about you. Here, you're not him are you? Not gone AWOL or nothing? Cos you do know I'd have to report you if you have? Serious offence, deserting. But, let me think. Are you officially back in Civvy Street yet? Now there's a puzzler.' He tapped his finger on his chin in a sarcastic pantomime of contemplation. 'Tell you what, I'll ask my young Lesley, she knows all about you rock and roll stars.'

'All right, Taff. Just tell me. What's the SP here? What you after?'

The officer's nostrils flared. He straightened up, beckoned for his colleague, who was waiting over by the police car, to join him, and said very slowly, 'What did you call me, *sir*?'

'I think you'd be better off knowing what to call me, actually, *mate*. O'Donnell mean anything to

47

you?'

A momentary cloud passed across his face. Why was this little cockney yob so confident? 'No. Nothing.'

'Anything wrong?' asked the other officer as he sauntered over, clearly bored with his lot. This definitely wasn't his idea of a good use of a Friday afternoon.

'Yes, I should say there's something wrong. This gentleman reckons I should know him. Name of O'Donnell.'

'O'Donnell?' the other man repeated, suddenly alert, dropping his head to get a look at the driver.

It was taking Brendan every ounce of willpower not to slam the car into first, shove his foot down on the accelerator, and get Catherine as far away as possible from this swede-bashing idiot and his stupid bloody machine. But he had to be sensible. Keep calm. Don't create a commotion.

'Yeah, that's right. I'm Brendan, Gabriel's son.'

The second officer didn't miss a beat. 'Of course, sir. Just see if you can take it a bit easier next time, eh?' He flicked a forefinger against the rim of his helmet. 'Remember, safety first and all that.'

'Thanks, I'll remember. Constable . . . ?'

'Medway, sir.'

'Constable Medway. Thank you. And I'll make sure I remember you and your family at this special time of the year.' He directed a look at the other man. 'And I'll make sure I remember your mate and all.'

'Thank you, sir.' Medway bent closer. 'Sorry for the misunderstanding; didn't recognise the motor.'

As he pulled away, Brendan caught the two

policemen reflected in his rear-view mirror. They were still standing in the road, their faces almost touching. The local bloke, now all stabbing, pointing finger and snarls, was very obviously having the better of it. It was amazing how much of a focus the promise of a Christmas bonus—rather than the threat of a punch in the face, or something a whole lot worse—could give an officer.

*        *        *

Luke jumped out of the car and shoved back the high, corrugated iron gates of the scrap yard. Brendan drove in, sending the two Alsatians chained up by the lean-to office into a frenzy of barking.

He wrenched on the handbrake. What on earth was he going to tell his father?

He lifted his chin at Luke, signalling for his brother to help him shift Catherine off the back seat and into the office, then snapped at Pete Mac to deal with the blood inside the car.

For once, Pete Mac was glad to do as he was told. He definitely didn't fancy being there while they tried to talk to Gabriel. There was no chance he'd even listen while they explained how it had all been an accident. He never listened. Probably wouldn't even if Catherine herself was to tell him.

No, the best plan was for him to give the car a quick clean, then make himself scarce. Stay well out of Gabe's way for a bit. Give the bastard a chance to have a few drinks and calm himself down.

*        *        *

Brendan stood by his father's scratched and rickety desk, just as he had done a long, bewildering hour and a half ago.

'I swear to you, Dad,' he said, showing the palms of his hands, an innocent man. 'I haven't got any other explanation. It just all went wrong. Kessler's boy started struggling with Pete and the gun went off. And I really, on my life, do not know why Catherine was there. All I know is she was suddenly in the middle of it. And she got hurt. Truly, that's all I know.'

Gabriel O'Donnell covered his still unconscious daughter with the tartan rug that was usually draped over the bulging springs of the battered sofa on which his sons had carefully set her down. He knelt on the floor beside her and stroked his hand lovingly across her blood-caked cheek in an unwitting echo of the gesture made less than twenty-five minutes ago by Sammy Kessler.

In his other hand, Gabriel held a blood-smeared tumbler half full of Jameson's. 'Luke,' he said, his voice gruff and halting from trying to hold his emotion in check. 'Go to the Albion. Get Stonely. He knows to keep his mouth shut.'

Luke's eyes flicked towards the glass in his father's hand. As usual, the whiskey had been the first thing he'd reached for. He knew he had to talk to him before he poured too much more of the stuff down his neck. He looked again at his little sister, willing her to wake up.

'Can Brendan go and get him, Dad? There's something I need to talk to you about.'

Gabriel knocked back the rest of his drink in a single swallow, screwing up his eyes as the liquor hit the back of his throat, and banged his glass down on the floor. Then he took his daughter in his arms. 'For fuck's sake, one of you fill that glass, and the other one of you go and get Stonely. And be fucking quick about it.'

Brendan, as wary as his brother when their father had a drink in him, said softly, 'I'll fetch the doctor, Dad.'

As soon as Brendan had closed the door behind him, Luke tore his gaze away from Catherine, and started talking; the words spilling from his mouth in a tumble of fear of his father and the shame of betraying his sister. 'Dad, she's been seeing him for nearly two months.'

Gabriel didn't react.

'Sammy Kessler. It's why I didn't want us to go over there today. Why I tried to stop us. I didn't want any trouble. I thought maybe we could talk to 'em. Work things out.'

Gently, Gabriel eased Catherine's head onto the arm of the grubby sofa, and scrabbled awkwardly to his feet. 'But you didn't think to stop her?'

Luke stared at the floor, unable now to face either his sister or his father. 'She wanted it kept secret.'

Gabriel walked slowly towards his son. 'Let me see if I understand you right, boy. I knock my pipe out earning a living, making sure you all have the good things in life, everything you want and need, and you keep secrets from me?' He cocked his head to one side. 'You *did* say it was a secret?'

'Yeah.' He could smell and feel his father's whiskey breath on his face, but still he couldn't look at him. 'She loved him, Dad. She showed me this photo. Down the coast somewhere. She knew

51

she could show it to me. Knew I wouldn't shout at her. They'd gone on a day out. Just the two of them.'

'Why didn't you stop her seeing him?' Gabriel's voice was thin, defeated.

'I tried to stop us going—'

'Today. The day I told you to take . . .' Gabriel leaned back against the wall. 'Told you to . . .'

Slowly, Luke raised his head and looked directly into his father's face. 'She's dead isn't she?'

Luke's only answer was the sight of the tears streaming down his father's face.

\*       \*       \*

The bottle of Jameson's in Gabriel's hand was now half empty, and logic was taking increasingly haywire paths through his shock- and booze-washed synapses. There were secrets, and lies, and things that didn't add up. Things he couldn't understand. Luke had kept a secret from him. And so had Catherine. And the boys had let that fucking idiot, Pete Mac, who couldn't wipe his own arse without a map, actually handle the shot gun. All that was bad enough, and he knew he'd have to deal with it all—deal with all of them—but what was haunting him, what Gabriel couldn't get his head around, was Eileen telling him that Catherine was indoors with her and Patricia.

If only she'd told him, he wouldn't have let the boys take that stinking thing with them. And he'd have never let Pete Mac go anywhere near the place.

It was all Eileen's fault.

And now his little girl was dead, and he had to

get Eileen out of the way while he cleaned up the mess.

He swallowed another mouthful of whiskey.

He should have had more control over them. Over Eileen, over Patricia, over Catherine . . .

But it was still him who had told them to take the gun. No matter how he tried to make it otherwise.

His tears flowed. Whatever else happened, Eileen must never, ever find out that he was as good as responsible for his own daughter's death.

Never.

He knelt down and tucked the tartan rug round Catherine's now cold, lifeless body, closed his eyes and asked God to take care of her soul.

Then he hauled himself to his feet. 'I walloped you boys once you were old enough to understand,' he said, staring down at the grubby, oil-stained lino. 'Kept you in order after your mother had spoiled you as babies. But Patricia and Catherine, your mother carried on letting them get away with things. And look where it's got them. Pat stuck with MacRiordan. And Catherine . . .'

He turned and looked at Luke, thrusting the glass into his face. 'You listen to me, boy. You do exactly as I say. You go and stop Brendan from bringing that drunken old bastard Stonely anywhere near this place, then the two of you, you get straight back here. And you bring Peter MacRiordan with you.'

As soon as Luke had left, Gabriel picked up his private telephone. 'Rosie, my love. Something's come up. I won't be coming round later. I . . .'

He tried to say something else, but couldn't. Sobs shuddered through his chest.

The woman on the other end of the telephone frantically tried to make sense of what was going on, but his blubbering and the booze were making his voice thick, his words barely audible. 'Gabe, darling, what's wrong? Talk to me, Gabriel, please. You're frightening me. Gabe, has Eileen found out?'

No answer.

'*Gabe. Has Eileen found out?*'

'No,' he managed to say. 'Not yet. God help me.'

\*        \*        \*

Brendan and Luke were back in the office within ten minutes. Dr Stonely had had a win on the horses, and had been as drunk as a ship's rat trapped in the rum store, and Brendan hadn't been able to rouse him from his chair, let alone lure him away from the saloon bar of the Albion.

Their father had just put down the telephone after finishing a second brief, equally confused conversation. He'd been speaking to his sister, Mary, who lived on his stud farm in County Kildare with her husband, Sean Logan. Gabriel had been arranging for his sister to be unwell.

Actually, Mary was far from unwell; she was a tall, strong woman—tough as a jockey's arse, most people would say—but she was always more than willing to help her brother. Sean Logan was a bit trickier, glad of Gabriel's patronage, but not exactly reliable with anything that might involve using his brains. But Mary would sort him out.

Gabriel motioned for his sons to be quiet and dialled yet another number.

'Eileen,' he slurred. 'It's me. Want you to go over

54

and stay with Mary for a few days.'

He paused, listening.

'You know, women's things. Sean's as useless as a two bob watch. She needs you, Eileen. Right away. Brendan'll sort out the ferry tickets. And Pete Mac can run you to the station.'

Luke waved both his hands and mouthed, 'He's not here.'

'Sorry, my mistake. Pete's busy. Luke'll take you.'

Eileen crossed herself. Please, please don't let him tell me to take Catherine with me. From the sound of it, he'd hit the bottle early today and would explode with temper if he found out she wasn't there.

She could have wept with relief when Gabriel said, 'And don't worry yourself about leaving us lot to manage on our own for a few days. Catherine and Patricia can look after us.'

'Patricia's gone home to get Peter's tea ready for him,' she said, glad of an opportunity to tell the truth for once. 'And before you say anything, she didn't go home in the fog by herself. Stephen Shea dropped by with an envelope for you and so I got him to drive her.'

When Gabriel didn't answer immediately Eileen felt the need to say something, anything to fill the gap. 'You're always saying he's the best driver you've ever met.'

'Yeah, he's a good man, Stephen Shea.'

'Are you all right, Gabriel?'

He looked at his daughter's body. 'Me, Eileen? Sure, I'm just grand.'

*     *     *

Eileen went slowly upstairs to her and Gabriel's bedroom, took a small leather case from off the top of the wardrobe and started distractedly filling it with things for her stay at the stud farm. Sweaters, a thick tweed skirt. Then she took a selection of bras, panties and underslips from her dressing table, but paused, clasping them to her chest, as she wondered why she was being sent over to Ireland this time.

She knew it was nothing to do with Mary Logan. Eileen would be the last person her sister-in-law would want around the place if she were really ill. There'd been no love lost between them for years, not since Mary and her mother had accused Eileen of plotting to steal away their breadwinner, when she had started walking out with Gabriel when she was barely sixteen years of age.

Maybe he wanted her to take one of his brick-shaped packages over again—the packages that contained *none of your concern, woman.* But it was obvious to Eileen what they contained. She wasn't stupid, and she'd realised a long time ago that the stud was as much to do with hiding profits from the London businesses as it was about breeding Irish horses. For Gabriel it was a purely practical decision; working on the principle that a middle-aged woman wouldn't draw attention to herself and so was less likely to be searched, it simply made sense to him—regardless of what she might feel.

Or maybe he was planning something big and just wanted her out of the way. It wouldn't be the first time she'd been treated as an inconvenience when he had a crowd around the house to discuss men's business.

Patricia would be disappointed, but Eileen knew there was no point in trying to argue with Gabe—there was no point anyone trying to argue with him—especially not when he had a drink in him. So, she was going and that was final. There was always another day to go shopping. And Patricia was learning to understand disappointment as much as her mother.

*     *     *

Pete Mac sat on the grubby, pink, frilled bedspread grimacing each time the iodine-soaked cotton wool made contact with his bloody nose.

'Oi, watch it! Be careful, can't you?'

'Aw, my poor Pete.'

'Poor? I'm not poor. Why does everyone act like I'm some sort of charity case or something? Like they're doing me a favour all the time.' Pete Mac reached into his pocket, pulled out a roll of notes and tossed it onto the pillows. 'I don't think that makes me poor, darling, do you?'

She picked up the money and smiled. 'Course not, Pete.'

'Good. Now get your clobber off, Violet, I need a blow job to calm me down, girl. I've had a right fucking day of it.'

## CHAPTER FOUR

Pete Mac lumbered into the office, pausing in the doorway to check Gabriel's mood. Seeing his father-in-law with his head in his hands, obviously nearing alcohol-induced unconsciousness, he held up the final edition of the *Evening Standard*. 'Here, see this? I reckon we pulled it off.'

'Where the hell have you been?' Luke, who was standing in the corner of the shabby lean-to, spoke to Pete Mac without once taking his eyes from the tartan rug covering the body of his sister.

'Had a few things to sort out, didn't I.' Pete Mac lifted his chin, proud of himself. 'Picked up a few bob from the girls—Anthony persuaded them back on the street where they belong—and then I . . . But never mind all that, have a listen to this.'

Pete Mac picked up the paper, cleared his throat and began to read—quietly so as not to disturb Gabriel. ' "*Following reports of gunshots this afternoon, two police cars attended the scene. Officers discovered evidence of blood on the roadway, but soon established that this had come from a pigeon, which, apparently, had been struck by a passing vehicle.*" '

He winked at Luke. 'Nice touch that, mate, stomping that thing's brains out. Good thinking. Plant the evidence, eh?'

'No thanks to you,' muttered Luke.

Pete chose not to hear him. ' "*The police are assuring locals . . .*" '

'I asked you where you've been, Pete.' This time Luke was looking right at him. 'I should have been here with Dad and Brendan, and . . .' His words trailed off as he turned and looked again at the tartan rug. 'But I had to drive Mum to the station so she could get the boat train.'

Pete Mac frowned, pulled his chin into his neck, and looked sideways at Luke. 'She's your mother, mate, not mine.'

Brendan, who'd been sitting on a straight-backed kitchen chair, with his elbows on his knees, his hands dangling between his legs, and his head bowed, sprang to his feet. He snatched the paper from Pete Mac's hand and threw it on the floor and grabbed Pete Mac by the collar. 'Ain't you even gonna ask how she is?'

Pete Mac pulled away from Brendan and glanced nervously over at Gabriel. He was slumped forward, his cheek squashed on the desk, snoring like a hog. 'Yeah, course, I didn't like to, you know, intrude. So, how is she?'

'She's fucking dead.'

Brendan only just managed to swerve out of the way as Pete Mac vomited in a spectacular arc right across the greasy carpet.

*         *         *

'For Christ's sake, Pete, be quiet.' Brendan was staring out of the window into the yard, smoking to cover the stench of vomit.

'But are you sure Gabe knows it was an accident? That I'd *never*, *ever* have intentionally hurt a hair of that girl's head? He's got to believe me.'

Luke, who was spreading sheets of the *Evening Standard* over the mess, paused and turned to Pete Mac. 'Please, Pete. Do as Brendan says. I mean it. You'll only make things worse if you don't keep your mouth shut.'

Pete Mac took a breath as if to speak, but just nodded.

Brendan pulled the window down a crack, flicked the cigarette outside then turned to face

59

them. 'Okay. Luke's got Mum off on her way to Aunt Mary, and now we know—finally—where everyone is, and that no one's had a tug or nothing.'

At the mention that he might just possibly have been pulled in by the law, Pete Mac gulped back another rise of bile in his throat.

Brendan raked his fingers through his hair. 'Now, we can get on.'

'So, what we gonna do?'

Brendan shook his head. 'In your case, Pete? As you're told, that's what you're gonna do.' He pointed at his mouth. 'So, zip that and wait till you're spoken to. Right?' He picked up the phone and dialled.

'Hello, Stephen? It's Brendan. I need to see you. Over here at the scrap yard, mate. Soon as you can. All right?'

\*     \*     \*

Stephen Shea was middle-aged, of average height and medium build. He had light brown hair, and a pleasant, if not particularly handsome, face. He wasn't loud, but was willing to have a bit of a laugh. He liked a pint, but wasn't given to getting drunk. He had a wife and a couple of grown-up kids, and lived in a neat terraced house off the Whitechapel Road. In other words, he was a regular, unremarkable sort of a bloke. But what set him apart was that, as far as cars were concerned, Stephen Shea was a genius: the best wheelsman in the whole East End, probably in the whole of the Southeast of England, according to those who knew about such things. That and the fact that he would have killed with his bare hands for his friend, Gabriel O'Donnell. Gabriel had looked after Sheila and the kids—Sheila, his childhood sweetheart, who'd married him despite the fact that she'd become Sheila Shea—when Stephen had been put away for a full handful for his part in a bungled bank job for which he'd taken the entire blame.

He hadn't even earned the gratitude of the two pathetically unsuccessful, small-time crooks who had screwed it all up, and who had since disappeared off the face of the earth—or rather to the south of Spain—warned off, according to rumour, by a furious Gabriel O'Donnell, who had very little time for amateur tosspots messing things up and getting the law sniffing round. Stephen still blushed at the mere thought of his involvement with the pair of knob-headed prats. But that was all in the past. Stephen had learned his lesson, and since that day had been employed by no one but the O'Donnells.

'Sorry, She,' he said, putting down the phone and looking longingly at the plate of corned beef hash, peas and carrots he hadn't even had the chance to taste. 'Got to pop out, babe.'

Sheila nodded with a little smile; she was nothing if not an understanding wife. 'Don't worry, love, I'll keep it warm for you. Make you some nice fresh gravy when you get back.' She touched his cheek with her lips. 'Time for just a quick cup of tea and a slice of cake before you go?'

'Sorry.'

'All right, go on. I'll see you later. And you look after yourself, yeah?'

Stephen Shea walked through the door of the lean-to office in the O'Donnells' scrap yard ten minutes later. He looked worried.

'If you're concerned about the takings from the street pitches, Brendan, on my life, I collected them all as usual, and dropped off the envelope round yours this afternoon. You can phone your mum, if you like. I had intended giving them to your dad like we'd arranged.' He couldn't help snatching a look at Gabriel, who was still sprawled, snoring across the desk. 'But he wasn't there. And then your mum asked me to drive your Patricia home because of the fog. And cos I didn't know how long it would take in this weather, I thought it'd be best to leave the dough there for when your dad got home later on.'

He hesitated before adding quietly, 'You don't have to worry. I told Eileen the envelope was full of receipts from that demolition job over Vicky Park way. And no need to worry about your Pat.' He was addressing Brendan rather than Pete Mac. 'She got home just fine.'

'Thanks, Steve. We appreciate you looking after her. And, as you can see, Dad got held up anyway.'

Stephen took another quick look at his boss. He was obviously out for the count. 'Yeah, and I don't wanna go upsetting him, Brendan. But if I can say—between us like—that Jewish mob what set up the betting pitches opposite ours. They were there again today. Opposite every single pitch. And every one of them had some big bloke minding 'em. West Indian looking some of them. Definitely not fellers I recognise from round here. I didn't know what to do. From what our blokes told me the takings are gonna be well down.'

'It's okay, Steve, Dad knows already.'

Stephen Shea looked relieved, and nodded as though that explained things. 'So, that's what you wanted to talk about.'

'No, this ain't about the takings, mate. Or the Kesslers. Not even their minders.' Brendan pointed to the tartan rug, rubbed his hand over his eyes, and sighed wearily. 'Stephen. We need a favour, mate. A right big one.'

*     *     *

It was nine o'clock on Saturday morning, yet despite the amount of alcohol Gabriel had consumed in his office the day before, and the half-bottle of Bushmills he had swallowed when he had come round after his sons had eventually got him home last night, Gabriel was now stone cold sober. He was standing in the big, basement kitchen of the family home, a cosy room that would have fitted more easily into an Irish farmhouse than with the 'contemporary' show home look favoured by Patricia and Catherine. He was holding aside the starched, white lace curtain that usually shielded the shallow window set high in the wall.

He looked up, watching the passing feet of people going on their way to do their ordinary, uncomplicated things in their ordinary, uncomplicated lives. The fog was as bad as it had been the previous day, deadening the sound of the passing shoes as they struck the pavement, making them sound as if they were bound in cloth like the hooves of funeral horses, muffled out of respect for the dead.

He let go of the curtain, looked at his watch, and then went over to the blue and white china-decked dresser, close to the telephone. He glanced across at his two boys sitting at the table. They were staring down at their untouched tea and toast: their half-hearted attempt at having breakfast, their failed crack at acting as if everything was normal.

Scrap, Eileen's big tan dog nuzzled up to him, hoping for a treat, a scratch behind the ear, or maybe even a walk, but Gabriel wasn't one to waste time on pets at the best of times, and on a day like this he felt almost murderous. 'For fuck's sake,' he yelled. 'Get this thing away from me, will you?'

Luke grabbed the animal by the collar. 'He's missing Mum.'

Gabriel was about to snap another obscenity at his son, when the telephone rang. Even though he had been expecting it, he still looked horrified.

He checked his watch again, took a moment to compose himself, picked up the phone, listened, and then let it fall from his hand.

As the receiver swung and twisted back and forth on its cord, knocking against his leg then against the side of the dresser then against his leg again, Gabriel closed his eyes, crossed himself and mouthed for God to forgive him.

Luke hurried over to his father and replaced the receiver gently in its cradle.

'Dad?'

'I know it's how it was arranged.' Gabriel's eyes were still closed. 'How we had to do it, but I still can't believe it's over. Not so soon.' He was speaking more to himself than to either of his sons. 'She's gone, God love her.'

64

Luke tried to steer Gabriel back to the table, to sit him down, but he pushed his son away and picked up the phone again.

Luke looked over at Brendan, but Brendan shook his head.

'Leave him,' he murmured.

Gabriel pressed his lips together, took a deep breath and dialled. 'Sean, it's Gabriel. I need to speak to Eileen.'

There was a pause, and then he spoke again. 'Eileen, I'm sorry to have to do this by phone, but there's some bad news.'

He couldn't go on.

Brendan took the receiver from his father's hand.

'Mum, it's me, Brendan. You'd better sit down. I've got something to tell you. No, please, let me finish, this ain't easy. You've got to come home. Right away. There's been an accident. A bad one. It was this morning. In the fog. It's Catherine. She's—'

He stopped speaking, trying to make out what was going on at the other end of the line. 'Mum?'

'Gabe, it's Mary here, whatever's wrong?'

'It's not Dad, Aunt Mary, it's me. Brendan. What's happened to Mum?'

'Your mammy's fainted. But she'll be all right. Sean's seeing to her right now, getting her a drink of water. Tell me, what's all this fuss about?'

'Aunt Mary, I've got some really bad news. It's Catherine. She's been in a car crash. A serious one. The car burst into flames. There was a terrible fire. And poor little Catherine . . .' Brendan gulped back his tears. 'Aunt Mary, she didn't get out in time. Aunt Mary, Catherine's dead.'

Pete Mac stood outside the door of his house in Jubilee Street, or rather the house that Gabriel had bought for him and Pat as soon as he had found out she was pregnant, and that they were—of course, no question about it, no point even mentioning it— getting married.

A. S. A. fucking P.

He stared at the immaculately black-leaded door furniture and sucked noisily at his teeth. He knew that having a whole house to themselves was a luxury that few couples in the East End could enjoy, especially couples as young as him and Pat. What with all the slum clearances, and the housing shortages that were still being blamed by the authorities on the war, and the overcrowding and multiple occupancy of homes that was simply accepted by most people as a way of life, they were genuinely privileged to have so much space to kick about in.

But Pete MacRiordan loathed the bloody place more than he could say. It was so nice, so tidy, so rotten, well, *just so*. Like Pat and her sodding knick-knacks, her poncy curtains, and her fancy bone china cups with their dinky little saucers.

Why couldn't she just leave the washing-up in the sink for once? Forget about it till he'd gone off down the pub? She could clear up then till her heart's bloody content. Why did she have to fuss about doing stuff while he was still around?

But that wasn't a question he was allowed to ask, because it didn't make sense, not in the world of the O'Donnells it didn't. Because in their world the

66

O'Donnells did exactly as they liked. But they told you what to do, and you did what you were told.

It was as simple as that.

Take this performance today. He'd said to them at the yard last night: why did it have to be him who had to tell Pat? Why couldn't one of them tell their precious sister the news? He knew she'd take it much better from one of them. But they hadn't even bothered to answer him.

It made him so mad, he felt like telling them what they could do with their so-called 'family business', and with the 'favours' they reckoned they did him all the time. But he couldn't, because now they had him good and proper.

It was bad enough when the only thing they'd had over him was him getting Pat up the duff before they got married. As if he'd have even dreamed of marrying the miserable bitch without them forcing him into it. Why he'd ever let her talk him into playing Vatican roulette, he'd never know, but he'd never do it again, that was for sure. It was French Letters or nothing from now on. Preferably nothing while he had young Violet to turn to. But now he'd made the mistake with the sawn-off, the O'Donnells really had something over him. They'd be on his back for the rest of his natural. It was a fucking depressing thought. He felt really sorry about what had happened to Catherine—she wasn't a bad kid—definitely, the best one of the O'Donnells. But he hadn't wanted to take the gun in the first place. That was Gabriel's fault. But would any of them listen? Course not. And it was why he had to do as he was told. It was a bloody farce.

Last night, when he'd got in, he'd had to tell

Patricia some old nonsense about a lump of scrap falling on him to explain away the bloody nose and all the bruising round his eyes. As if he ever shifted any scrap. Then, this morning, he'd had to feed her another load of old cobblers about why he was going into the yard so early. That was stupid in itself; he never went in before eleven. Especially on a Saturday.

As it was, Pat had hardly batted an eyelid over his injuries. Self-centred cow. But she'd had plenty to say this morning all right. She said he was selfish, waking her up so early. She didn't feel well. Felt sick or something. Like he cared.

Then he'd had to go to a phone box and call Brendan to make sure they all got their timings right, for when they talked about the 'accident'. After that he'd had to waste nearly half an hour driving around, just to account for the time it would have taken him to get into the yard, and for them to have told him about what had happened.

They reckoned all this palaver gave them all alibis. But if Shea was as bloody clever as they all said he was, then why did they need a cover?

And now he had to face Patricia with the next act in the circus.

He opened the front door, threw back his head and stared up at the pristine whiteness of the embossed paper on the hall ceiling.

Here goes. He puffed out his cheeks then called out, 'Pat, it's me, girl. I've got a bit of news for you.'

\*　　　\*　　　\*

'But she can't be dead.' Patricia stood in the hall, shaking her head, refusing to believe it. She was

68

wrapped in a thick candlewick dressing gown and had soft, warm slippers on her feet, but she was trembling as if she were standing there stark naked. 'She's seventeen years old.'

'Was seventeen years old, girl,' he said, with a sympathetic pulling down of his mouth.

Patricia felt as if she'd slipped into some strange parallel universe like you saw in the films, where everything was turned on its head, and where nothing made proper sense any more. 'And she couldn't even drive.'

'She could, Pat.'

Her head jerked up as if a string had been pulled. 'What? What're you talking about?'

'Luke had been teaching her.' He sighed disapprovingly, as if this were all his brother-in-law's fault. 'Doing it on the q.t. like, wasn't he. On that bit of waste-land behind the yard. It was his car she nicked to take out on her little jaunt. Silly girl, she wasn't experienced enough to drive in even good weather conditions. Not without supervision, she weren't. But in this fog . . . Well, it was a disaster waiting to happen, wasn't it, girl?' This time his disapproval was targeted on his young sister-in-law. 'Only, lucky she was by herself when she hit that wall, if you ask me. It would have been terrible if she'd hurt anyone else. In the accident.'

Patricia said nothing. She turned away from him and walked along the hallway towards the kitchen. She was going to throw up again, but this time it was nothing to do with morning sickness.

'Here, Pat,' he called after her. 'Any chance of a bit of breakfast, girl? Me belly feels like me throat's been cut.'

69

Pete Mac sat at the kitchen table. He wasn't exactly thrilled. After getting up so early, he was having to scrape by with a cup of tea and a bit of toast— hardly a breakfast for a man. And he'd had to make it himself. But even he had to admit that Pat did look a bit rough. She was still grasping the side of the sink, staring down at the water gurgling its way down the plughole.

He slurped the last of his tea, smacked his lips, and then wiped the back of his hand across his mouth. 'I'll have to be on my way now, girl,' he said. 'Got to get back into work, cos your lot are gonna be busy with other things today ain't they? Sorting out the funeral and that. So I'll have to be up the yard to take charge of the business.'

Pat stepped towards him. Her breathing was shallow as if she'd been running. 'Drop me round Mum's, Pete.'

'Aw, bugger.' Pete Mac stretched his lips across his teeth, grimacing and tutting at his own foolishness. 'That's something else I was supposed to tell you. Your mum, she's—'

'What?' Patricia leaned back against the sink, sweat beading on her forehead, unsure of how much longer she could stay upright. 'What's wrong with, Mum?'

Pete Mac looked affronted. 'Pat, will you, please, let me finish?'

'I'm telling you, Pete, if you don't—'

'All right. Your mum's over in Kildare with your Aunt Mary—'

Patricia opened her mouth but Pete Mac didn't let her get a word in; he had a story to get right.

'—who's ill or something. That's your Aunt Mary, I mean, not your mum. She's fine.'

With that, he stood up and left, leaving his dirty plate and cup on the table.

Patricia turned round, opened the tap and stuck her head under the cold water, letting it rush through her hair and down her neck, not caring that her dressing gown was getting soaked through.

He must have got it wrong. He must have. She couldn't be dead. She couldn't. Not Catherine . . .

*     *     *

Pete Mac stood outside the house pulling in lungsful of damp, foggy air to relieve his suffocation. He lit a cigarette and tapped his knuckles agitatedly against the wall, considering the day ahead of him. Maybe he should nip into the yard and phone Gabriel, let him know he was there, show him he was making an effort at a time of family tragedy.

He drew on his cigarette, holding down the smoke. He was going to have to come up with something to try and get himself back in Gabriel's good books.

## CHAPTER FIVE

Sammy Kessler hadn't heard a word from Catherine in well over a week. He was getting worried, really worried, and he wasn't feeling very proud of himself. Say she'd been hurt worse than he'd thought? He knew the gun had gone off, and that there was blood. But she couldn't have been that badly hurt. She just couldn't.

Maybe her dad had found out about them and had forbidden her from ever speaking to him again. He knew how his own father would react if he ever found out about them. Worst of all was the thought that she'd been so disgusted with him for leaving her to the mercy of those men, whoever they were, that it was she who never wanted to see or speak to him again—regardless of what her father thought.

If that was the way she felt, he couldn't say he blamed her. But he had to know.

He'd stood in the call box, just around the corner from his dad's haulage yard every night at six o'clock, waiting for the telephone to ring. They'd worked out their system soon after they'd met. Catherine would go to a friend's house, or another phone box, or even use the phone in her own home if the coast were clear, and she'd call him. Then they could speak to each other, like any other young couple, but without anybody knowing what they were up to.

Tonight, Sammy had been waiting for over a quarter of an hour, pretending every now and then to make a call, in a half-hearted effort to placate an angry looking man, who kept banging on the glass with the flat of his hand before finally giving up and stomping off, leaving a string of obscenities behind him. As far as Sammy was concerned, the man could have threatened to punch him on the nose and he still wouldn't have stirred from that phone box. He wouldn't even have let him in if he'd pleaded that he wanted to call 999. Sammy's need was greater. He had to speak to Catherine, to find out if she was all right, and to try and get her to understand why he'd panicked and run away.

Not knowing was driving him mad. He kept waking in the early hours, in a cold sweat, horrified by nightmarish visions of what could have happened to her after those men had taken her away. The dreams were becoming unbearable. Strange hands touching her body, her eyes pleading for mercy because she couldn't scream for help because of the gag they'd tied round her mouth. And the blood oozing around her. It was exhausting him. If he didn't do something soon people would start noticing. His mum would go on about him not getting enough rest. His dad would start accusing him of not pulling his weight. Then they'd start asking awkward questions.

He turned his wrist to catch the dim light from the bulb above his head, and looked at his watch.

Who was he kidding? She wasn't going to call. Not now. Not ever. Not till he explained. So, this was it. His last chance. He'd been putting it off all week, but the only option he had left was to try and contact Catherine through her brother—Luke, the one she said she could talk to. The one who knew that she and Sammy were friends, and that they were sort of seeing one another. But he had to be careful. Keep it light. Much as Catherine might think of him, her brother was still one of the O'Donnell boys.

Sammy flipped up the telephone directory, and searched through the listings for O'Donnell.

Sod it. There were half a dozen of them living at the Stepney end of the Mile End Road. Why hadn't he asked her for her full address? Because he hadn't needed it before, that's why. It wasn't as if her mum was planning on inviting him round for

Christmas dinner. He'd just have to call all of them.

He struck lucky on his fourth attempt.

'Hello, can I speak to Luke O'Donnell, please?'

'Who wants him?'

He hadn't thought this through. 'Er, John. John Smith.'

*John Smith?* Was he sure?

'Hang on, I'll get him.'

He heard some muttering, then someone said in a flat, dull voice, 'Ta, Brendan,' then, 'Ye'llo? Luke here.'

'Luke, I'm a friend of Catherine's. I think she might have told you about me. My name's Sammy.'

Luke turned his back to the table where Pete Mac was sitting staring at him with unashamed curiosity.

'Sorry, John, but I can't speak right now,' he said. 'Gimme a number where I can reach you and I'll call you later on.'

'Luke, please, listen. I need to know. Has your dad found out, or—'

'Honestly, this really ain't the time for this, John. Just gimme a number.'

The door at the top of the basement stairs opened and Gabriel stumbled down into the kitchen. 'Who's that on the phone?' His voice was thick from drinking.

Luke hurriedly scribbled down the number Sammy gave him and slammed down the receiver. 'No one, Dad.'

'Nothing to do with tomorrow?'

'No, nothing.'

Pete Mac folded his arms. 'It was some geezer, wasn't it, Luke? Reckons his name was *John Smith* if you can credit it. Sounds well monkey to me.

74

Who's ever heard of anyone really called *John Smith*? Not keeping any secrets from us are you, Luke? Feller calling you under a false name? What's all that about?'

Gabriel steadied himself with both hands against the table and looked into Pete Mac's face. His eyes were bloodshot and his focus was far from sharp, but his expression was clear enough. 'My wife's upstairs in our bed breaking her heart, while my daughter—your wife—tries to comfort her. And I'm going to bury my other daughter tomorrow morning. And we both know how she really died, don't we? So, do you think this is the time for your ignorant remarks?'

Pete Mac rose to his feet. 'Maybe it'd be better if I left.'

'You got something right for once,' Brendan hissed at him under his breath.

* * *

Pete Mac peered out at the world—or rather up at the grubby, cobwebbed ceiling—through swollen slits of eyes. He was on his back, in a lumpy bed, and his head was banging like a steam hammer.

And there was a bad smell, stale and musty, filling his nostrils. It was as if something had been soaked through, and then left in a screwed up heap to dry, far away from even a waft of fresh air.

Where the hell was he?

He heard soft snoring close to his ear, and, raising his head as far as the pain allowed, he swivelled his gaze sideways, trying not to move the rest of his body.

Violet?

75

He levered himself up into a sitting position, and hunted around for his watch on the clothes-strewn chair that served as a bedside table.

Quarter past eleven.

He wondered, for a brief, self-deluding moment if it was eleven at night, but the pale winter light slanting through the gap at the top of the curtains, where the wire drooped from a single, wonky nail, told him otherwise.

Shit! It was gone eleven o'clock in the morning. He'd been at Violet's all bloody night. And the funeral mass had started over an hour ago. And he was over in fucking Shadwell. He'd have to go straight to the cemetery.

He chucked the bedcovers off him, making Violet, who had still been asleep, wake up and begin complaining indignantly as the cold air hit her shoulders.

She stretched his name to three whining syllables. 'P-e-te. What d'you think you're doing?'

'I'm getting dressed, you daft cow. What d'you think I'm doing, tap dancing?'

'But your shirt . . .' The whine in her voice had levelled off into a sneer of disgust.

He picked it up off the floor and discovered it to be the pungent source of the really unpleasant stench. 'What the hell's happened to this?'

Violet snuggled back down under the blankets. 'Don't you remember?'

He turned and looked at her as if she were stupid. 'If I did, would I be asking?'

She smiled saucily over the edge of the covers. 'You brought a bottle of champagne round last night. And a bottle of Scotch. And after we—well, you—had polished off most of the whisky, you got

76

all, you know . . .' She turned her head and looked sideways at him in what she thought was a sultry imitation of the pictures she'd seen in her film magazines. 'Frisky. You told me to take off my clothes. And then you sprayed the bubbles all over me.'

She nibbled her bottom lip to stifle the giggle that was threatening to erupt. 'Trouble was, quite a lot of it went over you an' all. But you didn't care; you were too busy licking it off me bits to bother about your shirt. I wanted to rinse it out for you, but you were ever so insistent.'

She reached out and cupped his balls in her hand, squeezing them gently. 'Like a wild tiger you was, Pete, you filthy sod. Here, how about coming back to bed for a rematch?'

He pulled away impatiently. 'Leave off, Violet. Can't you see I'm in a hurry? Now get up and run an iron over this for me, while I stick me head under the tap and try and get rid of this bloody hangover.'

\*       \*       \*

Pete Mac abandoned, rather than parked, his car across the gates of the Catholic cemetery. He took a quick squint round, looking for the mourners, but could see only a group of formally clad men from the funeral directors, who were enjoying a smoke outside the chapel.

Bloody hell, not the chapel . . . Hadn't the requiem mass at St Joseph's been enough for them? Probably not, knowing Eileen. She'd be expecting every bit of knee bending, bell ringing and hymn singing that Father Shaunessy had to offer, and—just in case someone missed something—in as many venues as the old ponce could come up with. And, knowing him, he'd be more than happy to oblige. Anything to get a bit of extra wedge out of Gabriel.

Pete Mac puffed his way along the short path to the chapel, swearing that he would get himself back in shape, and stop drinking so much—first thing tomorrow morning. It would, after all, be impolite to refuse a glass or two at the wake. And, as he'd already missed the bit at the church, he'd better be on his best behaviour for the rest of the day. Keep his head down and play the game, do his bit as the caring, dutiful son-in-law.

He paused outside the chapel, pulled out a screwed up handkerchief from somewhere deep in his topcoat pocket and swiped it over his face. Despite the bitingly cold wind, and the heavy, grey-yellow sky, filled with the threat of snow, the short run had made him sweat, and had caused the stench from his shirt to waft up from his armpits like a miasma from some fetid, bodily swamp. Patricia was gonna just love that. Then he smarmed down the orange springs of his still damp hair with both hands, nodded to the undertakers, and wrenched open the heavy wooden door.

\*　　　\*　　　\*

The priest was well away, as if he'd been going at it for some time, and the place was packed, including the side and central aisles, where it was standing room only. As busy as Upton Park when the Hammers were playing at home.

Pete Mac looked across the sea of black clad,

heaving shoulders, the sobbing women with their veils and hats, and the misty-eyed men in their heavy winter overcoats. On one side of the chapel he noted a huddle of impressively senior coppers; and at the back, a clutch of cute little birds— friends of Catherine's no doubt, *very nice*—and spotted enough flattened noses, chiv marks and cauliflower ears, belonging to faces from both sides of the river, to start a full-blown bout of gang warfare. It was funny how a funeral had the so-called hard men coming over all sentimental; Pete Mac didn't get it himself, he thought it was all a bit effeminate. But, like he'd told himself, needs must. He had to take his 'rightful' place next to his poor, grieving wife.

God help him.

But how was he supposed to get to the front where the O'Donnells were sitting without having to barge his way through and make a right show of himself?

To his surprise, apart from the odd wrinkled nose, and a slight withdrawing as he passed by, most people seemed to be too lost in their own thoughts to bother with Pete Mac's lateness, or even the whiff from his shirt, and he managed to slide in beside Patricia with unexpectedly little fuss. Although a single look from her prat of a brother, Brendan, was enough of a warning to let Pete Mac know that he should expect rather more of a reaction a bit later on.

\*     \*     \*

While Pete Mac was wedging himself between Patricia and Luke, wondering how long he'd have

79

to sit on such an uncomfortable, arse-numbing bench, the three tearful, red-eyed young women at the back, whom he had rightly identified as friends of Catherine, were equally, if differently, preoccupied.

'Wonder which one's her boyfriend then, Jan,' sniffed the blondest of the three.

Janet dabbed at her nose with a soggy tissue and shook her head. 'He won't be here, Paul,' she sniffed back. 'He's Jewish.'

Pauline, taken aback, spoke more loudly than she'd intended. 'So?'

Bernadette, the third of the girls, and the only one of them from a Catholic family—though a long-since lapsed one—nudged Pauline in the side. 'Keep it down you two,' she said. She might not have been to mass for years—actually, not since the day her nan had insisted that her mother have her head wetted at the font—but she retained a fearful respect for religious practices. 'We are in a holy place, you know.'

'But what diff—'

'Don't you know anything, Pauline?' Bernadette swiped her eyes with the back of her gloved hand and leaned in closer to her friends so no one else could hear. 'That's what all that secret business was about. If Cathy's family had found out she was seeing a Jewish boy they'd have killed her.'

'Here, maybe it wasn't an accident. You don't think they did kill her, do you? You know, found out about them, and did her in.'

Janet, momentarily forgetting herself, rolled her eyes and sighed irritably. 'You really are dumb, ain't you, Paul? As if her own family would kill her. Bernie meant they'd go mad at her and put a stop to her seeing him.'

'Yeah, but you've got to admit, it is a bit fishy. I mean, she couldn't even drive, could she? So, why was she in the driver's seat of the car?'

Now it was Janet who leaned closer. 'That's where you're wrong again. If you must know, she could drive. I heard someone saying earlier. She'd been learning. With her brother. Luke. Him up there at the front.'

'He's bloody gorgeous.'

Bernadette looked appalled. 'Pauline, I'm sure you don't need reminding again, but we are at a funeral.'

'Yeah, I know, but look at him. I wouldn't say no.' She stood up, following the example of the rest of the congregation. 'I'd love to meet him. Do you think we'll be welcome at the do afterwards, Jan?'

'Oh, yeah, knowing Catherine's dad's views on us three, we'd be about as welcome as a dose of the pox.'

\*　　　\*　　　\*

As everyone filed out of the chapel towards the graveside, Pete Mac thought it wise to pre-empt any potential hostilities between him and Brendan.

'Surprised there's no newspaper people here,' he said, drawing Brendan to one side. 'Thought they'd want to at least report the accident, it being so tragic and everything.'

Brendan closed his eyes for a moment, dragging his fingers down his cheeks, then slowly buttoned his overcoat up to his throat. 'They've been warned off.' His voice was as cold as the wind that was now carrying the first flurries of snow, and it certainly didn't invite further conversation, but Pete Mac wasn't one to take a hint.

He flashed a simian grin showing pale pink gums and bits of the saveloy and chip supper that he'd shared with Violet the night before that were still stuck between his teeth. 'What, too many coppers here who want to keep their privacy? Who don't want to be seen at a do like this?'

Brendan felt too wrung out for this. What was wrong with MacRiordan that he didn't get anything right? He shook his head. 'Arse about face as ever, Pete. Why shouldn't police attend a *do* like this? It's a funeral. And Dad's a benefactor to all sorts of charities, and there's all sorts of people who wanna pay their respects to the family. All right? Plain enough for you?'

'Yeah, course. But why worry about the papers then?'

'Who said anyone's worried about them?' Brendan stared at his brother-in-law. Didn't the tosspot understand anything? Did nothing get through his thick skull? 'Clever people don't want their mooeys splashed all over the headlines. Not like them so-called Robin Hood heroes you read about in the *Evening News*.' He curled his lip in a sneer and spoke in a contemptuous imitation of an elderly woman. *'They've always looked after me and my old mum and we never have to worry about leaving our doors unlocked cos the streets are all safe with them around.* No. That ain't our style.' His voice was back to his own. 'And you should fucking well know that by now. We don't want a poppy show, we want privacy. Especially on a day like this. So, if only for the sake of Mum and Pat, break the habit of a lifetime and keep your trap shut. All right? Now get over there and stand with your wife, where you belong, God help her.'

## CHAPTER SIX

The hollow-eyed O'Donnells had led the mourners into the Star and Compass, the pub nearest the Catholic cemetery, a full half-hour earlier, but the proceedings were still very subdued. A wake for an elderly person—someone who'd had a good innings, whose life you could celebrate—that was one thing, but for a seventeen-year-old girl? That was another thing altogether. The food had hardly been touched, glasses barely lifted, and not a single note of an Irish ballad had been heard.

Eileen had been sitting in her own private silence. Since returning from Kildare the day after the accident, she had uttered only the words necessary to retain that solitude, to keep others at the distance she needed. But now she had plenty to say.

Ignoring Patricia and her sister-in-law, Mary Logan, she rose shakily to her feet and made her way over to Gabriel.

Pushing her way through the sombre group of awkward-looking men, who were standing with her husband, Eileen grabbed his wrist with such force that his eyes popped wide with astonishment.

'Why couldn't you let her live like other girls?' Eileen's voice came out as a tortured keen. 'Then there'd have been no need for her to tell lies. No need to go driving cars on her own. Going out and about God knows where.'

Gabriel, swallowing back the curses that were filling his mouth, said, quietly and politely, 'Excuse us, gentlemen.'

The men, putting Eileen's extraordinary behaviour down to grief—no one, not even his wife, spoke to Gabriel O'Donnell like that—nodded and muttered a ragged chorus of: *sure, of course, we're fine here*, and turned their attention to their drinks and a discussion of the racecard at Newbury.

Gabriel gripped her by the upper arm, and steered her over to a table in the far corner, indicating with a tip of his head for the occupants to move.

He sat her down with a shove, and stood over her, keeping his back to the room. 'You dare talk to me about lies? It was you who lied, Eileen. You knew she was going out. You told me she was indoors when she wasn't.'

'She was a young girl.' Eileen fumbled at her cuff for her handkerchief. 'She wanted to see her friends. Have a bit of fun.'

'What, like Patricia did, you mean?'

She looked up into the green, gold-flecked eyes of the man she had once loved more than life itself. 'You drove her to this, Gabriel O'Donnell. And you drove me to lying to you. You didn't let her move or breathe.'

He shook his head. 'No, Eileen. I won't let you do this to me. It's you who was in the wrong.'

'So, you were right, were you, making Luke lie to me, not letting him tell me about teaching Catherine to drive?' Images of her happy, laughing child, spinning around the house like a top, were making Eileen giddy. 'I'd never have agreed to her

84

doing that at her age.'

'Get up.' He cupped his hand under her elbow and steered her over to the bar, where Luke was standing with Brendan and Pete Mac.

'Luke,' said Gabriel, 'tell your mother why we kept Catherine's driving a secret.'

Luke gulped at his drink, giving himself time. What should he say? What did his father want him to say?

'She wanted to surprise you, Mum.' Another sip of his drink, a bit more time. 'Pass her test so she could take you and Pat out shopping and that.'

Eileen took her son's face in her hands. 'This is your sister's wake, Luke. If you're telling me more lies. If you're . . .' Her words dried up, her legs gave way, and Eileen O'Donnell collapsed on the pub floor: a shattered heap of black wool crepe and bitter tears of resentment.

Gabriel scooped her up as if she weighed little more than a child. 'Luke, get Stephen. It's time me and your mother were leaving.'

'All right, Dad, I'll come with you.'

*    *    *

In less than an hour, Eileen had been persuaded up to bed with a glass of water and a couple of the tranquillisers Dr Stonely had given her on her return from Ireland. Luke and his father were sitting at the kitchen table, much as they had been doing every day and night since what they now unfailingly referred to as the 'accident'. It was as if their denial of the reality of events somehow reshaped the truth of things, made them fit a more comfortable, or, at least, a more acceptable pattern.

Gabriel was in his shirtsleeves, his black tie loosened, and his braces dangling from his shoulders. He was nursing a very large whiskey, staring down into the glass as if it might hold the cure for his broken heart.

'Dad,' Luke said eventually. 'Can I talk to you?'

Gabriel let out a long, slow sigh. 'If you can tell me how to get drunk, so I can forgot this whole bloody mess, son, then talk away.'

'I'll pour you another drink.'

Gabriel held up his half-pint tumbler. 'I've got about a quarter of a bottle in here already.' He sipped at the liquor then took a bigger mouthful. 'Go on then,' he said, without looking at his son, 'top it up.'

Luke rocked his chair onto its back legs and lifted the bottle from the dresser behind him. He filled his father's glass almost to the brim and poured himself a double.

'Dad, someone told me something this morning. And it's made me think.' He flicked a look at his father. He looked as if his spirit had been drained out of him. His usually arrogantly handsome face was shadowed with loss. He could only hope he was listening, because he wouldn't have the courage to say this again. 'I reckon that since the accident it'd be all too easy for things to get out of control. That they could turn into something really serious.'

Gabriel hadn't shifted his gaze from his glass. 'Serious?' Even his voice betrayed his exhaustion. 'You're right there, boy. Because someone's gonna pay for this. Pay with everything they've got.'

'That's what I mean. And only you can stop it happening.'

Gabriel snorted, a soft roar. 'And, tell me, why should I do that?'

'It was an accident, Dad.'

'If she hadn't been with *him*, it would never have happened.'

Luke, wary of his father, but knowing he had no choice, risked going on. 'I've been thinking that maybe we should call a truce.'

Gabriel let out a humourless puff of laughter. 'A what?'

'With the Kesslers.'

Gabriel's hand flashed across the table. He grabbed Luke by the collar of his jacket, twisting it until it was tight up against his son's throat.

Luke could do nothing other than try to catch his breath. His father was capable of hurting people badly enough when he was sober, but, when he'd had drink in him, he was capable of anything.

'When I was younger than you,' Gabriel snarled, his face so close that Luke could see the flecks of saliva gathering in the corner of his father's mouth. 'I took a chance. A massive chance. I left your mother back home and came to this country, a strange place I'd never been to before, to see if I could get us a better life. A decent place to rear a family. And what did I find when I got here? Pubs and lodgings that had signs in the window saying "No dogs, no blacks, no Irish". I wasn't Mr Gabriel O'Donnell, a willing, hard-working man. No, I was Paddy. Mick. A stupid bog-trotting fool. Someone who was only given work because I was so poor I was prepared to do anything, and for less pay than anyone else. I learned my lesson then that nobody was going to make my dreams come true for me, boy. So I showed them all that I'd do it for myself.

Every fucking one of them.'

He let go of Luke, shoving him back in his chair. His sudden rush of energy spent.

'And you want me to do deals with the Kesslers? The fuckers who took away my child? The scum who think they can come back here and take away everything I've ever worked for?'

'It wouldn't be like that. They'd be more or less working for us. We'd make sure we kept control of things. Protected our interests.' Luke was speaking quickly, spilling out his words before his courage failed him. 'Have them buy moody scrap off us, say. At the right price. Or something else that'd tie them in. Make sure they were involved, but in a way that they couldn't cause any trouble for us.'

Gabriel sniffed dismissively. 'You have been thinking, son.'

'Look, Dad, you of all people, you know how this sort of thing gets out of hand. You take that first step and that's it. You can't go back. You're over the line. And then, before you know it, you're at war. Like with the mob over in Bermondsey. Businesses got neglected, some even ruined, but worst of all, people were killed, remember?'

'Remember? Yeah, I remember. People were killed. Just like your sister was.'

'And that's exactly what I'm talking about. Taking the gun with us, it was the step too far. The step that pushed it over the edge.'

Gabriel felt the guilt surging up in his chest. He looked his son directly in the eye. 'Are you saying,' his voice was low, 'it's my fault Catherine's dead?'

'No, Dad,' Luke lied, bowing his head, knowing his father should never have given them the gun. 'What I'm saying is, do you wanna start something

88

with the Kesslers. Have it all go off, and risk the business, and risk losing me as well? And Brendan? And the men who've been so loyal to you—they'd be targets right away. Men like Barry Ellis. Kevin Marsh. Stephen Shea. Anthony. And how about all the other blokes who work for you? And their families. And d'you wanna put Mum at risk? And Patricia . . .'

Luke ran his tongue around his parched lips. Should he be saying this? Why not, it was the reason he'd even thought of such a wild idea in the first place, why he was brave enough to be saying any of these things to his drink-fuelled, grief-maddened father.

'Dad, you know earlier, when I said someone told me something?'

No reaction other than another mouthful of whiskey.

'It was Patricia. While we were waiting to see if Pete Mac was gonna turn up for the Mass.'

'She told you what? That she married a fool?'

'No. That she's expecting.' He raised his hands. 'I know, I should have let her tell you herself. She ain't even told Pete Mac yet. But then nobody's acting exactly normal at the minute, are they?'

'Patricia's expecting a baby?' Gabriel was blinking as if someone had turned on the lights without warning him. 'When?'

'I'm not sure. But we've got to give this a try, Dad. For all our sake's, but especially for Patricia's.' Luke meant it. He wouldn't wait until there were more guns being flashed about and lives being threatened. He wouldn't let anyone harm a hair of Patricia's head. He'd swear to that on Catherine's grave.

89

'How's Mum?' It was Brendan, trudging down the stairs into the basement kitchen. He looked as exhausted as his father.

'She's resting. Dad got her to take some of them pills that Stonely gave her.'

Brendan dropped heavily onto the chair next to Gabriel's. 'Give us a glass of that.'

Luke tipped back and took another tumbler from the dresser. 'Everyone still down the Star?'

'Yeah, but Patricia was feeling a bit rough, so—'

'A bit rough?' Gabriel snapped. 'What's wrong with her?'

Brendan frowned, Christ the old man was losing it lately. 'Don't worry. She was upset, that's all. Like the rest of us. So I dropped her off home. Aunt Mary went with her to make sure she was all right.' He took his drink from Luke, eased off his tie and settled back in his chair. 'She'll be more use to her than Pete Mac.'

Luke poured himself a refill. 'Brendan, I've been talking to Dad.' He was speaking slowly now, cautious with his words. 'About how we should give it a go—cooling things down with the Kesslers. Before they get out of hand.'

Brendan slammed down his glass, spilling whiskey over the table. 'You *what*?'

'Look, we all know it'd be easy for us to go crazy. But like I was saying to Dad, think how it all went wrong with that team from over South London. They steamed in here with all them war surplus guns that were floating about, and—'

'And then Dad sorted it out.'

'Course he sorted it out.' Luke snatched a quick look at his father. 'Eventually. But how much damage did it do the business? And how many

90

people got hurt in the meantime? Really hurt. It makes sense for us to use our loaf over this, Brendan. We're doing well. Why risk losing any of it? This way we keep the power, and keep them in order at the same time. We'll be in charge, know exactly what they're up to. Plus a good weed out of anything they make. What do you think?'

'I'll tell you what I think, Luke. I think you've lost your fucking mind. On the day of your sister's funeral you reckon we should let them arseholes in on our business. Put our hands up in fucking surrender? Just like that?'

'No, not surrender. More like a truce. But on our terms. We say what we want, and what we're prepared to let them do. We set the rules. It's just like they'll be working for us. We win all round.'

'Dad,' Brendan appealed to his father. 'You can't tell me you're thinking about going along with this crap.'

Gabriel spoke for the first time since Brendan had joined them. 'What if I am?'

'Then I don't think you understand what he's saying.'

'Have I got eejit written here?' he asked, pointing to his forehead. 'I'm thinking about it, that's all. If they show proper respect, do what I say, then maybe I'll let them have a few crumbs off our table.'

'But—'

'But let them take a liberty—just once—and that's it. I'll kill every last one of 'em.'

'I'll organise a meet then shall I, Dad?'

Brendan's face was twisted with rage. 'What, they your new friends are they, Luke? Gonna nip round theirs for a cuppa and a chat? And hand over all the business while you're at it?' He turned to his father. 'You're upset, Dad. And you're tired. Wait till the morning and you'll see this can't be right.'

'Is that so?'

'Well, come on. A truce? With the Kesslers? After what's happened?' He leaned closer to his father. 'Please, Dad, don't do this.'

Gabriel drained his glass.

Brendan glared at his brother. 'I'm going out for some fresh air, something stinks in here.'

'Don't bother,' said Luke, unhooking his jacket from the back of his chair. 'I'm going out anyway. You stay and keep Dad company. Believe it or not, there's something he'll tell you, Brendan, that you might actually want to celebrate when you hear it.'

He turned and patted his father on the shoulder. 'I don't reckon Patricia'd mind.'

\*     \*     \*

Luke wasn't sure how long he'd been walking, but it must have been hours. The snow had blown itself out, but a freezing rain now angled down into his face, and had soaked right through the shoulders of his overcoat. His trousers were sodden, flapping about his legs, and his feet were squelching in his thin, Italian leather shoes.

He looked about him, noticing that the streetlamps had come on, and that the shop windows were leaking pools of light out onto the rain-slicked pavements.

Aldgate? How had he wound up here? He checked his watch. Ten to six. For him to have walked for so long and to have covered so few miles, he must have been walking in great blind circles.

Ten to six? He frowned. *Call me at six o'clock*, that's what Sammy Kessler had said.

There was a phone box across the road, on the corner of Mansell Street. Might as well get it over with. It had been that sort of a day.

He pulled out his wallet and searched for the scrap of paper.

*       *       *

'Hello,' said Luke; it was more of a question than a greeting.

'Yeah.' Sammy couldn't hide his disappointment. When he'd stood there in the phone box and the phone had actually rung he'd really believed it would be Catherine.

'It's Luke O'Donnell here.'

Sammy brightened up a bit. 'Tell me about Catherine.'

Luke kicked an empty cigarette packet into the corner of the booth. 'Maybe not on the phone.'

'We can meet then. Now okay?'

'Er, yeah. I suppose.' Luke peered out of the smeared glass of the telephone box. 'Do you know the Tun and Grapes up at Aldgate?'

'I'll be there in an hour.'

*       *       *

Luke sat at the far end of the short, curved bar by the fire. He was glad of the opportunity to dry his clothes, but the seat also gave him a clear view of the only entrance into the small, dark-wood panelled pub. Despite what he'd said to his father and brother, he was as unsure of what he was about to do as almost anything he had ever done in his young life, but if Sammy brought a team with him, at least he'd see them coming. And, if it did all go wrong, he wouldn't have much of an audience. Pubs in this area did little evening trade and always closed early. At this time of the evening, the bar was host only to him and a sparse gaggle of City stragglers, reluctant to go out in such awful weather to catch their homebound trains from Fenchurch Street. And, dressed as he was in his dark funeral clothes—so close to their office uniform—the place also offered him the small comfort of anonymity.

*  *  *

Luke was onto his third drink and spiralling down into the introverted misery of grief when Sammy Kessler appeared in the doorway.

Luke stood up, hand held out in unsure welcome. 'Sammy?'

'That's me.' Sammy looked him up and down as he walked across the pub. 'And you must be Luke. Catherine said she could trust you. Is that right?'

'Yeah. We always shared our secrets, even when we were kids.'

Sammy looked around the now almost empty pub. 'So, is she joining us?'

Luke's brow pleated into a tight frown. Christ, the bloke had no idea. 'I think we should get a drink.'

*  *  *

Sammy Kessler looked at Luke as if he were joking, as if he were playing some sort of sick prank. 'You're lying, right? Having a laugh?'

Luke shook his head. 'I wish I was. But I'm not. Catherine's dead, Sammy. We buried her today.'

'No, that can't be right. Why wasn't it in the papers?'

'It just wasn't.'

'Now I know you're lying. A death by shooting in a London street? It'd be all over the front pages. Why are you doing this?' He rose to his feet. 'You think you'll be able to split us up by telling me all this crap.' Sammy loomed over him, his lips turned back in disgust. 'And what are you going to tell Catherine, that I've run off with some Jewish girl because I can't marry a Catholic? Well, you won't get rid of me that easily, O'Donnell. I love her, and she loves me. Got it?'

Very slowly, Luke stood up and stared coolly into Sammy's angry face. 'What shooting? My sister was killed in a car crash. She drove into a wall in the fog. The car burst into flames. She didn't have a chance.'

'She did what? Do you think I'm stupid? Why didn't I hear about it? And anyway,' he allowed himself a knowing smile, 'she couldn't even drive.'

Luke was struggling to keep his voice under control. 'You didn't hear about it Kessler, because people round here know better than to run off at the mouth about the O'Donnells's private business. And, as a matter of fact, she could drive.' He took a deep breath. 'And don't you reckon it was a more dignified way to go than being left in the road to bleed to death, after being shot in the throat with a

95

sawn-off shotgun?'

Sammy raked his fingers through his hair, blinked and made jerky little movements with his head as though he were in pain. 'She can't be dead.'

'I know. But it's the truth. And we need to get our stories straight, Sammy. For all our sakes.'

'For all our sakes? Are you completely spineless?' Sammy stepped back, knocking his bar stool to the ground. 'I swear I'll kill you, O'Donnell. I'll kill all of you.' He stabbed a finger into Luke's shoulder. 'You especially. You were the one who was supposed to care about her. So if you know what's good for you, you'd better fuck off out of it.'

The barman moved hastily to the other end of the counter. The manager would be down to lock up soon, let him deal with this.

'No, Sammy, you listen to me. I cared about Catherine more than anyone'll ever know. And I thought you were supposed to and all.'

'I did. I do.'

'Then why did you leave her there? You didn't have a clue who we were. We could have done anything to her. Taken her away and done what we liked with her. But you ran away and left her.'

Sammy's face crumpled like a wet rag and tears trickled down his smooth, usually untroubled, cheeks. 'I had no choice.' He swiped angrily at his face with the back of his hand. 'It was a secret. No one knew about us.' He raised his head and looked, pleading, into Luke's eyes. 'No one but you.'

'The trouble with secrets is, Sammy, they come back to haunt you.' Luke's mouth was so dry his tongue was sticking to the back of his teeth as he spoke. 'And denying something don't make it go away.'

'What are you, a fucking nut doctor?' Sammy's face was contorted with rage at Luke, at himself, at the whole, rotten world.

'No, just someone who knows a bit about secrets, that's all, and a bloke whose sister's died for nothing.' He bent down and picked up the stool, setting it back on its legs. 'You've had a shock. We all have. But we can't just go off our heads. We've got to keep a lid on all this or the whole thing'll blow up in our faces.'

Sammy shook his head angrily. 'Why should I listen to you?'

'You'd better listen to me. Now, I don't know what influence you've got with your family, but I guarantee this.' Luke leaned forward and pointed his finger right into Sammy's tear-stained face, meaning every word as he hissed them out through clenched teeth. 'If this ain't gonna end in one big bloodbath then you do as I say. If you don't take the piss, I can make sure we leave you and your family alone. We'll maybe even come to an arrangement to do a bit of business with you. Something in the scrap line. In turn, you get your girls off our patch and move them somewhere else, and the same goes for the betting pitches. Nothing within spitting distance of us, right? But you go crooked on us, or try and have us over, take one step near our clubs, the spielers, or the protection, then I won't be held responsible. All bets'll be off. You got that, Sammy Kessler?'

'You're out of your head.'

'Why, because I wanna make sure we look after our own interests? Because I don't wanna lose any

97

more of my family? Think about it. The same applies to you. These arrangements mean there can be peace between us.' He put down his hand and leaned back. 'For as long as you lot do as you're told.'

'You are mad.' Sammy was looking at Luke as if he genuinely thought he had lost his mind. 'Even if I wanted to, how do you suppose I could ever explain these new *arrangements* to my old man?'

'Something'll come to you, mate. Or it had better, if you don't want all out war. I saw some of that when I was a kid. My dad took on some of the South London hard men, and do you know what, Sammy? He won. Hands down. But the claret that got spilt before it was all sorted out . . . You don't want to know.' He paused, letting it sink in. 'And I suppose you don't really want your family knowing about you and our Catherine either. So, how about you arrange a meet between your old feller and mine? You know my number.'

'You bastard.'

*      *      *

As Luke strode away from the pub he felt bewildered. On one of the worst, if not the worst day, of his whole life, he felt exhilarated.

He had always left most of the tough stuff to his father, to Brendan, and to the various thugs, hard nuts and foot soldiers who worked for them in the less public parts of their business. But that exchange with Sammy had got his heart pounding and his blood racing.

And now he needed a drink, a proper one, not a half-pint in some dodgy old boozer, but somewhere

98

he could be himself and could celebrate. And he knew exactly where he was going to have that drink: the Lagoon Club, on Dean Street, in Soho.

Paulie, a bloke he'd met in the City Arms on the Isle of Dogs, was the barman there, and he'd given Luke an open invitation to pop in and see him any time he fancied it.

Any time at all . . .


## CHAPTER SEVEN

The moment he stepped through the narrow, street level doorway of the Lagoon Club, Luke was overwhelmed by doubt. He'd just buried his sister, for Christ's sake, what the hell did he think he was doing going out to a club? Especially a club like this one.

A deep shame wedged itself in his chest like a brick. But, as he hovered at the top of the grim, South Seas mural-painted stairway, grief took over, usurping the brick with the taste of sour vomit. The grief wasn't only for Catherine, it was for himself— a man who didn't know who, or even what, he was.

He took a few tentative steps down towards the cramped underground space and the soulful sounds of a tenor sax that were soaring up from the smoky darkness.

As his eyes became accustomed to the muted lighting, Luke could make out a flamboyantly dressed, elderly man—floppy, velvet hat; heavy silk cravat, tied in a pussy cat bow at his throat; purple and gold brocade jacket—sitting in the corner facing the stairway. He was petting a pale pink poodle, perched delicately on his lap.

The man lifted his eyes and lazily surveyed the handsome youngster standing on the stairs.

'Varda the dolly old eek on the dish, Poppett,' he trilled to the poodle, wagging the dog's paw at Luke. And then, to Luke himself, 'Fancy a little bevie?' He paused, batting his sparsely lashed lids. 'Or something a bit stronger more to your taste? Me for instance?'

Luke couldn't. He couldn't go any further. Just as he hadn't been able to the last time. Or the time before that.

'Sorry,' he said over his shoulder, as he turned and made his way back up the stairs. 'There's been a mistake. Never realised the time. Got to go. Meeting someone. I'm really late. You know how it is.'

The man expelled a long, drawn out breath. 'Yes, sweetheart, I know exactly how it is. It's the story of my life, lovey. That's what all the good-looking ones seem to say these days. *Sorry*. Makes me feel like a right old meese omi-polone.' He lifted the poodle's ear and said in a loud stage whisper: 'Shame, eh, my little cherry? I was really bonar for him and all. It'll be a lonely old arthur for me tonight as usual. Ah well, let's have another little drinkette then, shall we? And perhaps, Poppett,' he sighed histrionically. 'I'll learn to keep my queeny old polari for them what appreciates it. Or for them what admits it.'

*     *     *

How could going into a room in your own home be this difficult?

Eileen made another faltering reach for the handle then, with all the determination she had left in her, she snatched at it, and threw open the door, waiting for the monster of grief to leap out of the shadows and devour her.

But there was no monster. Just a bedroom with a comforting glow, warming it like a soft quilt, as light from the streetlamp outside filtered through the cream lace curtains. Catherine had so loved that cosy radiance that she would never close the heavy drapes, not even in the heart of winter.

Eileen slipped off her shoes, crossed herself as if she were going into a side chapel for a moment of quiet prayer, and entered in her stockinged feet.

Making sure she disturbed no one else in the house, she clicked the door shut carefully behind her, turned on the light, and immediately felt a heart-leaping closeness to the daughter she would never see again. She looked about her—at the room that was still as much a little girl's domain as it was a young woman's, trying desperately to keep hold of the feeling of intimacy with her child. Then she walked towards the bed, the sheepskin rug soft and yielding between her toes. It was really little more than a raw, unfinished fleece, but Catherine had insisted on bringing it back from one of their trips to Kildare. She must have been what, seven, eight years old? Old enough to know her own mind and to get her own way.

Eileen stopped suddenly, drawing up one foot and sucking in a truncated hiss of breath. She'd trodden on something hard.

Bending down, she ran her fingers through the deep curling pile until she found it: a disc of white plastic, the size of a two-shilling piece, with a brass

101

clip stuck on the back. One of the cheap market earrings that Catherine had collected and cherished as if they were precious jewels. But however cheap they were, Catherine had looked lovely in them, especially when she'd worn them with matching loops of poppet beads wound around her throat and wrists.

Eileen touched the treasure to her lips and slipped it into the pocket of her pale blue, quilted nylon dressing gown.

Moving closer to the bed, she reached out and ran a finger across a poster pinned above the headboard. It had been carefully unstapled from the centre of one of Catherine's magazines, the marks from the metal still clear in the crease. It was an image of Catherine's favourite—the actor who played Kookie in the television programme *77 Sunset Strip*. He was leaning forward, combing his quiff of blond hair. She remembered how Catherine used to make them all laugh, saying how she'd go to Hollywood one day and meet him, reckoned she would sweep him off his feet, probably even marry him.

She'd never meet him now.

Eileen had to look away, unable to bear the thought.

Below the picture was a bookshelf, with chunky, green china rabbit bookends supporting a set of Lang's fairy books.

Eileen smiled through her tears. She practically knew them all by heart. Even when she could read them for herself, Catherine had still loved her mother to tell her the familiar stories over and over again, lulling her into a deep, child's sleep full of magical stories in which there would always be someone there to rescue you.

Eileen, now almost unable to control the whooping, shallow sobs rising in her chest, dragged her gaze away, lighting on the bedside cabinets— and more memories of Catherine, her precious girl. On one stood the Ekco transistor radio Brendan had brought home for her—after she'd driven them all half mad going on and on about how she couldn't live without listening to Radio Luxembourg —and a half-eaten packet of Spangles, its curling ribbon of paper wrapping winding out in front of it. On the other cabinet was her Dansette record player, its pale blue and cream leatherette lid still open from where she'd been playing her records. Catherine had always loved music, dancing about the house and singing at the top of her voice.

Eileen lifted the arm and took the top 45 off the stack on the turntable. She read the label: The Drifters. She knew them. 'Save the Last Dance For Me'. And knew the tune too. Then the next: 'Itsy Bitsy Teeny Weeny . . .'

A sudden flash of memory. The row she'd had with Catherine about the bikini she'd bought in the summer. She was as crazy over clothes as she was over music, but Eileen had forbidden her from wearing the thing to the Lido. And then, when she found out that it had cost her nineteen and eleven—nearly a pound for those ridiculous few scraps of material—she'd been angry with her all over again.

Why? Eileen wondered. Why had she denied her child such a small pleasure?

She went over to the cream and gold Melamine wardrobe and began sliding outfits along the rail one after the other. She unhooked a hanger and

103

took out a sky blue skirt, stiffened with a froth of net petticoats, so short it had barely come down to Catherine's knees. That had caused another row.

Had they really spent so much of the time they had together arguing?

Next: bright red toreador pants, with figured black ricrac down the outside seams.

Such a tiny waist.

Eileen touched the material to her cheek and then hung the trousers back on the rail.

It was almost too much: the feel and smell of her so close.

As she was about to close the wardrobe door, she spotted the old toffee tin tucked in among the racks and racks of shoes.

She bent down and picked it up, frowning at the brightly painted lid: a cartoon-like spaceman firing his ray gun at an enemy ship. Trying to remember. When had Catherine got this? Two, three Christmases ago?

Whenever it was, she'd still been a child.

Eileen carried it over to the bed, sat down and eased off the lid.

Photographs.

She tipped out a flutter of memories onto the lavender bedspread.

\*     \*     \*

Eileen was studying a picture of a chubby kneed toddler, with a sagging, knitted bathing suit, standing in a tin bath in the back yard that first summer after the war, when the door opened.

'Luke,' Eileen said, anxiously. She didn't know why, but she felt guilty, as if she'd been caught trespassing. 'I never heard you come in.'

'I took off my shoes. I heard Brendan talking to Dad down in the kitchen and didn't want to disturb them. Well, didn't really feel much like joining them, to be truthful. Sounded like Dad's had a skinful.' As he spoke, his eyes were fixed on the empty tin by his mother's feet. 'But then I saw the light on under the door, and I . . .'

'Wanted to feel near her?'

'Yeah. But I thought you'd be asleep by now. You know, the pills.'

'I didn't take them. Didn't want to be packed off into oblivion. I want to remember.' She patted the bed. 'Come on love, come and see.'

Luke sat on the edge of the bed and accepted each picture after his mother had finished putting together its story, drawing from it every possible connection with her youngest child.

'See that one,' she said, handing it to him to look at, while she carried on sorting through the piles of memories. 'The one with Scrap? She could make that dog do whatever she wanted. That day, she'd got out all her doll's clothes and . . . Oh look,' she interrupted herself. 'Here's a recent one. Looks like it's at the coast somewhere.' She held it at arm's length, turning it to the light, trying to understand. 'Now when was that taken? And who would have—'

'Mum.' Luke slid his hand over the shiny black and white snapshot, just glimpsing a smiling Catherine, her eyes sparkling, as she posed for whoever was taking the picture. 'This is too hard, for me. Too soon. Can we put them away? Please. Just for now?'

Eileen touched his cheek and nodded. 'Of

course.'

'Thanks. We'll look another time, eh? In a week or two maybe.' He stood up, helping his mother gently to her feet. 'You get off to bed. I'll tidy these away.'

Eileen nodded, and, with a brush of her lips on his cheek, and a whispered goodnight, she left him to it.

Luke waited, listening for his mother to open then close her bedroom door, and then shuffled hurriedly through the snaps. He slipped a slim stack of them into his back pocket and snapped the lid back on the tin.

*     *     *

The next morning, Luke—like his father and brother—didn't get up for breakfast.

Even though Luke had gone to bed almost immediately after his mother, he'd lain awake for most of the rest of the night, going back, time and again, to the photographs he'd smuggled out of Catherine's room.

As for Brendan, he'd stayed down in the basement kitchen with Gabriel into the early hours, trying to persuade his increasingly incoherent father that letting in the Kessler family was the stupidest thing he could possibly even consider doing, and that grief was clouding his judgement, stopping him from thinking straight. But Gabriel had drunk so much by then that he'd hardly heard a word of his son's arguments and pleas, and had eventually hauled himself up to bed, where he'd passed out on top of the covers without so much as taking off his shoes. Brendan had followed him up

106

not long after.

The only one of the O'Donnell household to be up and about on the morning after the funeral was Eileen.

When Gabriel had crawled his way up to their bed, Eileen, rather than lie there listening to him snoring, had got up and left him to it. She'd considered going back into Catherine's room, but didn't want to disturb Luke whose room was next door, so she'd crept downstairs and sat by herself in the ground floor front parlour, trying to see her baby on that last day—stretched out on the sofa while Patricia did her nails for her.

She'd tried so hard to grab hold of the happy moments—the laughter, the singing and dancing—but the emptiness kept opening up in front of her. And now she was down in the basement kitchen—rinsing her teacup, dressed and ready to go and see Patricia, who was carrying the one beacon of hope in Eileen's life—when the telephone rang.

Eileen answered it and then called up the stairs. 'Luke, are you awake? It's the telephone.'

'Who is it, Mum?' His words were heavy with sleep.

'A friend of yours. Look, you'll have to come and get it, I'm off to Patricia's. I'll see you later.'

Luke padded down the stairs in his underpants, his eyes barely open, and his hair sticking up in black tufts.

'Nnn?' he mumbled into the mouthpiece.

'Luke?'

'Yeah. Who's this?'

'Sammy Kessler.'

Luke was immediately awake. He looked over his shoulder to make sure he was alone. 'What's happening?'

'I've managed to convince Dad it's at least worth having a meet.'

'Right . . .' Luke said the word very slowly, the prospect of an actual, real life meeting suddenly seeming far less reasonable than it had done when it was just an idea. 'When?'

'In two weeks. December 13. It's a Tuesday, okay.' It wasn't a question.

'I'll make it okay.'

*         *         *

Mary Logan handed a cup of tea to her poor brother's aggravating dimwit of a wife and smiled sweetly—a smile that didn't reach her eyes. 'Can I make you a bit of something to eat, Eileen, my love?'

'Thank you, Mary, but I've no appetite for food.' Eileen, who was sitting on the sofa in what her daughter, Patricia, called her 'lounge', took the geometrically patterned, black and white cup and rested it on her knee.

Even on a gloomy winter's morning, the house was bright, stylish and welcoming. Before Pat and Pete Mac had moved in, the inside of the tall Victorian terraced house had been completely transformed. Following Patricia's strict instructions as to what was required, Gabriel had moved in a gang of men from the yard, and told them to get a move on before the wedding.

Their first jobs had been to strip out all the ornate coving and ceiling roses; to cover up the turned banisters and the panelled doors with hardboard—making sure to remove any old-fashioned brass door furniture and to replace it with modern, slanting plastic handles. Then they had concentrated on the basement kitchen, which, under Patricia's eagle-eye, they'd cleared of the deep butler sink, the wooden draining board, the Maid Saver, and the old black leaded kitchener, and had refitted with Formica and stainless steel units and a shiny Ascot heater. They'd then moved up to the ground floor where they knocked out the dividing wall between the front and back rooms, creating Patricia's spacious 'lounge'. The final job, and the one the men all agreed they really had better not tell their wives about in case they started getting any ideas, was to transform the smallest of the three top floor bedrooms into a proper, plumbed in bathroom with a lavatory and a separate wash basin. It was like something out of a film.

Patricia and Catherine had gone mad planning how to decorate the place, and it was the lounge that was to be the centrepiece of the whole project. The floor was covered in parquet—just right to show off the new orange and cream rugs; walls were painted white; Pucci print was made up into curtains; framed prints were selected from the range in Timothy Whites; and G Plan teak furniture catalogues, showing all the very latest in Scandinavian style were pored over, and a dining suite, sofa and armchairs, sideboard and tables were ordered. With the finishing touches of spider plants hanging from the ceiling in raffia containers; primary coloured glass vases full of flowers; ceramic dishes filled with fruit, a brass sunburst mirror over the hearth that now housed the electric fire; heavy pottery lamps with oversized shades;

109

and a television set placed in one corner as the main focal point, the room had been pronounced perfect by the delighted sisters and their admiring mother.

Almost a year later, Eileen would, if asked, have agreed that it still looked as fresh, airy and bang up-to-date as the day Patricia and Pete had moved in, but today it could do nothing to lift her spirits.

'Are you sure you won't have just a slice of toast?'

'Thanks all the same, Mary, but I don't think I'll ever want to eat again.'

'Not that Sean and I have ever been blessed, of course, but it must be a terrible thing, burying a child.' Mary breathed out the words as if in prayer. 'Although you should have something, Eileen; you must keep up your strength. What with Gabriel having you trek all the way over to Kildare to take care of me when there was nothing wrong—it's Sean I blame for that, getting everyone excited over nothing—and now poor Catherine.' She crossed herself ostentatiously. 'May God keep her safe in his bosom. And you still having to cope with the rest of the family.' *If you can be bothered to shift your lazy, scraggy arse, and get your men a decent bit of grub on the table, and find the time to do a few bits of washing for them, you spoilt bitch,* she thought to herself. 'You've got three strapping men at home to think of.'

Eileen said nothing, didn't even bother sipping at her tea. She just sat there, not really listening, while Mary talked and talked, not even noticing the sly, snide remarks that, as always, polluted her every other word.

'Look, Eileen, look who's here,' Mary said,

110

standing up and with a little clap of her hands, finally getting Eileen's attention. 'Here's our Patricia come down from her bed at last. And how are you this morning, my little love?'

Patricia, still in her dressing gown, with purple shadows under eyes, her skin deathly pale against her almost black hair that was plastered flat to her skull, walked into the room very slowly, as if worried that her head might fall off her shoulders. Carefully, she leaned forward and kissed her mother on the cheek.

' 'Lo, Mum.'

'Sweetheart. Look at you.'

'Sick again?' asked Mary.

'Yeah. Very.'

Eileen put her untouched tea on the floor, stood up and hugged her daughter. 'It was good of you to come back with Patricia yesterday, Mary,' she said, over her daughter's shoulder, meaning it. 'I hope you know I appreciate it.'

Mary treated her sister-in-law to another broad, lips-only smile. 'Glad to be of help, Eileen. Especially as you were in no state to help her yourself, dear.' She stepped forward and tapped Patricia on the back.

Patricia twisted away from her mother to see what her aunt wanted.

'And at least you only have yourself and the baby to think about for the rest of the day,' she said brightly, leading her over to one of the armchairs that stood on either side of the electric fire. 'I shooed that Pete Mac out of the house first thing.' She bent forward and turned on another bar. 'I mean, we don't need men around cluttering up the place, now do we?' *And we certainly don't need*

111

*Eileen clucking about like a distressed hen if she finds out what happened.*

Patricia flashed her aunt a look of gratitude for hiding from her mother the fact that Pete Mac was, yet again, on the missing list, and yet another night had passed without him sharing her bed, and that yet another day would pass without him finding out about the baby they were going to have.

If she hadn't felt so sick, so desolate at losing Catherine, and so totally and completely worn out by everything—including her well-meaning aunt's ministrations and her endless cups of tea—Patricia would have gone out and found Peter-bloody-MacRiordan. First she would have told him about the baby, and then she'd have told him his sodding fortune, and, finally, she'd have smacked him one right round his ugly, rotten mug.

Still, there was plenty of time for that. Pete, ever the bad penny, would turn up sooner or later. Just as he always did. Just as if nothing had happened. Expecting a smiling, wide-armed welcome, a hot meal on the table, and a quick fumble under the sheets, before he fell asleep as quickly and easily as an innocent cherub.

God he was a pig.

Patricia rubbed her middle protectively. But he wouldn't spoil this for her; she wouldn't let him.


## CHAPTER EIGHT

The big Daimler saloon stood at the front of a line of showily expensive, top of the range cars that had been parked in an otherwise unremarkable little

112

side street. Gabriel had got out of the front passenger seat—Stephen Shea having driven—instructing his sons and son-in-law to stay where they were until he sent someone to tell them otherwise.

Apart from the thin, bluish light pooled around the base of the single lamppost, the street was dark, cold and damp, and Gabriel was dressed accordingly in a heavy, immaculately tailored, navy overcoat, leather gloves and trilby. He looked every inch the wealthy, successful man.

Standing next to him on the pavement outside the terrace of narrow, ordinary-looking houses was Harold Kessler, barely five feet five and weighing in at a good fourteen stone, but as cocky as a six-feet-five, heavyweight champion. He was dressed similarly to Gabriel, but in shades of camel and brown rather than dark blue. Both men were flanked by big, silent minders, whose only moving body parts seemed to be their constantly vigilant eyes.

Kessler ground out his cigarette under the slightly stacked heel of his highly polished shoe. 'Chinatown, Mr O'Donnell? A strange choice of venue.'

'You've been away from the East End for too long, Mr Kessler.'

*Mr Kessler.* It stuck in Gabriel's throat to show even such superficial respect, but the meeting had been arranged and he would see it through to the end, however it might turn out. In truth, it was only pride that had made him turn up—pride that he was a man of his word. He could kick himself now for consenting to be in this bastard's company. He had only agreed to all this at a time of weakness:

113

Catherine's death, being told Patricia was expecting, and Luke going on and on about the trouble with the bloody south Londoners.

'Far too long.' Gabriel paused for a moment, taking time to pull himself together, as he realised that, as usual, when he was about to lose his temper, his accent had become far less Stepney and more markedly Galway. 'Or you'd know that what with all the bomb damage there's very little left in Limehouse of the old Chinatown.'

He indicated the terrace with a flap of his hand. 'Just odd remnants like this, and the occasional pub like the one across the road.' He clasped his hands behind his back and surveyed his surroundings. 'The gambling clubs and eating-houses are all moving over to Soho.'

Pleased with his show of superior knowledge, Gabriel allowed himself a brief hint of a smile. 'That's why I was able to pick up this place for such a fair price.'

'This place?' Kessler shrugged and spread his hands—an exaggerated parody of a gesture. He didn't get it. A small terraced house near the docks? Who would want such a hovel? 'So, this is where our discussions are to take place? In here?'

Gabriel nodded. 'That's right. Nice and private. Shall we go in?'

As Kessler took off his hat and inclined his head in agreement, Gabriel beckoned for his sons and Pete Mac to join him and his minders. Stephen Shea stayed behind to mind the cars.

Daniel and Sammy Kessler followed the example of the O'Donnell boys, and, along with their cousin Maurice, got out of their car to join their father, Harold.

Maurice was Harold's self-important, swaggering nephew. He had come down from Manchester to stay in London for a few days. That had been nearly a month ago, and he was now apparently staying on indefinitely, having been taken onto work for his uncle—purportedly in the haulage trade. Neither Maurice's mother nor father seemed to have any reservations about these arrangements, even though they were both well aware that Harold's businesses were all a bit on the dubious side to say the least. In fact, this turn of events had answered their unspoken prayers: maybe, at twenty-five years of age, he'd start making something of himself at last—anything, in fact. So long as it was something a long way away from them.

*     *     *

Once through the nondescript doorway, Gabriel was more than gratified to see the look on Harold Kessler's face. From the street outside, the terrace had been left to look like a row of small, individual dwellings, and so, to outsiders, it appeared as if they had entered a little two-storey house. But inside it was a very different matter. All the houses in the terrace had been joined up to form a complex of rooms and stairways running the whole length of the outwardly ordinary side street.

'Bloke called Chen did all this, over fifty years ago,' said Gabriel, indicating the central corridor lined with doors. 'A lot of betting used to go on, on this floor.' He paused to grin. 'Still does. But not on puck-a-poo—that was their game, the Chinese fellers—and there's no opium these days either.

115

But there are still plenty of girls and drinks to keep the punters entertained in the private rooms, where they can enjoy their brag, and their pontoon, and their poker, and, well, you name it they enjoy it. In fact, I'm surprised you didn't know about this place. I thought,' he considered his words, 'people of your religion enjoyed a bet and a good time.'

Kessler's eyes narrowed for the briefest of moments. 'No more than any other religion, *Mr* O'Donnell.'

'Quite so, Mr Kessler. Now, if you'd like to follow me.' Gabriel, slightly nonplussed by his faux pas, but also more than a little put out by the arrogant little fucker's cheeky response, inclined his head in a gesture of more or less apology and led the party of men along the corridor.

Maurice was the only one amongst them to pause and admire the series of black and white erotic etchings that had adorned the otherwise plain walls since the 1920s, before only slightly increasing his pace to join the rest of the group, as they followed Gabriel down the discreet spiral stairway at the far end of the marble floored passageway.

At the bottom of the steps stood a man whose neck looked to be about twice the circumference of his head.

'Thank you, Anthony,' said Gabriel, nodding to the man.

Antony immediately pushed open the heavy sliding door that he had been guarding.

The noise from the other side hit them like a wall.

Again Gabriel enjoyed the look on Kessler's face. 'Chen also joined up the cellars.'

They were in a massive, windowless, low-ceilinged, flagstoned space—a huge, cacophonous arena. The central area, marked off by a rough chalked circle, was quite bare, but around the perimeter of the enormous, brightly lit room stood a double row of metal and canvas chairs. The seats were nearly all occupied by expensively dressed men talking animatedly, but politely, to one another, and handing over large amounts of money to skimpily clad young women, all of whom had satchels slung across their shoulders. Behind the chairs stood more raucous gaggles of men, many of them in sailors' uniforms.

'A favourite place to spend their wages after a long voyage,' explained Gabriel. 'And not a bad choice either—placing your bets with a pretty girl and having her fetch you drinks, while you enjoy the company of your friends, before enjoying more . . . let's say, intimate pleasures.'

'But what are they betting on down here?' Kessler was puzzled—he could see no cards, no roulette wheel, no one-armed bandits, or any of the other illegal gaming machines usually favoured in 'private' establishments.

Gabriel was now really beginning to enjoy himself, having one over on Kessler. Maybe it wouldn't be such a bad arrangement after all.

He smiled warmly. 'Welcome to my boxing club, Mr Kessler.' He paused just long enough to register the man's expression of surprise, and, yes, there it was: a brief flicker of admiration. 'The soundproofing was a bit of a job, a nightmare in fact, and certainly not cheap, but worth it if you enjoy your privacy as much as I do.' He let out a pleasant, amused little puff of air. 'And bare-knuckle bouts do have a habit of attracting the wrong sort of attention.'

He looked Harold Kessler directly in the eye. 'The point of the bare-knuckle fight being, of course, to inflict the worst possible damage on your enemy—to kill him if necessary—in order to win. An ugly view of things, maybe, but, as I always say, better to reign in hell than serve in heaven.'

Gabriel held his gaze just a moment too long for Kessler's liking, making sure that the man felt the full discomfort of being in his power then, finally, when he thought he'd held him for long enough, he let him go, smiling at him again.

'Perhaps you'd fancy coming along as my guest to watch a few bouts one evening.' He winked matily. 'I'd make sure you picked the winner, you can be sure of that.'

Kessler returned his smile, and again shrugged and spread his hands. 'I like to do business with a man who knows the winner, Mr O'Donnell.'

Gabriel tried to decide if the little prick was being sarcastic, and was angry to realise that he couldn't actually figure him out. He felt his fists clench. Was he taking the piss or what?

The moment was saved by a pale, wiry man in his thirties. He was quite tidily dressed, but his clothes seemed just that bit too big for him, as if he had lost weight. From the dark smudges under his jittery, darting eyes, it was obvious he had something on his mind. He approached Gabriel with such humility that it wouldn't have been a surprise if he had actually buckled at the knee and gone for the full genuflection.

'Scuse me, Mr O'Donnell. Don't wanna be a nuisance or anything. But can I have a quick word?

118

If you're not too busy, like.'

'Sure, Ted.' Gabriel liked this. 'We're all friends here. Speak freely.'

'I've got a cotchell of groins, Mr O'Donnell. And a few loose diamonds. And some gold bracelets. All good gear. I did a grab in Hatton Garden yesterday cos I need a bit of dough for my old woman. My brief reckons I'm going down for a right lump, and I have to know she's got enough to last her, so she can look after herself and the kids.'

Gabriel nodded benevolently. 'It'll be a pleasure to help you out, Ted. You go over and see Anthony, tell him I said he's to take you through to the cashiers' room, and say I said they're to give you whatever price you say. I know you won't take a liberty.'

Ted did everything but kiss Gabriel's hand. 'Mr O'Donnell, I can't tell you—'

'Don't worry yourself, Ted. And don't worry about your family either. They'll be all right. You have my word on it.' He reached in his pocket and took out a roll of notes. He peeled off four fivers and handed them to Ted. 'Have that on the Scotch bloke in the second fight. My treat. You won't be sorry.'

With that, Gabriel turned to Kessler with a broad, handsome smile. 'Anyway, enough of all this, we're not here for the sport, now are we?' A pause, just long enough for the ambiguity to sink in and aggravate Kessler. 'So, if you and your sons and colleagues would care to join me in my office . . .'

*　　　*　　　*

'If it seems satisfactory to me, and this—' Gabriel

hesitated, considering his words, '—*venture* goes ahead, I think it goes without saying, Mr Kessler, that we both understand what we know is right and wrong here. What we should and shouldn't be doing. The ground rules—the code, if you like—that we should follow.'

Gabriel was sitting in a leather library chair, at an elegant Queen Anne desk, in a plushly decorated, wood panelled room that wouldn't have looked out of place in a gentlemen's club in Pall Mall. Harold Kessler was sitting on the other side of the desk in a deep-buttoned winged armchair. Both men were flanked by smoke-wreathed family members and their minders.

'We're neither of us stupid men, Mr Kessler, we're not mugs, and we're definitely not fresh in off the boat either. We both realise what I'm talking about. But let me set out the details for clarity, for everyone's sake.'

Kessler inclined his head in a gesture of permission that Gabriel wasn't entirely thrilled with, but he wasn't going to let his irritation show.

'You'll use your vehicle fleet to collect the scrap. There seems to be an endless supply of average stuff around, more than anyone can deal with, but then, Mr Kessler, there's the really good stuff, the stuff people would give their right arm for, the stuff for which you need the right contacts to get access to. A special sort of supply.'

Kessler was beginning to feel that he was getting out of his depth. Scrap wasn't his game. 'Explain.'

Gabriel looked at him, waiting for the show of respect.

'If you will,' Kessler added eventually.

'Okay. We—by that I mean, you, in this case—

120

graciously accept money from an investor—some posh type with more money than sense, who can't wait to get his jollies from the pleasure of mixing with real, authentic cockney villains.' He paused, leaned across the glass-topped desk and mouthed. 'Gangsters. Hoodlums. Faces.'

Kessler couldn't help but smile in recognition, he knew the type exactly, the ones who regularly risked their nice, comfortable lives just for the sake of a cheap thrill. Their preference could be for street corner tarts, illicit gambling, pretty boys, dope smoking in West London blues clubs, it didn't really matter, what mattered was that they thought it was *dirty*. And that was what they liked.

'Then,' Gabriel continued, 'with his money tucked away nice and safe in your bin, you buy something really tasty from a supplier. A very discreet supplier, of course.'

Kessler, intrigued, shifted forward in his seat. 'What sort of stuff?'

'Military scrap. Planes, army vehicles, that sort of top of the range type of gear. You view it whole, and then you collect it. It'll be cut up and stripped down ready—remember this is quality metal we're talking about—and you sell it on. Top dollar. Very nice. Very good profits to be had. Maybe even sell it to me. What with me being an expert in scrap metal . . . But, and here's the beauty of this game, you do not—repeat, do not repay the investor either his original stake or his cut of the profit.'

'What if they call the law? You know that sort, probably knows the Chief Constable personally. Probably plays golf with the feller and fucks his wife.'

'What if he does? A couple of plods turn up on

121

your doorstep, Mr Kessler, and you just straighten 'em out. Give 'em a nice drink. They take the bung *and* they put the frighteners on your investor— *"You wouldn't have anything to do with any illegal procurement of military property, now would you sir?"* The investor will now be shitting himself. He'll deny he's ever heard of you, let alone that he's given you any dough. And that's the beauty of you being the middleman, rather than him doing the deal with a known scrap dealer like me. *"All a mistake, sir. I see, sir. Long as you've not been wasting police time."* '

Gabriel smiled. 'And did I remember to mention that I'll be the supplier as well?'

At the sight of the greed lighting up Kessler's face, Gabriel couldn't help letting out a deep, self-satisfied sigh. Was it really going to be this easy taking control of the cheeky little bastard? It certainly looked like it. Perhaps Luke was right after all, this definitely beat going to war with them.

He took a moment to light a long, thick cigar. 'We're not, you see, Mr Kessler, like them ponces who might act like tough guys, but who just take a cut out of every job that's done by all the blokes on their manor, because they're too bloody scared to do their own dirty work. We love taking part, Mr Kessler, we love getting our sleeves rolled up and getting our hands stuck right down in the muck. That way, you see, we always know what's going on. We ensure that no one is taking a liberty. Because we really don't like liberty takers, Mr Kessler. We really don't like them at all.'

Kessler nodded courteously. 'I like the sound of the way you do business, Mr O'Donnell. And I'm

122

sure it can be mutually beneficial.'

'Glad to hear it. Now, if this arrangement is to proceed, this is what you do. You take your toms off our patch. You move them further east, up West, over the fucking river if the fancy takes you, but you *do* not stay on our patch. You can keep the betting pitches on the Shoreditch side, but not on the Whitechapel side, or down towards the docks. There's no shops opening there yet and I intend to make hay, as the old saying goes. You can keep your drinking club in Hoxton, open more round there if you like—again, well away from any of mine. But you'll use my gambling machines. Aw, yeah, and I'll be expecting a straight dollar in the pound on everything you earn.'

'Your machines *and* twenty-five per cent? I thought you said you didn't take—'

'I'm fair, Mr Kessler, but I'm not a fool. I said we don't take a cut from other people's jobs. We do take a cut, of course, from their businesses—the businesses that we might otherwise be running. We do own this manor, after all—and is there anything wrong with twenty-five per cent? Is there something unusual about that?'

Kessler looked at his sons and his nephew and flashed his eyebrows at them—they'd got off lighter than they might have done—and then shook his head. 'No. Nothing at all.'

'Good. But, I'll remind you again. Nothing of yours is to be within spitting distance of ours. And, if you get any trouble, say from the Eyeties over in Clerkenwell, then it's down to you to sort it out. But if you go monkey on us, Kessler, if you try and make a move on the spielers, try putting in a single one-armed bandit of your own in the drinking

123

clubs, touch *any* of the protection—even the soft foreign touches too scared to actually tell me if they're being had for payments twice over—I'll find out about it. And then it's over. I promise you that. So don't give me any agg, because I'm telling you, if you *do* give me any aggravation, I'll have you. War will be declared. And if that happens, you would be well advised to disappear from these parts as soon as possible. And you'd better make it somewhere one hell of a lot further than Notting Hill or even the south of Spain. I have contacts, Mr Kessler. In many, many places.'

Gabriel paused to tap the ashes from his cigar into a heavy crystal ashtray.

'So, what do you think, Mr Kessler?'

'Can we still sell Tanner a Pick straws and work the Shell game down the Lane?'

'Mr Kessler, I hope you're not being sarcastic. I asked what you think?'

'I think, *Gabriel*, that we have a deal. So, please, no more formality.' He beamed beatifically and held out his hand. 'Call me, Harold. Use my name. It's what people do when they're in business together. When they're colleagues. Might I even say—friends?'

'Harold,' said Gabriel, through his teeth, grasping the man's hand, and only just managing to stop himself from punching the squat, little bastard full in his ugly, grinning face. 'Nine o'clock. Time we went to meet the ladies.'

# CHAPTER NINE

Hidden away behind an anonymous door, in a street shabby even by Soho standards, and with only a small, dull brass plaque screwed to the wall signalling its existence, the inside of the Dahlia Club was a revelation. With its subtle lighting; blonde, maple wood interior; etched glass privacy panels, and deep leather banquettes, it had the glamorous feel of the Grand Salon of an elegant ocean liner. And even on this bitterly cold winter's evening, the fashionable venue was packed with what excitable gossip columnists would call *an exhilarating combination of high life and low life*. In other words, it was a place patronised by those who could afford it: a rich social mix of aristocrats, business people, and criminals. And with sufficient numbers of pretty young staff, glamorous entertainers, and ever-willing hangers-on in attendance—both male and female—to make everyone very happy to be there.

Yet, despite the crowd, there was one large, round table still unoccupied: the table that had been booked for the O'Donnell–Kessler party. Regardless of Luke's last minute reservations about what he had actually set in motion, and after a not entirely easy discussion with his father about the matter, he had booked the Dahlia so that the families could 'celebrate' their new business relationship after the meeting—if it went well. And Luke was, he supposed, glad to acknowledge that the meeting had gone well, or at least sufficiently well to satisfy his father.

For the time being, anyway.

*      *      *

An obsequious man in white tie and tails, who seemed anxious to show how overwhelmed he was to be receiving Gabriel O'Donnell in such a humble establishment, showed the O'Donnells and Kesslers to their table.

Gabriel was brushing away the maître d'hôtel's attentions with a pantomime of his own: a humble smile, a modest wave of his hand, and a self-effacing inclination of his head.

Both men knew it was all just an act. On his previous visit to the Dahlia, Gabriel had made sure he would be warmly welcomed back—despite the drunken behaviour of the bent-nosed, cauliflower-eared company he had been dining with that night—by palming the man two five pound notes. The man now had only wonderful memories of the privilege of serving Mr O'Donnell, plus the expectation, of course, that he would be equally well rewarded after serving him and his very slightly more sophisticated looking companions this evening. It was the way the wheels turned.

Gabriel, showing he was in charge of proceedings, acted the polite host and remained standing while Eileen, Brendan, Luke, Patricia and Pete Mac were seated. His lips twitched with annoyance as Kessler did the same, fussing around while his wife, Sophie, his two sons—Sammy and Daniel—Daniel's fiancée Rachel, and his nephew, Maurice, made themselves comfortable.

Gabriel insisted that Harold be the next to sit down, and only sat down himself after the various minders were accommodated at a hastily prepared table, which, while it might have been unfashionably close to the kitchens, gave the men a full, unobstructed view of the room. From there they could keep an eye on anyone who'd had a bit too much to drink and thought he might start playing the hard man. It was an occupational hazard for a family such as the O'Donnells that they would occasionally be challenged by foolhardy, drunken show-offs who wanted to impress their companions with their toughness. It was far kinder for a minder to accompany them out to the lavatory and give them a discreet warning or even a light kicking.

On the whole, the party seemed, superficially at least, to be glad to be there, although Eileen, still raw with grief and dressed in a sombre rather than glamorous black crepe, calf-length dress, had only gone along because she was too emotionally drained to argue with her husband. She had managed a stiff, polite smile when Harold Kessler had introduced his family to her, and again when she had been seated next to his wife, Sophie, as part of the strictly gender-divided seating plan.

Eileen found Sophie Kessler loud and showy, swathed as she was in crystal-sprinkled, floor length drapes of coffee chiffon that showed off every line of her handsomely curvaceous body, and with her fair curls piled on top of her head. Large diamonds flashed at her ears and on both hands. But, Eileen had to admit, she also seemed a decent enough woman, and watched approvingly as Sophie made sure that Rachel, her pretty, if over-primped and preened, future daughter-in-law, settled into conversation with Patricia, making sure that both the girls were at their ease.

'Here, Eileen.' She jumped to hear her name. It was Pete Mac, calling right across the table to her, waving his fork about as if he were conducting the band. 'I was just saying to Gabe here that he'd better watch out, cos he looks the right business in that new Italian mohair suit of his, don't he? And if he ain't careful he'll wind up getting captured by one of them pretty little cigarette girls. What a turn out that'd be, eh?' He grinned, looking about the table, checking that everyone was appreciating his wit. 'I mean, he might have forty-four years on the clock, but some of these young girls, well, they like an older man, don't they.'

Gabriel, wishing all kinds of evil on the idiot, closed his eyes for fractionally longer than a blink, and then flashed his teeth at Harold Kessler as if sharing a joke. 'Likes a laugh does my son-in-law.' Then he turned to his wife. 'You all right, Eileen?'

Eileen nodded silently and Gabriel returned to his conversation with the men.

Sophie looked at Eileen, put down her knife and fork, and touched her lightly on the back of the hand. 'Don't you fancy the sole, Eileen?' Sophie jerked her head at her husband. 'Typical of my Harry, barging in and ordering for everyone without even asking what they want. He thinks he's being helpful, but he's not, he's just being a nuisance. Does it all the time. Can't help himself from always having to be front of the queue.'

Eileen had probably been the only one who'd noticed the look of fury that had passed between Gabriel and Brendan, when Kessler had taken it upon himself to take charge of what everyone was eating, but she hadn't much cared, not on her own account. She had no appetite anyway.

'Shall we ask the waiter to fetch you something else? I'm sure it won't take a minute for them to rustle up something nice for you.'

Eileen smiled, more easily this time. So, she too was used to living with a difficult man. 'That's very kind of you, Mrs Kessler, but—'

'I told you. Sophie. Please.'

'Sophie. Like I say, it's a kind thought, but I'm not hungry. Thank you all the same.'

Sophie closed her hand over Eileen's. 'Harry told me the sad news this morning. I can't imagine what it must be like to lose a child. And in such an accident . . .'

Eileen could manage nothing more than a brief nod. She couldn't trust herself to speak without bursting into tears, and she didn't want to make a fuss, not in front of all these strangers. Gabriel would hate it.

'Children are always such a worry,' Sophie went on with a sigh. 'We try to protect them, wrap them up and keep them safe, but, in the end, we have to let them go, let them make their own mistakes. Take my youngest, Sammy, the one over there, sitting next to . . . Luke is it?'

'That's right.' Eileen's voice was little more than a whisper.

'You should see the way he's been carrying on lately. Girl trouble. It has to be. A mother knows. He's hardly said a word for weeks. But will he talk to me about it?' She tutted, somehow managing to express a mixture of frustration, resignation, and love for her child. 'Course he won't.'

'He does look pale.'

'Pale? That's not the half of it. He's not sleeping,

he picks at his food, and as for conversation at the dinner table . . . He might as well not be there. But, please, God,' Sophie picked up her champagne saucer, raising it in salute, 'maybe he'll meet someone at Daniel's wedding.' She took a long draft from the glass before setting it down, then slapped the table, her heavily ringed hand making a metallic clunk. 'Eileen, I've had a wonderful idea. You and your family, you must join us at the wedding. Next Tuesday. Be our guests. I'll send you an invitation. You must come.'

A wedding. Eileen said nothing. She just let the woman talk.

'For us, Tuesday's a lucky day for getting married, and not just because the caterers are cheaper midweek.' She raised her shoulders and winked, trying to draw Eileen into her joke, then reached across the table, tapping a perfectly painted Tangerine Pearl fingernail on the tablecloth by her husband's side plate.

'Harry, sorry to interrupt, but I was saying to Eileen, she and the family should come to Danny and Rachel's wedding. It would be a great way to seal this new business venture of yours. A real celebration.'

'What an idea.' Harry clapped his hands together, and pointed at Sophie, demonstrating to everyone his wonder and admiration for his wife. 'You're a clever woman. But I suppose that's obvious.' He grinned broadly. 'After all, you married me didn't you? And of course they'll all come to the wedding.' He raised his glass. 'The 20th, it's a date.'

Sammy and Luke's eyes met before they hurriedly looked away from each other; Brendan and Gabriel exchanged a tense, snatched glance, with Brendan willing his father to say the right thing.

Maurice noticed both connections with interest.

Then, Gabriel spoke. 'Thanks,' he said. 'And any other time we would have been honoured. But, with our recent unhappiness, it's probably too soon for us to go to a wedding.' He pointed his cigar— that he, like the other men, had been smoking throughout the meal—at Eileen, who was staring intently at her plate as if the untouched sole might have a message for her. 'Especially for my wife.'

Harold Kessler shrugged and spread his hands— a gesture that was beginning to annoy Gabriel in a very serious way. 'I understand,' he said generously, actually not understanding at all—they came out tonight didn't they? But who wanted them at the wedding anyway? He stood up and reached out to Gabriel. 'Still, today, today has been a good day.'

Gabriel also stood up, wondering what the little prat was up to now.

He might have known.

Harry put his arms round Gabriel and hugged him, the top of his bald head only just reaching Gabriel's top pocket handkerchief.

'Come here, come here,' he muttered into Gabriel's chest.

Gabriel stood there stiffly waiting for Kessler to let him go, but instead, he jerked back his head, cocked it to one side, and held Gabriel at arm's-length, exuding all the insincere emotion of a professional mourner hanging around for a free drop of the hard stuff after a funeral.

'We'll have a good future together,' he said, wagging his head up and down. 'A good future.'

Gabriel found a smile from somewhere. Was the little bleeder ever going to let him go?

He could have showered the band with kisses of gratitude when they stopped playing and the drummer performed a complicated roll to get everyone's attention, followed by the bandleader announcing the cabaret.

Gabriel and Harold—apart at last—took their seats as the main lights dimmed and the stage lighting turned from white to a deep, unsubtle mauve. The froufrou curtains lifted and a troupe of high stepping showgirls, wearing towering feathers in their hair, staggeringly high heels on their feet, and a brief scattering of sequins on their bodies, began kicking and wiggling to the Latin rhythms of 'Mambo Italiano'.

'Here, Luke,' snorted Pete Mac, elbowing his brother-in-law in the ribs. 'This is one of your favourites innit? One of the old ones they play down the Lighterman's Arms. At the drag shows.'

Maurice's ears pricked at the mention of the notorious Isle of Dogs pub that he had found within days of arriving in London.

Luke stood up. Christ, Pete Mac got on his nerves. 'Excuse me,' he said, stabbing a thumb in the direction of the lavatories.

Gabriel produced yet another smile. This evening was beginning to give him jaw ache.

A few seconds later, Maurice Kessler was on his feet. He pointed to his crotch, and mouthed to his Uncle Harold, 'Think I'd better join him.'

\*　　　\*　　　\*

Maurice stood at the urinal next to Luke and undid

132

his flies. Apart from an elderly attendant, who was busying himself polishing one of the big, three-sided mirrors, they were alone.

'So, feller, you weren't much taken by all them tits and arses flashing about out there then?' Maurice said in his broad, Mancunian accent, while studying Luke's penis as uninhibitedly as if he were considering which slice of porterhouse he fancied in a butcher's window. 'And that's certainly not the last turkey left in the shop,' he said approvingly.

Luke, shocked as much as embarrassed, turned his body away and concentrated on trying to finish urinating.

'That qualifies you as being more than well endowed I'd say. And I'll bet it makes you a right popular one with the boys.'

Luke's head jerked up. 'What did you say?'

'Come on, feller,' Maurice said, his voice low, amused. 'Anyone can see you're as bent as a nine bob note.'

'You what?' Luke flashed a look over his shoulder to check that the attendant wasn't eavesdropping. 'Don't be so fucking stupid.' He fumbled as he did up his trousers—his hands were trembling—and walked over to the washbasins.

'Are you saying you're not?' Maurice's voice was mocking, amused.

'Oh, I get it,' Luke said into the mirror, as Maurice again came and stood next to him, closer this time, his sleeve brushing Luke's back. 'You don't like these new arrangements. You're worried you might lose out, so you're trying to wind me up. Trying to cause trouble between the families so it all breaks down before it's even had a chance to get going.'

'On the contrary, feller. I'm just trying to be friendly.' Maurice winked at Luke's reflection and ran a finger up his spine.

Even through the layers of his jacket and shirt, and despite what he refused to admit even to himself, it made Luke shiver—a feeling of contracting waves that ran from the base of his throat, through his chest, right down to his groin.

He shook his head and pulled away. 'What's your fucking game, Kessler?'

'Game's a good word for it.' He paused, letting a wide grin spread slowly across his lips. 'You see, while I'm not exactly queer myself, I'm game for anything, me. Threesomes, foursomes. Older women. Younger ones. You name it, and I'm in there, feller. In like bloody Flynn.' He checked himself in the mirror, slowly admiring his own reflection. He liked what he saw—slim, but muscled build, just enough over average height to be described by most people as tall, and with a full head of dark, wavy hair that, because he'd kept it up until now, he was convinced he wouldn't lose. Not like his father and Uncle Harold who had both gone bald in their teens. He licked a finger and slicked back his eyebrows and then turned his attention back to Luke. 'And I've always fancied having a few innings batting for the other team. Something nice and intimate at first. A cosy little twosome. So, with a good-looking, well-endowed feller like yourself on offer—and a Southerner . . . Well, that'd be two new scores on my sheet in one go. And who knows, maybe I'll really like it.'

Luke stabbed his finger at his temple. 'You're sick.'

'Sick? No I'm not. I just think it's why we're here

on earth: to learn. And I aim to learn as much as I can before I go. And even if I go young, that'll be all right by me. I'll be England's answer to James Dean. A corpse maybe, but a bloody handsome one.'

'You are, you're out of your mind.'

'I'm glad I've met you, Luke O'Donnell, I've always liked a challenge.' Maurice put a hand on his shoulder.

'Get off me.' Luke shook himself free and threw a handful of silver into the tips plate.

At the sound of the coins hitting the dish, the elderly attendant, moving with surprising speed, proceeded to pump away at a fat rubber bulb attached to a silver-topped, cut glass bottle, spraying Luke's head and shoulders with sweet smelling cologne.

'Stop it. I don't want any.' Luke swished his hand around in the mist as if he could brush it away. Then he strode towards the door, about to leave, but then stopped and half-turned to speak to Maurice, knowing he had to deny those things— again—that he'd said about him.

He stood there, clasping the handle, looking over his shoulder at a whole gallery of grinning Maurices leering back at him from each of the row of triple mirrors that lined the wall opposite the cubicles.

'Here, Luke,' they all said. 'You know what they say about protesting too much, don't you, feller?'

\*    \*    \*

By the time Luke got back to the table, he knew he wouldn't be able to just sit there and join in the small talk. He had to get away. Get some fresh air. Blow away the vile stench of the cologne and Kessler's filthy insinuations.

'I'm sorry, everyone. I don't know what's got in to me, I'm feeling a bit strange.'

The sight of Maurice Kessler smirking at him made his stomach lurch.

'I'm going outside for a bit of air.'

'I'll go with you,' said Maurice. 'Make sure you're all right.'

'No, you stay where you are.' Hearing the panic in his own voice, Luke added more calmly, 'Enjoy your brandy.'

'Brendan'll go with you, Luke, won't you Brendan?' Eileen asked. 'He really doesn't look well.'

'I'm fine.'

'Brendan?'

'Okay.' Brendan frowned, noticing the look of amusement on Maurice's face. There was something about the bloke that Brendan really didn't like, and it wasn't just because he was a Northerner, or even because he was a Kessler. He just made Brendan's flesh crawl.

\*       \*       \*

Brendan and Luke stood outside the club, dragging on their cigarettes, blowing clouds of smoke and steamy breath into the freezing night air. Luke staring ahead, oblivious of his surroundings, concentrating on the pictures in his head; Brendan focussing on the passing punters, nodding at the accuracy of his predictions as he guessed which door each of them would slip into as they sought

136

out their own particular choice of illicit entertainment. Every one of the mugs was ready and eager to be separated from his hard-earned cash in the West End equivalent of the O'Donnells's places in the East End. The sorts of places that were as good as money printing factories, and that they were now planning on letting the Kesslers have a share in. It was like a bad joke.

Luke flicked his cigarette butt into the gutter. 'You know, Brendan, perhaps it wouldn't be such a bad idea if we went to this wedding.'

'What?'

'Mum seemed to manage all right tonight. And we wouldn't have to stay that long.'

'Have you taken leave of your senses?'

'It wouldn't hurt.'

Brendan turned full onto Luke and stared right into the eyes that wouldn't meet his. 'Hold on, I get it. *That's* what all this lark's been about tonight. I wondered why you've been up and down like a bride's nightie. It's the snatch innit? You've lost your bottle.'

Luke dropped his head back against the wall, puffed out his cheeks, and closed his eyes. 'I'm not like you, Brendan. This is all you've ever wanted, but you know I've never been sure about it. And as for this job, I honestly don't understand why Dad wants to take the risk. The streets'll be full of Christmas shoppers, plus we don't even know they'll be delivering the money that day.'

Brendan took his brother's face in his hands, making him look into his eyes. 'First of all, Luke, we're doing the job at seven o'clock in the morning. Not many shoppers around then, not unless they're

137

after lifting a couple of pints off a passing milk float. And second—yes, we do know it's being delivered on Tuesday; the clerk called Dad with the code word this morning. They've definitely brought the delivery forward because of the holidays.' He let go of his brother and rubbed his hands together like a stage villain. 'So, that's the wages plus all them lovely Christmas bonuses. Just think about it.'

Luke rubbed his own hands over his face. He felt as if he hadn't slept for a month. 'Look, Brendan, since the accident, I'm even less sure about how much I want to be involved in the business, it's—'

'Hang on a minute. *You're not sure how involved you wanna be*?' Brendan grabbed hold of his brother's arm, dragged him along the street and shoved him into the darkness of a narrow alleyway.

Luke, slipping and skidding on the muck-strewn ground, only saved himself from going over by clutching onto Brendan. 'Have you gone crazy?'

'Not yet, I've not, Luke.' Brendan pushed Luke away from him, sending him staggering backwards into the rough brick wall. 'But I might, so you'd better watch yourself. For someone who reckons he's not sure how fucking interested he is in the business, how come you were so quick setting up this little lot? Getting us hiked up with them bastards?'

'Brendan, don't do this,' said Luke trying to get past him, and away from the stink of whatever it was rising up from around their feet. 'You've been drinking, you don't know what you're saying.'

Brendan stepped forward, sticking his face up close to Luke's, blocking his escape. His breath stank of booze and tobacco, making Luke turn away. He hated the fact that his brother was getting

138

more and more like their father.

'Don't come this crap with me, Luke. First you cover up for Catherine when she was knocking about with that Kessler fucker, and now, because of you, we're tied up tighter than a duck's arse with his whole fucking family. So you're in it up to your neck, whether you like it or not.' He grabbed Luke's face between his finger and thumb, squeezing his cheeks so hard he could feel Luke's teeth through the flesh. 'Understand?'

Luke shook his head, and Brendan, exasperated, let him go.

'It's not like that.'

'Don't take the piss, Luke. Just because you're my brother, doesn't mean I won't get wild with you.'

'I know.'

'*I mean it*. You're in this with the rest of us.'

'But—'

'No, no buts. It's too late for that. And while we're at it, perhaps you'll explain what all that was about back in there, you getting all chummy with that prick's nephew.'

A noise at the top of the alley made Brendan pivot round.

'Oops, sorry, ladies,' said a mocking masculine voice. 'Didn't mean to interfere in your little lover's tiff.'

'Fuck off,' snarled Brendan.

At that moment, Luke was glad they were standing at the bottom of a dark, stinking alleyway. He couldn't have stood Brendan seeing that his cheeks had coloured up like a schoolgirl's.

'Temper, temper,' laughed the man, and then, addressing someone they couldn't see, said, 'Sorry,

Brian, we're too late, darling; someone's got our spot already. But maybe they might like a bit of extra company. How about it? Fancy that do you?'

Brendan spat on the ground in disgust. 'If you know what's good for you . . .'

'All right, sweetheart, hint taken.'

Brendan was ready to punch someone, and Luke was beginning to panic. Getting Brendan annoyed was never a good idea, but with the mood he was in tonight it would have been a really stupid thing to do. He had to calm him down.

'Look, Brendan, I promise, all I wanted to do was stop things getting out of hand. There's no edge to what I did, I swear. And surely you can't want it to be like it was before either—not knowing if there was gonna be axes smashing down the front door in the middle of the night; waking up to see a strange bloke standing over our beds with a gun in his hand.'

'We were kids then, Luke. Things are different now. We're men. Or we're supposed to be.'

'I know, and that's why we should be grown up enough to realise we've got to keep a lid on things.'

'If you're trying to pull that *Patricia's having a baby* old fanny on me, Luke, then don't bother.' Brendan leaned into him, his temper coming very close to turning physical. 'All this bollocks tonight: it's all your fucking fault. All of it. So don't even try that sentimental shit. It might have worked on Dad when he was too pissed and too upset to even know what day it was, but it's bloody obvious he's regretting it now. He's sitting back there gritting his teeth just having to talk to the stupid bastard, let alone being expected to go to his son's fucking wedding.'

140

Luke spoke as evenly as he could manage. 'Hasn't losing Catherine made you think, Brendan? Made you try and figure out what—'

'I get it. You really are a coward.'

'Thanks.'

Brendan sighed wearily. Rowing with Luke. What was the point of that? He'd had just about enough of this whole fucking night. 'I'm sorry, I shouldn't have said that.' He put his hand on his brother's shoulder. 'I know you're nervous about the snatch. It's only natural, first time being in the front line on a job like this. But you're gonna be all right.'

Luke let out a dry, humourless puff of laughter. 'D'you reckon?'

'Trust me. And it'll be a good opportunity to show me I was wrong, that you're not a coward.'

Luke felt like running a million miles away. 'Yeah?'

'Yeah. And anyway, it's good for you, learning new stuff.'

'What do you mean? Who've you been talking to?'

Brendan put up his hands. 'Blimey, Luke, don't be so bloody touchy. I'm trying to be friends here.'

'Sorry. You're right, I am nervous. But I still don't know why I've got to be part of it. Dad's got plenty of experienced blokes he always uses. So why do I have to go along? Come to that, why does *he* have to be there? He's not been on anything like this job for years. Always prides himself on being the businessman.' He put on a breathy imitation of his father's cockney-tinged Galway accent. 'I'm the brains, not the brawn.'

Brendan, despite his anger and frustration,

141

couldn't help but smile at the familiar impersonation—Luke had managed to defuse his brother's temper by mucking about ever since he was a toddler, saving himself from many a well-deserved clout.

'I'll tell you why, shall I, little brother? It's because this Kessler lark has got to him. He wants to show everyone, anyone who might have even the slightest doubt, that he's still a right tough bastard. Game as a bloody beigel. Heart like a fucking lion. And up for anything. Fuck the risk and bugger the danger. Plus, of course, there's one hell of a lot of dough involved.'

'Hasn't he got enough already?'

'There's no such thing, Luke.' Brendan put his arm round Luke's shoulder. 'Believe me. The more someone like Dad has, the more he wants. It's his nature.'

'I don't get it.'

'No, I know, mate. Different temperaments, eh? But think of the sort of expansion that kind of money can finance.'

Luke had nothing to say, well, not anything that would make sense in Brendan's universe.

Brendan punched him playfully in the guts. 'And, apart from Stephen Shea, Dad's gonna keep this one in the family. So, not only do we not have to divvy it up with any nasty, greedy outsiders, it'll also prove how loyal we all are to our dear old dad. You included, I'm afraid, Lukey boy. Good for his image, see. Show he's still got it—the bottle and the brains to pull off the big blag—and that his family stand by him, shoulder to shoulder, right there in the line of fire. That all enough of an explanation for you, little brother? They good enough reasons?'

Brendan wagged a finger at him. 'And, this is the clincher. It's the best buzz you can imagine. I know you don't believe me, but you wait till you feel the kick you get out of it. Better than sex, some blokes reckon.' He laughed. 'Not that red-blooded O'Donnells would ever agree with them sort of nutters, of course. But close enough for it to be bloody fantastic.' He started walking back towards the street. 'Come on, mate, let's go back in there and put on a show for Mum and Dad. Let everyone think we're loving it. I mean, one more lie can't hurt, can it?'

He looked over his shoulder and saw that Luke had made no attempt to move. 'Come on.'

It took Luke less than a minute to decide to follow his brother back to the club.

\*        \*        \*

The first part of the Dahlia's celebrated cabaret had ended, and the place of the long-legged chorus girls had been taken by couples doing their best to dance the Twist the way they'd seen the new dance demonstrated on television.

No one from the O'Donnell–Kessler party had moved onto the dance floor, they were still seated at their table, their numbers swollen by the minders, who, now that the meal was over and plenty of drink had been taken, had been invited to join them.

Luke distanced himself from Brendan by sitting well away from him, but he still watched as his brother fell so easily into making himself the centre of attention amongst the now substantial group of

143

men. He was making them all laugh out loud and slap their hands on the table.

Amongst the men, only Sammy Kessler seemed immune to Brendan's charms, as he put on joke accents, grinned and gurned, and acted out the story of how he and his friend, Baby Bobby Watts—the well-known son of the even more well-known Big Bobby Watts—carried off a two and a half grand con for the price of just three short trips to a rich but gullible junk merchant out in Essex.

Brendan explained how Baby Bobby had been the first to make the journey east to the salt marsh badlands a couple of miles outside Tilbury, introducing himself to the dealer as a Dutchman over on business in the nearby docks—business involving the disposal of a large quantity of top quality, green glass bottles. If only he could find the right customer, he could bring over unlimited supplies from Holland.

The dealer, rich as Croesus, but described by Brendan as looking like a cross between Fagin and the tramps who hung about in Itchy Park, would hardly give him the time of day. Who the hell wanted green glass bottles?

Disappointed, the Dutchman left.

A week later, Brendan turned up at the bloke's yard saying he could only hope that the dealer could help him. He had the possibility of making a killing, if only he could get hold of some green glass bottles, the *exact* size and shape as per the drawing—coloured in and everything—that Brendan showed him. In fact, he told the man, he could take an unlimited supply of the product, if only someone could get hold of them, but he'd heard that they were only available in Holland. His last hope, before making the trip over the water, had been dealers working in the vicinity of the docks in Essex. He wasn't going to be stupid about it, wouldn't be taken for a ride, but he would offer a very good price.

As soon as Brendan left, the dealer was on the phone. Sadly, he had no contact number for the Dutchman, but how difficult could it be to get bottles? But as he described the product to every contact he could think of, he soon discovered just why the man had been trawling the area with no luck. No bottles of the precise colour and description could be found. Other bottles, certainly, but those exact ones . . .

Then, just a few days later, a miracle happened: Baby Bobby turned up at the yard again. But—and he stressed this more than once—the dealer had to bear in mind that this was now a seller's market. The bottles were, so Bobby the Dutchman had heard, the most desirable commodity in the whole of the county. This meant, of course, that Dutch Bobby would need some money up front to show goodwill for the supply of his very desirable product.

He had the wedge in his hand before he could say Edam cheese.

Through that little deal, the boys had earned themselves a nice few quid, but, best of all, the bit that made them all laugh loudest, was the fact that not only did Brendan not deliver the items as promised, they never bloody existed. And if Baby Bobby—a born and bred Eastender, who got the earache if he even had to cross the river to go over South London for the day—was a Dutchman then Brendan would eat his clogs for him, and maybe have a windmill or two for afters.

'Come on, chaps,' said Kessler, with all the flamboyance that a short, fat man in his forties could muster. 'More drinks to celebrate our union with a family with such a genius amongst them.' He leaned forward and pinched Brendan's cheek. 'And a special one for this boy. A boy any father would be proud of.'

Glasses were raised and congratulations offered.

While Brendan accepted all the praise with convincingly good humour, Maurice Kessler took the opportunity to leave the testosterone-fuelled huddle to go and sit with Luke. 'So, do you fancy another drink then, feller?'

'No, I don't. I don't want anything from you.'

Maurice's face folded into an expression of knowing, easy amusement. He slipped his hand under the table. 'Sure I couldn't tempt you?'

It took Luke a moment to register that Maurice really was touching the inside of his thigh and that his hand was *creeping up towards his balls.*

Luke pulled away. 'Don't you ever . . .'

Maurice raised an eyebrow. 'Sorry,' he whispered. 'Must have slipped.'

Luke got up and went to sit with his mother on the far side of the table. The increased amusement on Maurice's face infuriated him, but Eileen was unaware of her son's discomfort. She was just glad of his company, especially as Sophie Kessler had been hijacked by an embarrassingly drunk Pete Mac, who was even now draping his arm over the back of the poor woman's chair.

Pete Mac sniffed loudly. 'Brendan's not the only one with stories to tell you know, girl.'

Sophie remained polite. 'Really?'

'And you lot . . .' he paused to belch. '. . . ain't the only religious ones either, you know.'

This time she offered a strained smile.

'I helped out at the church fête once. Even though I ain't really churchified meself. But I go along with it. It keeps the old woman happy.' He put his finger to his lips, joining her in his conspiracy. 'That's her—Pat—over there.' He waved and called across to her. 'All right, girl? You women like all that holy lark, don't you, love?'

He returned his attentions to Sophie. 'Anyway, like I was saying, I like to do my bit. So I helped out. Know what I did?'

Sophie had no idea.

'I put the frighteners on this little kid, who'd won everything all day. It looked like the little bugger was going to win the last race in the donkey derby and get the pick of the last of the decent prizes, the one they'd earmarked for the priest. So, you know the donkey he was riding in the derby?'

Sophie didn't, but thought it best to let him continue.

'I kicked it right up the jacksy. It went raving mad, like a wild bull it was. The kid couldn't get anywhere near it. That stopped him, the little bleeder.'

Pete Mac swigged at his drink. 'Should have given the kid a kicking and all really. Right little toerag he was. Wound up in the nick for doing gas meters. Got a couple of birchings by all accounts.' He smirked as if remembering some private joke. 'Mind you, girl, if the truth was told, I reckon Father Shaunessy would have preferred to have had the kid rather than the box of chocolates.' He nudged her roughly. 'The old goat's always enjoyed the company of the altar boys, if you know what I mean.' He grinned broadly. 'His wrist's so limp he can hardly bless himself.'

Sophie's expression had frozen into a tight, thin-lipped grimace. 'I'm sorry, would you excuse me, Mr MacRiordan.' She lifted her chin and gestured to her husband. 'Harry, would you mind calling me a taxi. I don't want to break up the party, but I'm very tired.'

Pete Mac huffed loudly. Silly tart. There he was being nice, even about to ask her if she needed any help up the synagogue—not that he'd actually intended doing anything, but it was a nice thought - and what had she done? Blanked him, that's what. Well, she knew what she could do, the miserable bitch. He'd show her be rude to him.

He wasn't sure how, not this minute, but he'd show her all right.


## CHAPTER TEN

It was bang on 7 a.m. Stephen Shea manoeuvred the simple, workmanlike van, bearing the proud legend: *Thomas Simpson and Sons Plumbers. Estab. 1924. Commercial and Private work undertaken*, into the dead-end service road at the side of the tall, West End office block in a street at the back of Oxford Street. Most of the lights were off at that time of the morning, but, exactly as they had expected, there was a lamp on in the service reception, a plain square room furnished with functional office basics, at the rear of the building.

Inside the room, Gabriel, who was sitting in the

passenger seat, could make out a middle-aged man wearing the uniform of the Corp of Commissionaires. He had his elbows on his high, clerk's desk, as he sipped from a green enamel mug, and pored over the back pages of the *Daily Mirror*. He didn't even look up as the van drove past.

'Ready lads,' Gabriel said, as he pulled his full-face balaclava down to his chin, nodding to Stephen Shea to do the same.

Brendan, Luke and Pete Mac, sitting on the narrow benches that had been installed along the insides of the back of the van, followed suit.

'Here we go then.' Gabriel crossed himself, picked up his canvas bag, and burst out of the van and through the door of the office.

This time the uniformed man did look up, momentarily more baffled than scared. He put his mug and paper on the desk and rose to his feet. 'What's all this then?' he asked in the tones of a displeased sergeant major questioning a show of high jinks amongst the new recruits. 'What do you want?'

'To wish you a Merry Christmas, of course,' said Gabriel in a fair imitation of a Glaswegian accent.

Pete Mac couldn't help it, he burst out laughing. 'You a Scotchman? You sure, Gabe?'

Gabriel spun round. 'Shut your fucking mouth,' he spat, his accent now slipping all over the British Isles.

'Look out!' yelled Stephen, who was supposed to be guarding the door, but had been the only one to notice the commissionaire picking up the telephone.

Gabriel was on him with the speed and

determination of a lurcher after a hare. He grasped the now terrified man's shoulder with one hand, shoved his face flat on the desk with the other—sending the mug flying across the room and spraying tea all over the lino-covered floor—then pulled out a leather-covered cosh from his pocket and whacked it down on the back of the now terrified man's neck. The combination of fear and the lead-assisted rabbit punch knocked him out cold.

Stephen Shea looked at his watch and called over to them from the door. 'They'll be here in less than half an hour.'

Gabriel nodded. 'Right. Concentrate. You, Pete, you bring the things from the van. Brendan,' he jerked his head at the internal, half glazed door. 'You have a quick shufty round the corridor. The cleaners should have gone by now. But just in case there's anyone nosing around out there who wants to be a hero . . . Stephen, take off your balaclava and get ready to greet the security van.' He paused. 'You sure you're still all right with that?'

Stephen laughed. 'Won't I be one of your victims myself?'

'Good man, Stephen.' Gabriel turned to his son. 'Now, Luke, you get his uniform jacket off.'

Luke stood there, staring down at the man, stomach-churning visions of Catherine lying in the road coming unwanted into his head. 'He's bleeding.'

'And you're a bleeding nuisance,' offered Pete Mac, coming back in with his arms full. 'Move yourself Luke or you'll get us all nicked.'

Gabriel spoke softly. 'Ignore him, Luke. Just do as I say.'

Luke didn't answer, didn't trust himself to speak, he just got on with it.

While his son pulled off the man's jacket, Gabriel set out the ropes, cloths, and the can of petrol Pete Mac had fetched from the van.

\* \* \*

By the time the wages van arrived, the commissionaire had been tidied away behind a run of lockers in the adjoining changing rooms, where, in a little over ninety minutes, chattering office workers would be stowing their umbrellas, bags, and heavy outdoor footwear. He was bound to a metal and canvas chair, gagged and trussed up like a turkey, and had just over half a gallon of petrol soaked into his trousers. It had mingled with the urine he had released involuntarily when he had come round and realised what was happening to him; the humiliation, fear and fumes had filled his yellowing eyes with tears he couldn't even move to swipe away.

\* \* \*

Seeing the plumber's van that was blocking his way into the service road, the driver of the wages truck tutted impatiently, told his guard he wouldn't be a minute, got out of the cab, and slammed the door angrily. This was a good start. Knowing his luck he'd get held up on every single drop—and he had enough of them to do, what with everyone getting paid early because of the holidays.

'Here, mate,' he called to the man who was leaning against the door, puffing on a roll up.

151

The man was Stephen Shea. He was wearing a bulky overcoat to conceal his body shape; a flat cap, pulled down hard to his eyebrows; thick, milk bottle glasses shoved up high on his nose; and a chunky muffler knotted about his chin. His own mother would have had trouble recognising him. 'Yeah?'

The driver pointed at the van that was blocking his path, stopping him from getting bloody started for the day, never mind finished. 'You the plumber, are you?'

'Sorry, pal, can't help you. Busy all day, see. Got all my jobs mapped out for me by Hitler's mother back at the yard. I'd love to help you, but she'd have me guts for garters. See, what with this cold snap, and Christmas and everything . . . You know how it is. Sorry.'

The man rolled his eyes. 'Look, mate, I ain't got a leak, I've got a delivery to make. And your van's in the way. So, you gonna move it for us or what?'

'Well, I've not really finished yet. Frozen pipes, see. Terrible mess in the Ladies' toilets.' He wrinkled his nose, making his glasses waggle up and down. 'The governor's fault for turning the boiler down, if you ask me. Like an igloo in some of them offices.'

'Do us a favour, mate, we won't be long,' pleaded the driver. 'Go on. I've got Christmas presents to collect for the missus.'

Stephen flicked his roll-up into the gutter. 'Well, so long as you're not. Cos, to tell you the honest truth, I've not actually even been inside there yet to have a look. Wanted a quiet smoke first, see. But if I don't get in there and get it sorted out before them office wallahs start turning up, I'll never hear the bloody end of it.'

'Thanks, you're a good 'un.' The driver gave him a double thumbs up then trotted back to his vehicle. He backed out onto the public road, and Stephen—very obliging—pulled out after him, peering myopically through the distorting lenses of the glasses, allowing the security van to turn round and reverse back in before him, thus swapping places on the service road.

The plumber's van was now effectively the cork in the bottle, blocking the way out for the wages van until Stephen was good and ready to let them go—not that they'd actually be able to go anywhere. Well, not for a while they wouldn't.

\*　　　\*　　　\*

The driver and guard jumped out of their vehicle and made their way into the service reception, both more than ready for a quick, reviving cuppa. Five minutes wouldn't hurt, not now they'd got the van out of the way.

\*　　　\*　　　\*

Gabriel was sitting at the desk, with the enamel mug set in front of him. He was wearing the commissionaire's uniform jacket and the balaclava. The two men could see his sleeves—dark serge, buttons and braid—but the balaclava was hidden behind the open Daily Mirror that Gabriel was holding up in front of him, and apparently studying intently.

'Morning, Stan,' grinned the driver, winking at his guard. 'If only this lot realised how useless you are, you deaf old git, they'd chuck you right out on your arse.'

Gabriel dropped the paper. 'Is that any way to talk to a man who probably fought in Flanders' poppy-covered fields for the likes of you?'

The guard's jaw dropped in an involuntary parody of cartoon surprise. 'What the—' was all he managed to say before Brendan stepped from behind the door and took hold of him, pulling his arms tight behind his back.

Pete Mac grabbed the driver.

'Don't even think about making a fuss, just answer me nice and even like,' said Gabriel, flicking his eyes towards the door. 'I heard you out there. You were talking to someone.'

The men glanced nervously at one another, but said nothing.

Gabriel sighed, disappointed by such an unhelpful response. 'Take them through to the lockers, lads.'

Brendan and Pete Mac marched them into the corridor.

Their eyes widened as they saw Stan gagged and lashed to his seat. Their nostrils twitched.

Gabriel took a lighter from his pocket and held it to the commissionaire's petrol soaked groin. 'You can smell it, can't you? What is it do you think? Petrol, maybe? Very dangerous that can be, especially with a naked flame around.' He made a show of putting the lighter back in his pocket, picked up the petrol can, and held it in mid-swing as though he were about to fling the contents over the driver. '*Well*?'

The driver nearly lost control of his bowels. 'It was a plumber.'

Gabriel turned to the guard, who averted his gaze before he spoke, ashamed of his own cowardice.

'That's right,' he said. 'There's a plumber out there. Bloke with a cap.'

Gabriel nodded. 'Ah, the truth at last—very sensible.' He tossed Luke a length of rope. 'You. Go out and see to him. Make sure he's not going anywhere.' Then he jabbed a finger at the guard. 'And now it's time to take a look in that vehicle of yours.'

'Wait, please,' the driver pleaded. 'Can't we just vanish? Can't you let us make a break for it and—'

Gabriel interrupted him with a raised hand. He then put his finger to his lips to indicate that the man should keep schtum, and took out his lighter again. But this time he sparked it up, and held it right under Stan's nose. 'Don't think so, lads. Do you?'

\*       \*       \*

With Gabriel directing, it took them less than twenty minutes, a fraction more persuasion, and only the minimum of fuss, to get the van opened up for them; to tie the two men to the legs of the desk; to transfer all the money from the wages van to their own—far more than they'd been expecting, the driver having been contracted for extra Christmas drops—to make sure they'd left nothing incriminating behind—and then to drive sedately out of the service road.

It took just a further half an hour to reach a boring looking Morris shooting break, which was to be the vehicle they would use to drive in a time-consuming, nerve-wrackingly circuitous route, finally reaching their slaughter—the flat in Kilburn where they would divvy up and stash their haul—by about a quarter to eleven that morning.

So far, there had been just the one slight hitch, and even then no one except Pete Mac knew about it.

He had thought that while he was tying up the driver, the bloke had muttered at him a bit sarcastically, and so Pete Mac had taken against him. When they were all outside, packed and ready to leave, he had starting running back towards the office, patting his supposedly empty pockets, calling over his shoulder that he was sure he'd had a packet of fags with him, and had better just check. Evidence and all that.

Safely inside and out of earshot of the others, Pete Mac had given the driver a right bollocking about manners, called him a cunt, and had then struck him round the side of the head with a knuckle-duster, catching him on the temple.

Picking up presents for his wife was now going to be the least of the van driver's worries over Christmas. The fractured skull, internal bleeding, and subsequent brain damage would be of far more concern.

Pete Mac's only response to the bloodied and unconscious man, who had flopped forward as far as his bindings allowed, was a slightly giggling, 'Ooops!' But when the guard's bowels gave out in terror, dreading it would be him next, Pete Mac wafted a hand in front of his nose, and gasped.

'You dirty bastard. What is it with you two's manners? And what the hell did you have for fucking breakfast?'

156

Pete Mac was just about to escape from the stench, disappear out into the fresh air, but he couldn't let the guard get away with it, or else he'd think he'd one over on him. So he turned round, walked back over to the desk, and stamped his heel as hard as he could, full in the man's crutch.

*         *         *

Eileen and Patricia were struggling through the bustle of bag-laden Christmas shoppers in Oxford Street. Neither of them looked very pleased to be there.

'God, I've not got the heart for this, Patricia. Not this year.'

'Look, Mum, it's nearly quarter to twelve. These crowds are only going to get worse. How about calling it a day?' She pulled her mother gently out of the way of a hot chestnut seller's glowing brazier. 'We've got the turkey ordered from Marston's, Alfie Simms is delivering all the veg, and you made the cake and the puddings ages ago. I can pop out tomorrow and get the last few bits down the market.'

Eileen slipped her arm through her daughter's and drew her close. 'You're a good girl, Pat, but come on, let's get this done. The men won't just be expecting a Christmas dinner with all the trimmings and everything else we can cram on their plates. Big kids that they are, they'll be expecting something to unwrap waiting for them under the tree.'

Patricia knew that her mother was kidding herself, that all their efforts were actually nothing to do with what the men wanted, but were about her feeling the necessity to go through the motions, to do what they did every year, to make the house and table look the way Catherine used to love at a time of year she used to adore. 'If you're sure you're up to it.'

Eileen's lips compressed in sadness as she held back the tears. 'Hark at you in your condition worrying yourself about me. It's me should be looking after you, darling.'

'You're letting us stay round your place over the holiday.'

'*Letting* you? I couldn't think of anything I'd want more.'

'Except having Catherine back, eh, Mum?'

That did it, the tears spilled over onto her cheeks. 'Yes, love, apart from that.'

'Come on, Mum. If we're brave enough to put up with those men of ours, we're brave enough to face the crowds in Selfridges.' Patricia took out her hankie and dabbed away the dampness on her mother's face. 'Might even have a quick look at the maternity dresses, eh?'

Her tone didn't carry the conviction of her words.

*     *     *

While Eileen and Patricia half-heartedly compared the length of men's cashmere scarves, just a few miles away, in an historic synagogue on the edge of the City of London, Daniel Kessler was bringing down his foot on a linen wrapped glass, shattering it with a loud, satisfying crack.

Cries of 'Mazel tov!' echoed around the ancient walls as Sophie Kessler, tears of joy rolling down

158

her cheeks, threw her arms round her husband's neck.

'Harry, our little Danny, a married man—how can it be possible?'

'I'll show you the bills for the wedding if you really need proof. Now, come on, let's get to the hall and get some of that food and champagne down us before your sisters guzzle it all.'

*     *     *

As the wedding party bustled around outside, getting into the fleet of cars waiting to take them to the reception, Kessler sniggered to himself like a schoolboy who'd just heard a grown-up talking about willies. He hadn't thought that much could have topped O'Donnell falling for the idea that he'd brought his family back to escape the threat of more riots, rather than realising he'd had little choice but to leave Notting Hill once Rachman had decided to take over. But today was special, his eldest son was now a married man, a man who would one day be more than capable not only of taking over the family businesses, but the O'Donnell bastards' businesses into the bargain.

He couldn't have been a happier man.

*     *     *

Patricia had, after not much argument—she hadn't the energy for it—allowed her mother to pay for the late lunch they had both done little more than pick at. The excitement and enthusiasm of everyone surrounding them had done nothing to lighten their mood.

159

Patricia stood up and began buttoning her coat. 'Mum, can I say something?'

'You know you can say anything to me, love.' Eileen wasn't looking at her daughter, she was concentrating on easing her gloves over her fingers.

'I know I've got to try and think of the baby as a new start, but it's Pete, Mum. He's just so . . . Aw, I don't know how to explain it.' She flapped her hands in exasperation. 'I know it sounds daft, but he's just so flipping big. Like a great big bull crashing about and making a mess, and not listening, and always doing what he wants and never thinking about telling me when he's coming home, and . . .' Her arms dropped to her side as her words ran out. Her chin dropped almost to her chest. 'It's like he just doesn't care about anything but himself.'

'I know, love.' Eileen gave up on her gloves and shoved them into her pocket. Her youngest might have been taken from her, but she still had a duty to her other children. She couldn't abandon them by allowing herself to wallow in self-pity; she had to try for their sakes. Be it by buying them silly gifts or trying to help them make the best of a not very good situation.

'We all have our burdens to bear, darling, but, when you think about it, we're better off than a lot of women. At least our men provide for us, look after us, and protect us. They might not always be the most sensitive to what we're feeling, and not bother much about asking what we want from life, but they do work hard. That's why they need to relax, have a few drinks—maybe even a few drinks too many. Let their hair down. And we . . . we just have to try and understand them. It's the price we

160

pay.' She paused, summoning the final justification. 'And better than living in some hovel in Ireland with no water or electric.'

Patricia bent down and began gathering up her bags from under the table, not as convinced as her mother apparently was as to what was worth the sort of price they were paying.

*     *     *

When Gabriel had led them into the slaughter earlier that day, they had all—even Luke—been chuckling like monkeys, with their arms full of shopping bags: an ordinary group of chaps paying someone a visit at Christmas time. Luke had been surprised, to say the least, by the inside of the pleasant, little two-bedroom flat.

On a highly polished dining table there were muslin-draped plates of sandwiches, cheese and biscuits, and fruit. And around the plates were neatly laid out tins of beer with an opener and glasses, and four thermos flasks—which they soon discovered where filled with whiskey-fuelled coffee and tea—and even a home-baked cake, complete with jolly, if amateurish, Christmas icing showing a snowman standing next to a lop-sided fir tree.

They had dumped the bags on the floor—all carrying the names of high street chains, department stores and even one or two from Dublin, just what good Irish lads coming over to England to see their families in Kilburn would be carrying—and threw themselves onto the armchairs and sofa.

'Jesus, Stephen,' grinned Gabriel. 'I thought I was getting too old for all this.'

161

Stephen grinned back at him. 'You too old, Gabe? Never.'

Gabriel opened one of the glossier, string-handled bags and lifted out a brick of bank notes. He tossed it over to Stephen. 'Just that would be enough to finance opening that drinking club I've been thinking about over Plaistow way.'

Stephen clapped his hands around it, weighing it appreciatively. 'Happy Christmas, Gabe.'

'And to you, my friend. Now let's have a drink. I might make my living out of crime, Stevie, old son, but I am passionate about me leisure. I just need a glass in my hand and a fucking great wedge in me bin. What more could a simple man like me ask for?'

Luke, who, up until now, had said very little, opened one of the cans and poured the cold beer down his throat. The excitement of the robbery had both shocked and excited him, disturbed and thrilled him. He had beamed like a tickled baby one minute, and had shaken like an abandoned one the next. But now he just felt drunk from the combination of adrenaline, too many slugs of warm, hip flask whiskey in the van, the two cups full of thermos flask toddy he'd gulped down without it barely touching the sides—now all topped up with the beer.

'Here, Brendan,' he said, 'who was that copper? You remember, the one who helped us out when that other one stopped us for speeding?'

'Medway,' said Brendan without a pause.

'Yeah, Medway, that was his name.' Luke put down his can, ripped a stack of notes from one off the bags, tore off the paper binder and threw the money in the air. 'Happy Christmas, PC do-us-a-favour Medway. To you and yours. Have a Happy-bloody-Christmas, mate.'

'Good thinking, Luke, very good,' said Brendan, smiling indulgently as he took the opener from the arm of his brother's chair. 'I told you coming on this job'd be good for you.' He popped a can for Gabriel and then one for himself. 'That'll be a sensible thing—showing him our appreciation.'

'You're not really gonna bother treating him are you, Brendan? I reckon he was a right flash fucker.'

Brendan looked coolly at his brother-in-law; he spoke quietly, slowly, his restraint not hiding his disdain. 'He did us a favour on a very difficult day. And we're going to say thank you. You see, that's the problem with you, Pete. You don't get it, do you, the old back scratching bit? Or the idea that you should keep your word?' He paused, sipped at his beer. 'When it's in the interest of the family, you act nice. It keeps things sweet.'

'What, like I tried being nice to that Kessler's old woman? The ungrateful, stuck-up cow.'

'What're you going on about now?'

'That Kessler bitch. She didn't want to know in the Dahlia Club, did she? Making conversation with her I was, all polite and everything.'

Gabriel wasn't really listening to what they were talking about—something to do with coppers and polite conversation, or something—but he was confident Brendan could handle it, whatever it was. And, anyway, he had other things on his mind. He looked at his watch and smiled as the telephone rang, right on time.

'Here, Gabe,' said Pete Mac, all saucer-eyed. 'You don't think that that's Danny Kessler calling us for advice about what he should be doing on his honeymoon tonight, do you?' He pumped his elbows and waggled his hips suggestively. *'Go on my son, give her one!'*

Gabriel didn't respond to Pete Mac, instead, he calmly checked his watch again, and with a deep, satisfied sigh, he stood up.

'It's for me,' he said, and went out in the hallway to answer the phone.

*　　　*　　　*

'Gabriel, thank God you're all right.' It was a woman's voice, soft and concerned.

'I'm just fine and it's good to hear from you, my love. It's been quite a day.'

'Is everything at the flat okay for you? Enough to eat and drink for everyone?'

'Couldn't be better. Everything's perfect as always, my angel, except of course that you're not here. It's empty without you.'

There was a contented pause as the praise was accepted with pleasure. Then, 'I'm glad.'

'Glad you're not here?'

She heard the smile in his voice. 'Don't tease me, Gabriel O'Donnell. Now, are you managing without me?'

'Rosie Palmer, how could I ever manage without you, my darling?'

He put down the receiver and went back into the boys with a warm smile on his face.

They all knew better than to question him, but he spoke before they even had the chance.

'Pete Mac was right,' he said, now sternly straight-faced. 'It was the Kesslers. But they didn't want my marital advice, they wanted my blessing.

So, I think a toast is in order, lads.' He raised his can, using it to make the sign of the cross in the air, and said very solemnly, 'To Danny Kessler, his lovely bride and her new family.'

When the others burst out laughing, Gabriel tried to hold his serious expression, but failed totally. He threw back his head and shouted out loud, 'May they all behave themselves or rot in hell like the dogs they are!'

## CHAPTER ELEVEN

Brendan pulled on the handbrake and smiled. It was a fine, bright afternoon, the kind of day that lifted your spirits, with the sky the sort of inspiringly cloudless blue that, when you looked out at it from behind the car window, made you think it might just be July, that you could walk outside with rolled up shirtsleeves and feel the heat of the summer sun on your back.

But appearances can be deceptive. Outside it was still winter, so cold and crisp that, as he got out of the car and breathed in, Brendan felt as if he were taking down great gulps of iced mountain water, making his lungs contract from the shock of it. Although, it had to be said, what he was inhaling on Shoreditch High Street, was a very long way from the pure air he'd tasted during his childhood stays in Galway and Kildare. Because the high street on which Brendan was standing was on the 'wrong' side of the ancient wall—the old Roman barrier that, while no longer visible, was still most definitely there, dividing the world of wealth and privilege that was the City, from the shadowy streets of the East End that occupied its backyard—a place where working people spent their lives manufacturing goods and providing services for their privileged neighbours.

As always, when Brendan parked so close to the City boundary, he wondered if, one day, he might cross that divide, and make it meaningless, be accepted for who he was, and not just because he had a thick roll of notes in his pocket. But, for now, he was satisfied with taking his neighbours' money in exchange for providing them with the means to meet their three seemingly inexhaustible needs—booze, betting, and whores.

He issued a final instruction to the two men inside the car, then crossed the pavement and stood outside a busy builders' merchants.

As if summoned by a bell, a brown-overalled assistant appeared by his side.

Brendan slipped him two pound notes and the man smiled and nodded. 'Course,' he said. 'Don't you worry about a thing, Mr O'Donnell. It'll be a pleasure to keep an eye on your motor. A real pleasure.'

The exchange was also a pleasure for Brendan: a further strengthening of his reputation as being a man with enough scratch in his pocket to be generous, and confident enough in himself to know that his bidding would be done.

He patted the assistant on the shoulder, turned and beckoned for Luke and Pete Mac to get out of the car and join him.

Brendan was now striding along, with his brother and brother-in-law flanking him, heading east towards a narrow alley, which threaded through to a cobbled cul-de-sac that anyone unfamiliar with the area would probably never have realised was there.

At Brendan's signal—a raised, leather-gloved hand—they came to a halt at the top of the short, block turning, and, despite their familiarity with the street, stood and weighed up the situation, taking their bearings as carefully as if they were on a military reconnaissance.

The roadway was flanked on one side by the high, almost windowless walls of a sweet factory; the other by the wide-open front of a furniture finishers, where they could see bow-backed men and boys working in a way that they never would. At the bottom of the street, was the dull brick façade of the incongruously named Bellavista club.

Being mid-afternoon, the little street was busy with the traffic and sounds of manufacturing, and the air was filled with the sweet, heavy scent of boiling sugar, mixed with the equally sweet, yet somehow acrid stench of toxic polishes and glue. The labourers and craftsmen in the furniture workshop, used to such comings and goings, flashed envious yet cursory glances at the three men standing at the top of the street in their expensive, unstained clothes, presuming they were just more lucky buggers who could chose to spend their afternoons in the Bellavista Club rather than having to worry themselves about the finer points of veneers, finishes, and rotten lacquered brass fittings.

They were right in one way, the three men were going into the club, but they weren't being seduced by the bold neon light over its door that winked its

167

saucy, candy-floss pink come hither, promising as it did a business very different from the production of cough candy twists and dining-room suites. The trade in which the club specialised was, in actual fact, quite prosaic: the sale of alcohol to those whose thirst could not be satisfied by the everyday licensing hours extended to drinkers in other more 'regular' establishments—and that wasn't what attracted them either. Well, not exactly.

'Right, lads,' said Brendan, shooting his spotless French cuffs and smoothing down his thick black hair, which was no longer greased into a quiff, but was allowed to fall forward in a fashionable, more natural style. 'Let's get ourselves inside and explain the new arrangements to Mr Johnson.'

\*       \*       \*

Brendan put his palms flat on the brick wall on either side of the door, rocked back on his heels, judged his distance, and then rammed one chisel-toed Chelsea boot, square and flat footed—*smack!*—against the hinge side of the door. It would have been easier kicking in the lock side, but he knew kicking the hinge side would cause more damage, make more impact, lend more drama to their entrance.

It took him two more goes to send the door splintering in on itself with an at first slow creak, and then with a swift, dusty *whhhump!* as it finally surrendered and hit the floor.

Luke threw a look over his shoulder. Not one of the workers—being used to some of the club's drunker customers acting very badly indeed—had been foolish enough to show even a hint of curiosity.

As Brendan brushed any stray specks of grime from his sleeves, he tutted with concern. 'Not much care being taken of these premises, is there, lads? Shame, prime location like this. Think we'll have to explain our insurance policy to Keithy Johnson all over again, don't you?'

Pete Mac grinned. 'Here, that was good, Brendan—*insurance policy*. You make us sound like the men from the Pru.'

\*　　　\*　　　\*

Despite its grandiose name, the Bellavista was little more than a very large, low-ceilinged room, having once been the workroom and store for a gown manufacturer who had long since retired to Hendon. It was no longer packed tight with whirring industrial sewing machines, and hissing Hoffman presses, but was fitted out with plain wooden tables, kitchen-style Windsor chairs, and a functional, undecorated bar from which over-priced, unbranded drinks were served in not very clean glasses. There was a single, evil-smelling lavatory that was generally ignored, the customers preferring to risk the elements rather than the stench, and to relieve themselves in the corners of the alleyway outside.

And yet most of the tables were occupied, and by surprisingly smartly turned out customers; some were playing cards, one was flicking through the early afternoon City Prices edition of the evening paper, but most were happy to be simply drinking, smoking, talking and laughing, passing their time with like-minded men.

169

There were no women in the room.

And no one except the man behind the bar seemed all that disturbed or interested, as Brendan, Luke and Pete Mac entered the place, walking over the kicked-in door with as little heed as if it had been the unpolished doorstep of the mother of their worst sworn enemy.

Why should the customers have cared? If it had been a police raid they'd have known about it, would have been given plenty of advance warning to get out, as more than a few of the customers were in the force themselves. So, best just to keep their heads down, keep their eyes on their drinks, and maybe get a bit of free entertainment thrown in. Let sleeping dogs lie and all that. That's the ticket. Have another sip. Chin, chin!

The bystanders had it right; the object of the O'Donnells's visit wasn't anything to do with any of them. The O'Donnell boys and their knuckle-headed brother-in-law were there to see the man behind the bar—Keithy Johnson, the sole owner and proprietor of the Bellavista drinking club.

Keithy was an overweight, crop-headed man in his fifties, who looked as if he hadn't seen daylight for at least the past thirty years, and had not exerted himself physically for the past forty. But who now, from the panic in his eyes, the sweat on his top lip, and the way he was wringing the grubby glass cloth through his hands, looked as if he couldn't decide whether he should run like the clappers or just give in and cack his pants right where he stood.

'Keithy, old son,' said Brendan, hoisting himself up onto a cheap, bamboo barstool, and nodding for Luke and Pete Mac to stand either side of him. 'I know we could have rung the bell and all that, but I thought I might do you a favour, let you know the sort of mood I'm in before we begin.' He smiled his handsomely disarming smile—Keithy's new best friend. 'Just so you wouldn't make the mistake of going and upsetting me, like.'

Keithy gulped—a stranded codfish with no way back to the sea—took out a bottle from under the counter and held it up for Brendan's approval, careful to shield its well-known label from everyone else in the room. 'This suit you?'

Brendan shook his head.

'It's okay,' Keithy assured him. 'It's the proper gear, not the shit I serve them lot.'

'We're not here to drink, Keithy,' said Brendan, offering the man a sad downturn of his lips and a regretful shake of his head, all the while holding poor, distraught Keithy's gaze without so much as a blink. 'We're here to chuck you out.'

'You're here to what?' Keithy Johnson looked from Pete Mac to Luke and back to Brendan. 'You're having me on, right?'

'Not really, mate. No.' He leaned forward. 'Look, you saw how we came steaming in just now. Well, what sort of protection could you ever hope to get that could insure you against that? And as you know, Keithy, we're the only insurers round here anyway, so what's the point you trying? And— I dunno—we just want the club. Simple as that. So now it's ours.'

'But you can't—'

'I'm sorry, Keithy, but we can. And, let's face it, let's put our cards on the table and be honest here, you've got no one to blame but yourself. Pete Mac came round here only last week offering you all

171

sorts of extra protection, all kinds of help, but would you accept it? No, course you wouldn't. Thought you could have one over on us, didn't you?'

'That's not what happened. You know I couldn't afford the sort of money he was talking about.'

'Yeah, course I know. I ain't fucking stupid.' Brendan leaned back from the bar and grinned. 'Good plan of mine, eh?'

'Please, Brendan . . .'

'Anyway, perhaps you could have afforded it if you'd stopped playing the gee-gees.' Brendan put on a suitably rueful expression. 'Betting always was a mug's game.' He leaned forward again and whispered. 'But don't you go telling no one I said that, will you Keithy? Don't want me profits going down, now do I?' He winked as he settled himself back on the stool and folded his arms.

'Now, you either tell everyone a nice little story—I dunno, your wife's dying or something. Ask them all to leave nice and quietly, and say the club'll be closed for a day or two. Then you follow them out that front door—or rather, what was the front door. That, or we have to help you on your way. And you wouldn't like that, Keithy, old son, you have my solemn word on it.'

Keithy grabbed the edge of the bar as if it would give him safe anchor. 'Brendan, please.'

'*Sorry?*'

He shook his head, getting his words right. 'I mean, Mr O'Donnell, please. Don't do this to me. It's the wife, she's—'

'Ugly?' suggested Pete Mac.

'Nice one, Pete,' said Brendan, still staring unflinchingly at Keithy, who was now sweating as if

172

it really were July.

'Come on, gentlemen, please.' He held up the Scotch again. 'Why don't you let me pour you all a nice drink?'

'Because we don't fucking want one,' said Brendan. He snatched the bottle from Keithy's hand and tossed it over his shoulder, an unwanted chip wrapper thrown into the wind. 'Time to get to work, lads.'

It took just a few minutes of bottle smashing, table kicking, and chair launching for even the most hardened drinkers amongst the Bellavista's clients to get the message that they were being invited by the O'Donnells to vacate the premises as soon as their booze-decelerated bodies could manage.

Only Keithy and Herbie—the dozy, elderly potman who had only just returned from the ripeness of the lavatory—were left behind to defend their territory, and once Pete Mac had raised a splinter-ended chair leg to Herbie's face, it was just Keithy.

Keithy hadn't been expecting Brendan's first punch, a right jab straight to the cheek. But he did try to avoid the second. No chance. It threw him off balance, sending him windmilling into the shelves of glasses behind him.

He staggered to his feet, the blood pouring down his face from a split eyebrow sending rivulets of red into the deep creases of his podgy cheeks. He leaned back on the lower shelf, not even noticing the shattered glass. 'Please. Leave now, chaps. Before some of the customers come back to see what's going on. Some of them are coppers you know.'

173

'Coppers? In an illegal drinking bash? Never! Next thing you'll be telling me is that some of them were kaylied.' Brendan, his hands still gloved, reached in his pocket. 'Go and stand by the door and keep an eye out, Luke.'

Luke hesitated, guessing he was being got out of the way. He wasn't entirely sure whether he was pleased or not.

'Now, Keithy.' Brendan turned back to the bloody, frightened man, smiling at him with just his mouth—all white teeth and steady, emotionless gaze. 'Do you know what I always love about Christmas time? Have done ever since I was a nipper? Any idea?'

'No Bren . . . Mr O'Donnell.'

'Well, I'll tell you, shall I? Having all that fruit, that's what. The grapes, and tangerines and nuts and that. Smashing. A real treat. In fact, I love the nuts so much I've kept my very own pair of nutcrackers in my pocket, just in case I should ever be lucky enough to come across any on the off chance. Then I'd be ready, see. I mean, you know how it is, it'd be a bit of sorry situation if I didn't have me equipment with me, now wouldn't it?'

Keithy gulped and nodded, blinking back the blood that was trickling into his eye.

'Trouble is, I'm a bit out of practice, not had any nuts since what, must be Boxing Day. Weeks ago. So maybe I should get in a bit of practice, eh, Keithy? Reckon that'd be a good idea?'

Keithy's mouth felt as if it had been glued shut.

'What's that Keithy? Can't hear you, mate. Here, tell you what, you can give me a hand. *Your* hand. And it won't only be a bit of practice for me, it'll be a little reminder for you and all.'

Brendan grabbed Keithy's hand, and yanked him across the bar. His eyes narrowed and his voice dropped. 'A reminder to do as you're fucking well told.'

'No, Mr O'Donnell, please.'

'Don't do this, Keithy, don't get me wind up, or I might just have to practise on your fucking nuts and all.'

Luke heard Keithy Johnson's screams and felt an involuntary, shameful stirring in his groin. Brendan was right: despite what Luke had always protested, there was an excitement in this business that he was beginning to get used to. And to like.

It was a fact of which he wasn't proud.

*         *         *

Brendan put his arm round Luke's shoulders, guiding him back towards the car. 'All right, Luke?'

'Yeah.'

Brendan squeezed him. 'Good, good. Now,' he said over his shoulder to Pete Mac who was tacking along behind, swigging from the bottle of single malt that he'd liberated from under the counter. 'Nip round Charlie Taffler's and tell him we're ready for him to start the refurb. And tell him quick as he can, Pete. He's got two weeks tops.' Brendan turned back to his brother. 'I right fancy the idea of having a bit of a do after we've sorted out the scrap deal with the Kesslers.' He grinned nastily. 'Be good to have somewhere nice and new to take our nice new friends, eh, lads?'

*         *         *

Harold Kessler wasn't a fool, he understood the value of good quality scrap in a still scarce market, but he looked about him and wondered what the hell he was getting himself into. This place didn't feel right.

Here he was on a dark, miserable afternoon— one of those days when the sky was like a dull, heavy lid, not letting more than the feeblest of the last of the dying light in through the cracks—with the bitterly cold weather doing its worst to freeze his arse off, and the slicing, icy wind slanting the rain down between his neck and collar, and squelching into his shoes. And what was he doing? Standing on a tiny airfield in the open mouth of an arc lit, corrugated iron hangar, somewhere out beyond North London, in a place where the suburbs had finally petered out, leaking into a scrubby, brown-grassed countryside. It was a place Harold Kessler didn't recognise, hadn't been to before, and didn't much want to come to again.

And then there were the men. There must have been nearly a dozen of them. They made Kessler really nervous. He'd been told by O'Donnell to bring along no one but family, that it was to be hush-hush, too important to risk anyone else finding out about it. Yet all these dungaree-clad men, clambering about on an aeroplane that filled up almost the entire space inside the hangar, could get a good enough look at him to identify him and grass him up anytime they felt like it.

Then there was the more immediate threat the men presented: they could come running at him right now if they had the mind to, with their spanners and hammers waving above their heads, knock him to the ground and take everything off

176

him as easily as picking an apple off a tree. Kill him even. He might as well have had a target painted on his arse by way of invitation. And here he was, standing there like a fucking lemon, while his car, his one means of escape, was parked deep in the shadows where he couldn't even see it.

He wished he was somewhere else, somewhere that was warm and dry, maybe sitting by a fire with a double Scotch in one hand and a nice little bird in the other. In point of fact, he would have been quite happy to have been sitting indoors with Sophie. Anywhere that meant he didn't have to look at Gabriel O'Donnell's self-satisfied mooey, as he stood there, looking down from his six feet bloody two, or whatever he was, pretending not to notice the cold and rain.

'Isn't this a bit, well, how can I say . . .' Kessler looked around him as he searched for the right word, '. . . casual?'

'Trust me,' said Gabriel enjoying the man's discomfort. 'Just be said and led, Harry. Just be said and led. Casual's a good thing to be.' He chewed at the damp end of his cigar, which, he'd made a loud point of promising Harold Kessler, would remain unlit while they were in such close proximity to the aircraft; speaking to him as if he were a nervous, elderly relative who needed to be reassured.

'I promise you,' Gabriel continued, 'casual's a very good thing to be.'

Kessler hated this, hated feeling like a lost tourist being offered obvious, patronising advice by a know-all bastard of a local.

'See, when you act casual, Harry,' Gabriel said, now in smiling, benevolent parent mode, 'no one's

177

suspicious. It's the jumpy ones that interest them, the ones they watch. It's the nervous ones what become their prey.' Still smiling, he sighed, studying the unlit cigar with a show of regret for the smoke he wasn't able to enjoy. 'Now, shall we get down to business? You look like this weather's getting you down.'

*     *     *

Gabriel's smile didn't last very long. He had gone from patronising to bloody annoyed in a few brief moments. And now, after nearly fifteen whole, perishing minutes of wasted time, his lips were twitching with irritation, and he was feeling something that was a very long way from casual.

They were still standing outside the hangar, but were no further forward with the deal, despite Gabriel having patiently run through the details— again and again.

What was this fool Kessler expecting from him? He was doing the bloke a massive favour even letting him get a sniff of this deal. *And he had the cheek to question him?*

He hadn't liked the rude, arrogant little runt before this had happened, but now . . . Now he would happily have pulped his stupid face for him, taken real delight in feeling his knuckles smash into the bones behind his smooth, fat, baby chops.

Why had he listened to Luke's old fanny about truces and deals with these bastards? He must have been out of his head. The boy had little more than an amateur's experience of the inside running of the business, and yet he'd let him talk him into getting hiked up with this load of crap.

178

He was having to stand here, like a spare prick at a wedding, going over the details of a deal that anyone with any brains would have blessed him for, would have snatched off his hand to have been even a little part of. Did Kessler really not get it? Or was he just acting like the aggravating little turd he really was? If it wouldn't have meant losing face, he'd have walked away. Left him there, done up like the kipper he was: no guts and two faces.

Kessler's lips were moving again, and Gabriel knew he'd better listen, even if he had long since realised that whatever the fool was going to say would be about as much use as two penn'orth of fucking tripe.

'So, tell me, Gabe, how do I know that the scrap I take away in my trucks is the metal that they've cut off that plane in there? Where's my guarantee that justifies my investment here?'

Back to this.

Okay . . .

Gabriel breathed out slowly and drew his fingers down his face, doing his best to hold his temper. 'Like I said, Harry, one of the reasons I brought you along this afternoon was so that you could test the goods in whatever way you chose—magnets, chemicals, filter papers, you name it. That testing's for all our sakes. You do it before you give me half the dough you got from your investor. And before I pay that half over to my contact to seal the deal. Right, so far so good. Then, when my contact's team've got rid of all the identifiable parts, and cut it up, and it looks nothing like the plane it once was, *then* it'll be nice and ready for your trucks to collect, and you can test it again. Just the same way. Or different. Up to you. If you're happy with it, my

179

contact gets the other half of his payment. Then you deliver it to me and I sell it on. If we do get stiffed in that last part of the deal, I'll suffer as much as you do, Harry, because that's when me and you get our bit of poke out of it. That's why I'm leaving the testing to you.' He stabbed his cigar at Kessler, wishing it was alight and that he could stab it in the arsehole's eye. 'As a matter of goodwill.'

'How do I know I can trust the cutting team?'

'How do we know we can trust anyone, Harry? Because we believe someone's word, that's why. And because the team know I'd kill them if they tried to have one over on me.'

Kessler turned down his mouth, jerked his head to one side, and flashed his eyebrows. He then leaned back, still keeping his eye on Gabriel, and whispered something to Daniel and Maurice. Then he nodded and said to Gabriel, 'Okay. We test twice. Agreed. My boys know what to do. And if they're satisfied—*if*—then Sammy's sitting over there in the car,' he inclined his head towards the shadows thrown by the beech hedge that ran the length of the hangar, 'with the first half of the investor's money on his lap. But, remember, we'll still be testing when we collect.'

Gabriel found a smile from somewhere. Even if the little tosspot still didn't seem to have fully grasped who was on whose side and what they were actually doing, why couldn't they have got to this point a quarter of an hour ago?

'Of course, Harry. That's understood. That'll benefit us both. Now, Brendan, Pete, you two go with Daniel and Maurice. And Luke, you go and sit in Harry's car. Keep Sammy and the money company till its time to fetch it over.'

*     *     *

With the testing finally completed to Harold Kessler's idiosyncratic satisfaction—he still had only a cursory understanding of what they were actually checking for, his attention and business acumen not really extending to anything more complex than straightforward blags, pimping, and bullying of various kinds—he and Gabriel stood outside the hangar. They were making falsely chummy conversation, both, in their different ways, relieved that this first deal was at last about to get off its backside, and both eager to get back into the warm.

And Maurice, good nephew that he was, had volunteered to trot off into the shadows to tell Sammy and Luke that Uncle Harold was at last ready to hand over the money to the O'Donnells so they could pay the supplier.

Ten feet away from the car, Maurice slowed down. He could make out the two figures sitting in the back seat, and a finger being jabbed angrily into someone's face. But which of them was doing the pointing? And why was he so upset?

He crept forward. From five feet away he could see—and hear—quite clearly.

Sammy was *very* upset with Luke.

Maurice stood there, watching. And listening.

He smiled, enjoying himself as voices were raised and he heard some very interesting references to someone called Catherine, and how much Sammy had loved her, and how it was all the O'Donnells's fault she'd died.

181

Catherine?

Wasn't that the O'Donnell girl who'd wound up fried to a crisp like an overdone fish supper?

He listened a bit longer.

Yes, it was her all right.

*His cousin Sammy had been going with young Catherine O'Donnell?*

Who'd have thought it?

*And the O'Donnells were somehow involved in her death?*

This was good. The sort of information that could prove useful in all sorts of ways. He'd definitely file this away for future use.

*     *     *

When Maurice eventually stepped forward and tapped on the car window, Sammy Kessler and Luke O'Donnell sprang apart in shocked surprise, guilty as two monkeys caught with their paws stuck in the sweetie jar.

'All right, fellers?' Maurice beamed down at them, as he opened the back door. 'Nice and cosy in there are you, while we do all the work?'

Sammy was about to protest, but Luke beat him to it.

Pushing the door open wide, he shoved Maurice out of the way. 'Piss off, you flash, Northern bastard.'

'Hold on there, feller. Hurrying off like that, anyone'd think you've got some nasty secret you don't fancy sharing.'

*     *     *

Gabriel didn't so much as blink as Brendan took the bag from Sammy Kessler, and nor did he intend to show himself up by checking that the brown, leather attaché case contained the full, agreed amount. That sort of behaviour was for mugs: men who didn't consider themselves frightening enough to know that the likes of Harold Kessler wouldn't dare try to take the piss.

Kessler was finding it a bit more difficult to hide his feelings. He had just handed over half of a very big wedge that he had acquired—admittedly with unexpected ease—from his investor: a posh, self-important City type, who had become a regular user of Kessler's whores, but who, on their first meeting, had treated Kessler with little more respect than he had the toms.

But when Kessler had 'accidentally' engineered another meet, and had explained his proposition to him, the man had suddenly become his friend, slapping him on the back and explaining what a good chap he'd always found Kessler to be, and how he was never averse to a little tax free investment if any should come his way. He'd acted as if they'd known each other since their days at prep school, rather than from a chance encounter a few weeks before, when Kessler and Daniel had been collecting the takings from one of their street brasses.

It might have been easy for Kessler to get the money off the bloke, but why had he just gone and handed over half of it to O'Donnell? For the promise of a pile of scrap that, although he was paying for it, he was going to hand back over to O'Donnell, who was then, supposedly, going to sell it on and share the profits with him?

183

He must be out of his mind. If this went wrong he'd make O'Donnell wished he'd never heard the name Harold Kessler. He'd show O'Donnell mess him around. But he had to keep up his image, even with this lanky Irish schmuck. Needed to take control of the situation. Show him what was what.

'This is a good day's work we've done here, Gabriel,' he said, as they walked back towards the cars. 'The first of many such deals, God willing. So, how about we all meet up to celebrate one evening next week? My treat. We can go to Marlino's, a restaurant I know on Greek Street. Owned by good friends of mine. They'll look after us, give us the best of everything.'

Gabriel, who had decided that this was the perfect moment to light his cigar, puffed rhythmically, staring at the slowly burning tip, indicating with a lift of his chin that Brendan should answer for him.

'Good idea,' was Brendan's response. 'We can take the ladies out to dinner at your mate's gaff, whatever it's called, and then us chaps can go and visit our new club. You might have heard of it: the Bellavista.'

Kessler actually stopped in his tracks. 'The Bellavista? I thought that was Keithy Johnson's place.'

Pete Mac came in with the timing of a pro. 'It was,' he said.

# CHAPTER TWELVE

Eileen O'Donnell and Sophie Kessler settled themselves into the soft, cream leather upholstery in the back seat of the Daimler. They were waiting for Stephen Shea to go back inside Marlino's restaurant so he could find out what was keeping Patricia and Rachel.

'Pretty girl, your Brendan was with tonight, Eileen.'

'She seemed nice.' Eileen was vague, preoccupied in the way she often was these days.

'Serious, is it?'

'Sorry?'

'Wake up, Eileen,' Sophie laughed gently. 'Brendan and his girlfriend?'

Eileen gave a tiny shrug that barely disturbed the sapphire mink stole she was clutching round her shoulders. It was now four months since she had buried her child, and she was wearing black, but this dress was floor-length, stylishly fitted, and adorned with a glittering ribbon bow of diamonds at her shoulder. 'They never last long,' she said, turning to Sophie, doing her best to be sociable, 'not with Brendan.'

'Daniel used to be like that: different girl every week. You don't know the relief when he settled down with Rachel. I only wish my Sammy would do the same. Since he broke up with that nasty little madam who broke his heart, he's been moping about like he'll never meet anyone ever again. I keep telling him: you're young, you'll find plenty of girls. But will he listen? Kids, eh, Eileen?'

Sophie peered out of the window of the parked car onto Greek Street, wondering if they were ever going to get away. She was getting to like Eileen, like her far more than she'd ever expected, but trying to have a conversation with her wasn't exactly easy. She wasn't blaming her, she couldn't begin to imagine what it must be like to bury your child—mad as they drove her at times.

She tried another tack. 'Your Luke seeing anyone?'

'No one I know about.'

Another dead end.

Sophie patted Eileen's hand. 'I really am sorry about this.'

'It's okay, I've only the dog to worry about.'

In the darkness, Sophie could just make out the tears brimming in Eileen's eyes. 'You know,' she said briskly, 'I'll bet it's that Rachel titivating again. But why bother? With Harry and Gabriel taking the boys off to this drinking club, Rachel'll be tucked up fast asleep in bed before any of them start thinking about making their way home.' She looked at her watch and tutted impatiently. 'Quarter to eleven; this is getting silly.'

'It's all right. I know what girls are like.' Eileen's voice was small, distant, as her mind filled with the familiar pictures of Catherine, sitting in the big, cosy basement kitchen with scrunched up toilet paper twisted between her toes, tongue nipped between her teeth, as she painted her nails the latest startling shade. Her hair—before she and Patricia had their outrageous urchin cuts that Eileen thought were more suited to little boys than to young women—wound over big, fat rollers to straighten out its pretty, natural curl, and a thick

186

white paste of face pack smeared over her lovely features.

She would have been eighteen years old on New Year's Eve.

Sophie gave a little laugh. 'Not having been blessed with daughters, Eileen, I'm having to learn—fast—about modern girls. Like why Rachel dyes that beautiful hair of hers that auburn colour. And, for goodness sake, why she's started going on at Daniel to get his hair straightened. Straightened! Can you believe it? Honestly, tell me, Eileen, what's wrong with a head full of tight fair curls?' Her smile broadened as she remembered. 'When he was a baby, he was like an angel. People used to think he was a little girl. Him and Sammy get it from me, of course. My ringlets were nearly white when I was a toddler.' She chuckled throatily. 'I tell them to think themselves lucky that they never got their hair from their father.'

Eileen wasn't really listening, but she heard enough to murmur her agreement.

'Who knows, perhaps Danny and Rachel will have some good news for me one day soon. And maybe I'll have a granddaughter to fuss over. And then I'll become an expert on modern girls, and begin to understand Rachel at last.'

Eileen let out a long sighing breath. 'I don't think any of us understands anyone. Not really.'

Sophie didn't know what else to say.

*        *        *

Stephen Shea was waiting in the restaurant's lobby, casting self-conscious glances at a fancy-handled door displaying a plaque of a woman wearing a

187

wide picture hat, a crinoline dress, and carrying a parasol over her shoulder.

He would do anything for Gabriel—had done things he wouldn't be prepared to speak about to anyone, not even to Sheila—but hanging around outside a ladies' lav like some dirty old man?

What on earth was taking them so bloody long?

*　　　*　　　*

Inside the powder room, Rachel leaned into the gilt framed glass and tidied her plucked and arched eyebrows with a tiny, tail-handled tortoiseshell comb, while Patricia—barely five months pregnant but feeling like an overheated, shapeless sack of spuds next to the slender, boyishly-figured, Rachel—perched uncomfortably on the edge of a dinky brocade chair that wouldn't have looked out of place in a kindergarten.

Patricia picked up one of the many lipsticks that had spilled from Rachel's bag and widened her eyes as she wound out its metallic lavender core. She hadn't seen anything like that colour before. It was gorgeous. Catherine would have loved it.

'Rachel . . .'

'Take it, I've got loads.'

Patricia dropped the lipstick as if she'd been caught trying to pocket it. 'No. It's great, but I didn't mean—'

Rachel lowered the miniature comb, and narrowed her eyes at Patricia's reflection. 'What's wrong?'

Patricia cast around for the right words. 'Rachel, do you ever talk to Daniel? About his work? Well, not his work exactly. But when he goes out. And stays out late. You know, like tonight. With the men going onto Dad's club. Do you ever wonder what he's getting up to?'

'No.' Rachel drew in her chin, looking at Patricia as if she were stupid. 'Why should I?'

'You know. In case he's . . . Aw, you know.'

'No, I don't actually.' Rachel paused to stuff the little comb back into her make-up pouch, and to scoop all the lipsticks back into her handbag, her pretty lips stuck out in a not very attractive pout. 'I get all the money I need. I've got a house that he's letting me get done up however I want. I have a great life. What's to wonder about?'

'I know all that,' said Patricia, wishing she hadn't started. 'I've got all that too, but, I mean, Daniel. Himself. Isn't he sometimes—'

'He's the best part of it all,' Rachel gushed. 'And that's why I always make sure I look good. Dye my hair the colour I know he loves. Wear the sort of clothes that drive him wild.' She let her glance slide up and down Patricia for a long, embarrassing moment, her expression clearly implying that it wouldn't do any harm if she made a bit more of an effort—maybe a nice tight roll-on. 'And that's why I've decided not to have kids. Well, not for a long time yet.' Her words were as pointed as her look had been. 'Because my Danny is wonderful. And more than enough for me. I'm not like a lot of girls, you see, Patricia. I don't need a houseful of brats to make me happy. And nor does Daniel. I'm everything he needs. Everything.'

Rachel turned back to the mirror, and Patricia watched her as she teased out the Jackie Kennedy flicks of her glossy, tinted hair, part of her wishing that Pete Mac was *really wonderful* too. But another

189

part of her was wondering if maybe Rachel was a fool. Or a liar. Or just hard as nails, and prepared to put up with anything for her *great life.*

*     *     *

'That was good of you, getting Shea to take the girls home,' Kessler said, as Gabriel ushered him through the door of the Bellavista. 'But we could have put them in a cab. I'd have paid.'

'That's a generous offer, Harry. But Stephen's a loyal servant, and I like to feel there's someone I know and trust taking care of my wife, and that she has a safe journey home.'

Kessler swallowed the insult, and changed the subject. 'Well, will you look at this?' As he stepped inside the completely refurbished club, he whistled as if he were genuinely impressed. 'This has certainly changed.'

He waited for Gabriel to walk ahead, leading them into the once bare barn of a place that had now been transformed—with the help of a team of brickies, plumbers, carpenters and electricians, many yards of crimson velvet and gold netting, and some very clever lighting—into a passable likeness of a galleried, turn of the century bordello.

Satisfied that Gabriel was out of earshot, Kessler whispered under his breath to his son. 'This really has changed, Daniel.'

Daniel refused to be impressed by the new, glitzy décor, or by the fact that the place was so busy. 'Don't make any difference to me, Dad. Never been here before. Never felt the need to.'

'Take my word for it, son, it's changed, all right—a lot. Just look at it.' He did the wide-armed, shoulder-shrugging thing, and said quietly, 'It's not just some rotten old bash any more, where you can come along to pour cheap turps down your throat until you get sick to your stomach. It's a place where you can have a drink, fuck a whore, and get a dose thrown in for luck.'

Daniel held his arm to his face and snorted his laughter into his sleeve.

'Mind you, Dan, even I wouldn't mind having to make an appointment with the pox doctor's clerk, not if it was the price of having a taste of that one over there.' Kessler pointed to a raised, padded bench, where a row of young women in various states of revealing dress were sitting smiling prettily for the mug punters.

Daniel followed his father's gaze and grinned. Of course, the little one with the heavy breasts, and the wild halo of gorgeous red, wavy hair—a pint-sized Rita Hayworth just like she was in the old films he loved to watch.

'Just look at the body on her,' marvelled Kessler. He puckered his lips and kissed the bunched tips of his fingers. 'She'd make a blind man see, that one. You should get in there, Daniel. God knows, it's not as if you'll be fighting off your brother, the miserable sod. I don't think he could get it up if you played the national anthem, the mood he's in.' Kessler leaned closer to his son. 'Here, why not try and get Sammy to enjoy a bit of company, eh, Dan? Cheer the little fucker up a bit.'

He shook his head—a man bewildered by his youngest son's behaviour—and began making his way over to join Gabriel and the others at the bar. He tossed a departing thought over his shoulder. 'For your mother's sake, Dan. She's been worrying about him. You know how she gets.'

*       *       *

Daniel looked around for Sammy and spotted him sitting alone at one of the little gilt tables set around the edges of the room. He had the expression on his face of a man who sucked lemons for a living, but that apart, he had a drink in one hand and a cigarette in the other.

He was all right; and it wasn't as if he was being held prisoner.

Daniel turned his back on his sour-faced brother and eased his way through the crowd of men smooching with the smiling come-on girls. He stopped in front of the bench where the rest of the girls sat waiting to be selected—items on a shelf, barely one step away from meat on a slab—and fixed the redhead with a smile.

'What's your name then?'

'Nina. What's yours?'

'Daniel. Drink, Nina?'

'Love one,' she said, sharing a quick look with her companions. This was a touch; the customers were usually at least twenty years older than this one, and not nearly as attractive. And even though blonds weren't really her type, and, if she had a choice, she preferred them to be really tall, he did have a great body. And she'd always liked fit-looking men. That was why she really liked the O'Donnell boys: tall, dark and hunky. Perfect. But from the day she and the other girls had been brought into the revamped club, it was made clear that the O'Donnells were not going to bother with the likes of them. So this one was a real bonus.

192

'Friend of Mr O'Donnell's are you?' Nina said, running a fingernail down Daniel's cheek.

'Business associate.'

Bingo! Loaded!

'I've not seen you in here before.'

'No, my wife don't let me out much,' he said, taking her by the hand and leading her towards the bar.

'Cheeky.'

'No, just honest. I'm a married man.'

'That's nice.'

He shrugged. 'It's all right, I suppose,' he said, helping her up onto a stool, well away from where his father was sitting—not because Daniel had anything to hide from him, but because he didn't want to be anywhere near the O'Donnells or that idiot Pete MacRiordan.

He put his hand on Nina's back, and pulled her close, fantasising about the heavy, creamy breasts that bulged out over her neckline tumbling out into his hands, and thrilling at the touch of the slippery red satin dress against his skin.

Rachel was going to be a good little wife, and a good little mother—his own mother would make sure of that—but if Daniel had had a choice in the matter, Nina was far more like he'd have chosen for himself.

She leaned into him, her arms pulled together to accentuate the swell of her breasts. She had used the same move ever since she'd been thirteen years old and had realised the power of her body. When, after some misdemeanour or other, rather than sending her on the dreaded trip to the headmistress's office, her flushed-faced geography teacher had let her off with nothing more than a garbled warning and a not completely unpleasant grope after the final bell. That had all happened a full, incident-packed, and instructive three years ago. Nina had learned that one school lesson very well indeed.

She giggled prettily as she sipped the sickly fruit punch that Daniel had bought her, the only drink she and the other girls were allowed—so they would keep sober and their minds on their work.

'Look,' she said, 'look at these little see-through sticks. I love these.' She tossed her thick red hair over her shoulder, swishing it against the satin, dropped her head to one side and held a plastic cocktail stick up against one of the crimson shaded wall lights.

'See,' she said, her small, childlike teeth pearly white against her pink, smooth gums. 'It's a naked lady; look, you can see her little titties. Not as big as mine though are they?'

Daniel cupped one of her breasts in his hand. 'You're right there, sweetheart,' he murmured, burying his face into her neck under the thick curtain of her hair.

'I collect these and cash them in,' she said, moving so that her knee slipped in between his thighs. She heard him moan softly.

'It's how I get paid. I love the lime green ones best, they're worth more cos they're the ones what come in the champagne cocktails. Do you like champagne cocktails, Daniel?'

'Love 'em.'

'Shall I order you one then?'

She felt him nod against her throat.

'Champagne cocktail over here for the gentleman,' she said to the barman with a knowing look.

'Champagne cocktails? In a near beer joint?' It was Maurice.

Daniel jerked upright and looked over Nina's shoulder into Maurice's grinning face. 'How long have you been standing there?'

'Do you mind?' Now it was bloody Brendan O'Donnell standing behind Maurice. What were they doing, forming a queue?

'Our Champagne's the genuine article.' Brendan wasn't happy.

Maurice half turned, looked at him and grinned. 'Can we have a steward's enquiry on that, feller?'

'Look, Maurice.' Brendan really didn't like this bloke. 'We're meant to be having a nice evening here.'

Maurice turned right round and inclined his head. 'So, you got yourself a proper licence for this place then, eh?'

Brendan snorted like a pony let loose in a field; surely even an idiot like him knew it was impolite to ask that sort of a question—any sort of a question—when it was none of your business. 'I have friends.'

'Friends?' Maurice smiled. 'I'll say you do. That one having dinner with you tonight at Marlino's. Very nice arse. How much does she charge an hour then?'

Daniel, seeing the expression on Brendan's face, stepped in. 'What is this?' He peeled Nina's arms from round his neck. 'It's like having a fucking audience, and a bloody noisy one at that.'

Maurice spun back round to face his cousin. 'Audience, eh? Well I wouldn't mind watching if you're up for it.' Then back to face Brendan. 'What

195

do you think Brendan? You game?'

Brendan looked at Maurice as if he was as funny as a bit of string, and then said to Daniel, 'I'm sorry

to interrupt you—and Nina—but I want to talk to you. Privately. About business. D'you mind, Maurice?'

'He don't mind,' said Daniel. 'Maurice, go and get yourself a drink. Nina, I'll have to make it another time, darling.'

Nina did her big eyed, imploring little girl with big breasts thing, and Daniel crumpled. Her expression was just like Rachel's when she wanted him to buy her something. And he was a sucker for it.

Bloody birds.

'Hang on.' He dipped in his pocket, whispered something in her ear, and slapped her on the backside.

She nodded, smiling up at him as she accepted the money he slipped into her hand, kissed him on the cheek, and snatched the precious lime green stick from his drink. Then she wiggled her way over to Sammy Kessler with a cute, bye-bye jiggle of her fingers.

'This had better be good, O'Donnell,' Daniel said to Brendan. 'I was ready for that.'

Brendan leaned back on the bar, and folded his arms. 'You didn't have to pay, you know, Daniel, you're my guest here this evening.'

'It's okay' he said, his eyes following her across the floor, 'I only gave her enough to make sure she puts a smile on my brother's face. Sammy's been a bit down lately.'

'Yeah, well,' said Brendan hurriedly, 'families

196

can be a worry.'

'Right,' he agreed, pulling himself together. 'You said you wanted to talk business.'

'I do. There are two more planes coming our way. It's all happened a bit on the quick. If you're going to be involved, we need the money by Monday night. Can you produce?'

Daniel nodded calmly. 'Sure.'

Brendan hid his disappointment. He'd intended catching him out, have a reason to row the Kesslers out of the deal. Show his father how useless they were. It would have been a good first step towards getting rid of this ridiculous arrangement—which he fully intended to do before he took over the business. And, at the rate his father was drinking, that wouldn't be too far into the future.

He looked into Daniel's eyes, wondering if he was telling the truth, whether he really could get another investor willing to cough up enough of a stake by Monday.

Daniel Kessler was also wondering: about why Brendan had put the deal to him, rather than Gabriel O'Donnell speaking to his father? He disliked the O'Donnells as much as he reckoned they disliked him and his family, and he didn't trust a single one of them. But, for now, he reckoned it made sense to pretend that he couldn't have been happier than being in the bastards' company. It'd give him a chance to watch and learn. Figure out what the fuckers were up to.

Daniel looked about him. 'The club looks like it's a big success, Brendan. Congratulations. You must be very pleased.'

The compliment caught Brendan off guard. These Kesslers were as slippery as bloody eels.

197

'Thanks. Let me get you another drink.'

As Brendan turned to catch the barman's attention, his own eye was caught by something else. Maurice—the slipperiest of the lot as far as he was concerned—had taken himself over to Luke, and was grinning like a wolf as he made an exaggerated show of pointing out to Luke that Nina was draping herself all over Sammy Kessler. As for Sammy, he obviously wasn't interested in the girl, and was making a right song and dance of trying to get rid of her.

Brendan shook his head. Why had his dad done this? He should have known that inviting the Kesslers to the club would cause nothing but trouble.

Nina was now taking Sammy's refusal of her services as a personal challenge, especially as that mate of the O'Donnells had paid her so well to entertain his brother. She'd bloody well entertain him if it killed her—the other girls'd take the right piss if she couldn't at least get to sit on the dozy bugger's lap.

'What's wrong, handsome? Bit shy are you?'

Sammy flicked her hand off his neck. 'I said, just get away from me . . .'

'Don't be like that, lover, your brother gave me a little present to be nice to you. Wasn't that kind of him?' She rubbed her hand over his fly, smiling broadly as she felt his erection. 'Here, you! You might pretend you're not interested, but this little chap can't lie, now can he?'

Sammy was on his feet. 'Keep whatever he gave you. And here.' He stuck his hand in his trouser pocket and pulled out a roll of notes. He licked his thumb and peeled off two fivers. 'Take that *little present* and all. From me. But just piss off. Got it?'

Nina was disappointed, and a bit scared. This weirdo was a friend of the O'Donnells after all, and pleasing him certainly wouldn't have done her any harm, but displeasing him would be a very big mistake.

'I'm sorry, I just thought you wanted to have a bit of fun.'

Sammy straightened his tie, and combed his hair back with his fingers. 'Forget it, all right?'

She smiled. As always, she'd quickly bounced back and was looking on the bright side. She didn't really mind that much. The O'Donnells were good to work for—she reckoned she earned them anything from £50 to £400 a week—and they not only allowed her to keep a tenner for herself, they looked after her as well, always had plenty of minders about the place, and they didn't have too many disgusting sorts for her to deal with. So, as long as she kept getting paid, they could do or not do as they liked. In fact, it actually made a nice change. Before the Bellavista, she'd only ever worked as a come-on girl before, satisfied with her bit of commission on the drinks, but since she'd been here there hadn't been a single evening when she hadn't been expected to go upstairs to the private rooms with at least half a dozen different men, and sometimes with a lot more. Not that it bothered her, not really, but it could get boring.

Still, she'd better give it one more go. 'Are you absolutely sure, sweetheart? I can do anything you fancy, you know. I'm very versatile.' She looked up at him through her heavily mascaraed lashes. 'Well, so I've been told.'

Sammy sucked in his breath through gritted

teeth. What was it she didn't understand? He wanted Catherine. Not some cheap tart.

He took her by the shoulders and started shaking her. *'Will you. Just. Leave. Me. Alone?'*

'Jesus.' Daniel slammed his glass down on the bar.

Brendan put up his hand to stop him. He didn't want the Kesslers and their minders getting upset over one of his girls. That would be a right show up. 'It's all right, Daniel. If she's upsetting your brother, I'll sort it out. Okay?'

Brendan was over by Sammy and Nina before Daniel had a chance to reply. A few curious eyes followed him, but men getting angry at tarts wasn't exactly big news to the sort of punters who used the Bellavista.

Brendan put on a concerned expression. 'You don't look very happy, Sammy. Anything I can do?'

Sammy said nothing, he just dropped his hands from Nina's shoulders and stared at Brendan as if he could kill him.

'Not upset you has she, mate? Or maybe you prefer a brunette. Or a blonde. Whatever you fancy.'

'No thanks.'

'Suit yourself, but it would be my treat.'

'I'm not interested in your whores. Got it?'

Brendan raised his hands. 'Fair enough. Just being friendly.'

Nina had her head bowed, but she was sneaking looks at one man then the other. What now? What should she do?

Maurice was watching the three of them. He was enjoying himself. The O'Donnells and the Kesslers doing business together? How was that ever going to work? And knowing what he knew about Catherine O'Donnell and his cousin Sammy, that could make the situation explosive. And then there was Luke: he was convinced he was right about him. He grinned happily. Why had he ever thought that coming down to London was going to be dull?

He went and stood beside Luke, and said quietly, 'That's an interesting little scene, eh, feller? A man who won't take a beautiful woman. Even as a gift.'

'Fuck off,' muttered Luke, and barged his way over to his brother.

'Here, let me help you out here, Brendan.' Luke grabbed hold of Nina's hand and dragged her across to the stairway that led up to the private rooms. 'That's one less problem to worry about,' he called over his shoulder.

She giggled with relief, feeling as if she'd just won the Littlewood's jackpot. Not only was her problem of what to do next solved for her, but she was going upstairs with *Luke O'Donnell.* Perhaps she'd really cracked it this time. This could put her into a different league all together. Make her practically one of the family.

\*       \*       \*

'You all right now, Sammy?' asked Brendan.

'Yeah. Terrific.' He sounded more angry than relieved as he edged past Brendan. 'If you don't mind I'll go over and say goodnight to me dad.'

Brendan sighed wearily as he joined Daniel Kessler back at the bar. This was getting to be like a game of pass the sodding parcel, with little Nina as the prize.

He picked up his glass and took a swig of whiskey.

'Good job you dealt with that,' Daniel said. 'Don't want a reputation for trouble in a new club.'

Brendan downed the rest of his drink in one. 'Just didn't want your brother Sammy making a fool of himself.'

Daniel bristled. 'It was your brother what surprised me.' He said it tonelessly.

'What?'

'Luke. Going upstairs with that bird.'

'She's a good clean girl. All our Bellavista girls are.'

'No, not that he's gone with a tom—I was thinking about giving her one myself—but that she's a bird. According to our Maurice, Luke's the other way.'

It took every last bit of Brendan's self-control to stop him from kicking Daniel Kessler until he'd never be able to go with another woman again. Instead, he snorted as if he'd just heard the funniest joke ever. '*Luke?* That's a laugh,' he said. 'Right comedian your cousin.'


## CHAPTER THIRTEEN

Sammy found his father still sitting at the bar with Gabriel. 'Dad.' His voice betrayed his weariness. 'I'm going home.'

'All right, wait for me outside, son.' Harold Kessler had had quite enough of O'Donnell's club and his drunken ramblings, and was glad of an excuse to escape.

'Gabriel, the Bellavista, it's a great place.' Harold clapped him on the shoulder. 'And I've had a wonderful evening. It's been a real celebration. But you'll have to excuse me. It looks like my youngest has downed one too many of your very generous cocktails.'

Gabriel screwed one eye tight to help his focus, and nodded, unclear as to what he was agreeing to, but mellow enough to want to make everyone happy—until someone upset him.

*    *    *

'Oi, Sammy!' Harold Kessler spotted his son just as he turned into Folgate Street, heading in the direction of Bishopsgate.

'I'm getting too old for this,' he puffed, catching up with him. 'Forty-one and the body of a sixty-year-old. Maybe I need some exercise.'

'Or learn how to say no to fried fish,' Sammy snapped back.

'What's wrong with you?' Kessler took hold of his son's overcoat, stopping him. 'I told you to wait for me outside the club.'

He twisted round, snatching his coat from his father's hands. 'I'm not drunk, no matter what you think, or said to O'Donnell. But I am angry.'

And he was. Sammy Kessler had a burning resentment that he was stoking up ready for it to burst into raging flames. He loathed the O'Donnells and their fucking idiot of an in-law Peter MacRiordan more than he'd hated anything or anyone in his whole life.

Since Catherine had died, their brief time together as a couple had taken on more of a reality than it had ever had when she had been alive. He had completely rewritten those few weeks, including forgetting that he'd left her bleeding and alone in the road. And that, if he were honest, he had known deep down that even in his dreams they would never have wound up together. His family would never have stood for it. But right now, with the mood he was in, Sammy Kessler was fit to blame anyone for his having lost her. Anyone except himself.

Sammy, taller than his father, loomed over him. 'Why should we put up with this, Dad? Why?'

Kessler backed away, his hands at his chest, his head to one side. 'Don't go getting upset with me, son.'

'I'm not upset with you. Well, maybe I am. But what I wanna know is why we have to listen to them O'Donnells. It's like we're a bunch of twats hanging about waiting to be told what to do.'

Kessler sighed. This was just what he needed: Sammy getting all emotional. The boy was turning out to be too much like his mother. Always getting worked up about something or other: where they lived, girlfriends, and now the bloody business. Like he knew anything about it.

He reached up and put an arm round his son's shoulders. 'Bide your time, Sammy. Just bide your time. Things'll work out. You see if they don't. Your brother Daniel'll see to it.' His face creased into a chubby baby's grin. 'He's already organised a new deal for us. Tonight. Two more planes. How about that? And, when we're ready, we're gonna—'

'We're gonna what? Let 'em piss all over us? What's happening to us?' Sammy was snorting like a bull, as the familiar images of the sawn-off shotgun, Catherine sprawled out in the road, and what he now knew to be the O'Donnell boys, sliced into his brain.

He couldn't work with the O'Donnells. He wouldn't.

'Dad, we should be cutting proper deals. Of our own. Like back in Notting Hill. Ones that work for us. Nothing to do with them Irish cunts.'

Kessler looked at his youngest child as if he were missing one or two links in his chain. 'Look, Sammy, son, you did a good job at the airfield the other day, a very good job, but that doesn't mean you can—'

'I did a good job?' Sammy could hardly believe this. 'What, sitting in a car with a bag of money on my lap? How hard's that? You must really think I'm stupid.'

Kessler was getting fed up with this, and he was cold. Even the thought of going back to the Bellavista was beginning to seem inviting. 'No, not stupid, Sammy, but when you decided you didn't like it round here, what did you do? You went running back to Notting Hill. What was I supposed to think? You made a choice then. A choice that went against what I thought was best for you. And what happened? You came running right back. I was right. Of course I was. I'm your father. I know. Just like I know now, by the way you're acting, that you're not happy. You hardly speak, you don't eat. And back there in the club—you didn't join in. This is business, Sammy. You need to change your attitude. Then perhaps I'll listen to you. You can't be half-arsed in our line of work. It's too dangerous. Especially with the O'Donnells breathing down our necks.'

205

'But that's exactly what I'm talking about. Why do we have to have anything to do with them?'

'Because, like it or not, son, this is their toby, and they're the ones with all the power.' He reached out, patted his boy's cheek and winked. 'For now, eh.'

Sammy clenched his fists. Why couldn't his father see what he was doing? 'Look, Dad, say I come up with something that'll get us a real stake; enough for us to be able to ignore the O'Donnells?'

Kessler smiled benevolently. 'Sounds good, son.'

'I've got plans.'

Kessler pulled his collar up round his throat and looked up at the sky; it was starting to rain again. 'I'm sure you—'

'Please, will you just listen to me? There's these people; they're bringing them over the channel. From India. Like our family came from Russia.'

'So they're rich? These Indians?'

Sammy hesitated. 'And there's other stuff we should be getting into. The strip clubs and near beer joints. They're earning hand over fist.'

Kessler smiled, a picture of the compassionate elder. 'Of course they are. All over London. But d'you really think there's room for more?'

Sammy dropped his chin. This was getting him nowhere.

Despite himself, Kessler couldn't help feeling sorry for his son. 'Listen, Sam, it's good to know you're taking an interest. I've been worried about you. So has your mother. All this moping about. But what's the rush? Let's just bide our time, eh? Take it easy.'

Sammy's head flicked up. 'But say I come up with something that'll knock that arrogant bastard

O'Donnell right off his perch?'

'Do that son, and you've got my ear.'

Sammy could feel his excitement rising. He had his father's interest at last. 'I'm meeting a man tomorrow afternoon.'

Kessler's magnanimous smile dissolved into condescending nodding and patting. 'Good for you, son, good for you.' Then he shrugged down into his coat, more than ready to get out of the rain, and away from such a pointless discussion, even if it really did mean going back to the Bellavista. 'Now, if you don't mind, I think I might nip back to the club. Dry off and have a drop of brandy to keep out the cold. But if you don't fancy it, don't worry; you get yourself off home. Go up on the main road and find yourself a cab.'

\* \* \*

Kessler was handing over his damp coat to the hatcheck girl, when Maurice appeared at his side.

'All right, Uncle Harry? Sammy calmed down now has he?'

Kessler rolled his eyes. 'You know how he's been, Maury. I don't know what's wrong with the boy. One minute he's shooting off to West London, then he's back. Now he reckons he knows what's best for the business. What does he know? He can't even look after himself.' He rolled his eyes. 'Hark at me, I sound just like his mother.'

Maurice flashed his teeth. 'I think it's nice you care about your son. I hope he knows how lucky he is.'

Kessler—the perfect father—looked suitably modest. 'I know one thing: he's going to take

207

forever getting a cab at this time of night, especially in this weather. And if he doesn't manage to find a cab, and he gets home soaking wet, and then he gets himself a cold, I'll never hear the end of it. Your Aunt Sophie'll nag me till I become a scientist and find a bloody miracle cure for him.'

Maurice was still smiling, but inside he was urging the old windbag to shut up. 'Uncle Harry,' he jumped in, while Kessler was taking a breath. 'I'll go after him. Keep an eye on him for you.'

Maurice was treated to the triple bonus of a shrug, a patted cheek, and a hug. 'You're a good boy, Maury, a very good boy. Your parents should be proud.'

Maurice accepted the praise with appropriate humility and left the club at a trot with a cheery, 'See you later, Uncle Harry.'

Kessler was a man blessed. He'd tell that piss tank Gabriel O'Donnell how his big-hearted nephew had given up the rest of his evening just to sort out his cousin. That'd show him what a fine family the Kesslers were.

*       *       *

Luke was sitting in one of the Bellavista's upstairs rooms on a clean, but hard and narrow bed—punters weren't encouraged to spend too long up there—with Nina's child-sized arms wrapped around his neck.

He had only taken her upstairs to prove a point to Maurice, and would have been less than happy to know that Maurice had disappeared into the night in pursuit of Sammy Kessler, without giving Luke O'Donnell so much as a second thought.

208

'It's okay,' Nina cooed into his ear. 'It happens sometimes. But I won't tell no one.'

'Tell no one what?'

'That you can't . . .' She flicked her eyes downwards. 'You know.'

'Who said I can't?'

'Well, you've not even undone your—'

'Just shut up!' Luke fired the words at her through clenched teeth, ripped open his flies, grabbed Nina by the hair, and shoved her face down into his lap. 'Now do your job.'

Despite the shock at his sudden violent change of attitude, Nina did her professional best.

As she eventually managed to get his flaccid penis to show interest in the ministrations of her tongue and lips, tears poured down Luke's face, falling onto her glorious red hair in sparkling rainbow droplets.

He threw back his head, his eyes pinched tight— from humiliation, but also from passion—not wanting to watch the back of her head as it worked up and down, yet finding himself unable to resist her attentions.

Why was he doing this to himself, and to this girl who didn't even look as old as his little sister?

Luke shuddered to a squalid, unsatisfactory climax, wishing he could wipe away his disgrace and degradation as quickly and easily as he knew the girl would be spitting his semen into one of the scratchy paper handkerchiefs, which she'd snatched from the bedside table before she gagged on the indignity of having a stranger's taste in her pretty young mouth.

He'd known ever since he could remember that this was just one of the ways his family made the

209

money that gave them their nice, comfortable life, but Luke swore to himself that he would never do anything as sordid as this again. But, somewhere deep inside him, he knew he was kidding himself, and that one day he would do something far worse than having a paid tart suck on his dick. One day, he would step over the line that marked the end of all the lies, but that also marked the point of no return.

And that thought terrified him.

Her work done, Nina tried to make conversation with him; he might be a bit strange, what with all that crying and carrying on and that, but his family did own the place, and she didn't want to seem unsociable. But Luke would have none of it. He just tidied up his clothes, blew his nose and stumbled out of the room and down the stairs, leaving Nina on the bed to count her spoils and to hide a few of the notes in her roll-on. It was all so confusing tonight, and what with all the comings and goings, nobody would miss the odd couple of quid.

\*　　　\*　　　\*

As Luke took the last three stairs in a single stride, he crashed into Pete Mac.

Pete Mac waggled his eyebrows and grinned. 'Saw you coming down, Lukey boy, and thought I'd take your place. Money that little whore's been raking in for nothing tonight, she might as well do us both a favour, eh?'

Luke felt just about ready for the likes of Peter MacRiordan. 'If you take even one step up them stairs, Pete, I'll tell Dad. Then you'll really be in for it. We all know about your bit of stray, but going with toms, with our Pat being in the family way? Who knows what you'd be risking?'

Pete Mac clicked his tongue against his teeth. This was bloody typical. The whole bloody family could get their end away with any scrubber they fancied, and no one would say a word. But if he felt like having a bit on the side, all hell broke loose. Bleed'n' hypocrites.

Good job Violet was always ready and willing. In fact—he looked at his watch: ten to one—he might as well go round there now. Nothing more was happening here tonight, and Gabe was too pissed to notice who was in the club and who wasn't. So, he'd just say his goodnights to Brendan, and explain that he was off home to check on his beloved, pregnant wife.

*    *    *

As Pete Mac ambled along in the now sheeting rain—there wasn't much that had him moving at more than strolling pace—to pick up his Zodiac that he'd parked under a streetlight in Folgate Street he suddenly sped up. There, just a few yards in front of him, up on the corner, was Maury, the only Kessler he had any time for—a right comical bugger. He was holding open the door of a taxi for that miserable fucker, Sammy. And he was telling the driver to take them to the Drake, a late night drinking spot off Gerard Street. A right bloody hole, but where you could drink twenty-four hours at a stretch and no one said a word, a bit like the Bellavista before Brendan had persuaded his old man to spend all that poppy doing it up. Pete Mac wouldn't mind a bit of that before going round to Violet's.

'Here, Maurice,' he bellowed, far louder than necessary. 'I'll have some of that, mate. Wouldn't mind a few more swift ones before getting off home.'

'Sorry, feller,' said Maurice with a wink. 'Got a bit of family business to sort out.'

Rather than being offended, Pete Mac grinned. Maurice, the cheeky Northern bastard, was obviously up to something.

*     *     *

Maurice presented Sammy with a second extortionately priced triple 'Scotch' that smelled more like something you'd use to strip varnish with than enjoy drinking, and treated himself to another small sip of his pint of vile, supposedly imported lager. Maurice planned to keep his head clear—it was Sammy he wanted drunk and loose tongued. And from the swivel-eyed look on his face, the plan was working. So much so that if he didn't jump in now, there'd be no point, Sammy wouldn't be able to tell his arse from his elbow.

'I know all about you and Catherine O'Donnell.'

Sammy's head jerked up. 'Me and Catherine?'

'That's right, feller. Luke told me.' He was only partly lying, as he had heard the words from Luke's very own mouth, when they'd been at the airfield. Even if he had been speaking to Sammy rather than him at the time.

Sammy suddenly felt very sober. It was bad enough that the O'Donnell boys knew he had been seeing their sister, and that he'd left her bleeding in

212

the road. But now Luke was blabbing to Maurice—Sammy's own cousin. What would the rest of his family do if they found out? Not only a Catholic, but an O'Donnell. His mother would never forgive him. And as for his father . . .

Sammy tapped his thumbnail against his bottom teeth. He had to straighten things out with Maurice, make sure he kept schtum. And he had to bring his father to his senses. Make him realise how stupid it was to do business with the O'Donnells. And do it quick—before one of them opened his mouth and dropped him right in it.

'You look shocked, feller.'

'Not shocked, disgusted. I can't believe he told you about me and Catherine.' He picked up his drink and swallowed down a mouthful, squinting at the taste and the burning in his throat. 'That family, I'm gonna have 'em.'

Maurice patted his cousin's shoulder. 'You need a plan, Sammy, lad. And money. It always takes money.'

'Tell me something I don't know.' Sammy went to pick up his glass again, but shoved it aside in anger. 'I need a proper stake. Big enough to show Dad he's gotta take me seriously. And enough to make people take notice of us, show 'em we're a family to be reckoned with. Then we get shot of them bastards, and have nothing more to do with them—whether we stay in the East End or not.'

Maurice leaned forward and spoke quietly. Not that anyone in the Drake was interested in anything other than the contents of the glass in his hand. 'We could do a bank.'

'Who could?'

'Me and you. That'll show your old man what

213

you're made of. And start priming the pump.'

'What, us two?'

'Listen, feller. It's easy. In the morning, we stroll into any boozer on the Bethnal Green Road, and see who fancies working. Get ourselves a little team together. Then, one of us goes in the bank, pretending to change a note, and checks out the place—makes sure there's no coppers hanging about or anything, checks the lie of the land. That kind of thing. Then he comes out, gives the others the SP and they steam in with pickaxe handles, make the bank clerks shit themselves. Then they hand over whatever we want.'

A bank job? With Maurice? Sammy was now feeling that while he might have sobered up a bit, he had probably gone off his nut at the same time. 'You're having a joke, right?'

'No.' Maurice sounded as if he didn't understand Sammy's problem with the plan.

'Look, Maury, that sort of thing might still work up in Manchester, but we've moved on a bit down here. Ever heard of bandit glass?'

'Don't get flash with me, feller.'

'I'm not getting flash. I'm just wishing I'd kept my mouth shut.' He covered his face in his hands. 'What a fucking mess.'

'Blimey, Sam, calm down, feller.' Maurice shuffled his chair closer to the table. 'How about this? You lived over in Notting Hill. They reckon there's a fortune being made in property over there. Say we go and get ourselves some of that?'

'Right. Course. Property. I'll get myself a pin-striped suit, a bowler hat, and an umbrella shall I? I'm sure Mr Rachman won't mind.'

Maurice looked blank.

'It's all tied up already. Like everything else that's worth any dough.'

Maurice didn't look pleased. He leaned back in his seat and took his time lighting a cigarette. 'Well, if you're not interested. And you don't mind that slag Luke shooting his mouth off about you and his sister to anyone'll listen. Then what can I say?'

Sammy studied his cousin, watching him as he flicked his cigarette lighter—on, off, on, off—feeling sick at the thought that if the whim took him, Maurice could bubble him anytime he wanted.

He took a deep breath, letting it out long and slow. It killed him to do this, but now his monkey, two-faced cousin knew about Catherine he had to keep him sweet, on side.

'Sorry about that, Maury. Nothing personal. I'm just a bit jumpy, that's all. And I am interested, as it happens. I might even be one step ahead of you.'

'Come on then, feller, I'm all ears.'

Was telling this to Maurice as stupid as he thought it was?

Probably.

'There are these two blokes. Blokes I've been thinking about going to see for a while now.' *Yeah, when I was thinking about how I was going to set up somewhere a long way away so I could be with Catherine.* 'And I reckon now might be the time. Come along if you like. Say we leave around noon tomorrow?'

# CHAPTER FOURTEEN

Sammy sat in the passenger seat, barely registering the twists and turns of the country lanes, as Maurice struggled to manoeuvre his sleek, silver Jensen at worryingly fast speeds through the wintry countryside.

When he had made the decision that he was going to stay long term with the London branch of his family, the car had been bought for him by his parents. It was probably as much a bribe to leave Manchester for good, as a gift to wish him well, Sammy thought, because, as far as he could see, the showy vehicle was the one single thing about his cousin that was of any worth or interest. And he couldn't even handle *that* properly.

Sammy lit a cigarette. Perhaps they were trying to get rid of their son in a more permanent way than just moving him to the other end of the country. He, of all people, knew that car crashes were a good way to get rid of something embarrassing.

He wound the window down a crack to take the smoke, and stared out at the twiggy, almost leafless hedgerows, wondering what it would have been like to have made this journey with Catherine.

Or even alone. Maybe he would have taken some pleasure in having a break away from the East End, from the O'Donnells, and from Maurice and the rest of the bloody family.

It now seemed the accepted thing that his dad and brother treated him as if he was as useful as an arse with a headache, while his mother apparently saw him as someone to be fussed over as if he had some terrible disease. It was driving him off his head.

And now he had to sit here, listening to Maurice's boring bollocks as he babbled on and on. The sound of his nasal northern vowels was bad enough, but if he said: *So, you and Catherine O'Donnell then, eh, Sammy, feller, that's one for the book, that is, a right turn up, a Catholic girl and an O'Donnell* just one more time, Sammy honestly thought he might lose control, and tell his cousin: *Okay, that's it, tell whoever you like about me and Catherine, because I don't care any more. I loved her. And I still do, and there's nothing any one can do about it.*

Then whatever happened, surely it couldn't hurt him any more than he was hurting already.

He ground the heels of his thumbs into his eyes, trying to wipe away the visions of Catherine's body sprawled across the filthy tarmac.

Why *not* throw Maurice that additional little tit-bit? Tell him how she was murdered by her own family? How could telling the truth make things any worse than they were now?

Sammy almost laughed. Because he was weak that's why. A grown man who couldn't face up to his own family. But he would face Catherine's family, the ones who'd made him admit that terrible weakness in himself. That was why he was sitting here, being driven by a maniac through the Kent countryside, on the way to meet some people who, Sammy could only pray, would help him get rid of the O'Donnells from of his life. And maybe, who knew, with a bit of luck, would help him get rid of the O'Donnells—full stop.

217

'Oi, Sammy lad, are you listening to me, or what? I asked you, who are these blokes we're meeting? I don't want to look like a prick when we get there, now do I?'

In Sammy's opinion, Maurice couldn't look like anything other than a prick, but he wasn't going to start getting lairy with him. Not yet, not while he needed him to keep his mouth shut.

Sammy aimed his cigarette butt out of the window at the trunk of an ivy-covered oak. He missed.

'They're two cousins.' His voice was weary, almost defeated.

'Like us, eh, feller.'

'Yeah, like us. Their name's Baxter. Joey and Chas. They're Londoners, but they got this place out in the country a few years back.'

'Why the move to the country?'

'Got to like the area, so the story goes, when they used to come down here as kids, hop-picking with their nan.'

'What they like then, these Baxters?'

'They run a small, South London outfit. They're hard—'

Maurice snorted loudly, interrupting him. 'You're having me on, right, Sam?'

'How d'you mean?'

Maurice flashed Sammy a disbelieving look. 'Why would a cockney want anything to do with South Londoners? My old feller always said you lot north of the river prided yourselves on being,' he put on a mock posh accent, '*superior* to the likes of them.'

'I might have been born in the East End, Maury, but Notting Hill was always my home. Where I felt

218

I belonged. Until I met—Here, slow down.' Sammy stopped himself from saying any more. Maurice had enough on him already.

He consulted the roughly scribbled map he'd had propped up on the dashboard like a party invitation since they'd left Stepney Green. 'If this is right, I think we're getting close.'

*      *      *

The Four Aces roadhouse was a large, single-storey, wooden building with broad, shallow steps leading up to the veranda, which ran along the whole front elevation. It was painted a dark, sludge-like green that helped it blend almost organically into its idyllic riverside surroundings. The only thing that made it stand out as being something of a cuckoo in its verdant nest was the blue and pink neon sign, fashioned in the shape of the eponymous hand of cards, flashing on and off over the door. But even that had an odd, cheerful charm in the gloomy, grey light of the February afternoon.

Maurice sent up a shower of gravel as he sideslipped the Jensen into the car park, and came to a scrunching halt in the lee of an ancient-looking arched stone bridge, which spanned the foamy, rushing waters of a chilly-looking weir below.

Apart from a battered, open-backed truck, and a few small family saloons, the car park was empty, but it was easy to imagine such a spot being packed out in fine weather, as day-trippers took their refreshment, while watching their laughing, splashing children playing in the river.

'This looks a right dump,' was Maurice's only

219

comment as he locked the car. But as he followed Sammy inside the Four Aces, Maurice had to admit that it was an intriguing sort of a place. Homely, but chaotic.

It was filled with an apparently random mix of furniture: scruffy leather armchairs; slightly wonky, overstuffed sofas; assorted wooden tables and chairs; low, three-legged stools; long carved benches; and what looked like old church pews. Any of the dark stained floorboards not hidden under furniture, were covered by scatterings of threadbare rugs. And with the quirky ornaments and lamps, cushions and tasselled drapes, stuffed creatures under glass domes—all sizes from a tiny wren on a willow branch, to a large, barrel-chested monkey dressed in a smoking jacket and matching braid trimmed hat—it seemed the owners must have spent much of their time scouring markets and auction rooms. Either that or they had a lot of elderly relatives who had chosen to leave them all their old junk in their wills.

It took two massive log fires to heat the big space, one at either end of the long, single bar that ran along the back wall, and they were doing their job well, the place was as cosy as an intimate front parlour.

A pair of lurchers, stretched out in front of one of the fires, with their chins resting on their long elegant paws, opened their eyes and pricked up their ears as they observed the visitors. They appeared too lulled by the warmth to spring to their feet and make a stand. But anyone taking their apparent passivity for granted might have come unstuck, as they were as ready as any snarling Alsatian to protect their masters' territory.

'Okay, boys, *stay*,' snapped a whip-thin, frail-looking man.

The lurchers sighed in whispery canine unison, relaxed their ears and closed their eyes, returning to their twitching doggy dreams.

The thin man was sitting at an old kitchen table. He was playing dominoes with a man who, if he hadn't been so fat, could have been his identical twin brother.

The thin man focussed his pale-eyed gaze on Sammy.

'The name's Sammy Kessler. I'm here to meet Chas and Joey Baxter.' He was well aware that he was talking to Joey himself, *and* that his fat cousin Chas was sitting there across from him; Sammy, like a lot of people, knew these two by reputation.

'Mind pointing me in the right direction?'

'You've found them,' said fat Chas, flicking a double blank high into the air, and catching it with a chubby knuckled snatch, his South London accent grating on Sammy's nerves almost as badly as Maurice's Northern one. 'Who's the other bloke?'

'This is my cousin. Maurice Kessler. He's down from Manchester. Living with us in London for a bit.'

Chas's face folded into a thousand creases. He was smiling. 'Best thing to do with Manchester—leave it.'

Maurice's eyes narrowed very slightly. *The cheeky fat fucker.* But he didn't like anyone thinking they could upset him—not that easily. So he winked at Chas. 'A sense of humour,' he said. 'I admire that in a feller. Just like I admire this place. Very original. Shows imagination.'

221

Chas and his skinny cousin looked at each other, weighing up if the Northern git was taking the piss. It wasn't easy for them to tell. They weren't accustomed to such exotic company.

They stood up. 'We like it,' Joey said. 'Right, business. We'll go somewhere private.'

Chas nodded for them to follow Joey, who, moving with surprising speed for someone who looked so physically frail, was already over by the door.

They went outside, round the back of the roadhouse, where barrels and crates and empties were stacked in apparently disorganised chaos, but there were no weeds sprouting, or bits of broken glass, so it was all, no doubt, in businesslike readiness. It was beginning to look like a bit of a trademark with the Baxter boys—things looking chaotic.

'Hands against the wall,' puffed Chas, winded from the effort of their short walk.

Sammy and Maurice didn't move, instead they just stared, questioning what they'd just heard. *Hands against the wall*? Was he sure?

Joey laughed and shook his head as if he were dealing with a pair of daft five year olds. 'You didn't think we'd let you onto our turf without searching you, did you?'

This was going well. Maurice wanted to join in with his laughter—but not because he was amused. If it took the Baxters's fancy they could put a bullet through the back of their skulls, drag them into the woods, and have them safely buried all within the hour. Have fucking daffodils planted on top of them ready for Easter. And no one would know any different.

*Because no one knew they were there.*

So much for Sammy and his big fucking plans.

Maurice wasn't so much relieved as genuinely taken aback when all they got was a very professional frisking.

'Clean,' said Joey to Chas, snapping Maurice back to attention.

'Fair enough,' said Chas, 'let's go.'

'Hang on,' said Sammy, grabbing Joey's arm, and flashing a worried look at Maurice. 'We came to talk to you.'

Joey stared at Sammy's hand on his shirtsleeve. Despite the cold, and him being such a slight man, he hadn't bothered with a jacket, and didn't appear at all uncomfortable even with the wind whipping across from the water meadows on the other side of the river, but he *definitely* appeared put out by the fact that Sammy had taken the liberty of touching him.

'I know, Mr Kessler,' he said, eyes still fixed on Sammy's hand. 'That's where we're going— somewhere we can talk. We keep our business private.'

Sammy withdrew his hand, sticking it deep into his overcoat pocket. 'Right. Good.' He spoke as if it had been his idea all along to go off somewhere.

Chas sniffed loudly and spat a great gob of green snot into the grass. 'Follow us. And make sure you keep up.'

As he put the Jensen into first, Maurice was about to make a smartarsed remark to Sammy about the state of the beaten up flat-back truck that Joey and Chas had clambered into, but when it took off at a gravel-spraying lick, he turned down his mouth and nodded his approval. 'Souped up.

223

Nice touch. Full of little surprises them two, ain't they, feller?'

*       *       *

They drove at speeds that made their earlier drive look like a Sunday afternoon jaunt with the Mothers' Union. After forty or so stomach-churning minutes they arrived at a little boat yard on an estuary. It was a long way from the main road leading them back to the safety of the Blackwall Tunnel and the 'right' side of the river.

Maurice parked the Jensen next to the truck on a piece of rough ground, hurriedly locking the doors so that he and Sammy could keep up with Chas and Joey, who were already halfway along a short jetty against which a tatty-looking boat had been moored.

Sammy was beginning to have serious doubts about all this. The other craft in the tiny marina were clean and spruce, their brass gleaming even in the thin, afternoon light, and their natty little flags flapping and snapping proudly against the wintry sky. It seemed a miracle that the rust bucket they were about to climb onto could actually sit in the water, let alone sail anywhere.

Maurice held back a snigger as Chas heaved himself down through the hatch after Joey, like an over-sized cork being shoved into a bottle, and then gestured for Sammy to be his guest and go next.

As Sammy's feet hit the floor of the cabin, he stared about him in surprise and didn't feel too bad at all.

Maurice landed next to him. 'Here, this is a bit

of all right, feller.'

That was an understatement. Compared to the exterior, the inside of the four-berth motor yacht was a palace, decked out with highly polished cherry wood, and with subtle tones of soft pink and grey in the immaculate upholstery.

'Don't like to have anything too flashy looking on the outside,' said Joey matter-of-factly. 'People get to thinking you're rich, and then they wonder where you get your few quid from.'

Maurice looked about him, nodding his approval. 'Very clever, feller. And this is a right handy bit of kit. Take it wherever you want, carry whatever you like, and all without attracting too much attention.'

Chas and Joey exchanged one of their glances, and Chas signalled for their guests to sit down. 'Niceties over,' he said. 'When we heard you wanted to see us, I must admit we were surprised. From what we understood, you Kesslers are all nice and cosied up with the O'Donnells.'

Sammy didn't hesitate. 'My family are doing some business with them.'

'The O'Donnells are a powerful outfit.'

'I know, and I know you had trouble with them a few years back.'

'When we was only based in Bermondsey.'

Maurice sniggered. 'What, before you went international, feller, and came down to Kent?'

Chas steepled his fingers over his great, fat belly. 'It was a nasty business. People got hurt.'

This time Sammy paused for a moment, looking right into Chas's puffy, piggy eyes. 'People died.' Another pause. '*Your* people.'

'They did.'

225

'And that's why I thought you'd be the perfect choice for me to do business with.'

'What business?'

'One or two bits of business actually, jobs that'll earn us enough of a stake to put a stop to the O'Donnells thinking they can act as if they own us. Enough to really shock them into realising who and what they're dealing with. And you can be in on it.'

'What sort of jobs?'

'All sorts.' Sammy had promised himself he would bide his time, wouldn't say too much too soon. 'I'm talking big money. And—' he added the clincher '—I'm talking about you helping us destroy the O'Donnells.'

'Sorry, but I think you're wasting our time. We've got our own interests to think about.'

What was going on? This wasn't what he'd expected. 'But—'

'But nothing. We don't need to start messing about with all that old Wild West fanny again, do we, Joe?'

'No, Chas, we don't. I had enough of all that shooting lark a long time ago.'

'In fact—' Chas hauled himself to his feet and jerked his head for Joey to do likewise '– I think we've gone far enough with this conversation.'

'You don't understand.' Sammy was now standing next to him. In spite of the cold, he could smell his own nervous sweat. 'There'd be plenty in it for you.'

'We're doing all right as it is, thank you. Come back another time maybe. When you've actually got something to talk about, something that don't involve playing Cowboys and Indians. And make sure it's something that's worth the agg.'

226

Maurice was close to exasperation. Some big scheme this was turning out to be. He tried to think of something to say that might repair some of the damage, and that might recover a bit of their self-respect.

Sammy beat him to it.

'I've got something to talk about now. And it would just be the beginning. On my life, when I said about you helping us destroy the bastards—I meant help us destroy their businesses. I wasn't expecting nothing else.'

More exchanged looks between Chas and Joey.

Chas sighed theatrically. 'We'll listen for two more minutes.'

'Right. It's a warehouse. It'll look like it's been stuffed full of furs. *After* it goes up like a rocket display on bonfire night. A warehouse that you two could have shares in. And . . .' He let the words dangle for a moment or two. 'In the future, let's say, I might also be looking for a way of disposing of some unwanted remains.'

Joey grinned, flashing more gold than teeth. 'So, *you're* gonna do the O'Donnells?'

'I'm not saying that.'

'Sorry, perhaps that was jumping the gun.' His grin spread even wider. 'As you might say.'

Sammy held up his hands. 'No, you're right, Joey. Cards on the table. You two know how them bastards work, which might prove very useful to me. And you two've also got a grudge against them.'

'True,' Chas said, plonking down on his seat—back in the chair in every sense. 'And?'

'And . . .' Sammy was speaking slowly but thinking in overdrive. 'That's where I might be useful to you. And if I maybe did want to get rid of some unwanted rubbish at some point in the future . . .'

'I don't think we'd be averse to lending a hand then—*after* the event, like—do you, Joe?'

'No.'

'In fact, we might know a man you might wanna speak to.' One of Chas's already piggy eyes disappeared in a wink. 'Posh bloke. Goes hunting and that. Mate of his runs the kennels for the hounds. They feed 'em on raw meat; make sure they keep their hunting instinct. So, if you ever did want to dispose of that rubbish . . .' He let the idea sink in. 'Please, let us know. We'd be happy to make the introductions. That's right, innit, Joe?'

They were the most words that Chas had said in one go since they'd met him. He was obviously excited.

'Chas. Joey.' Sammy held out his hands in open-palmed gratitude. If this went the way he hoped, it might just be the answer to his problems. 'You've almost embarrassed me now, making such a kind offer. Thank you. I'll remember your words. And, I swear, once I've got the stake together, I'm gonna finance the plans I've got that are gonna show up the O'Donnells for the two bob merchants they really are. And by the time we've finished, we'll be the only people anyone'll do business with in the whole East End.'

Chas and Joey exchanged another glance, while Sammy stared into the middle distance visualising bits of the Irishmen disappearing into a mincing machine. That would definitely get his father's attention, show him what his son was capable of. And maybe revenge on the O'Donnells might just begin to wipe away some of his guilt.

*     *     *

Just over seven weeks later, on a dull but dry Saturday evening in late March, Sammy and Maurice sat in the Jensen in a deserted side street in the East End's garment district. They were watching through binoculars as a colleague of Joey and Chas Baxter expertly set fire to a warehouse off the Commercial Road, a warehouse which the Baxters and the two Kessler cousins now owned in everything but name. The name on the papers being that of Susie Farlow, the young, widowed sister of the barmaid from the Four Aces.

A month after that, Mr Walter Jenkins, a bored, unhappily married, middle-aged loss adjustor, was sympathising with the young and lovely Mrs Farlow as he stared down the front of her blouse at her very attractive bosom. He told her how sorry he was that everything she'd inherited on the sad and premature passing away of her husband—the money which she'd invested in the warehouse—had literally gone up in smoke, when all the contents and fabric of the place had been destroyed in the devastating fire. But he hoped that the cheque would be of some compensation.

Susie Farlow, looking suitably mournful, but ever so grateful, didn't mention that the late Mr Farlow had been beaten to death by one of her boyfriends, a man who'd taken exception to his girlfriend being a married woman. And Mr Jenkins—oblivious of such complications—became quite excited at the thought of the charming, grateful, available young woman, and of the nice big cheque that she held in her dainty little hand.

He even began to wonder if he might perhaps offer her a more personal kind of comfort.

So smitten was he, in fact, that even if he *had* discovered that the few valuable contents of the warehouse—a couple of low grade mink coats, a box of squirrel stoles, and a half a dozen very old-fashioned musquash capes—had actually been removed and sold before the fire had happened, and that all that was left in the store at the time of the 'accident' were a few scraps of offcuts and a load of burnt rabbit skins, he would probably have ignored the evidence of his own eyes. For Mr Jenkins was a man fuelled by a dream: a fantasy of escaping from the insurance industry and from his dismal marriage.

As for young Mrs Farlow, who had been well paid for her work, she was actually tempted to go on a second date with Mr Jenkins. The first, which she'd initially seen as a necessary chore to prevent him from becoming difficult, had actually turned out to have been rather pleasant, unused as she was to men like Mr Jenkins. But, on reflection, she thought that doing so would probably have been pushing her luck with the Baxters. And so she did as they told her, and disappeared out of the country for an extended spring holiday, going to stay with one of their business associates who lived in a little Spanish fishing village called Fuengirola.

Mrs Farlow had made a wise choice, striking it very lucky indeed by choosing to go and stay with the Baxters's colleague.

Billy the Brick—so named for his early apprenticeship in famously daring smash-and-grab raids, before his graduation to more sophisticated,

230

not to say much better paid, crimes—had been lying low in his charming, newly purchased, seaside villa, and was missing female company; well, female company of the sort that had blonde hair, a saucy laugh, and a reassuringly familiar, South London accent.

And the widow Farlow fitted the bill perfectly.

She soon settled in, and the holiday just seemed to go on and on. It wasn't long before Susie had plans for their little fishing village retreat. Using her pay off from the Baxters, she opened a real novelty of a place, a genuine English pub complete with a dart board on the wall, plenty of Red Barrel on tap, and roast beef and Yorkshire pudding on the daily menu.

Billy the Brick thought she was gorgeous, but bonkers, but Susie had an idea that it might just catch on.

*       *       *

Back home in England, the money that Susie Farlow had accepted in the form of Mr Jenkins's compensatory cheque had been tidily laundered and divvied out. Sammy Kessler had thanked the Baxters, and told them he was looking forward to doing business with them again very soon, and popped his share into a thick manila envelope.

The next morning, he waited for his mother to start clearing the breakfast things, and then asked if he could have a quiet word with his father.

Expecting yet more nonsense from his youngest son, Harold Kessler very reluctantly followed Sammy and Maurice into the front parlour, leaving Sophie to her chores.

Making sure the door was tightly closed, Sammy handed his father the envelope full of money, plus an edited explanation of recent events—playing down the role of the Baxters somewhat, but playing up the fact that this was only the first of the many scams that Sammy was planning. Scams which would get them a big enough pot to get them right out of the O'Donnells's circle of influence once and for all.

'I mean it, Dad,' Sammy said, tapping the bulging manila. 'There's gonna be plenty more where that little lot came from.'

Maurice had been right: this time Harold Kessler was listening to his son. He was listening very closely indeed.


## CHAPTER FIFTEEN

It had been a week since Sammy Kessler had handed the envelope full of money to his father, and now, with an eye to his plan of severing every last tie with the O'Donnells, and of repaying every bit of hurt they had inflicted on him, Sammy suggested that he and Maurice should pay a visit to the Bellavista.

They arrived at the club accompanied by two dishevelled looking men, who appeared to have had more than their fair share of booze before washing up in the narrow Shoreditch cul-de-sac.

One of the two bullet-headed, but immaculately

dressed, door minders, put out his hand to stop them entering, looking Sammy and Maurice's companions up and down with obvious disapproval.

'These chaps with you, Mr Kessler?' The doorman couldn't keep the contempt from his voice.

'These gentlemen,' said Sammy with great solemnity, 'are my personal friends.'

Had the two strangers not been with members of the Kessler family, they would never have made it through the door—the O'Donnells were clear on this: mysteries weren't welcome anywhere near the new Bellavista—but the bouncer had a problem. He could just wave them in and risk them making nuisances of themselves. But that wasn't a good idea, not when his bosses kept stressing that they were trying to make the place *more classy*. He could insult them by keeping them on the pavement like idiots, while he checked with Brendan whether he should let them in or not. But that would upset the Kesslers—and maybe the O'Donnells. Or he could refuse them entry, point blank.

In short, he could start a fight by doing anything other than letting them waltz right in. And that might cause a fight anyway.

Great.

The bouncer puffed out his cheeks. It was no good asking his colleague, his brains stopped in his ham-sized fists. No choice but to take a chance and hope that the Kesslers would keep an eye on their mates. And so, with his metaphorical fingers crossed, the minder ushered the four men through. But, just to be on the safe side, he waited a few diplomatic minutes, and followed them into the club so he could warn Brendan about what he had done, and to promise him that he only had to shout and he and his mate would be right by his side.

Brendan took in the information without a word, not even bothering to get up from his bar stool to go over and greet them. He could see all he wanted from where he was—for now.

But it soon became clear that the strangers were not exactly respectful guests. Their voices were loud; their gestures over-extravagant, and their attitude towards the O'Donnells' bar staff was dismissively arrogant. None of that would have been too much of a problem for Brendan—not in normal circumstances. In fact, treating the bar staff with a measure of disdain was as good as an established business policy of the O'Donnells. But when it was tanked up pals of the Kesslers, who thought they could come bowling into his club and act that way, it made Brendan start twitching.

Finishing his drink, he checked his tie and hair—peering ostentatiously in the mirror behind the bar—and strolled over to where the four men were standing in the middle of the dance floor. As he passed by, customers nodded and smiled at him, eager to show their companions that they knew one of the owners—one of the notorious O'Donnell family—*in person*.

Brendan extended his hand to Sammy Kessler.

'Evening chaps,' he said, cracking a handsome grin at Sammy. 'You and your friends are more than welcome to come and join me and my brother for a drink at our table.' The grin softened into a warm smile; he was the good-natured host, gesturing with a lift of his chin to where Luke was sitting by himself sullenly nursing a very large whiskey.

One of the Kesslers's drunken companions slapped Brendan hard on the shoulder. 'Thanks all the same, moosh,' he yelled, turning heads all round the bar. 'Rather sit with a bird, if you don't mind. I mean, this is a fucking knocking shop, ain't it?'

He folded an arm round the other drunk's shoulder and they staggered over to the girls' bench to check out what was on offer.

Brendan just managed to keep his lips stretched into a thin approximation of a smile. 'Your mates are a bit Brahms, ain't they, Sammy? Sure they ain't had enough?'

Sammy returned Brendan's mouth-only smile. 'Thought that's what clubs like this were for, selling over-priced booze, renting out whores, and generally having one over on the mug punters. But maybe you're right, maybe I had better make sure they at least stay upright. I mean, wouldn't want the Bellavista getting a bad reputation and forcing the law to make an official visit, now would we? That'd be bad for business wouldn't it, eh, Bren?'

Brendan wanted to punch Sammy Kessler right in the face, but this wasn't the time or the place to do it. Especially as he had a very strong hunch that starting a ruck was exactly what the swaggering little twat wanted him to do. And even though every time he looked at the bloke he wanted to hit him—just the thought of him having been anywhere near his little sister made Brendan want to put his hands round the bastard's throat and shake him till his brains rattled—he wouldn't give Kessler the satisfaction of letting him know he could upset him.

He managed to keep what was left of his smile

plastered to his face. 'No one ever likes to get an official visit, Sam,' he mugged.

'You're right there, Brendan.' Sammy turned to his cousin and winked. 'So, reckon I'd better get over to them other two, Maury. Case they do something silly. But there's nothing to stop you from joining Brendan and Luke *at their table*. Go on, go and enjoy yourself.'

'You know, Sammy, I think I will.' Maurice flashed his eyebrows at Brendan, and rubbed his hands together in eager anticipation. 'Right, a taste of the O'Donnell hospitality . . . I'll have a large Scotch, please, feller. And make sure it's Scotch, eh? Cos I can't be doing with the Irish.'

Brendan walked over to speak to the barman, knowing he had to get away from that saucy, big-mouthed fucker before he landed him one right in the middle of his sneering, Northern gob. Sammy Kessler was bad enough, but there was something about his toerag of a cousin that Brendan could feel crawling all over his skin like a slime-trailing bug. He was a nine carat piece of shit.

Maurice, on the other hand, had a very different opinion of himself—he was feeling rather pleased with what he'd achieved: winding up Brendan O'Donnell like an over tight clock spring without so much as breaking sweat. Nice.

Time to move on and see what he could do to his little brother.

\*       \*       \*

Maurice snatched up a chair, set it down close to Luke, and straddled it like a horse. 'So, how're you doing then, feller?'

236

No answer.

'Fair enough.' Maurice began whistling along to the crackly recording of Bobby Darin singing 'Mack the Knife', enjoying the knowledge that he was making Luke feel uncomfortable just by being there.

Still accompanying Bobby, Maurice linked his fingers and stretched out his arms, right under Luke's nose, cracking his knuckles loudly.

He stopped whistling abruptly, pointed at Luke and said, 'Just out of interest, don't you ever feel like asking our Sammy about, you know—him and your sister?'

Luke stared about him, gathering his words, his lips stretched tight across his teeth. He then returned to studying his drink. 'I ain't got the first clue what you're talking about.'

'It's all right, Luke, me cousin's told me all about her.'

Luke lifted his head and looked directly into Maurice's smug, mocking eyes. 'What are you on about?'

Maurice paused, the little smile playing about his lips somehow making the silence suggestive. 'I hardly mean your Patricia, now do I? It's Catherine I'm talking about.' He looked over his shoulder. 'So, where's this drink I was promised then, eh, feller?' He turned back to Luke. 'Mind you, I don't know if you'd really want to hear what he's got to say. Not really. Some of the things he told me about her . . .' He narrowed his eyes, pouted his lips and shook his head. 'Like how she loved to get—'

A sudden, loud squeal, as one of the two drunks pushed a young brunette off the bench, sending her crashing backwards into the wall, distracted

237

Maurice for a brief but crucial moment.

Luke swung back his arm and punched him—hard—on the side of the head.

'Are you sure?' Maurice, clutching his temple, spun round. He stuck his face right into Luke's and grabbed him by the lapels. 'Have you lost your fucking mind? I could rip your head right off your shoulders with just this one hand, you pathetic little queer. I like a grin with the best of them, but you have just overstepped the fucking mark.'

'Leave it, Maury.' It was Sammy. He was pulling Maurice to his feet. 'I think it's time we joined the others.'

Maurice let go of Luke, but poked him hard in the chest. 'Touch me, would you, you Irish ponce? I'll have you later.'

Brendan was standing in the farthest corner from the door looking fit to detonate with temper, as Kevin Marsh and Barry Ellis sprawled on the floor in front of him, grappling with Sammy's two companions. Fists were flying and girls were screaming. It was like a scene from a Saturday morning Western at the fleapit.

There was a sudden explosion of glass and a chorus of high-pitched yelps from the girls, as one of the drunks managed to pull off Barry's shoe and aim it at the row of optics behind the bar.

At the sound of the bottles smashing, the door minders were inside in a flash.

'That's it,' hollered Brendan. 'Out.' He grabbed the shoe thrower by the hair and dragged him to his feet, pushing him towards Sammy Kessler. 'And it might be an idea if you and your cousin go with them and all.'

'You're chucking us out?' Sammy shook his head

pityingly. 'That would be one big mistake, O'Donnell. Our two families are trying to be friends here, and what are you doing? Mugging us off. Treating us like punters. What would your old man have to say about that d'you reckon?'

'He's not here is he?'

Luke, still rubbing the sting from his knuckles from where he'd punched Maurice, joined his brother in the middle of the chaotic scene. 'All right?'

'Fine,' said Brendan, not taking his eyes off Sammy. 'Kessler, you and your cousin and your two piss artist mates, get out. Now.' Then he put out his arms, and, with the minders flanking him, began marshalling the four unwanted guests towards the exit. He turned his head and called to his brother. 'Now the cabaret's over, make sure everyone's got a drink, Luke.'

Barry and Kevin, their shirt tails hanging out, their hair in their eyes, and with only three shoes between them, stood on either side of the door like glowering ushers at a shotgun wedding.

'Come on, lads,' said Sammy, seeing the other three out onto the pavement, as he straightened his collar, 'let's get away from here. We don't have to put up with O'Donnell's old guyver.'

Once Sammy had stepped outside, Brendan tried to shut the door on them, but the drunk whose hair Brendan had grabbed had other ideas. He moved with unexpected speed, sticking his foot in the jamb, and lurching back inside.

Before Brendan knew what was happening, the man had raced through the lobby and back into the main part of the club, and was clambering over the girls, hauling himself up onto their bench,

239

scattering them around him like a frightened flock of screaming, multi-coloured gulls.

'You O'Donnell fuckers,' he hollered over the music, waggling his outstretched arms like a tightrope walker as he battled to keep his balance on the narrow seat. 'You wanna watch your arses. Cos I'm coming back here, and I'm gonna set fire to this bastard place. I'll show you throw *me* out.'

With that he lurched off the bench, shouldered his way back through the crowd and fell through the front door, slamming it loudly behind him.

Outside on the pavement, Maurice put an arm round the supposedly drunken man's shoulder and hugged him warmly. But the man was no longer drunk, he was, like his supposedly equally intoxicated mate, completely sober. The four men walked steadily and calmly towards the top of the cul-de-sac.

'Regular little fire brands you South London lot, ain't you, feller?' said Maurice. 'And not bad actors, eh, Sammy? They should go on the telly, shouldn't they? There's good money in that.'

'And there's good money in causing aggravation for them Irish cunts and all. Here lads.' Sammy gave each of the two men a wad of notes. 'Give my regards to Chas and Joey, and tell them I'll be in touch.'

'Very nice job, fellers,' said Maurice, pulling open the door of a phone box on the corner of Folgate Street. 'I'll only be a minute, Sam. Just got a quick call to make. Might as well wind them right up, while we're at it. Here, hold on.' He beckoned the two men to come back. 'Can either of you two show me how to do an Irish accent? Just for a laugh like.'

240

While all hell was breaking loose at the Bellavista, Gabriel was sitting in front of a frill trimmed, kidney-shaped dressing table, taking sips of Jameson's in between knotting his paisley tie. The drink was supposedly an alibi, his cover to convince Eileen that he'd been in the club with the boys. But even he was beginning to wonder if he was getting to be as dependent on the stuff as his father had been—and that was a long time before he'd finally run off for good and left them all to fend for themselves.

He stood up and slipped his arms into the jacket Rosie was holding up for him. Then he turned and pulled her close.

'I don't know what I'd do without you, Rosie Palmer.'

'So long as I make you happy, love, that's all that matters to me.' She dropped her chin, her heavy dark hair falling about her face. 'And Ellie, of course.'

'I know you miss her, Rosie,' he said, stroking her soft, pale cheek, 'but she's better off over there. She couldn't be at a better school than St Anne's. And you know Mary would rather have her eyes plucked out than have anything bad happen to her. It's for the best, my angel, you know that.'

'I know, and I'm not complaining, honest, Gabe, but . . .' Rosie gently pulled away from him and fetched his cigarettes and lighter from the bedside table.

He tucked them into his pocket. 'Tell you what, Rose, how about if I get Mary to fetch her over

241

next week?'

Rosie's eyes welled up with tears. 'Really? Next week?'

'Why not?'

'You're so good to me.'

He smiled down at her, loving her in his own way, but knowing he'd never understand why she was prepared to sacrifice so much for him. He hadn't wanted the bother of another child, so what had she done when she'd fallen pregnant? She'd as good as given her up. For him.

He could never care so much about what someone else wanted. Never.

Rosie undid her wrapper and let it fall to the floor, showing off her ripe, plump body, the body that made Gabriel forget all the everyday nonsense that drove him mad and that, he would say, justifying his thirst, drove him to drink. 'You deserve a proper thank you for that.'

Gabriel felt himself harden. 'You're a beautiful woman, Rosie Palmer, a truly beautiful woman.'

\*　　　\*　　　\*

The next morning, Gabriel went into the yard early. He wanted privacy, so he could speak to his sister about organising the trip over from Ireland.

He had just put the receiver back in its cradle, when the door was pushed open and Gabriel saw Brendan and Luke framed in the opening. They were staring at him, eyes wide with surprise, as if they'd been caught burgling the place.

Brendan spun round to say something to someone behind him, but he was too late.

'You should have heard the piss-taking accent.'

242

Gabriel heard Barry's voice saying from outside, and then sliding into a mocking Oirish lilt. 'See, dey weren't punters, dey weren't even our mates. Sure wasn't it all—'

'All right Barry,' Brendan cut in.

'Let him finish.' Gabriel was on his feet, looking over his sons' shoulders. 'Come in here, Barry. You too Kevin. Now, what were you saying?'

Barry and Kevin sloped up the steps into the shabby lean-to office like schoolboys caught smoking behind the girls' lavs. Barry looked at Brendan, pleading with his eyes for a signal to tell him what to do.

'Go on,' Brendan said flatly.

Luke could barely stand to listen.

Barry gulped then said, all in a rush and in his own cockneyfied Dublin, 'Them blokes who turned up at the Bellavista. They weren't really drunk; they were just there to cause trouble. Show us up. They were paid to do it. They work for them blokes that the Kesslers owned that warehouse with.'

Gabriel tipped his head to one side and held out his hands—totally confused. 'What blokes? When? And what warehouse?'

Barry looked at Brendan again. Knowing he'd said too much, but what could he do—risk a good hiding from Gabriel? At least Brendan would only give him a bollocking for shooting his mouth off.

He lowered his eyes and began, very slowly. 'There was a bit of a ruck in the club last night.'

'Tell me you don't mean the Bellavista.'

'Sorry, Gabe.' Barry dropped his chin. 'Sammy Kessler, and that flash cousin of his, they came in with these two blokes. Then, right after they left, one of the arseholes phoned the club. I answered it.

He was taking the piss, putting on some stupid accent. But I know it had to be that Northern ponce.'

'I said, *Barry*, what blokes and what warehouse?'

'The fur *wa*rehouse. The one that got torched. The one they say Sammy Kessler bought with the Baxters. And the blokes last night, they work for the Baxters and all.'

'*The Kesslers and the Baxters are working together?*'

Barry nodded miserably, but did his best to limit the damage of the bad news. 'Only Sammy and his cousin though, Gabe. Not Daniel or the old man.'

Gabriel stared. 'Aw, so that's all right then, is it?'

'Well, no . . .'

'Anything else I should know about? Anything else you weren't planning on telling me if I hadn't been here early?'

Barry was wishing he was in a damp, dark cell somewhere having lighted matches poked down his toenails. 'When we threw them out of the Bellavista, one of them came back in, shouting the odds about how he was gonna torch the gaff.'

Gabriel dropped down into his seat. 'That's it, we've lost control. Why did I ever think them whoresons would know how to behave? I should have known they'd take my kindness for fucking stupidity.' He smashed the side of his fist onto the desk. 'And if anyone's going to set light to my fucking properties it's going to be fucking me.'

He fumbled around trying to get a cigarette out of his packet, his hands were shaking with temper.

Luke lit one of his and gave it to his father. 'What you gonna do, Dad?'

'Do? I'm gonna tell that fucker Kessler his

fucking fortune. That's what.'

Brendan was tempted to urge him on, get him even wilder, make him realise that this was the moment they should break with the Kesslers once and for all. Even get another dig in about the drugs he was sure the Kesslers would start dealing, if they didn't shift themselves and get the business sewn up first. But one look at his father's face, and Brendan knew it was best to keep quiet.

Gabriel's cheeks and throat had gone a lurid, purplish red and the veins in his neck were bulging and throbbing as if he were about to have a seizure.

Brendan judged it right: he would have to bide his time.

Luke, on the other hand, had more immediate plans.

*     *     *

While Gabriel was coming close to boiling point in the scruffy lean-to in Bethnal Green, the objects of his fury—Sammy and Maurice—were in the Jensen speeding along peaceful country lanes. This time it wasn't wintry, rural Kent they were driving through, but the Essex countryside, and the hedgerows and trees were in their full spring glory.

'Easy there, feller.' Maurice was beginning to regret agreeing to let Sammy drive. They were racketing along a rutted farm track that the dry spell had rendered as solid as jagged chunks of concrete. 'This isn't a bloody truck.'

Sammy's face didn't give away a flicker of irritation, he just dropped down a gear and lowered the speed. Anything rather than let Maurice back behind the wheel.

After a few more minutes being tossed and bucketed around they came to a straight stretch of metalled road that led directly to a beautifully proportioned, red brick Tudor farmhouse.

Chas and Joey Baxter—resplendent in vests and braces, with a variety of fresh cuts and slightly older scabs standing out against their pale skin in the slightly chilly, but clear morning light—were waiting in the magnificent front porch to welcome their guests like a nightmare parody of a pair of postcard seaside landladies.

*     *     *

'Thought it was Kent you two fellers liked,' said Maurice, sitting back in a huge carved oak armchair and looking around the great hall with undisguised admiration. 'What with all that jolly London hop-picking with your old gran and that. So, what brought you out here to Essex?'

'Pea-picking. Near Ongar,' said fat Chas.

'What, with your nan again? She sounds a good old girl.'

'All right, Maury,' said Sammy, 'we're not here for family reminiscences. Let's listen while Chas and Joey tell me how they're gonna double my money for me.'

Joey did something with his skinny weasely features that was the closest they'd ever get to a genuine smile. 'Only way to guarantee that, mate, is to fold it in half and stick it back in your britch.'

Sammy laughed politely and looked to Chas for a sensible answer.

'Come and see our barn,' was his unexpected reply.

They eventually reached the traditional Essex barn by fighting their way through a tangled spinney, with briars and brambles lashing their faces—the explanation for the Baxters's scratches and scabs.

Chas, in his usual laconic way said that they used a different route each time they went to the barn so as not to beat a single, detectable path from the house. But that there were plenty of tracks for four wheel drives, as well as a whole series of anonymous little lanes crisscrossing along the back that could easily be accessed by the trucks, and plenty of quiet spots to transfer their loads into the Jeeps.

Joey heaved open one half of a pair of tall double doors and flicked a switch. They all blinked as a fluorescent glow lit up the whole, triple height space. As with the Baxters's boat, first impressions of the barn had been deceptive. Outside a piece of architecturally interesting agricultural history, inside a thoroughly organised system of alphabetically labelled, well-lit, open metal shelving with corresponding filing cabinets and rolodexes: all in all, a well-thought out system for delivery and distribution.

Joey pointed into the air with a bony finger. 'This, chaps, is set to be the biggest porn warehouse in the Southeast. We fitted it out using our cut from the warehouse. Always good for business to put some profits back into the firm.'

'Why Essex?' asked Sammy, adding hurriedly, 'And I'm not talking about the pea-picking. Why not Kent? Surely the sort of gear you're talking

247

about comes over from France.'

'Good point. A lot of it does. And that's why everyone would expect us to bring stuff in over the Channel, what with us being based in South London and Kent. But we decided the Harwich route in from Holland is the way forward. There's a lot of gear available over there. A lot of the real hard stuff.'

Sammy could feel the excitement. This was smelling just right. He knew the sort of money that the dirty bookshops brought in in Soho. If he could start supplying them direct . . . 'Okay. Say we provide as many lorries as you want, maybe even organise ourselves a few regular runs taking stuff out to Holland or Belgium. Good, legit cover plus some extra bunce into the bargain.'

Chas and Joey shared a look. 'Sounds very possible,' said Chas.

Sammy took a breath. 'Like I say, I can provide the vehicles and drivers, as many as you need. But there is one slight problem. I'm going to have to ask for a bit of help financing the first run. That's why I'm offering you a sixty–forty cut on this one.'

'Eighty–twenty,' said Chas without missing a beat.

'Seventy–thirty.'

'Done.' Chas spat into his fat palm and slapped it against Sammy's.

'But, after that, fifty–fifty, okay?'

'Fifty–fifty,' said Joey. 'And, when this takes off and starts bringing in the dough like I know it will, there's something else you might be interested in.'

\*     \*     \*

Chas had settled himself down to enjoy the sun on a circular bench under a huge mulberry tree on the lawn at the side of the house, while Joey escorted Sammy and Maurice back to the Jensen.

'And it's got other benefits,' Joey said, as Maurice unlocked the car. 'It looks a nice, straight down the line business. But it's a very useful way of rinsing through the profits from trade like this.' He turned and looked in the direction of the barn. 'And a good way of shifting the merchandise about. We're setting up in South London as we speak. And just think how nice it'd be for you to set up something so visible in the East End, before them O'Donnell cunts get a look in. Hit them where it hurts. Their pride, their pockets, and their fucking balls.'

'Kesslers's Cabs, eh?' Sammy raised his hand in goodbye to Chas, and then shook Joey's bony claw. 'It's a thought. But I'll have to think about it. See how much we get out of this film and book lark first. Then see if I can afford to diversify.'

'Sammy, mate, you won't be able to afford not to.'

\*      \*      \*

Gabriel snatched up the phone from his desk. 'What?'

'It's me, Gabe, Eileen.'

'Not now.' His voice was full of pained exasperation. 'I've got—'

'Sorry, Gabe, this is important. Patricia's round ours, and she needs Peter to take—'

'Hang on a minute, Eileen. Calm down.' He put his hand over the mouthpiece and rolled his eyes.

249

'Stephen, where's Pete Mac got to?'

'I'd put money on him being round that Violet's drum again,' said Stephen, avoiding Gabriel's gaze by concentrating on folding his *Sporting Life* into a neat oblong.

Gabriel nodded wearily. 'Me too.' He took his hand away from the phone. 'Sorry, Ei, he's out seeing a bloke about a contract.'

'Well, can someone find him? Patricia's gone into labour.'

'Don't worry about Pete Mac, I'll send Stephen.' Gabriel put down the phone. 'Stephen, get round my place and get our Patricia to the hospital, will you.'

It wasn't a question.

Stephen stood up, and shoved his paper in his jacket pocket as he made for the door. 'I'll take me five minutes.'

'Steve,' Gabriel went on with a sigh. 'When's he going to get rid of that little scrubber? It's all beginning to seem a bit too serious.'

'You want my genuine opinion on that, Gabe? It's not serious at all. He's just a lazy bastard, who can't even be bothered to sniff out a fresh bit of skirt to mess around with.'

Gabriel put his elbows on his desk and buried his face in his hands. 'All I've ever asked is that my family should be happy. Is that too much for a man to ask?'

# CHAPTER SIXTEEN

'I don't think I'm going to able to get in tomorrow afternoon, Pat,' said Eileen softly, smiling down into the hospital cot, as she gently tucked the blankets around the new love of her life, her baby granddaughter, Caty. 'Got a few errands to run. But I'll be here in the evening to see you, okay?'

Patricia, who hadn't said much during the visit, grabbed her mother's hand. 'Mum. Will it get better now I've had the baby?'

'Better? Course it will, darling. It's not even been a week yet. All that soreness and pain'll soon be nothing more than a bad memory now you've got your precious little bundle.'

'I'm not talking about that.' She pressed her teeth into her bottom lip, biting back the tears. 'I mean with Pete. Will he grow up a bit now he's a dad?'

Eileen sat down on the high-backed bedside chair and squeezed her daughter's hand. 'I honestly don't know, Patsy, love. I don't know if men ever grow up, not in the way we have to. Now you have a child, you'll soon realise, it's women, mothers, who keep things going. We might only be quietly in the background, while it's the men making all the noise and fuss, but really we're the strong ones—we have to be. We keep it all together. We don't just clear off down the pub if the mood takes us, or if things get too much, like they do. We just get on with it.'

Patricia buried her face in her hands. 'What have I done?'

'Ssshh, love, don't cry. It's not all bad.'

'No?'

'No, course not. It's the way we get what we want. Our home, and our life with our family. And it's the way we get to keep it.'

Patricia dropped her hands and looked pleadingly at her mother. 'I'm sorry, I'm just so miserable. And I keep thinking about how much Catherine would have loved the baby. Mum, I miss her so much.'

'So do I, darling,' said Eileen, wiping her daughter's tears with her fingers. 'Every single minute of every single day, God love her. And when I think of some of the people on this earth who wouldn't even be missed . . .'

'She was so funny, wasn't she? Always mucking around, making us all laugh. She could get Dad to do whatever she wanted, remember?'

'She was our baby.'

'And she really would have loved little Caty wouldn't she?'

'Yes, darling, she would.' Eileen kissed her daughter on the cheek and stood up. 'I'd better be off now, or the nurse'll be after me. We've already had an extra ten minutes.'

'Do you think Dad'll be able to get in tomorrow afternoon if you can't?'

'I'm not sure, Pat.' Eileen took one more look at the baby. 'I think he might be a bit busy. You know, what with work and everything.'

*     *     *

As she walked out of the ward, Eileen had to keep her lips pressed tightly together to stop her

252

screaming to the world, 'Of course he won't be able to get here tomorrow afternoon. *Of course he bloody won't.'*

*     *     *

Eileen had told her daughter the partial truth: Gabriel was busy the following afternoon. But not with work. He was sitting on the sofa in the front room of the neat, ground floor, two-bedroom flat in Kilburn with his mistress, Rosie Palmer.

'You seem edgy, Gabe,' Rosie said, throwing him a glance over her shoulder, as she rearranged the table full of cakes and sandwiches yet again. 'Is it seeing Ellie? It'd be understandable if it was. It's been what? Three months since you last saw her?'

'No,' he said, 'it's Eileen.'

'She'll be caught up with the new baby.'

'She's that all right.' He rubbed a hand over his chin, absent-mindedly checking for signs of stubble. 'The first time we went in to see Pat, we were driving home after, and she said how glad she was that the baby was a girl.'

Rosie repositioned a plate of glossy pink cupcakes and turned to face him. 'You can't blame her for that, can you, love? Think about it. She lost Catherine, and now she has a new baby to fuss over. A little girl. I can't begin to think how I'd feel if anything ever happened to Ellie. It's hard enough not having her here with me all the time. But to lose her forever . . .'

Gabriel stood up, his soft towelling dressing gown flapping open, showing a body that, despite his boozing, was still well muscled for a man in his forties. 'You're a good woman, Rosie,' he said,

253

pulling her to him. 'Good and generous. That's why you don't understand the way a woman like Eileen thinks. She said she was glad the baby's a girl, because it means she won't be involved with the business. She was looking down on me. Looking down on what I do.'

'Don't condemn her, Gabe. Women don't always realise what you men have to put up with. Or how hard you work. But it's not our fault we don't understand.'

'Eileen understands all right. She knows where the money comes from, and she's only too happy to let me pay all the bills. She doesn't say no to that.'

Rosie reached up and stroked his neck. 'Don't upset yourself, Gabe, not today. Please. Why don't you go and get dressed? Ellie's going to be here soon.'

\*       \*       \*

Rosie was ready and waiting on the front step when the taxi arrived twenty minutes later.

She ran down the path and wrenched open the back door.

Mary Logan, Gabriel's sister, stepped out onto the pavement, followed by a pretty little girl in a school uniform, her hair braided into two shiny, blue-black plaits.

Rosie's hand flew to her mouth. 'Sweetheart,' she sobbed, and bent down to fold her in her arms.

Gabriel came up behind the little group.

'Say hello to your daddy,' said Mary, removing the child from her mother's hugs and guiding her towards Gabriel.

'Hello, Daddy,' said the little girl, peering up at

254

him from under the brim of her bottle green hat.

At the corner of the street, hiding like a sneak thief in the shadow of a red and white striped watchman's hut by a hole in the road, Eileen O'Donnell stood watching the touching scene of family reunion. Tears were flowing unchecked down her face. But it wasn't because she was watching her husband scooping up his supposedly secret daughter, making her pigtails swing around her head, while his whore stood beaming, full of happiness, by his side, and her bitch of a sister-in-law, Mary Logan, encouraged the pair of them.

No, it was looking at the child that tore her heart apart.

Eileen hadn't had a glimpse of her for nearly two years and knew that she must now be almost ten years old—the whore had had her when she was little more than seventeen years old. And now she was a schoolgirl in her sweet, convent uniform, so full of life, yet so shy with her daddy, a man she rarely saw.

*And she was the living image of Catherine.*

It was all Eileen could do to stop herself from rushing over and snatching the child up in her arms, to cover her little face with kisses, to steal her away from that woman.

She watched as her husband's whore suddenly held up her hand, and said with such a joyful smile, 'Hang on, darling'—*darling* to *her* man— 'I can hear the phone. You and Mary sort out the taxi and get Ellie's bags, and I'll go and answer it.'

Ellie, her name was Ellie.

Such a pretty name for such a heartbreakingly beautiful little girl. She hadn't known her name before. There'd been no one to ask. Everything

255

Eileen knew about her had been found out by standing behind half-closed doors when Mary was over from Ireland to see Gabe, sneaking looks at notes in pockets when sending clothes to the laundry, and listening to whispered phone calls.

The worst part of it had been all those other people knowing. It didn't bother Eileen that they were probably laughing at her stupidity and foolishness. No, it was knowing that they could tell her so much about the child, but that she wasn't able to ask them. And it hurt even more since Catherine had died. Hurt so much it drove a knife through her heart; made her ache like she had a stone in her chest and a lead weight in her stomach.

A brief moment later, the whore was back outside on the step, and this time not looking nearly so happy. In fact, she looked as if she had just been slapped around the face.

'It's for you,' she called to Gabriel, who was taking his change from the cab driver. Her voice was low, measured, but Eileen could still make out every single word.

'Me?'

She nodded. 'It's Luke.'

'*My* Luke?'

She nodded numbly and stepped aside to let him into the hall.

\*　　　\*　　　\*

'Sorry to call you when you're round there, Dad.'

'I don't want to even start discussing the ins and outs of that right now, boy. Just tell me what the fuck you want and then get off this phone.'

256

'You said you wanted to talk to Harry Kessler.'

'I said I was going to tell him a few things.'

'That's right. To sort this all out.'

'Luke—'

'Dad, I've contacted him for you.'

'*You've done what?*'

'And he's agreed to come to the yard to see you. Half ten, Monday morning.'

'He's *agreed?*'

'Dad, I bet he's as wild with those boys of his as you are.'

'Luke, I don't think you begin to realise what someone being wild really means. But if you don't get off this phone, *now*, you'll realise a lot sooner than you could imagine. Now don't you ever, ever, call me on this number again. Do you understand?'

'But Dad—'

'Listen to me, Luke, because I don't intend repeating myself. I'll swallow seeing the no-good bastard now you've arranged it. Because I don't want one of my family being made to look a fool. And I'll even give him a fair hearing, waste time listening to his crap and his lies. But, I swear on this, son: if you tell anyone about me being here— *anyone*—I promise you, you'll regret it for the rest of your life. *Got it?*'

*     *     *

Gabriel sat alone in his office, his face set like a hollow-eyed Celtic carving. Harold Kessler had just smarmed and shrugged and spread his arms through a ridiculous two hour meeting.

Kessler was going to give his boys a talking to, tell them what was what, sort it all out, and everything was going to be hunky-fucking-dory . . .

Brendan had stormed out in disgust, and Luke had gone running after him, calling for him to stop, but Brendan wouldn't listen. He just jumped in his car and screeched out of the yard.

Kessler had made some smartarsed comment— *boys, eh!*—that made Gabriel want to stub out his cigarette on the man's fat, smug face. Then he'd laughed, and he'd fucking shrugged—again—and he and his poxy sons—flashy, over-confident Daniel, and the shifty looking younger one, Sammy—and that aggravating arse of a nephew of his, Maurice, had left.

And now what was he left with? Another compromise for the sake of so-called peace. That's what.

Gabriel could hardly believe he'd actually agreed to give them another chance.

And why had he done it? Because he'd let a tearful Rosie, *Rosie of all people*, for Christ's sake, persuade him that peace was better than the alternative, and that she wanted the father of her child, the man she loved, to stay safe.

Well, if this was peace, he'd hate to see what war with the bastards would be like.

He should have talked to Mary about it, not Rosie.

No, hang on, no he shouldn't. What the hell was he even thinking? He shouldn't have talked to anyone. He never used to; never used to take any notice of anyone but himself. He was Gabriel O'Donnell, head of the family, the boss, number one, a law unto himself.

And now he was giving that stupid fuck another chance.

*For the sake of peace . . .*

He reached for the Jameson's. He hardly knew what to think any more; all he knew was that he needed another drink.

A bloody big one.

# September 1961

# CHAPTER SEVENTEEN

The man dug his fingers deep into the rigid knots of muscle in Gabriel's neck, and then worked his hands up and down his soap-slicked back.

Gabriel didn't flinch, didn't swear, didn't even try to make himself more comfortable on the marble massage slab. He was too incensed to be able to register anything other than his hatred of the Kesslers and his anger at what they had done— what they had so contemptuously dared to do. After he had given them that final opportunity to behave—an opportunity in the name of fucking peace . . .

When the masseur indicated that he had finished his routine by stepping away from Gabriel and collecting up his sponges, soaps and scrapers, the seven men—Gabriel, Brendan, Luke, Pete Mac, Barry Ellis, Kevin Marsh and Stephen Shea— secured their towels around their waists, and made their way through to the refreshment room of the municipal baths. Gabriel visited the baths every Wednesday morning, because he could. Because he, unlike lesser mortals—the mug punters, who spent their Wednesday mornings in factories, workshops and offices—was the one who decided what he did with his time. But on this particular Wednesday morning his sense of superiority, his knowledge that he was in control, while others were being controlled, had been shat on from a very great height. By the Kesslers.

And he didn't like it. He didn't like it one fucking bit.

The seven men sat on wooden loungers waiting for the tea and toast they had ordered. Their toast would come topped with the various combinations of eggs, beans and tomatoes offered by the baths' tiny kitchen. Usually, the snacks were a simple but enjoyable treat. And usually, the post-steam relaxation time would have been easy and companionable, interspersed with occasional jokes and wise cracks, and maybe with coded discussions about bits of business that had to be attended to, but not today. Today felt drawn out. A void waiting to be filled.

It was, as it was so often, Pete Mac who cracked first.

'Well, you know what they say, Gabe.' His voice echoed round the high, white and green tiled walls of the bathhouse like that of a Tyrolean yodeller in full throat. 'After the Lord Mayor's show comes the shit cart. And this time it looks like it's Kessler who's driving the fucker.'

Gabriel was just about to shout at his son-in-law to stop his non-stop, bloody aggravating, idiotic, bollocks-for-brains, smart mouthing, but a man came into the room, unknowingly saving Pete Mac from Gabriel's temper.

The man was wearing a white knee-length apron over baggy shorts and a vest, and was holding two plates of double poached eggs on toast, decorated with dainty slices of tomato and sprigs of cress. He smiled pleasantly and held out the plates for inspection so that they might be identified and claimed by their rightful owners.

Slowly, and without fuss, Gabriel took a deep breath, rubbed his hands together then folded his arms and jerked his head at the door for the man

264

to get lost.

The man hesitated for a brief moment. Tentatively, he experimented, putting down a single plate of food on one of the wooden side tables.

Still without a word, Gabriel swiped at it with a sweep of his arm, sending it crashing onto the duckboarded floor. Soft, orange-yellow yolk dripped down between the slats.

The man decided, pretty sharpish, that discretion was definitely the better part of valour, and he left, taking the remaining plate with him, closing the door with the faintest of clicks.

At last, Gabriel spoke. 'Almost a year he's been back here in the East End. And for nearly all that time I've tolerated the donkey's arse. I've let him get away with his stupid, niggling little tricks, turning a blind eye, pretending I've not noticed his pathetic, two-bob scams. Nearly a whole. Fucking. Year.' Gabriel sat on the edge of the wooden lounger shaking his head. A man disappointed by his own stupidity. A man proved right in his own misgivings about his misplaced generosity.

No one in the room felt like disagreeing, or even agreeing with him for that matter. Not even Pete Mac.

'I've put up with them and I've kept my mouth shut. I must have been out of my bloody mind. I can't believe I've been so stupid. I let that bastard have the world. And what thanks do I get for it? How does he repay me? He pisses all over me and takes a fucking, diabolical liberty. That's how.'

Gabriel's forehead furrowed into a deep frown, as if he were trying to make sense of it all. 'I even cocked a deaf ear when it was obvious he thought he was tucking me up over the betting shops. And then there was all that shit about why he came back to Stepney. Worried about more riots? Bollocks he was. I knew all along he was scared off when Rachman moved in. Well, he's gonna be in for a shock. He's gonna think that that bloke and his henchmen are fucking nursemaids by the time I've finished with Harold Kessler.

'Kevin, pour me a whiskey, and go through it again. Properly. Bit by bit. I don't need figures, just the ins and outs.'

Looks were exchanged between the other men in the room as Kevin fetched a bottle and Gabriel's preferred Waterford crystal tumbler from a black leather holdall in the corner of the room.

They often enjoyed a snifter stirred into their tea after a steam, but this was different. And if Gabriel was about to get drunk and go potty about the Kesslers, then it was probably best he did so in private. Brendan stood up quietly, went over to the door, stuck his head outside, and said something that the rest of them couldn't make out. Then he shut the door again and wedged a chair firmly under the handle.

Kevin handed Gabriel his drink. 'Right, let's see,' he said, 'we all know that there's been plenty of whispers, talk about the Kesslers thinking of branching out, that they fancied making money from this new game, this minicabbing lark—'

'Tell me,' Gabriel cut in, 'did I stop his fucker of a son getting into bed with the Bermondsey lot? Did I say a word when they opened their betting shops? Complain they were taking away my business?'

'No, Gabriel,' said Kevin automatically.

Pete Mac's mouth was open before anyone could stop him. 'No, that ain't right, Kev. Once the betting shops started coming in, Gabe said he didn't want anything to do with them. He said the street pitches were okay—no books, no taxes, no betting duty. But the shops . . .' He turned to Gabriel. 'I remember it clear as day. You weren't interested. Said they could get on with it. They could have them. And anyway, if you ask me, the shops'll never amount to anything. Not in the long run. Dingy rotten holes. You wait and see, most people'll agree with me in the end. Everyone prefers the street corner pitches or going down the track. Nice day out, few drinks, something to eat. Much—'

Brendan was on his feet. *'For Christ sake, Pete.'*

'What?' Pete Mac looked hurt.

'First of all, it was you what said—'

*'Shut up. All of you.'* Gabriel threw back the rest of his drink. 'Listen to Kevin, will you. I don't care about the fucking shops. I just know I never gave them permission to do this minicabbing. And I want to know what's behind it. There must be some reason they'd risk upsetting me. There must be something. Something I should be having.' He held out his glass for a refill. 'I know Kessler's got lairy, but not even asking my permission . . .'

Kevin poured him another drink and waited until he was sure that Gabriel had finished speaking. Only then did he continue.

'The honest truth, Gabe, is that I've heard it's gonna turn out to be more than a good earner.'

Gabriel looked to Stephen. 'What do you think?'

'Sorry, Gabe, I can do whatever you want me to do with a motor, but you know what I'm like on the

267

business side.'

'Take a guess then.'

'All right, if you really want my opinion, and if I'm being honest, I can't see it. I mean, would you trust some bloke you didn't know, in a motor you don't even know was his, or insured, or in decent nick, to take your wife home from shopping up the West End? Course not.'

Kevin ventured on. 'But that's not the half of it. You've got to think it through, to understand how it can work.'

'Have we?' Pete Mac sneered and was ignored by everyone.

'You see,' Kevin continued, 'it's not only the cabbing itself that brings in the dough—although that shouldn't be overlooked. There's plenty of money out there. Times are good. So there's more and more call for taxis and that. But it's the sidelines that can be *really* profitable—and useful. That's why I reckoned it *w*ouldn't do any harm to consider it as something we should be getting into.'

Gabriel stretched out on his lounger, the whiskey beginning to relax him—just as it always did until he went over the edge of drinking too much of the stuff. 'Tell me, Kevin, these sidelines. What would they be now?'

'There's all sorts, Gabe. Cabs taking the high-end tarts to their punters—'

Pete Mac grinned. 'Tell you what, lads, I'll volunteer to drive that shift meself.'

Again they paid no attention to him. 'Moving the strippers round the circuit, making sure they don't moonlight—we all know the serious sort of dough the strip joints are bringing in these days. Then add in shifting the blue films and dirty book stock about. And we all agree that's gonna be bigger than any of us ever dreamed of, a right bloody goldmine. And then there's collecting the takings from the spielers and the drinking clubs. Very discreet, nice and quiet.' Kevin laughed, unable to believe the beauty of it. 'Can even do that with legit punters on board. And the cab office itself, that's sweet as a nut. That could be used as a sort of central office. Use it for taking "bookings" if you like, for any of the other businesses. Good cover for all kinds of things—even setting up the odd long firm. Especially as you've been talking about wanting to get out of using the scrap game as a front, Gabe. So, I reckon, whatever way you look at it, setting up a minicab office is not only a good idea, but it's got the added bonus that you could close the yard down, soon as you like, and not miss it one little bit. And that's why it's all the more important to have it all tied up, nice and watertight, right out of Kessler's thieving hands.'

Kevin hesitated, weighing up whether he should carry on.

Why not? Gabriel was wild with the Kesslers, not him. He was only being helpful, and he'd be doing Brendan a favour by planting a few little seeds . . .

'And, of course, there's the final icing on the cake, the cabs could give us a very tasty little screen for delivering drugs.'

Gabriel narrowed his eyes. 'I've never had anything to do with that filth, and I never will. You know that, Kevin Marsh.'

Kevin added hurriedly. 'I know what you've always said, Gabe, but this is different. It's not any of that bad stuff, it's just these pills and that. Bet it's not much different from that blood pressure

269

gear you get from old Stonely. And it's all the go in the clubs and dance halls and that. I'm telling you, straight up, it ain't nasty. I mean, even my old girl takes it. Brilliant stuff. Me dad says it cheers her right up. You can—'

Gabriel spoke over him, staring into the middle distance. 'A bit of respect, that's all I expected from them. If they'd have asked, it might have been different. I might have said, open the business. Not big time, but go ahead. But what do they do? They think they can fucking mug me off without me saying a word.'

He stood up and started pacing. 'I don't know who they think they are, but I'm telling you this. We're going in to this minicabbing, and they're getting out of it. We're having it all. Every single bastard bit of it.'

He hurled the half-empty tumbler at the wall, smashing it off the tiles. 'I'll show them break my rules. I'll break their fucking necks.'

Luke's mouth had gone very dry. 'Dad, do you really want to do this?'

Gabriel's answer was to turn to Stephen Shea. 'Did you drop Eileen anywhere today?'

'No, Gabe. When I phoned, she said she was taking the little 'un out to the park.'

Gabriel looked at Barry Ellis. 'Go and find Mrs O'Donnell, Barry. Get her home. Now.'

Stephen Shea stood up. 'I can get her if you like.'

'No, you're all right, Stephen. I've got something I need to discuss with you.'

Pete Mac couldn't resist it. 'Why send anyone, Gabe? Why don't you just call her a minicab? I bet Kessler would do you a good deal.'

270

As had become their habit, whenever the weather was as fine as it was on this lovely late summer day, Sophie Kessler and Eileen O'Donnell were spending a couple of hours in Victoria Park, enjoying the fresh air and the rare luxury in the East End of a green, open space. They were sitting on a bench in the children's playground. Eileen was holding onto the handle of a high-wheeled Silver Cross pram as she and Sophie watched three young children busily working away in the sandpit with their swirly-patterned rubber buckets and spades.

'When Harry first said I should meet up with you, Eileen, that I should make friends, it'd be good for business—you know what he's like, organising everyone—I really wasn't sure about it. I thought we might go shopping once or twice. But this,' she smiled fondly, 'this isn't what I expected at all.'

'A lot of things haven't turned out how I expected in life, Sophie. Do you know, my Catherine's been gone nearly a year.' She closed her eyes and crossed herself. 'May God rest and keep her soul.'

Sophie took Eileen's hand. 'Let's hope you see no more trouble.' She craned her neck to peer into the pram at the sleeping baby. 'And, thank God, you have the gift of young Caty.'

Eileen took a pack of du Maurier's from her handbag and offered it to Sophie. 'Cigarette?'

Her hand hovered over the packet. 'I should be getting back, to do a few jobs, but it's such a lovely day. Oh, go on then.'

She and Sophie lit up and, sat smoking in

companionable silence, watching the children playing.

'Is Rachel feeling any better about her news yet?'

Sophie blew smoke out of her nose and huffed. 'Hardly. All she keeps going on about is losing her figure and turning into an old woman before her time. Why does she think my boy married her—to be a fashion plate? He wants children, a family. I'm telling you, she needs a lesson, that one, on what it means to be a Kessler. On what it means to be a proper wife. But I don't think she'll ever be like one of us.'

'Young women think differently nowadays.'

'Differently? You're right there. Honestly, Eileen, since the day she found out it's probably going to be twins, she's been acting like she's lost her mind. A blessing like that and she weeps and wails like a mad thing.' Sophie bent forward and stubbed out her cigarette on the gravel. 'I'm popping in to see her later this afternoon.'

'Give her my love, and tell her I'm thinking about her.'

'I will, Eileen, thank you. Right after I've given her a good talking to about the ridiculous names she's coming up with. You should hear them. What's wrong with traditional names? Proper names? And I know she needs her rest, but I think she might be turning out to be lazy. She could be getting things ready, but she just sits about doing nothing and then complains the time's dragging.' She shook her head. 'It's not fair, is it? For her it's dragging, but me, if I had another twelve hours a day, I still wouldn't have enough time to do everything I have to.'

'But you'll find plenty of time for those babies.'

'Course I will.'

Eileen stood up to adjust the blanket over her sleeping granddaughter. 'You should see the boys with Caty. Not six months old and she already has them eating out of her hand. I worry sometimes that we might be spoiling her.'

'You don't spoil your children by loving them, Eileen.'

'No, but you should see the things they bring home for her. I reckon it would be good for her to have a brother or sister, so she could learn to share. And Patricia shouldn't wait too long before thinking about the next one. It's not good to have too big a gap.'

Sophie laughed. 'So, you fancy another grandchild, eh, Eileen?'

Eileen wrinkled her nose good-naturedly. 'I admit I do keep hoping. And a grandson would be nice. Still, there's plenty of time and it's her and Peter's business. I'd never interfere.' Her smile broadened as one of the children in the sand pit, a little fair haired girl, wagged a chubby finger at the two small boys she was playing with, instructing them on the proper way to create a sandcastle even though she was barely big enough to lift the sand filled bucket.

'But it doesn't stop me from hinting that I think she should get a move on. Still, I'm lucky that Patricia lets me have Caty as much as she does.'

Sophie chuckled—a light, girlish sound for a woman who was now officially in her forty-first year. 'And our children are lucky having mothers who are happy to mind their children for them. I know I'm lined up for having the twins as soon as

273

Rachel brings them home. Giving her time to go to the hairdresser's and to the gown shops—or whatever they call them these days.'

'Mrs O'Donnell.'

Eileen and Sophie both turned round.

Eileen frowned. 'Barry? Is something wrong?'

Barry Ellis gate-vaulted the metal railings and strode over to the pram. He smiled down at the sleeping child and picked her up. 'I'm taking you and Caty home, Mrs O'Donnell.'

The baby's eyes opened and her face began to crumple into trembling, teary folds.

Eileen tried to take her from him, but he wouldn't let her go.

'Barry, what's going on? You're frightening her. You're frightening me.'

'Sorry, Mrs O.' Barry started striding away. 'Orders from the boss.'

'How about the pram?'

'Sorry, it won't fit in the car. We'll have to leave it.'

Eileen spoke to Sophie over her shoulder as she hurried after him. 'I don't know what this is all about. I'll give you a call.'

Sophie was on her feet. 'You get off, Eileen, I'll wheel the pram round to mine and you can collect it later.'

'But it's a long way,' puffed Eileen, trying to catch up with Barry and her granddaughter.

'A long way? What d'you think friends are for?'

# CHAPTER EIGHTEEN

Brendan checked his now collar-length hair in the rear view mirror, pausing for a moment to admire his new look, then threw open the driver's door, got out of the Jag and took a lungful of autumn air. He smiled—a man pleased with himself and his lot. 'All right, lads, time to put on the show.'

Luke, Pete Mac, Kevin and Barry followed him round to the back of the car, and waited while Brendan opened the boot and handed each of them a meat cleaver and a short-handled lump hammer. The last in line was a reluctant-looking Luke.

Pete Mac narrowed his eyes at his brother-in-law and released a sharp, disdainful breath. 'Not got the wind up have you, Luke?'

Luke wasn't so much scared as terrified—not by what they were about to do, but by where it all might end—the almost inevitable outcome of more blood being shed, and war being declared between the families. 'We shouldn't be doing this.'

Brendan put his hand on his brother's shoulder. He was a man who wasn't going to let anything or anyone stop him. Not even his brother. Not now. Nor would he have him sowing seeds of doubt in the minds of the others. 'Hold up, Luke, what am I thinking of, mate?' His voice was light, almost playful. 'Give us them things here.' He took the knife and hammer from his brother and tossed them—*who could care less?*—back into the car. 'I'm so revved up, I'm getting myself all confused. We've got to have someone make them calls. Might as well be you, eh?'

Pete Mac looked from Brendan to Luke and back again in slack-jawed amazement—*you what?* —while Kevin and Barry avoided looking anywhere but down at the pavement.

'Here, cop this.' Brendan took a canvas bank bag full of coins from the boot. 'You're on phone box duty while we sort out the drivers on the late shift. All right?'

'Brendan—'

'I said, *all right*?'

*      *      *

Brendan bowled up the black and white tiled path of the tall, three-storey house in Burdett Road. He was followed by Pete Mac, Barry and Kevin. Not one of them made any attempt to conceal the tools they were carrying.

Brendan rat-tatted nonstop on the knocker until the door was opened by a woman wearing a crossover apron and a turban; she was carrying a scrubbing brush in her chapped and reddened hand.

'What the bloody hell d'you think you're up to—' she began, her words drying as she saw the cleavers and the hammers that the four men were holding as nonchalantly as if they were knives and forks.

'Get your old man out here,' said Brendan. 'Now.'

'But he's having a kip, he's on—'

'Lates. Yeah, we know, darling. Just get him.' He stuck the hammer in the jamb and pulled his lips back in a travesty of a smile. 'And don't even think about trying to shut that door on me.'

The woman disappeared along the passage, and they heard some mumbling and cursing from a room at the back of the house, and then some accusatory screaming in reply.

Brendan was just beginning to grow aggravated by the delay when a man appeared in the hallway. He was wearing a tatty striped dressing gown that didn't quite meet across his gut—a belly that must have cost him a fortune to have cultivated to such proportions—and which gave them a full, unwelcome view of his greying Y-fronts, his sagging string vest, and his hairy, drooping breasts.

'So, Mr Wade,' Brendan began politely. 'You're doing the late shift for the Kesslers.'

The man, not the brightest of souls, smiled craftily, showing a set of brown and rotten teeth that made Brendan take a step backwards even though he was well out of reach of the man's no doubt stinking breath. 'Why d'you wanna know? Got a bit of private for me, have you?'

'No, I've not got a bit of private for you, I've got a warning. This time it was your tyres . . .' Brendan used the paper-thin, sharpened cleaver to point over his shoulder to the man's Consul that was parked on the street behind them. 'Next time . . .' He flicked the knife forward and hooked it into the web of the man's string vest. 'Who knows what might get slashed? And I'll tell you what, a little tip for you. If I was you, I'd be careful if you've been claiming on the sick, or on the old Nat King Cole, while you've been driving for that mob, because you know what people are like, don't you. They get jealous and the fuckers go and grass you up.' He shook his head sadly. 'People, eh, Mr Wade. It'd be

277

a right bugger though, wouldn't it, if you did get bubbled? I mean, I can just imagine how hard it must be to survive on them poxy handouts in the first place, but being nicked cos you was claiming, and all . . . Well, that'd be a double dose of bad luck, now wouldn't it?'

Brendan shook his head in sympathetic solidarity, and then turned to address his three menacingly silent companions. 'Here, I've had a great idea.'

He turned back to Wade, who had finally cottoned onto what was happening, and was just about ready to fill his Y-fronts. 'I reckon if you wasn't working for the Kesslers, then you'd probably be all right. And,' he grinned happily, a man with a brainwave, 'you're never going to believe this. I might even know of a proper cabbing job you could have. With a decent firm and everything. Our firm. The O'Donnells. I'm sure you've probably heard the name. And I might be able to get you a deal on four new tyres.'

'Look, mate—' Wade began.

'Mate? I'm not your fucking mate.' Brendan was on the man before he knew what was happening—drawing the blade of the cleaver down his cheek with one hand and aiming the two-pound hammer through his front window with the other.

Wade's wife, who had been spying on events from behind the net curtains, screamed and bawled in terror as the glass exploded into the room, and the hammer went whirling past her and smashed into the radiogram that stood against the far wall.

Wade swiped his hand down his face and looked stunned at all the blood. 'I've got kids in there.'

'And I said, *I'm not your mate.* All right?'

'But if I . . .' he whined, his words petering out as he realised he had no idea how he was going to finish his miserable, feeble sentence. In fact, Wade was so slow that, until he felt the blood trickling down his belly, he hadn't even cottoned onto the fact that Brendan had swiped the cleaver down his string vest, slicing off his left nipple like an unwanted blemish on a ripe fruit.

'What the fuck have you done to me?' he bleated.

The four men answered him by turning away and walking off down the path.

Brendan paused at the gate as he heard Wade's wife begin cursing and yelling at her husband.

He looked over his shoulder at the now shocked and blood-streaked man, who was still standing on his doorstep as if bidding farewell to his unexpected visitors.

'She's got a right gob on her, your old woman, ain't she, Mr Wade? So, if you do make the sensible decision and come and work for us, you will make sure she don't ever come near the office or phone us up or anything, won't you? Cos we don't want her spoiling the tone of our business, now do we?'

\*　　　\*　　　\*

Just as the young woman looked up to see what all the noise was about, the door flew off its hinges and came smashing into her desk; it was immediately followed by four aggressive looking men barging into the tiny Brick Lane office and surrounding her.

Her eyes were wide with surprise and alarm, but when she spoke there was a tough confidence in her voice that she'd learned from being dragged up in a family where any sign of fear could earn you a battering.

'Oi, you,' she demanded, looking from one man to the next. 'What the hell do you think you're up to? Mr Kessler'll skin your arses for you when he sees that door.'

'Fuck Mr Kessler,' said Brendan evenly. 'Now, if you know what's good for you, get out.'

'But I've got cabs to send out.'

'Are you stupid?'

'No, I'm not actually. Here . . .' She stood up, sticking her little fists into her waist. 'Are you anything to do with these calls I've been getting all afternoon?'

Brendan put on a mocking, puzzled face. 'What calls would they be then, sweetheart?'

'For moody jobs, that's what. *All bloody afternoon* I've been getting them. I've been sending cars all over the bleed'n' shop. And there's never any passengers when they get there. And two of the drivers got jumped when they got to the addresses I was given.'

'What a shame,' said Brendan shaking his head. 'Now fuck off.'

'I said, I ain't stupid. It was you, wasn't it?' She gathered up her things, pushed past a grinning Pete Mac, and tottered out of the office on her black patent heels—*keep looking confident.* 'And I'm telling you,' she shot over her shoulder. 'Mr Kessler's gonna go raving mad when I tell him you kicked that door in, and what you did to his business today.'

Brendan winked at her. 'Aw, I do hope so, babe. And you won't forget to tell him it was Brendan

280

O'Donnell what did it, will you?'

'No, I won't forget.'

'You sure you got the name right? Brendan O'Donnell. And take a good like at me mooey and all, while you're at it. I want you to be able to pick me out when Kessler shows you me picture in his photo albums of special friends.' He walked over to her, grabbed her by her upper arms and gave her a shake. 'So, let's see how really clever you are, shall we? What's me name?'

'Brendan O'Donnell.' She was in pain, but she kept her chin up high and her voice strong and steady.

'Good. Very good. And remember, tell him that Brendan O'Donnell said: Challenge us would you, you cunts? Excuse my language, darling. And say we've had a little chat with most of his drivers, cos we're running the minicab business in this toby from now on.' Another wink. *'O'Donnells's Car Services.* Got a nice ring to it, ain't it? And we've got a nice office and all. Not that far from here as it happens. Just round on the Bethnal Green Road. A sight better than this shithole.' He let her go, and shoved her staggering backwards, smack into the filing cabinet. 'But then what would you expect from the Kesslers?'

'You bullying pig,' she muttered, rubbing her shoulder.

'Save your breath, love, and, if you know what's good for you, you wanna wire in and get out of here.' Brendan turned to Kevin Marsh and held out his hand. 'Petrol can, please, Kev.'

\*          \*          \*

281

Brendan took his pint from Barry, and raised it in salute to him and Kevin. The three men were elated, and the only three men in the whole, tatty Hackney Road pub not even glancing at the blank-eyed girl on the stage, who was see-sawing one of her grubby, stiff-footed black stockings back and forward between her legs in a desultory imitation of bringing herself to a climax.

They had far more exciting things to get off on.

Kevin took a long slow swallow of his Guinness and decided it was time to introduce a note of caution. 'You really are stone-bonking positive Pete Mac and Luke don't know about this, are you Brendan?'

Brendan raised his glass again, closed his eyes and lifted his chin—a grin illuminating his handsome face. 'I told you, Kev, I'm absolutely fucking positive.'

'I'm sorry I'm being so twitchy, but you know I've never felt right about Pete Mac. It's the same with all them MacRiordans. Mouths bigger than the Blackwall Tunnel, the lot of them. And as for Luke, he's got no, you know, interest in this sort of thing . . . Aw, you two know what I mean.'

'We do, Kev, we know all too well, mate. But don't worry, it'll all be fine.' Brendan couldn't stop his grin widening. 'And if this supplier is as good as he reckons, we're going to be busy boys—very rich, busy boys. So, drink up, lads.' Brendan's voice was now artificially stiff, formal. 'I need to sort out a few things with Dad for the morning. And we've all got an early start.'

\*       \*       \*

282

Pete Mac threw back the covers, plonked down his feet on the sticky, matted surface of the bedside rug with its faded image of a collie dog, and raked his fingers up and down his stubbly pink chops.

'Come back to bed, Petey. Please?' She dragged out her words through, what were for him, her almost unbearably sexy, pouting lips.

'Don't do this to me,' he whimpered in reply as she rubbed her chubby little hand over his stiffening penis. 'You know I've got to get back home tonight.'

Violet was a dookie mare, didn't even know the meaning of housework, but she had the sort of round, soft body on her that Pete Mac had always dreamed of, and she never, ever complained about anything. And she loved him, the dozy cow.

'And I've got to make some business calls, Vi. You know they can't manage without me.'

'You are so clever, Pete.'

He kissed her lightly on the top of her bleached and matted beehive and padded over to the phone that was half hidden by all the lidless bottles and jars that cluttered up her dressing table.

His call was answered almost the moment his finger left the dial. 'What's going on tomorrow, then, Brendan?' he said, only half paying attention, as Violet was now stretched out on the bed in front of him. She licked her fingers and then slowly and deliberately began massaging herself to a far more convincing climax than the stripper had managed in the pub where Brendan had been drinking with Barry and Kevin just an hour before.

Pete Mac gulped.

'You still there, Pete?'

'Er, yeah. Anything I need to know about?'

283

'You're joking, right? And while we're at it, where did you disappear to tonight?'

'Thought I deserved a break. After all the effort I put in today. Fifteen drivers' houses we went round.'

'Right, and so you decided to spend a bit of time with your wife and little girl, did you?'

'Yeah.' Pete Mac's voice had reduced to a low, ecstatic groan.

'Yeah, sure you did, you lying fucker. Now, you just kiss that soapy tart Violet *night, night* and get round ours. Right away, Pete, I'm warning you. We've got plans to go over for the meet tomorrow.'

Violet was now using both hands.

'But, Brendan,' he said thickly, 'it's nearly ten o'clock.'

'Are you arguing with me? Do you really want me to have to tell Patricia what you get up to when you go amongst the missing all the time?'

Pete Mac slammed down the phone and stared at it. He was fed up with being treated like an idiot by them hypocritical fuckers.

He strode over to the bed, pulled Violet's hands away from her crotch and rammed himself into her.

Two minutes later he was getting dressed.

'Sorry, Vi, got to go, darling. Duty calls. You know what it's like. And I've gotta pop home for a bit, or she'll only get the hump if I don't show me face again.'

Violet sat up and pulled the creased and grubby sheet up to her chin. 'That wife of yours is so mean to you, Pete. So spiteful.'

'Yeah, I know, girl. She's a right bitch. Here.' Pete Mac put his hand in his pocket and chucked two fivers on the bed. 'I know it's not the same as

284

me staying over, but you treat yourself tomorrow to one of them baby doll nighties I like you in.'

He pulled open the bedroom door. 'And make sure it's a red one. One of them you can see through.'

## CHAPTER NINETEEN

Gabriel O'Donnell blew on his hands, rubbing them together to get them warm, as he led the way through the stable yard. He strode past the row of ragmen's pony stalls, his breath vaporising in the air, and on past the grander trotting racers' boxes, then along the path, and out onto the open marshes.

Although they were no more than a few hundred yards away from the traffic on the A13, the early morning Thames-side scene that stretched out before them could have been set in the heart of the countryside. The sky was a muted, duck egg blue, tinged on the horizon with pink and yellow, and the mist lay low over the soft, tufted grass, making the elegant trotting horses that were being exercised in their full, gleaming rigs look as if they were wading their high stepping way through a pale grey sea.

As one of the big-wheeled sulkies sped past them, Gabriel raised his eyebrows in approval. 'Nice bit of kit that, Stephen, light and fast. And the bay pulling it, he's a real beauty. Worth keeping an eye on for the next big race.'

Stephen Shea nodded. 'That's Micky Lee's rig, one of the travellers who winters over Canning Town way. They've got some good horse flesh between them all right.'

Gabriel and Stephen came to a halt by a line of vans that had all been parked facing in the one direction to form the edge of an improvised flapping track. Halfway along the line, a wiry youngster in his early teens was perched on a stripped down, lightweight scrambling bike, ready and eager to rev up and drag the lure for the assorted lurchers and greyhounds that were howling and yelping through the wire-reinforced windows in the backs of the vans. Even the existence of the lures—dead and bloodied rabbits, safely stowed away in a sturdy wooden chest on the back of a flat-back truck—wouldn't be apparent after the event, the bodies having been thrown to the dogs both as a training reward and as a means of disposing of the evidence. If everyone did their job—and they would—there wouldn't be a single clue that the illegal meet had ever taken place at Burton's Farm. Although such thorough precautions were probably a bit excessive, as no one without relevant business of some kind or other would be visiting the place, and that included the police.

Run as it was by a loose network of characters—best avoided unless you were either family, an invited guest, or, at the very least, known to be 'sympathetic' to their way of life—Burton's was a very private place. And the likelihood of some innocent civilian stumbling on it by mistake wasn't exactly likely. Especially not with the size of the bull mastiffs that were chained to the main gate.

By the vans, huddles of men were standing around smoking, talking, and placing bets with Kevin, who had arrived an hour earlier, when the mist had been more like a fog, and when it was still barely light. Some of the men were smartly dressed like Gabriel and his companions—suits, shirts and ties, velvet collared overcoats, neat, freshly brushed hats—while the others were more casually attired in rough working clothes, but with flashes of gold on their hands and wrists, and across their ill-matching waistcoats. And every one of them seemed to have plenty of money to place on the first race of the morning.

Gabriel pulled his collar up about his ears and stamped his feet. 'It's a grand morning, Stephen, and more fun than hanging about in some betting shop. More profitable too. Nice big bets, no records, no taxes.' He looked about him, savouring the fresh air. 'But I can't say I'm not worried about leaving things back at the yard and the cab office.'

'Don't worry, Dad.' It was Brendan, who had just strolled over, with a smile on his face and a lurcher straining on its leash. 'Anthony's at the yard with some of the lads and Luke's keeping an eye on the cabs. And not even the Kesslers would be stupid enough to try anything with the blokes I've left there watching the place.'

He jerked the yelping dog back to heel with a sharp rip of the lead. 'And Luke's got young Sherry to look after him if things get really rough.'

Gabriel snorted. 'It's not a joke, Brendan.'

'I know, but as well as the heavies, there are at least half a dozen drivers in and out of there who could throttle a bloke with one hand if they had a mind to.'

'Maybe.'

'Come on, Dad, relax, have a bet, pretend you don't know what hound's gonna win.'

'Talking of hounds, where's that Pete Mac got to again?'

Brendan was wondering that himself. After the ear bashing he'd given him last night he thought even silly bollocks MacRiordan would have got the message to toe the line for once. 'Probably spending a bit of time with Pat and the little 'un.'

'Yeah, course he is, son. And Kessler's gonna just ignore the fact that we torched his cab firm yesterday afternoon.'

\*     \*     \*

Pete Mac had actually been up and dressed since seven o'clock that morning, unusually early for him. Since becoming a father he rarely stirred before nine, making sure he left all the baby lark to Patricia. But today, as he parked his car near the synagogue at Stepney Green, it wasn't even a quarter to. He was parking there because it was just a short stroll from where he was going to prove to the O'Donnells that he was a man who could handle himself, and that he deserved a bit of respect for once. In fact, after he'd finished today, they wouldn't be able to ignore him or laugh at him—not any more they wouldn't.

He left the car and walked round the corner, stopped a few yards from his target and pulled out a packet of Capstan Full Strengths from his coat pocket.

A big, serious looking bloke was standing by the gate. He'd expected some sort of minder, but this one was a great big bugger. Typical that, little blokes making up for their own shortcomings with oversized foot soldiers.

288

As casually as he could manage, Pete Mac stuck one of the cigarettes in his mouth, and then made a performance of patting his pockets with his left hand. It made him look as if he were putting out some weird, peripatetic fire that had taken hold in his clothing.

He then walked on, but paused by the man at the gate, leaned forward slightly, and said, 'What an idiot, eh? Forgot me matches. You ain't got a light on you, have you, mate?'

The man narrowed his eyes for a brief moment, weighing up the situation, and judging Pete Mac to be just a passing prat, said in reply, 'Sure.' He pulled out a sizable Ronson lighter that looked like a toy in his huge hand, and charged it up.

Pete Mac knew he had to act quickly, before the man realised what was going on, and before he, Pete Mac, had the chance to bottle it. He pulled his right hand out of his pocket and smacked the man full in the face with a heavy brass knuckle-duster.

Automatically, the man raised his arms to protect his head, and Pete Mac slammed him in the kidneys, sending him staggering into the railings.

Pete Mac started speaking at Olympic speed before the big bastard had a chance to gather his wits about him. 'I'll mark your card, mate. We can do this one of two ways. You either piss off and disappear, or I'll lift my right hand like this—' he began to raise it '—and ten big angry Micks'll be by my side before you know what's hit you. Oh, and nine of them think you've been screwing their old woman.'

The man spat, aiming the gob right by Pete Mac's feet. 'Think I'll leave you white folks to it.'

Pete Mac, the adrenaline kicking in, ushered him

grandly onto the pavement—'A wise choice, sir'—
then swaggered up the path and smacked the flat of
his knuckle-dustered hand, just the once, on the
front door.

Sophie, who was sitting at the kitchen table
drinking tea with her daughter-in-law, was
immediately on the alert. Harry had warned her
that there might be some sort of trouble, and had
insisted that Daniel and Rachel came to stay with
them. And Rachel hadn't stopped moaning since
she'd shifted her lazy arse out of bed . . .

Another knock.

'Who's that at this time of the morning?' wailed
Rachel. 'Daniel said Lincoln would knock three
times if he wanted to speak to us.'

Sophie pulled her housecoat around her and
lifted her finger to her lips. 'Just keep schtum for
me, all right?'

Another single knock. 'Sophie, I'm scared.'

In truth, so was Sophie, but her pride and her
protective instincts were stronger. 'Rachel, darling,
don't worry yourself, all right? It'll be Lincoln
wanting the lav or something. If you're really
panicking, pop upstairs to my bedroom. There's a
phone on the bedside table. Give Danny a call.
And I'll go and have a look round the front room
curtains and see who it is. Then I'll be right up. Go
on. Hurry yourself.'

The knocking grew more insistent.

Sophie smiled. 'There, I knew it'd be Lincoln.
But you go on up anyway. It's time we got ourselves
dressed.'

She saw Rachel safely up the stairs and walked
along the hall towards the front room where she
could get a good look at what was going on, and

see if it really was Lincoln making so much noise.

She made it halfway along the passage when one of the glass panels of the front door at first cracked and then shattered inwards.

She ducked and screamed, but then her hand flew to her mouth to stop her noise, as a man's hand covered in gingery hairs, reached inside and flailed around searching for the latch.

Not knowing where she found the courage, Sophie sprang forward and shot the bottom bolt before the man could undo the latch.

'For fuck's sake,' she heard him complain. 'If that's the way you want it.'

Sophie stood there, appalled, now convinced she'd never be able to move from that spot, as he kicked and shouldered the door.

It soon began splintering around the lock, and then, as if it were little more than matchwood, it crashed back against the wall, wood and glass shards gouging into the embossed wallpaper like knives.

Pete Mac grinned happily to himself. Brendan wasn't the only one who could bash in a door.

Sophie took no more than a few seconds to register the face of Eileen and Gabriel's schlub of a son-in-law coming towards her, and her power of movement rapidly returned.

Deciding she would be better off making a dash for the safety of the front room and it's heavy, panelled door, rather than trying to reach the stairs—*please God, he might not even realise Rachel was up there in the bedroom*—she flung herself back along the hall.

It was the wrong decision.

She crashed into the pram that had been

291

cluttering up the hall waiting for Eileen to collect it, and went sprawling onto the floor. Pete Mac grabbed her by the arm, dragged her to her feet and shoved her into the front room.

Now he was in there with her, and it was him who was shutting the door. Locking her in there with him. And he was undoing his flies . . .

Sophie grabbed hold of the mantelpiece, not sure if she was going to vomit or pass out.

Pete Mac saw the look on her face as he released his penis from his underpants.

'Don't kid yourself, you silly old cow,' he sneered as he released a dark, steaming stream of urine into the dried flower arrangement adorning her carefully polished fireplace. 'As if I'd want to dip me wick in what you've got to offer,'

Pete Mac sighed contentedly. 'That's better,' and tucked himself back into his underwear. 'Now, where shall I begin?'

'Why are you doing this?' Sophie's voice cracked with fear.

He was about to tell her to shut her mouth when he thought about how Brendan had behaved yesterday, about what he'd said to the bird in the Kesslers's cab office. How it had made him look the right business.

He folded his arms—the big, brave man. 'The name's Peter MacRiordan. Remember me, do you darling?'

Sophie shook her head, pretending she didn't. Hoping that was the right thing to do.

It wasn't.

He looked angry. 'Well, you should, you stupid mare. We met at that posh club, Gabe took us to. And I was really nice to you. Talked to you and everything. But you offended me. Do you know that? Treated me like I was a prick. But I suppose that's just natural for the likes of you; that you think I'm just the oily rag.' He stuck a finger in her face. 'Well, I ain't. And you'll remember me now though, won't you? And you'll tell your aggravating little squirt of an old man that no one, *no one*, ever messes with Peter MacRiordan.'

'Please, I don't feel well.'

'You don't feel well? What is it with you women? Always fucking moaning about something or other. I'll show you don't feel well.'

He paced around the room, picking up things and letting them fall to the floor.

He hated the fucking place. It was the sort of front parlour he'd never had as a kid, but that people like this always had. The sort of place that was so *nice*. Stuffed full of poxy photos and little fancy, stupid ornaments and all that shit; chairs you weren't allowed to sit on in case you squashed the sodding cushions; and a bastard piano. Who the fuck needed a piano when you could have one of them hi-fis? It wasn't as if the arseholes couldn't afford one.

He knew the type of kit he'd get himself if he had their sort of money—he'd have one of them bachelor pads. But while he wasn't exactly short of a few bob, he had expenses. A lot of expenses. Violet's flat for a bloody start.

Maybe when Gabe saw what he was capable of he'd start giving him a fairer whack, a decent cut in the business. When he'd finished here, Gabe'd have to take him seriously then, all right.

Quite calmly Pete Mac strolled over to the piano and lifted the lid. He reached inside his overcoat and took out the hammer that Brendan had given him the day before to put the frighteners on the drivers. Then, with his tongue poking out between his lips to aid his concentration, he began to systematically work his way along the keys.

Sophie, trembling in the corner, and with her back to the wall, knew this was her chance.

Keeping her eyes fixed on him, she felt her way slowly along the wall towards the door. Waiting for the hammer to fall, to disguise the sound of the handle turning, she slipped out into the hall and shot up the stairs.

Pete Mac, absorbed as he was in trying to destroy the piano, kept his focus on the job, but he did speak, or rather he shouted. 'Don't worry, darling, I ain't stupid. I'll be up to see you later. And perhaps you might look a bit more attractive in a different nightie. Red's me favourite colour if you was wondering.'

\*       \*       \*

It took Sophie an agonisingly long couple of minutes to persuade Rachel to open the bedroom door to her, and, when she eventually let her in, Sophie was ready to strangle her. But when she saw the fear on her daughter-in-law's face she could only hug her.

'Have you phoned Danny yet?'

Rachel shook her head. 'Couldn't.'

'That's all right,' Sophie sounded relieved. 'Now don't worry.' She put her hands on Rachel's shoulders and looked her steadily in the eye. 'Now, you sit yourself over there.' She steered her gently in the direction of a pink Lloyd Loom chair by the window. 'Okay?'

Rachel nodded, her lips pressed tightly together.

'Good. Now I'm going to move the dressing table in front of the door, and then I'm going to work out what we're going to do. Okay?'

Another nod. 'Yeah.'

Thank God someone was.

*        *        *

Despite it being barely a quarter past nine in the morning, Gabriel had already swallowed almost a whole hip flask full of whiskey, and had really started to relax, especially as everyone seemed to be having such a good time. The big men over from Ireland were already asking when the next meet was going to be, and Kevin had taken a sack full of dough. Not bad for a few hours enjoying yourself in the fresh air on a fine autumn morning.

Maybe he should think about retiring or at least spending more time over in Kildare at the stud farm. He could get Rosie a little cottage somewhere close by and she could see more of young Ellie.

It wasn't as if Eileen could care less if he wasn't around so much. All she cared about was Patricia, the baby, her precious boys, and visiting the bloody cemetery all the time. It was morbid, that's what it was. The way she carried on, it was like she was the only one who had ever loved Catherine. The only one who mourned her. What had she said to him when he'd told her to stop being so miserable? He thought for a moment, but couldn't quite remember —it would have been something nasty and bitter. But he was clear on one thing: he was a man, a

295

successful man, and a man with needs. He didn't have to put up with her selfishness. In fact, he might pop round Rosie's later, have himself a few drinks and get himself a bit of affection for a change.

*       *       *

'There,' puffed Sophie. 'That should do it.'

Unused to any work heavier than stripping the beds ready to be collected by the laundry van, Sophie was out of breath from the exertion of dragging the dressing table, her husband's tallboy, and the bedside tables, over to the door.

She'd have felt more secure if she'd have been able to add the wardrobe to the barricade, but she knew her limitations. 'Now, let's think. What next?'

Rachel was cowering in the chair, her shoulders hunched, her knees up to her chin, and her arms clasped round her legs. 'Listen to all that noise he's making. Why don't the neighbours do something? Why doesn't someone come and help us?'

Sophie knew exactly why. This was the sort of neighbourhood where the likes of the O'Donnells and the Kesslers weren't interfered with. And if one of the O'Donnell mob had the hump with the Kesslers, then that was their business. Sensible people stayed well out of it.

'They must be out, love,' she said brightly. 'You know, shopping and work and that. But someone's bound to be back soon. Here, you're looking a bit pale, why don't you stretch out on the bed and try and get a bit of rest? Stop worrying yourself, I'll see to everything.'

Sophie stretched the phone lead as far away from the bed as it would go, cupped her hand over the receiver and whispered, hoping that Rachel wouldn't be able to hear the fear in her voice.

'Eileen?'

'Sophie, I'm really sorry. I know I should have come round for the pram—'

'Eileen—'

'Really. I hope it's not in your way, but Gabe's practically had me and Pat prisoners, these past—'

'Eileen, this is *not* about the pram. It's Peter MacRiordan. He's downstairs, and he's—'

'He's what?'

'Let me finish, Eileen, please. I'm telling you, he's downstairs destroying my home. And me and Rachel are stuck up here in the bedroom, with the furniture blocking the door. And I can't phone Harry. He'll just come flying home and kill him stone dead. You know how he is. And then he'll kill me for letting him in after what happened yesterday.'

'You'll have to slow down, Sophie, I don't understand. What happened yesterday?'

'There was a bust up. The boys set fire to the cab office—'

'No, that can't be right. Luke's there right now.'

'No, Eileen, *your* boys set fire to *our* office.'

'Jesus, Mary and Joseph.' Eileen crossed herself. 'How about Danny? Can't he stop him?'

'I thought of that. But can you imagine what he'd do to him when he realises how he's upset Rachel. Eileen, I can't have my husband or sons getting in trouble over him. Please, just get someone round here to come and take him home. Please.'

'Okay, I'll—'

'Oh, Eileen,' Sophie interrupted her. She sounded close to tears 'I've just had a thought. Say he recognises the pram down in the hall, and thinks I've got Patricia up here with me.'

'He wouldn't recognise his own daughter unless she was in her mother's arms.'

Sophie flinched as another loud crash reverberated through the house and Rachel started whimpering like a baby. 'Eileen, the man's going mad. Just get us someone round here. *Please.*'


## CHAPTER TWENTY

Eileen was shaking as if she had a fever. She didn't understand what Pete Mac was up to, but she knew she had to stop him. He might have been a fool, but he was a big fool. And the thought of the sort of damage he was capable of inflicting made her feel sick. And the trouble that he'd cause if either Harold or his and Sophie's boys turned up and caught him there.

But Eileen didn't want her boys involved either. This whole business was complicated enough as it was. She'd just have to get hold of Gabriel.

But finding him was another matter.

After phoning everywhere else she could think of, all Eileen had left was the cab office. It was a long shot, but maybe Luke knew where he was.

'Sherry, put Luke on.'

'Sorry, he's not here at the minute, Mrs O. Try a

bit later.'

'Listen to me, Sherry, I need to get in touch with Mr O'Donnell.'

'Sorry, can't help you.'

'I'm not messing around, Sherry.'

'Give us a break, Mrs O. You know what he's like. He'd go off his head.'

'And *I'll* go off my head if you don't tell me.'

'But he'll sack me.'

'Sherry, who do you think got you that job in the first place? And how many chances do you think an unmarried mother like you would have of getting a decent little number like you have there? Sitting in a nice clean office, answering the phone, and chatting to big handsome drivers all day. Think about it, Sherry.'

Sherry Driscoll rolled her eyes. If only Mrs O. knew the half of it. She'd been in the job just one week, since the day the cab office had opened, and she'd already witnessed all sorts of goings on. There were the toms and the betting—they were obvious—but there were other things, things she hadn't quite worked out yet. And that was without the four great big blokes Eileen's old man had posted outside the office because of something— again, she didn't know what—that had kicked off yesterday.

But none of that was Sherry's business, so, of course, she'd never mention it. And anyway, she didn't want to upset Mrs O. She was all right. She'd known Sherry since she was little, and had never looked down her nose at her like the other neighbours. Not even when she had the baby. In fact, it was Mrs O'Donnell who'd persuaded her husband to give her the job in the first place . . .

She took a deep breath. 'He told Luke that if anything happened, he'd be over the flapping track.'

'Right. And where's that?'

'That's all I know Mrs O. I swear on my little one's life.'

'Okay, Sherry, thank you. You're a good girl.'

She laughed. 'But not as good as I should have been, eh, Mrs O'Donnell?'

As Sherry put down the phone, Luke came into the office swinging a carrier bag from the baker's next door. 'Breakfast,' he announced, holding the bag up for inspection. 'What d'you fancy?'

Sherry giggled, flapping tracks and the threat of Gabriel going bonkers at her temporarily forgotten. 'Anything'll do me, Luke, you know that.'

Luke smiled at her. 'Got just the thing,' he said, fishing out a white paper bag from the carrier. 'Two lovely, big fat doughnuts.'

His smile widened as she took them from him as eagerly as a child. He felt great, so much better than he'd felt for ages. Brendan had promised him that he'd kept his word yesterday—that not one of the Kesslers' drivers had been hurt. Just warned off till it was all sorted out. And Luke couldn't have been more pleased. He'd said all along that that was the right way to go about things. Beatings and slashings got them nothing but more violence. But now it was looking as if Brendan had come round to his way of thinking at last, and could see that things could be dealt with by acting like civilised adults rather than mindless animals.

And who knew, maybe, eventually, Harold Kessler could be persuaded to cut his losses, and pack up and take his family—including that prick

Maurice, with a bit of luck—back over to West London.

Luke was even looking forward to getting more involved in the business if it could be more like this minicabbing lark.

And there was another reason to feel pleased with the world. He liked spending time with young Sherry. She was funny, clever, and certainly much better company than he usually had to put up with.

He looked at her, as she smiled up at him, licking her sugary lips with the flickering tip of her little pink tongue. She was pretty, really pretty. And nice. He couldn't help wondering if, with someone like her, he might feel different.

If it was an illness, like they said it was, then surely it could be cured. It wouldn't be like it was with Nina, that brass from the Bellavista. Sherry was different.

She giggled at him over the top of her doughnut as jam oozed out and dripped onto her chin.

His smile faded.

Who was he trying to kid?

\*   \*   \*

Eileen was still trembling as she dialled the number, praying it would be Sean Logan and not Mary who answered.

'Hello, there.'

She instantly recognised the ponderous tones of her husband's slow-witted brother-in-law. Thank goodness for that; he wouldn't even think of questioning her.

'Sean, hello, it's me, Gabriel's Eileen.'

'Eileen! How are you, love? Well are you?'

'I'm just grand Sean, but—'

'I'll get Mary for you, shall I?'

'No, no you're all right, Sean. You don't need to go bothering Mary. It's just that me and young Luke here are trying to think of that place where you all went flapping that time you were over.' She put a light little laugh into her voice. 'Sure, isn't it driving the pair of us mad trying to remember.'

Silence.

'You know, Sean.' For Christ's sake did the man have spuds for brains? 'The flapping track, with the lurchers and the betting.'

'Oh, the flapping. Of course. I remember. Wasn't that a great day?'

'And it was *where*, Sean?'

'Burton's Farm, down on the marshes. Beckton way. Where they keep the ragmen's horses and the trotters and pacers. Nice feller that Gerald Burton. A real gentleman. Came from over here originally, you know. Kerry, I think it was. Or it might have been Wexford. No, I tell I lie, it was—'

'Sorry, Sean, I have to go.' She had the receiver back in its cradle before he had the chance to take her any further round the map of the Republic.

Her mind was on places closer to home, but far more inaccessible. How the hell was she going to get to Burton's Farm?

She let out a humourless breath of laughter. She'd take one of their bloody cabs, that's how.

Yeah, they'd be queuing up to take her to interrupt their boss while he was doing business.

She'd just have to be careful how she went about it.

She picked up the phone again.

302

Sophie could hear Pete Mac moving along the hall towards the living room at the back of the house. She could only hope he had enough things left to smash, that he wouldn't grow bored and come up after them before someone came to stop him.

She stared at the phone, willing it to ring. Why hadn't Eileen called back?

She called her number again, but it was engaged.

She flicked a quick glance at Rachel. She was so pale it was beginning to frighten Sophie. If something happened to her or the twins she'd never forgive herself.

It was no good; she'd have to call someone else. But who? It had to be someone who could calm the situation.

Harry or the boys would go stark raving mad at such a lack of respect, and she really didn't want them involved, but what choice did she have?

*     *     *

Downstairs, Pete Mac had decided that all his exertions had made him a little peckish, so he stomped through to the kitchen that led off the living room at the very back of the house.

He opened the pantry in the corner, and tossed a few packets of this and that over his shoulder, scattering their contents over the blue and white vinyl floor tiles.

'What the hell's all this shit?'

He lumbered back along the hall to the bottom of the stairs and shouted at the top of his voice. 'Don't suppose you've got any pork pies have you, darling?'

This was it. He was at the bottom of the stairs. She had to do something fast. She snatched up the phone and rang the haulage yard.

*     *     *

Eileen dialled the cab office again. 'Sherry, it's Mrs O'Donnell, I—'

'Mum. Is that you? It's me, Luke. Are you crying? What's wrong?'

*     *     *

Just twenty minutes later, Eileen had been grabbed by the shoulder and was being steered by a very angry Gabriel away from the track towards the stable yard at Burton's Farm. Groups of men cast sly glances at them, wondering what possible reason a wife could have for turning up at the flapping, and why O'Donnell didn't have better control of her.

Brendan, Kevin and Barry just made sure they busied themselves with other things.

'Did you send Peter over to Sophie Kessler's home?' she demanded, as she tripped over the hummocky grass in her totally unsuitable court shoes. 'She has Rachel with her for God's sake. A young pregnant woman. And he's going mad round there, smashing the place to pieces. I had no choice, I've had to send Luke to see what he can do, but you'll have to go round there and—'

He stopped suddenly and swung her round to face him.

She could smell the booze on his breath, could

304

see the high colour of his cheeks. His blood pressure would be through the roof again. She wondered how she could have been so foolish as to think there was any point in coming here, in even trying to talk to him.

'You're a stupid woman, Eileen.' He was walking towards her, looming over her, driving her backwards into the stable yard. 'First of all for even thinking I'd send Pete Mac to do something like that, when we all know he has shit for brains, but worst of all, you're more than stupid for sending Luke round there after him.'

'What else could I have done?'

'Why would you think a pathetic mummy's boy could do a man's job?'

'Don't speak about him like that.'

'Stop protecting him, we all know what he is.'

'What, a decent boy, who hates all your bullying and lies?'

Gabriel shook his head. 'He's the one who's living a lie.'

Eileen felt years of resentment bubbling up inside her. 'What lie's that then? That he has a secret mistress just like his loving daddy?'

Gabriel grabbed her again, this time with both hands. 'What filth has that boy been telling you?'

'Nothing. Neither of the boys has told me anything. Neither of them even realise that I know about the dirty slut. They've been protecting you for all these years. Don't you understand?'

'You're lying to save him as usual.' He pushed her away from him, sending her staggering sideways into a stable door, and causing a ripple of whinnying alarm through the horses. 'Now, get out of my sight. I've got work to do.'

Eileen felt her mouth go dry. He couldn't mean it. 'But what about Sophie? And Rachel?'

'I'll sort it out when I'm good and ready.'

\*     \*     \*

The telephone calls that Sophie and Eileen had made to their sons were just minutes apart, but Luke's Mini had been no match for Daniel's Jaguar—or for his incandescent rage at the thought of Peter MacRiordan going anywhere near his mother and his pregnant wife.

Daniel reached the house a good ten minutes before Luke. He jumped out of the car, leaving the engine running and the door swinging on its hinges without so much as a backwards glance.

Pausing for a teeth-gritting moment by the smashed front door—*the door to his parents' home*—he took in a deep, angry snarl of breath and barrelled into the hall.

He found the bastard sitting at the kitchen table—*his mother's table. And he was fucking eating.*

\*     \*     \*

As Luke hovered on the front doorstep he could hear loud, male hollering and grunts from somewhere at the back of the house, and female screams and wailing from somewhere upstairs.

With the first prayer he had uttered since Catherine's funeral playing on his lips, Luke ran along the hall towards the kitchen.

Pete Mac was curled up on the floor, moaning in pain, as he tried to protect his head from the tyre lever that Daniel Kessler was using to beat him.

306

Luke launched himself across the room at Daniel. 'Stop it. Leave him alone. You'll kill him.'

Daniel whipped round and smacked the lever across Luke's shoulder.

'Don't, Daniel. Stop! There are women upstairs. Can't you hear them screaming? Stop it.'

'I'll give you fucking women upstairs.' Flecks of saliva showered from Daniel's mouth and his arms flailed around as he lashed out again at Luke.

Biting his lip to stop himself yelling from the pain, Pete Mac dragged himself over to the table, and hooked the lump hammer from off the chair, where he had left it while he was eating. Then he hauled himself back across the floor, and, using all his remaining strength, he swung it back and caught Daniel right behind the knees with the full length of the handle.

Daniel roared in anger and surprise, and went down like a prize fighter with a glass jaw.

Luke wasn't sure how he managed it but, somehow, he heaved Pete Mac out to the Mini, and got him away from Daniel before his adrenaline had him back on his feet and he started attacking them again.

*     *     *

'Honestly, Mum.' Luke flinched as Eileen dabbed iodine-soaked cotton wool on his bloodied cheek. 'Sophie and Rachel are both fine. They never even came downstairs. I swear they didn't.'

She glared at Pete Mac who was slumped in the carver chair at the head of the kitchen table. His face was a pulpy bloody mess, but she had no sympathy with him. 'Fine? How can they be fine

with that maniac on the loose? If I was a man I'd—'
She froze at the sound of the street door opening
upstairs, and Gabriel and Brendan chatting and
laughing about the money they'd made and how
they could do with a decent fry up after their
morning on the marshes.

'At least try to sit up straight,' she hissed at Pete
Mac. But he was in too much pain to listen.

Gabriel stopped at the top of the stairs and
stared down into the kitchen. 'What the fuck's
happened to you two?'

'I tried to tell you,' said Eileen, collecting up the
basin of bloody water, the cotton wool and the
iodine off the table. 'I knew there'd be trouble.'

He moved slowly down towards them. 'Who did
this to you?'

Pete Mac lifted his head with a groan; one of his
eyes had closed completely, and there was a wide
gash across his eyebrow like an open, rosebud
mouth. 'Danny Kessler.'

Gabriel dropped down onto a chair, leaned
forward, and banged his tightly curled fists on the
table. 'So, stopping their cab firm wasn't enough of
a message for them. And they think they can get
away with this do they? Making a fool of me.'

He looked over his shoulder at Brendan, who
had sat himself halfway down the stairs. Brendan
knew his father well enough to understand that,
when he was in a temper, being well out of arm's
length was the most sensible place to be.

'Brendan, go and find Stephen Shea. Tell him to
drop whatever he's doing. Say that the job I talked
to him about—the plans have changed. I need it
seeing to right away. *Right away*, got that? And tell
him I haven't had the chance to go and get the gear

off Welsh Billy. He'll have to collect it himself.'

Brendan was immediately on his feet and heading back up the stairs, glad to be getting away, but with no idea as to what was going on.

Why didn't he know about this job the old man was talking about? And Welsh Billy? He was the bloke who supplied the explosives and detonators for all the big blags; he got quality stuff from his old contacts in the mines and sold it all over the country. Everyone in the game knew Welsh Billy.

But no one had even so much as mentioned anything about a bank job to Brendan.

\*   \*   \*

The reason no one had mentioned the job was because Gabriel wasn't planning one. He had other plans for Welsh Billy's specialist supplies.

## CHAPTER TWENTY-ONE

'Look, Rach,' moaned Daniel. 'I know it's gonna take a while to get over the shock, but can't you at least try to get some sleep?'

He was on his side, rolled up tight as a winkle in its shell, with the bedclothes pulled up over his head, trying to shield his eyes from the light, while Rachel sat there next to him, bolt upright, drinking yet more tea, and with yet more tears spilling down her pale drawn, cheeks.

He didn't get it. They were back in their own home, on the far side of Stepney Green, well away from Harold and Sophie's place. They had Joshua and Winston sitting outside the house in Joshua's car, ready and waiting to deal with any trouble— and still she couldn't bear the thought of having the lights out, even with Daniel there beside her.

And now he was seriously in need of some sleep.

'Look, love, you know Joshua ain't like that Lincoln—who I swear I will kill if I ever set eyes on again. And Winston, he's a right good bloke and all. Sweet as a nut, the pair of them. You're safe. Trust me. Now come on, you must be as knackered as I am. Why don't you close your eyes for a little while? You'll feel much better if you get a bit of kip. And it'll be good for the babies and all.'

Rachel's chin wobbled. 'It's not just being scared,' she said, putting down her cup, and turning her head so he couldn't see her fresh crop of tears. 'And I am tired, but . . .'

'So, what is it? Why don't you tell me?' He was no longer bothering to hide his irritation. 'Come on, Rach, what the bloody hell's the matter here?' He threw back the covers and dragged himself up against the headboard. 'Just tell me. What the fuck's up?'

Rachel began weeping loudly and miserably.

Here we go, more snivelling; Daniel was really getting annoyed now. All right, she'd been scared stiff by that fucker MacRiordan, but, when all was said and done, he hadn't gone anywhere near her. The prat probably never even realised she was there. So, what was wrong with her?

He rubbed a hand across his sore, red-rimmed eyes. 'Rachel. Please. I'm sorry I swore at you.' He put his other arm round her. 'And, I promise, I won't ever let anyone scare you again. All right? And when I've finished, they're not gonna know what's hit them. And, may I drop down dead if I'm lying, they will never, ever go anywhere near you again.'

'I told you,' she whimpered, swiping at her tears with the back of her hand. 'It's not just that horrible pig breaking into your mum's.'

'Then what is it?' He was now really having to fight to keep his voice even and his temper under control.

'You don't . . .' She paused for a big snotty sob.

'. . . fancy me any more. You're always out.' She was now wailing loudly.

'Yeah, out working.' He put his hand gingerly on her swollen belly. 'Working for you and the babies.'

'That's not true, Danny. You can't stand the sight of me any more. I'm all fat and ugly. I know I am.' She drew in a deep, shuddering breath. 'And you don't love me.'

'Course I love you.' Daniel pulled her close, desperate to stop her noise. 'I've just been busy that's all.'

'Do you really love me?'

'Yes.' He pressed his lips to her forehead. Even though he was exhausted, he was also a bit ashamed of himself. It wouldn't hurt to pay her a bit more attention. She was such a pretty girl; a bit dopey maybe, and certainly not much cop indoors as far as cooking and cleaning was concerned. But that was okay, he hadn't married her for her brains, and they had the money to get someone to do the cleaning and that for them.

'Here,' he breathed into Rachel's ear, tickling her and making her smile through her snotty, juddery tears. 'You still getting them cravings for, what was it? Cream cheese platzels?'

311

She shook her head. 'Chopped herring beigels,' she said, somehow oddly shy with her husband. 'The ones they do at the top of Brick Lane.'

'All right,' he said, pinching her cheek as if she were a baby. 'I'll go down Brick Lane and get you one right now. No, two. How about that?'

Panic flashed across her tear-stained face. 'No, Danny. Don't leave me here by myself. Please.'

'All right.' He stroked her hair gently. 'Stick your coat on over your nightie and come with me.' He smiled and winked. 'So long as you don't tell Mum I was out driving on a Friday night.'

'But it must be nearly midnight. And how about your knees?'

'My knees are just fine,' he began, punctuating his words with little kisses planted all over her face. 'And if my beautiful, sexy, gorgeous wife wants a beigel . . .'

\*      \*      \*

Daniel guided Rachel tenderly down the stairs, out of the front door and along the path to his Jaguar. It didn't cost anything to be nice, did it? And if it meant he could get some shuteye into the bargain, well, that was a right win double wasn't it? All bets paid, everybody happy, thank you very much, ladies and gentleman, and goodnight.

He was just about to nip across the street and have a word with Joshua, to let him know where they were going, when Rachel let out a little yelp of anguish. 'It's my bag! I forgot my bag!'

'Blimey, Rach, you gave me a right turn. And what d'you want your bag for? I've got money on me.'

'It's not my handbag I want, it's my other bag.' Her eyes were pleading with him. 'My special bag. For the hospital. It's got all the things they said I've got to take with me.'

He stepped back in alarm and goggled at her stomach. 'Here, you've not gone and . . .' He lifted his gaze and looked into her eyes. 'Have you?'

'No, course I've not. I've got weeks to go yet. But say I do go into labour? Please, Daniel, get my bag for me. *Please*? They said I had to have it with me. Just in case.'

'All right.'

She smiled, relief flooding through her. 'It's up by the bed.'

'You don't have to tell me, Rach. I've tripped over the bloody thing every night for the past three months.' He handed her the car keys and pecked her on the lips, even more relieved than she was. Her going into labour—that would have put the right bloody tin lid on the night, that would. 'You get yourself inside the car in the warm, beautiful, and I'll be one minute. Okay?' He pointed to a metallic blue Zodiac parked discreetly across the street, well away from the glare of the streetlights. 'Josh and Winston are over there, keeping an eye on things.' He flashed a double thumbs-up at the car. 'Okay?'

She nodded. 'Okay.'

\*     \*     \*

Rachel eased herself slowly into the passenger seat of the Jaguar and shivered. The bright, cloudless day had left a really chilly night in its wake. She'd have to see if Daniel could get them that central heating put in before the winter started, like her Auntie Becca had up in her new flat. Some people moaned about being moved into the tower blocks, but Rachel couldn't understand why. The flats were fantastic, all light and airy, and the council certainly hadn't skimped on the mod cons. She wouldn't mind a nice new place for herself, once the twins were born. Somewhere out in Essex maybe. Anywhere would do, really, so long as it was a long way away from Danny's family—especially his interfering old cow of a mother.

With much huffing and grunting Rachel stretched across and slipped the key into the ignition. She'd get the heater running and have the car warmed up in no time, all ready for Danny. And she'd try and be a bit more understanding about his job. It wasn't his fault his dad made him work every hour God sent. And if she gave in—just a bit—then so would he. And they'd have everything worked out to suit them for once. Instead of his rotten mum and dad.

As she turned the key, something on the floor caught her eye, making her pretty forehead crease in bewilderment, but, before she had a chance to organise her confusion into coherent thought, there was a blinding flash of light followed by a loud whoosh of air.

The explosion could be heard over half a mile away.

Rachel and her unborn babies hadn't stood a chance, and, despite Daniel's belated, guilt-driven good intentions, her marriage hadn't either. The last thing Rachel had seen in her short, not very fulfilling life, was a skimpy pair of scarlet, lacy knickers poking out from under Daniel's seat.

They belonged to Nina.

What Rachel—or Daniel for that matter—hadn't seen, was that both Joshua and Winston were slumped back in their seats in the Zodiac, and that both of them had had their throats slit from ear to ear.

*       *       *

Stephen Shea went out to the car to fetch the last of the shopping, while Sheila put the kettle on. He knew they'd needed piles of food when the kids were still at home—there had always been a houseful of their mates wanting something to stuff into their teenaged empty caverns of bellies—but five bags full for the weekend, just for the two of them? She'd bought enough grub to feed the street.

He smiled to himself. She'd always liked to keep a good table had Sheila, and, he had to admit, he was looking forward to one of her classic belt busters of a Sunday dinner tomorrow. Roast fore rib of beef with all the trimmings, Yorkshire pudding, and a nice little dob of horseradish on the side. Smashing.

It made his mouth water just thinking about it.

He was bending down with his head stuck in the boot, making sure that nothing had escaped from the final two bags, when the hand clapped over his mouth.

'Let me mark your card for you, Shea,' someone hissed into his ear. 'No fuss or the boys'll have to go in and have a word with your missus. A serious word. They're behind me, ready to go in there right now to make sure you don't make a fuss. Got it?' As he spoke, the man was stroking Stephen's throat

315

with a long, thin blade.

He nodded carefully.

'Very sensible. Good. Come on then, we're going for a little ride.'

\*　　　　\*　　　　\*

Sheila looked up at the kitchen clock. What was Stephen up to now? If he didn't hurry up the tea would be stewed and he hated that. He'd either be chatting to some kids playing outside, handing over all his loose change for them to go and buy sherbet dabs from the corner shop; or one of the neighbour's motors would be playing up, and he'd be out there with his head under the bonnet getting his decent clothes covered in grease, fixing it for them. The trouble with her Stephen was he couldn't say no to anyone.

Well, she'd have to say no for him. She took off her apron—Sheila wasn't the sort to go out in the street looking untidy—and went outside to bring him indoors.

\*　　　　\*　　　　\*

She didn't get it. What was going on? The car boot was wide open, the last of the shopping had disappeared, but there was no sign of him.

'Michael,' she called over to a blond-haired, scabby-kneed ten-year-old, who was standing with a group of boys all trying to peep up the skirt of a girl who was swinging herself round a lamppost from a length of rope. 'Have you seen Mr Shea?'

'I never seen him,' said Michael, blushing the colour of a scarlet lollipop. 'And I never nicked no

316

shopping either.'

'I don't care about the shopping.' She marched over and grabbed hold of him by the sleeve of his jumper. 'Tell your mother you can keep it. All of it.'

'I never give it to me mum.'

'Just tell me, Michael. If you know what's good for you, and you don't want me to call the coppers, where's Mr Shea?'

Michael looked to his friends for support, but they'd all scarpered. His bottom lip started wobbling, as he thought about the hiding he was going to get from his mother for showing her up. 'There was these men. One of them had a knife. And we went and hid behind Teddy's dad's car till they'd gone, and I sort of took—'

'Michael.' Sheila started shaking and she felt her knees begin to buckle under her. 'Help me indoors. There's a good boy. To the phone. It's in the back room.' She summoned up all her strength. 'Now.'

\*　　　\*　　　\*

'I swear on my life that I had no idea that girl would be in the car.'

'That *girl* was my fucking wife.'

'I'm sorry, it was a mistake.'

'A mistake? So, it would have been okay if you just blew me to fuck, would it, you cunt?'

'No. It was on a timer. Set for the early hours. Something must have tripped it. Maybe the spark from the ignition.' Stephen was doing his very best to keep still; every time he moved, the ropes binding his naked body to the hard metal chair just seemed to get tighter. But he couldn't stop himself.

317

He gulped hard, trying to get some moisture into his dry, claggy throat. He had to try to work himself loose.

He'd worked out that they were in some sort of a lockup—bare brick, no windows, freezing cold. And from the noise over head, it was possibly in a railway arch. Or maybe down by the docks. But he didn't have a clue where.

'And it was all right for you to slit Joshua and Winston's throats was it?'

'I never—'

'Used something like this did you?' Daniel held up an old-fashioned cut throat razor.

Stephen felt totally humiliated as a hot stream of urine gushed from him, pooling on the indented seat of the metal chair, and soaking his legs in reeking degradation.

Daniel wrinkled his nose, flipped out a handkerchief from his top pocket and held it to his face. 'Here.' He handed Maurice the razor. 'Get him talking.'

Slowly and deliberately, Maurice began slicing a thin layer of flesh from the inside of Stephen's thigh.

The blade was so sharp that, at first, Stephen felt no pain, but then, as the urine trickled down onto the exposed tissue, he couldn't stop himself from crying out, from letting them know they were hurting him, that they had got to him.

Daniel paced up and down the small cramped space. 'Pain. Not good, is it?'

'No.' Stephen managed to gasp.

'So, how about the pain I feel? You murdering my wife? Killing my two babies before they was even born? Don't that count? Was that all right?'

'*No.*'

Daniel spun round and stuck his face up close to Stephen's. 'Tell me, I'm really interested. If it wasn't all right for you to do that, was it all right for that slag O'Donnell to order you to do it?'

'It was nothing to do with him. It was me. I did it.'

'But you said you never did Josh and Winston.'

'I didn't. I don't do things like that.'

'Then who?'

Stephen said nothing.

Maurice held up the blade to the bare overhead bulb, examining its edge. 'He's loyal, Dan, you gotta hand that to the cunt.'

'This is a waste of time.' Daniel turned his back on them and walked towards the door. 'Do him. We'll have the others later.'

He reached for the handle, but still not quite able to leave, he turned and watched as his cousin calmly and precisely removed his top clothes and put them on a hanger, which he then hooked onto a nail, before slipping into a pair of brand new pale blue overalls. He then began searching through a full-sized, carpenter's tool box.

Without turning round, Daniel opened the door just wide enough to leave, and said only loud enough for himself to hear, 'I'm glad you're my cousin and not my fucking enemy.'

*　　*　　*

Maurice whistled tunefully as he unloaded the newspaper-wrapped packets from the back of the van, and ferried them over to the high corrugated iron fencing that surrounded Gabriel O'Donnell's

319

scrap yard.

He grinned and winked at Sammy, who had collected him from the lockup in Silvertown, and who was now sitting, ashen-faced in the driver's seat.

'Not exactly them posh hounds that the Baxters told us about, eh, feller? Shame really. Still, the Alsatians'll just have to do, won't they?'

He lobbed another package over the fence, and peered through a small hole round a rusted rivet holding two of the sheets together.

'Pity I never thought to bring a camera, Sam, I bet your Daniel would have enjoyed a memento of this little scene.'


## CHAPTER TWENTY-TWO

Barry Ellis wrenched on the handbrake, and yawned: his head shuddering, and his jaw pulled down until it nearly touched his chest. 'Won't be long, Sand.'

'Good. You look worn out.'

'It was worth it.'

Sandy played it coy. 'D'you think so?'

'You kidding? How randy were you last night?'

'Been nice if we could've stay a bit longer, wouldn't it?'

'Babe, you know I promised Gabe I'd feed 'em this weekend . . .' Barry reached across and began stroking her thigh.

'Oi, you. Less of that. Get a move on and we can get home and have a little—' She lowered her chin and looked up at him through her lashes '—*sleep* before I get the dinner on.'

'Now look what you've done to me.' He took her hand and put it between his legs. 'How am I meant to get out of the car with this?'

Sandy smiled: a crooked, saucy leer. 'Who's gonna be around to see you at this time of a Sunday morning? In fact . . .'

Sandy had his flies undone and had her face in his lap before he even had the chance to answer.

\*       \*       \*

'Blimey, that sea air certainly got to you, girl. But you're gonna have to let me go, or them dogs'll wake up starving and start barking their heads off. Then someone'll complain, and Eileen'll get to hear about it. Then she'll have a go at Gabe cos she's always saying he's cruel to 'em. Then he'll bloody slaughter me for not being here to feed them last night, and for getting him in trouble with his missus.'

'All right, Bal, you don't need to write a list. I know. But you remember.' She winked and clicked her tongue at him. 'It's my turn when we get home.'

\*       \*       \*

After what Barry Ellis saw when he went in to feed the dogs he wasn't exactly in the mood to pleasure his wife. Not only did one of the Alsatians turn on him, ripping at his forearm, as it protected what was left of the freshly butchered meat it had been thrown the night before, but the sight of the other dog gnawing at what remained of Stephen Shea's half-eaten head was an image that would haunt

321

Barry Ellis's dreams for the rest of his life.

*       *       *

Sandy Ellis beckoned frantically for Anthony to get himself over to the car and to help Barry up the steps to the O'Donnells's front door. She had no idea what had happened—her husband certainly wasn't in a fit state to tell her anything. But she knew enough about his life to realise that, when things looked as if they'd gone as wrong as this, she had to get herself into the driving seat and get him round to Gabriel's as fast as she could. She'd driven once or twice before. She could manage. She had to.

*       *       *

'Whatever now?' Eileen, red-eyed and white-faced, was sitting at the kitchen table in her dressing gown, when she heard the urgent banging on the door. She lifted Scrap's head from her knee and went to see who on earth would be calling before eight o'clock on a Sunday morning.

*       *       *

'Really sorry to bother you, Mrs O'Donnell,' sniffled Sandy, as Anthony eased Barry onto a chair.

'That's okay, Sandra. You sit yourself down.' Eileen was distracted by the look on Barry's face. What was it? Fear? Disgust?

'I'll be outside, Mrs O,' said Anthony, happy to be leaving Eileen to it. 'Bang on the door if you

322

need me.'

'Right, thank you.' Eileen sat down, unable to tear her gaze from Barry's wide-eyed stare, waiting for him or Sandra to explain, as she absent-mindedly fussed Scrap, scratching him behind his silky ears.

But no one said anything.

'All right, Sandra,' Eileen said eventually. 'Are you going to tell me what all this is about? Or do you want to give me twenty questions?'

Sandy flicked a nervous glance at Barry. 'Is Mr O'Donnell up yet?'

'He's not been to bed, Sandra. None of us have.' She lowered her eyes, making a show of concentrating on Scrap. 'The boys're all out looking for Stephen Shea.'

A shadow clouded Barry's eyes. He covered his face with his hands and began weeping silently.

Sandy didn't know what to do, she just knew she wanted to give the responsibility of all this to someone else, to make this nightmare go away.

'Me and Barry, Mrs O'Donnell, we've been away for a couple of days. Down Eastbourne—only one night, mind—and we came back really early this morning, so's Barry could feed the dogs up the yard. Like he'd promised Mr O'Donnell he would. And . . . I don't really know how to say this. But, from what Anthony got out of him when he was helping him in from the car, I think Barry might have found him.'

From the top of the kitchen stairs, there was a loud cry of delight, as Sheila Shea, gasping with relief clapped her hand over her mouth. 'You've found my Stephen,' she said, through shaking fingers.

Eileen leapt to her feet, and Scrap—put out to lose his tickles yet again—lolloped over to Barry in search of a bit of fuss.

The animal-like scream from Barry Ellis, as soft old Scrap licked his hand, was the most heart-rending sound that Sandy would ever hear in her life.

\*　　　\*　　　\*

Brendan tossed down an envelope on the battered desk. 'There you are, Dad.' His voice was full of quiet rage. 'A nice tidy death certificate from Dr Stonely. And only a pony. Not a bad price to cover up the murder of a good and loyal friend. And I've told Ernie Carson we want a closed coffin. Not that there's much left to go in it.'

Gabriel, his head bowed, looked at his hands. 'These have dug holes, carried lumps of metal most men couldn't even lift, and they've beaten respect into people. They've earned us a good life. But what good is all that when your friends suffer?'

'No good at all, Dad. We've gotta finish this shit with the Kesslers once and for all, corner the pills market, and—'

Gabriel's head snapped up. 'So, it's drugs talk again is it? At a time like this?'

'Times are changing. It's you who always says that if we're not looking after the customers then someone else will be. And there's plenty of customers for this sort of gear. If we're not careful, we'll be leaving the way open for them cunts to step right in and take the lot. Believe me, Dad, I've—'

'Oh, I believe you, boy, but don't you dare start trying to get clever with me. I've said no, Brendan.

324

Over and over again. And I mean no. When I'm dead and buried you can run this business whatever way you want. Sell whatever shit you like to whoever you like. But while I'm alive, I'm in charge of this firm, and you'll do as you're told or you'll get out.'

'Maybe I will get out. I've just about had enough of all this.'

'Don't talk bollocks, Brendan.'

*     *     *

The Star and Compass was playing host yet again to a wake where the O'Donnells were in attendance. Although this time the funeral hadn't been for one of the family, it had been for what was left of Stephen Shea, and a lot of serious drinking had been done.

Brendan O'Donnell was sitting with Kevin Marsh and a hollow-eyed Barry Ellis.

Brendan was still fuming at his father's refusal to even give him so much as a proper hearing. 'So, it looks like we'll have to carry on as we are. Keeping it from him like we was fucking kids doing something naughty. I just don't get why he's so fucking pig-headed about it.'

'It's simple.' Kevin tipped his head back, and watched the smoke ring he'd just blown rise and disappear. 'He's getting on, Brendan. We're young. We can see the future. He can't.'

'Yeah, I suppose. But it means we'll have to think about other ways of getting ourselves bankrolled.' He reached across and helped himself to one of Kevin's cigarettes. 'I heard a whisper that Sammy Kessler and that clown of a cousin of his have set up some sort of a porn deal. That it's really earning. Perhaps it's time we thought about moving in on it. Taking it over. How do you fancy that?'

Barry Ellis took a deep breath and spoke for the first time. 'I'll do anything—anything it takes—to have them bastards.'

Brendan stood up. 'Time for another round, I reckon.'

*     *     *

Brendan went over to the bar and clapped his hand on his brother's shoulder. 'All right, Luke?'

'Great.'

'No need to be sarcastic. Now, what'll you have?'

'You're very chirpy, considering we're at a funeral. What you up to?'

'Nothing that need bother you, Luke. But you might like to know that I had a little chat with Dad the other day, and he said I've got to either do as I'm told or get out. You might like to remember that the next time you start whining.'

Luke put down his drink, turned to face his brother and looked him directly in the eye. 'Well, why don't you get out? Before it's too late. I don't know about you, Brendan, but I've had a bellyful of this. We're burying Stephen for Christ sake. *Stephen*. A week after the Kesslers buried that poor girl and her babies. And what happens next? Who's gonna get blown up? Chopped up? Shot to bits? What other lies are we gonna be expected to tell? What shitty story about how someone's died?'

'Luke—'

'No, I'm not listening any more. I think getting

out of all this is about the most sensible thing any of us could do.'

'Fine. Go on then. Do it. Go and earn peanuts. Wear cheap clothes. Go to the only clubs you'll be able to afford. The clubs where you won't be safe, where you'll get nicked.'

Luke could taste the bile rising in his throat and the sweat gathering in his palms. 'What rubbish are you talking now, Brendan?'

Brendan looked at him pityingly. 'And you've got the neck to talk about lies? You're a one-off, mate, you really are.' He shook his head in wonder, tightening the grip on his brother's shoulder. 'Listen to me, Luke, I know about you. Tumbled you years ago. But I don't care. You're my brother, and I love you whatever you are, whatever you do. But I ain't having you acting like some hedge-crawling tinker. You're an O'Donnell, Luke. Have some pride in yourself.'

'Let go of me, Brendan, before one of us says something he regrets.'

'Fuck you. You please yourself.'

'I will.'

'Good. Piss off then. Go on.'

Luke shoved past his brother and swerved his way through the crowded pub and out of the door.

Pete Mac, glass in hand and head still bandaged from his beating from Daniel Kessler, sauntered over to Brendan with a concerned smile on his face. 'You know what you've gone and done now, don't you, Brendan?' He sounded regretful, almost sad.

'*What?*' Brendan barked at him.

'You've gone and upset your brother.'

It was only the presence of Pete Mac's mother-in-law, his wife, and the grieving members of the Shea family that saved him from getting a good kicking and an even more serious head wound than he already had.

*       *       *

'Are you sure he's in there, Maury?'

'Sammy, feller, I followed him here from Shea's funeral do meself. I sat outside the place in a cab, and watched as he came running out of that pub like he had a pack of hounds up his arse. Then his big brother Brendan started off after him. But then he gave up—just stopped chasing him, like he couldn't be bothered any more. But he did shout up the street after him. Hollered out that he could fuck off and get on with it. Then young Lukey boy disappeared round the corner and slipped into a phone box, made a call, waited a bit, then got picked up by a car—one of their firm's I suppose—and I said the immortal lines to my driver, Follow that cab. The driver didn't even crack a smile, the miserable bastard. He just gave me a lecture about how minicabs are killing his trade. Like I give a fuck now our business is finished.'

Sammy Kessler slid his gaze in the direction of the club doorway. 'But you're sure he's in there?' He was sounding nervous. 'I don't want to go inside if he's not. That'd just be wasting our time.'

Maurice did his best to hide his smile. 'Sammy, I told you, Mr Luke O'Donnell esquire arrived here in Dean Street precisely twenty minutes ago, when I phoned you from that phone box right there on the corner of Old Compton Street. And he has not left the premises since. Okay?'

328

Sammy nodded, breathing heavily and shifting about like a boxer waiting for the bell to tell him to come out fighting.

'So, do you want me to come in with you then, feller?'

Another nod.

'Thought you might.' Maurice smirked with amusement, but he didn't really get it, why some fellers would rather face a grizzly bear than enter a room full of nice peaceable men all having a quiet drink and a bit

of a dance, in happy, friendly preparation for having a bit of something else later on.

Sammy was on the defensive. 'What d'you mean, you thought I might?'

'Nothing. Don't be so touchy. Come on, feller, welcome to the Lagoon Club.'

'Thanks Maurice, I couldn't think of a nicer way to spend the evening.'

\*　　　\*　　　\*

Sammy edged his way around the dimly lit room until he was standing just a few feet away from Luke.

Luke was by himself, staring at the dancers, self-consciously tapping his toe to a booming recording of Johnny Kidd and the Pirates blasting out 'Shaking All Over'.

Sammy eased up right behind him and hissed in his ear, *'Oi, you, O'Donnell.'*

Luke jumped as if he'd just been plugged into the mains.

Breathing like a long-distance runner with a bad case of asthma, Luke turned slowly to face his tormentor. He didn't find it easy to swallow, but knew he had to if he was going to spit out the single word that would probably be all he could manage. 'Yeah?'

'I just wanted to catch up with you, that's all, Luke. Let you know that I'm gonna have you. All of you. I'm gonna ruin your lives. Just like your lot ruined mine, when you murdered Catherine. And I'm gonna have you for killing Danny's Rachel. And their babies. Then I'm gonna ruin your brother's life. And your brother-in-law's life. Your mother's life, and your father's, and your big sister—'

'All right, Sam.' Maurice tutted at him with about as much passion as someone who'd made a mildly bad choice from his sock drawer.

'Fuck off, Maury.' Sammy was shouting now, his eyes wide and shining with anger, oblivious of being in the club and of all the men who had turned to watch as he stabbed his finger into Luke's terrified face—the men who were wondering if the strangers were about to raid the place, and whether they'd be wise to make themselves scarce.

'And I'm gonna start by telling your old man your dirty little secret. Tell him that his big brave son's nothing more than a shirt-lifting nonce.'

Luke drew back his fist, but Sammy grabbed his wrist before he could unleash the punch. 'I don't think so, do you, nancy boy?'

Tears began to brim in Luke's eyes. 'Please, don't. Please.'

'You stinking coward.' Sammy shook his head in disgust and let go of him. 'What you gonna do to stop me? Get down on your knees and beg?'

Luke did the only thing he could think of. He

shoved Sammy away from him as hard as he could, and fled into the crowd of gawking onlookers, disappearing, unseen by him or Maurice, through an open door at the far end of the room. The second time he'd run away from the truth in one night.

Sammy looked slowly around him, sneering at every gaze he met. 'And what d'you lot think you're fucking looking at?'

'Don't know, sweet lips,' said a flamboyantly dressed, elderly man sitting in the corner by the stairs with a pale pink poodle on his lap. 'Hasn't got a label on it.'

Even Maurice winced as Sammy barged over and smashed his fist into the old man's nose—shooting up the stairs before anyone could stop him.

'Well, dearie me,' said Maurice, with a flash of his eyebrows, but then made sure he took the stairs two at a time, hightailing it after his cousin, before anyone had the chance to start anything.

The more perverse part of Maurice was tempted to stay behind, to charm his way out of being associated with Sammy and Luke, and maybe make a proper night of it, but with the mood Sammy was in, he thought there might be a bit more action on the cards elsewhere, and he didn't want to miss out on the fun.

But, as he stepped out onto the pavement, Maurice saw that Sammy was far from up for it. He was leaning against the wall, his head back and his eyes closed.

'You all right there, feller?'

'I couldn't help myself down there, Maury. Hitting that old bloke. The way he looked at me

331

made me feel sick.'

Maurice thought for a moment. 'Hang on, Sammy, lad,' he said, holding up a finger to his cousin. 'How about if you wait here, and I go down and straighten it out for you? Make it all right.'

'Would you?'

'I'll be two secs.'

Sammy lit himself a cigarette, and Maurice sprinted back down the stairs into the club.

A group of men were fussing around the man with the poodle, dabbing at his nose with wet handkerchiefs, and pressing refills on him for his Gin and It.

Maurice had a quick shufti round. No sign of Luke.

'Let me through,' said Maurice firmly.

A hefty man in his thirties—more than a match for Maurice—stepped forward. 'Why?'

'I wanted to have a private word, to apologise for my friend. Explain why he was so nasty to that poor old bloke.'

The man with the poodle spoke, gesturing with a jaded flap of his hand. 'It's okay, let him through.'

Maurice squatted down in front of him, and patted the little pink poodle gently on the head. 'Nice dog,' he said, and then sighed dramatically. 'Look, feller, sorry about that. You just got yourself in the middle of a lovers' tiff that's all.' He held out his hands, throwing himself on the mercy of the man's understanding. 'He is so jealous.'

Then he leaned right up close to the man and whispered. 'If you even think about sending one of these goons up after us, I'll wait for you, and rip this fucking mutt's head right off it's scrawny neck and shove it up your arse. Then I'll kick you so hard in the crutch that your dick'll be sticking out of that filthy old gob of yours. Okay, feller?'

The man's chest heaved in a weary sigh as he dabbed at his still bloody nose. 'I've heard it all, and suffered it all before, sweetheart. So I'm not going to change the habit of a lifetime, and start worrying about nasty boys, who think they've got to duff me up to prove what fine strong men they are, now am I? And I certainly don't want to get any of my dear friends here in trouble with Lily Law. We have enough of that just trying to walk along the street minding our own business.'

Maurice almost smiled in admiration. He had to hand it to the old poof; he certainly had balls.

\*     \*     \*

Back upstairs on the pavement, Sammy was drawing heavily on his cigarette, and glaring at passers-by, daring them to say just one word to him.

'All done,' said Maurice. 'I told the old feller you was sorry and dropped him a score for his trouble.'

'Thanks, Maury, I appreciate it.'

'It was a pleasure, Sam. Anyway, I see it as my job. Spreading joy and happiness. In fact, let's spread a bit more, let's phone Lukey's old man for him.'

\*     \*     \*

The barman at the Star and Compass gasped in disbelief. 'If you think I'm passing on *that* message, after the amount of booze that's been swallowed in here since they came in this afternoon . . . No, what am I saying? I haven't even *heard* any message. I haven't even had this phone call.' It was hardly news about Luke O'Donnell being the other way, but saying so to his old man? What was this bloke on the phone, out of his bloody mind?

'Wait, please, don't cut me off, feller. Just get Gabriel O'Donnell to the phone and there's a fifty in it for you.'

A *fifty?* That got his interest. This bloke was serious. 'Make it a ton.'

'All right, a ton.'

The barman couldn't believe his luck. A hundred sovs, just for answering the phone? 'I'll get him right away.'

'Hang on, what's your name. So's I know I'm giving the money to the right bloke.'

'Lawrence.'

'Lawrence. All right, Lawrence. The reward's as good as yours, feller.'

\*       \*       \*

The thought of the hundred pounds had imbued Lawrence with a reckless courage, and he found himself persuading Gabriel O'Donnell that the caller had stressed how it was a private matter that no one but Mr O'Donnell could deal with.

Gabriel's immediate thought was that it was something to do with Rosie, and he was behind the bar with the phone in his hand, demanding to know who was speaking, before Lawrence had even finished.

'It doesn't matter who I am, O'Donnell. Just think of me as a friend.'

Gabriel cupped his hand over his other ear to

334

block out the noise of the drunken mourners singing their sorrowful ballads from the old country. 'Kessler, I know that's you. What do you want, you Northern ponce.'

'Sorry, O'Donnell. Never heard of no Kessler. Northern or otherwise.'

Maurice felt a bit miffed; he'd thought he sounded just like one of the soft, Southern nancy boys from the Lagoon Club, thought he'd done a really clever accent. 'My name's Oliver, if you must know, but my friends call me Olive. And that's what I'm calling you about. Friendship. You see, your lovely boy Luke, he's a friend of mine. A really special sort of a friend.'

When Gabriel had stopped yelling obscenities at him, Maurice carried on in an admiring lisp, 'You're very butch aren't you, Mr O'Donnell. Oh, by the way—no, wait, hang on, don't go, Mr O'Donnell. One of the barmen there, Lawrence, that's his name. He's one and all. As a matter of fact he was the first one to give your Luke a seeing to. Make sure you look after him, won't you, Mr O'Donnell, because you do know it's illegal, don't you? And I'd hate to think he could blackmail your son. I mean, it'd be terrible if the law was to find out his dirty little secret, wouldn't it? And if it got in all them naughty Sunday papers . . . That'd be horrible, wouldn't it?'

Maurice was still speaking, but Gabriel wasn't listening. He had dropped the phone and was moving slowly towards Lawrence—who was pulling yet another pint of Guinness as he daydreamed about the motor he was going to buy himself with his hundred notes.

Lawrence's body was found two months later by a gang of kids. They'd been experimenting with their first packet of Player's Weights, in the privacy of a derelict house on the Barking Road, and had been unfortunate enough to investigate where the disgusting stench was coming from—anything rather than having to persevere with the fags, which had been making them feel seriously unwell.

The association between their queasiness from the taste of the cigarettes and their first sight of a dead body—and a badly decomposed one at that—had been enough to make lifelong nonsmokers of them all.

The body itself was never identified, probably because Lawrence's wife never reported him missing. It suited her too well, him being out of the picture. She'd always fancied being a landlady of her own pub, having her name up over the door. And the owner of the Star and Compass wasn't *that* bad looking. Not really. And, as for the landlord— at his age, he was delighted, not to say surprised, to have a woman back in his life. Any woman.

It was just a shame he'd lost such a good barman.

## CHAPTER TWENTY-THREE

When Luke finally got home, it was nearly half past four in the morning, and he was shattered. He had hidden away for hours, like a frightened, cowering animal, in a cubicle in the Lagoon Club lavatories, waiting until the music had died down, and he'd heard the bar staff clearing away for the night. He had spent the next hour or so wandering around the streets of Soho, eventually going to sit in a twenty-four hour greasy spoon, where he nursed cup after cup of dark orange tea.

The thought of going home any earlier and having to face people had been too much for him to bear—especially if Sammy Kessler had done what he'd threatened, and had actually called his father.

It was just impossible to think about.

It would be easier in the morning, when he'd had a rest, time to pull himself together.

Or perhaps it would make more sense to pack a bag right now and leave for good.

Unfortunately for Luke, he didn't have the luxury of making that choice; as he let himself in through the front door, he heard his father yelling at him from the basement.

Luke stood in the hall, his eyes closed, accepting the inevitability of what was going to happen to him. But dreading every moment of what he was about to face as he made his way down to the kitchen.

He stopped halfway down the stairs, and took in the scene below him. His father—sitting there in just his vest and trousers, lids half-lowered, hair falling over his forehead—had obviously carried on drinking long after the funeral had finished.

'Get down here,' he snarled, banging his glass on the table.

Luke moved slowly down towards his fate. 'Where's Mum and Brendan?'

'In bed. So don't think they can protect you.'

'What from? More of your bullying? Your fists?'

'I said, get down here.'

Luke did as he was told, too scared of his father not to, but also because this was it: this was when he would say the things he'd never dared say before. Things he had to say before he lost his courage and started despising himself even more than he did now.

Gabriel rose unsteadily to his feet and took a step towards him. 'Why couldn't you just keep it a secret?'

'What, like you keep your whore a secret? Not much of a secret when everyone knows, is it Dad?'

'So it was you who told your mother about Rosie. I knew it was, you miserable, snivelling little shit.'

'No. It wasn't me. I'd never hurt Mum like that. Don't you understand? I'm not like you.'

'No, you're not like me, more's the pity. You're a vile, stinking pervert.'

Gabriel's hand lashed out.

Luke flinched, thinking his father was going to strike him, but he didn't. Instead, he seized Luke by the collar, dragging his son towards him, making him wince with pain, his body still sore from the beating he'd had from Daniel.

'Why couldn't you be a man?' Gabriel was shaking him.

'What, and follow your example? No thanks, Dad. I don't want to be a bully. Or a drunk. Or a womaniser.'

'Shut your mouth, you . . . you abomination.'

'Abomination am I? Been listening to that old hypocrite Father Shaunessy again, have you, Dad? That beast'll tell you anything so long as you keep

338

giving him money.'

Gabriel raised his hand, but Luke stood his ground, refusing to lower his gaze.

'Do you know what, Dad? Hard as it is, this thing about me that I'm gonna have to somehow come to terms with—and all the lies I've had to tell; the fear of being caught out; or being put away by some little creep of a copper with a grudge—I'm glad I'm different. And shall I tell you why? If I hadn't realised how much you despised what I am, I'd have hero-worshipped you. And then I'd have turned out like you: a self-obsessed animal. Just like you're making Brendan into. Believe me, you disgust me far more than I could ever *begin* disgusting you.'

That was it, it was too much for Gabriel; he clenched his fist and laid into his child.

As he kicked and beat his son, tears poured down Gabriel's face. 'I have to do this. Do you understand me, boy? It's for your own good.'

\*       \*       \*

When Gabriel had finished with him, Luke was lying unconscious and bloody on the kitchen floor.

Gabriel gave him a final departing kick, and then hauled himself up the stairs, bellowing at the top of his voice: 'Get that piece of shit away from me, I can't stand the sight of him.'

Eileen and Brendan were down in the kitchen before Gabriel had slammed the street door behind him.

\*       \*       \*

339

'Mum, please don't make me say it again. I don't need to go to the hospital. And I definitely don't want Dr Stonely anywhere near me.'

'But you were unconscious.' She turned to Brendan who was sitting next to her. 'Tell him.'

'Luke, why don't you let me take you to casualty?' Brendan didn't sound very convinced about what he was suggesting. 'You can say you got jumped in the street.'

Luke shook his head, and wished he hadn't. It hurt. A lot. 'Please, Mum, don't worry. I'll be fine.'

'Luke, I want you to see someone.'

'Okay. Tell you what, I'll see the law. He's gone too far this time. I'm gonna have him over this. I'm gonna drop him right in it.'

Eileen couldn't look at him, didn't know what to say, but Brendan did. 'Don't talk stupid, Luke.'

'Stupid? Is that what you think I'm being?' He put his hand to his lip that had split open and had started bleeding again. 'Give us that flannel, Mum.'

Eileen handed it to him. 'Don't you two start your arguing as well, don't you think I've got enough to worry about?'

'And why do you think you've got so much aggravation, eh, Mum? It's him. And I can't bear to see the way you all put up with it. The covering up for him. The way nobody ever dares—'

'Luke,' Brendan was on his feet, his anger about to tip over. 'Like Mum said, don't start.'

'Why not? Why not tell some truths for once about the great Gabriel O'Donnell? Start letting everyone know what—'

'Don't listen to him, Mum, he's not thinking right.'

'Me not thinking right? I've never been clearer.'

340

He turned to his mother. 'Why do you put up with him?'

'He's my husband.'

Brendan grabbed his brother by the arm and dragged him to his feet. 'Luke, you're knackered, mate. Let's get you up to bed, eh? Sleep it off. Stephen's funeral's upset us all. And we're—'

'Let go of me, Brendan.' Luke shook him off. 'You're getting as bad as him.'

'He's our father.'

'Her husband. Our father. What a wonderful man! And I'm meant to be proud of that fact, am I? When he brags about what he does just like it's any other business. And how he's so kind and generous to everyone.' Luke threw back his head. 'We all *know* it's just a load of bollocks.'

'Luke!' Eileen crossed herself. 'Will you mind your language?'

He took hold of his mother by the shoulders. 'A bit of swearing, is that what really worries you, Mum? Not the violence, and the fear, and the bullying? Look at you, you're terrified of him. Terrified. Just like all the little boys, who're too scared of that other stinking hypocrite, Father Shaunessy. Too petrified to tell people what he does to them. How they put up with all his crap because they're so scared of him. Just the same as you with Dad. And just like you haven't said anything over all these years, when you've known all along that your husband's had another woman, and that—'

Even as the words came spilling out, Luke was regretting them. And he was almost glad when his mother whacked him round the face with the back of her open hand. But he still couldn't stop himself

341

from saying all the things he had bottled up for so long.

'Where d'you think he is now, eh? Who's bed has he run off to?'

Another slap. 'I said, *he's your father!*'

'Oh, yeah, and I'm so happy about that. So glad to be the son of a man who as good as killed his own daughter.'

Eileen recoiled as if Luke had slapped her back. 'What did you say?'

'You'd better sit down again, Mum, there's a lot more you need to know.'

Brendan stepped between them, and closed his hands round his brother's face, forcing him to look into his eyes. 'No, Luke. No. Don't do this. Please.'

'It's too late, Brendan. I told you, I've had enough.'


## CHAPTER TWENTY-FOUR

When Gabriel eventually came home on Monday morning—three days after knocking his own child to the floor and kicking him senseless—Eileen calmly set a place for her husband at the breakfast table, and told her sons to make themselves scarce as she needed to speak to their father.

Gabriel was sitting with his chin propped on his fists, unshaven, stinking like a rancid brewery, and still, very obviously, drunk. Wherever he'd been on his bender, it was clear that he hadn't bothered taking along clean clothes or a razor.

Luke, his face puffed and bruised, and his eyes peering out of yellow and purple slits, was happy to leave; he couldn't stomach the idea of spending any more time with the arsehole of a man who called himself his father, and had only agreed to stay at the house at all over the past few days because his mother had been so mad with grief. But she'd calmed down now, and he was satisfied that he'd done his job: he'd told her the truth. At last.

Brendan wasn't so sure about leaving them alone. According to what Anthony had told him, Gabriel had lost his temper during Stephen's wake at the Star and Compass, and, for some unknown reason, had taken it out on the barman. He had dragged him out from behind the counter, punching, kicking and threatening him, right there, in front of everyone, not caring who saw or heard— miles away from their own manor.

Then, when he'd got the bloke outside, Gabriel had beaten him unconscious. And, as if that wasn't enough, Gabriel had bundled the bloke into the boot of his car, and had driven off with him.

And all that before going home and starting on Luke.

Brendan really did need to find out what had happened. And why. And if his father had made any other stupid mistakes. Stupid mistakes got you in trouble with the law. And he definitely didn't want the old man ballsing things up for him. Not now. Not when he'd got Kevin and Barry ready and primed to fuck over Sammy Kessler for his porn business. The business that was going to fund their move into big-time supplying.

But Eileen wouldn't hear of Brendan staying, and she led him over to the stairs as if he were a little boy. 'Go on, son. Leave us. I'll be just fine. I'm not a fool, I can see he's drunk. But there are things I have to discuss with him. You can ask him all the questions you want, *after* I've had a chance to talk to him.'

Brendan looked at his watch. 'All right. I've got one or two things to do. But me and Luke'll be back at dinner time, around twelve, to make sure everything's all right. Okay?' He turned to his brother. '*Won't* we, Luke?'

'If you say so.'

'And, Mum, don't go winding him up, will you?'

*     *     *

Eileen pushed a cup of weak tea liberally laced with whiskey towards her husband. She had no intention of helping him to pull himself together. For once, she didn't want him sober. So, as soon as he had finished drinking that, she gave him another one, this time not even bothering with the pretence of including any tea.

She sat and watched him as his eyelids began to flutter, knowing what she was going to do, knowing what she had to do.

Eileen looked at the clock. Nearly half past ten. The boys would be back by noon. Maybe earlier.

She shook him roughly.

Gabriel came to, groaning pathetically. He staggered to his feet; his bladder bursting.

'I want that glass filled when I get back from the lavatory,' he said, stumbling across the room.

'You're very flushed, Gabriel,' she said gently. 'You really don't look well. I'll get you your pills.'

'I don't need that crap,' he snarled from the top of the stairs without even bothering to turn around to look at her.

344

'Gabe, you've not taken them since we buried Stephen. You don't want the next funeral to be yours do you?'

*     *     *

When he returned from the lavatory, Gabriel's flies were still open, and his shirt was hanging outside of his trousers. He looked a mess.

Grudgingly he took the pills from his wife and swallowed them, downing them with the half-tumbler of Jameson's she'd set in front of him.

'Get me a refill.'

'Are you sure you really want one, Gabe?'

He lifted his head and glowered at her. His eyes were out of focus and sweat was trickling down his face. 'I'm your husband, woman. The man of this house. Now fetch me another fucking drink before you feel the back of my hand.'

Eileen had to steady herself as she got up to fetch the bottle from the dresser. She had never feared him physically before. Not once. Not even over at the flapping. She'd just put that down to the drink.

But then he'd never beaten his own child into unconsciousness before either.

During the past few days she'd learned a lot of things she hadn't known before about the man she'd been married to since she was barely sixteen years of age.

'The drink, woman. Now.' His words were sliding into one another in a drawl of increasing incoherence, and he was blinking as if the light were hurting his eyes. 'I said. Woman. Drink.'

'I'm fetching it.' Eileen had her back to him, as

345

she stirred the liquid around the glass with her finger, which she wiped on her skirt.

'Why? Why did he have to turn out like that?' he wailed as Eileen handed him the glass, as if his lack of understanding had lent him momentary lucidity. 'Look at the life he has. Here. Beautiful home. Money in his pocket. You're blessed. All you. I've given everything. All you. This what happens. How yer pay me back. Pathetic little queer.'

He gulped greedily at the drink, then stopped and spat it out over the table. 'Wass wrong? Tastes like muck.'

'That'll be your breath. You stink like a hog.'

His head jerked up, he couldn't believe he'd heard her right. 'What did you . . .'

'Nothing. Nothing important.' She took the glass off him. 'Here, I'll get you another.'

Gabriel held the palm of his hand to his head. He didn't feel right.

She gave him the glass, folding his fingers around it. 'And as for me being blessed, I suppose some would say that I am. But me, I think of myself more like a bird in a cage. Sure, I love that I have my food and water and a nice clean place to live, but do I want my babies to live in the cage with me? No. Freedom, that's what I want for them. It might be too late for Brendan, but Luke might still have a chance.'

'Freedom?' Gabriel swallowed another mouthful of his drink then paused to look at the glass. Perhaps it didn't taste too bad. He knocked back the rest of it.

'Yes, Gabriel, freedom. From you.'

'Eileen, I feel—'

'Tired?'

He tried to shake his head, but it was too heavy.

'Well, you should be after all the stuff you've got inside you.'

She sat down, putting a small brown bottle on the table in front of him. 'Brendan got me these tablets. Well, more like capsules I'd suppose you'd call them.'

'Ehhh?' Gabriel could barely make sense of what she was saying.

'They're drugs. You know, those things you hate. They were meant to help me sleep. As if I'd ever sleep again. It was our little secret, because we knew you wouldn't approve. You swallowed three of them, when I told you I was giving you your blood pressure medicine. And now I've been mixing more of the insides of the pretty little things into your drinks. Sure, don't they say that mixing your drinks is bad for you?' She laughed. 'Another secret. So many in one house. And I put up with all of them. And with your lies, your drinking, and your whores. All our married life. But this, I can't take this. I won't. Not any more.'

'I don't . . .' His mouth had stopped working, and his head was lolling forward.

'You know, when I was a girl I used to ask my mother to tell me stories about the old days, but she wouldn't. She said they'd make me too sad. That they were stories of even worse poverty than we were living in. Stories about families fighting one another for nothing more than a few crumbs from the rich men's tables. And stories of things that went on behind the closed doors of so-called decent people. Stories that hid secrets behind lies. You know, I really thought I was going to have a better life living here with you. My God, I was a

347

fool.'

He managed to raise his head and slur a few barely intelligible words: 'How 'bout your lies, Eilee . . .'

Then his head flopped forward onto the table and he began to snore through his wide-open mouth.

With quiet dignity, Eileen rose to her feet, picked up the cushion she had been sitting on—the one she had fetched especially from the front parlour—lifted his head by the hair, and slipped the thing onto the table. Then she pushed his face into the cushion, and held him down—in his drunken, drugged, disgusting stupor—until she was sure he was dead.

As she held him there, she was crying, but it wasn't for Gabriel O'Donnell that she wept, or even for what she was doing, it was for her children, and for Sophie's daughter-in-law, and for her unborn babies.

*      *      *

Eileen rinsed out Gabriel's glass under the tap, poured herself a measure of whiskey into it, and sat herself down by the dresser to make the first of the telephone calls.

'Is that Rosie Palmer,' Eileen asked, surprised at her own composure.

'Who is this?'

'I can hear you're a Dublin girl from your accent.'

'I said, who this is?'

'In good time. There's a question I want to ask *you* first. How could you let him send your child

348

away from you? How could you do that? You're that child's mother. And you act as if she's of no more value to you than a dog that's being sent to the kennels.'

'I don't have to listen to this, I—'

'I thought you wanted to know who I am.'

There was a silence at the other end.

'Well, I'll tell you, shall I? I'm Eileen, Gabriel O'Donnell's widow.'

She heard a gasp.

'That's right, you heard me, his widow. I've just murdered the evil bastard. Killed him stone-cold dead. Just like he as good as killed Catherine, may God rest her. And all those other poor souls. I stopped him. Before he could kill anyone else. I really think I've done everyone a favour, don't you—Rosie Palmer?'

As she put down the phone all Eileen could hear was a sound like a cornered creature screaming in pain as it was being ripped apart by dogs.

She took a moment to think and to sip at her drink, and then she made the other calls.

\*　　　\*　　　\*

Satisfied that she had accomplished all she could at home, Eileen put on her coat and left the house, fixing a note with a drawing pin to the front door, and then closing it securely behind her.

\*　　　\*　　　\*

Eileen knelt down and crossed herself, taking in the familiar, slightly damp fug of the confessional.

The grill went back and she said, 'I appreciate

349

you coming here for me, Father Shaunessy.'

Then she crossed herself again. 'Bless me, Father, for I have sinned. It is one week since my last confession, and nearly twenty-five years since I last told the truth. And now I've killed my husband.'

She laughed, a blank humourless sound. 'Don't bother to absolve me from that last one, Father. That wasn't a sin, that was a duty. But now, let's get on shall we? We don't have much time.'

*     *     *

Eileen stepped out of the confession box, and looked the priest levelly in the eye. She could see he was stunned. Well, he was about to be totally and completely bloody horrified.

'And while we're at it, Father—you know, telling the truth and all that—maybe it might do your own soul a bit of good if you confessed to a thing or two.'

Father Shaunessy was as white as a freshly laundered altar cloth. 'Whatever's got into you woman?'

'What's got into me *Father* Shaunessy, is that I'm sick to my stomach with lies. I'm up to here with hypocrisy, and God forgive me, I think I'm even sick of life itself. I've seen and heard too much. But I know what really sickens me most of all. It's you. For what you did to those little boys.' She held up her hand. 'Don't even try and deny it. My son told me everything. Do you know, the poor boy's even wondered if what you did to him had anything to do with the way he's turned out. God love him.'

'I don't know what you think you're doing—'

350

Eileen ignored him and just kept on talking. 'I thought very carefully about whether I should tell the police about you. But when I thought it through, I realised that it wasn't the answer, that it wouldn't do any good. They'd call me, or rather the children, liars—those who'd be brave enough to come forward, that is; those who wouldn't feel too ashamed to speak about the wicked things you'd done to them. The things you'd forced them to do. And it would all be covered up. And they'd send you off to some other parish, where you'd just get up to your filth there instead. Well, I'm warning you, Father, if you do it again—ever, to any child— I'll find a way to kill you too. You have my solemn word on that, Father Shaunessy. My solemn word. So, it's up to you. You decide what happens. And, as long as you behave, you're safe. For now. But put a foot wrong and I swear, you'll be sorry.'

'Eileen, I won't have you speaking to me like this.'

'Won't you now? Is that so? Do you know, Father, I think there should be an eleventh commandment—thou shall not bully. I mean, just think what the world would be like if there was such a thing. Think how much better it would be. All the control and the power the likes of you have over fearful people and children weaker than yourself—it would just disappear.' She snapped her fingers. 'Whooof! Up like a puff of smoke. Now wouldn't that be a more Christian sort of a world?'

'I think you've lost your reason, woman.'

'No, Father, I've just found it.' She pointed to the stained-glass window high above the altar. 'Take a look at that beautiful picture up there. What does it say to us? The meek shall inherit the

351

earth. And isn't that what we're supposed to believe? Words that'll keep us down. Under control. But we know, don't we, deep down, that it's all rubbish. And sure, it's not much of a place to inherit anyway, now is it? Meek or otherwise. I mean, honestly, Father, who'd want to inherit a shithole like this?'

'Eileen! Remember where you are.'

He reached out to take hold of her arm, but she stepped away from him, putting a row of pews between them.

'Don't you dare touch me.'

He held up his hands. 'All right. Keep calm. You can't be feeling well, Eileen, that's what it is. You're unwell. Now, why don't you sit yourself down? I'll go and tell the housekeeper to make us both a nice cup of tea, and we can have a little chat.'

'Don't waste your time thinking about slipping away to call the police, Father.' She held her arms wide. 'There's no point. Sure haven't I already done it myself? I told them they could find me here at half past twelve. Made sure I gave myself just enough time to get my last few jobs done. Like my confession and like telling you a thing or two.'

'Mum?'

It was Luke calling to her.

She turned around to see both her sons, hurtling down the aisle towards her and Father Shaunessy.

'Let me talk to her, Luke,' puffed Brendan. 'Before you say anything to anyone, Mum, don't worry. We can sort this out. It's gonna be all right. Nobody needs know.'

'What, like nobody needed to know about Catherine seeing Sammy Kessler? Or about how she died? Or about Luke and the way he is—God

352

forgive him. Or about your father and his whore. And your little half-sister, Ellie?'

Brendan's face contorted like a wax mask held in front of a fire.

'Don't look at me like that, son. I know you knew everything all along, and that you thought I was a fool. And you were probably right. But I have to believe that although I might be a foolish person, I'm not a bad one. I have to believe that I'm better than he was. That there's a chance for children to be better than their fathers. If they really want to be.'

'Thank God!' shouted Father Shaunessy, as two men in police uniform and two men in plain clothes strode into the church.

The uniformed men were fiddling awkwardly with their helmets, knowing they had to wear them when they were on official business, but they were in church. So, what were they supposed to do?

The plain-clothes policemen just looked generally embarrassed by the whole situation.

'Sorry, Mr O'Donnell, sir,' said one of them, waving his identification at Brendan. 'We had a phone call. But I'm sure there's been some sort of a mistake.'

'No, there's no mistake.' Eileen turned to the altar again and crossed herself before turning back to the policemen. 'It's all true. I've killed my husband, and I'm giving myself up.'

All four policemen looked as confused and astonished as if she'd just started speaking in tongues.

The officer who'd spoken was the first to pull himself together. 'I'm sure . . .' he began. But his words petered out. He genuinely had no idea what

353

to say next.

Eileen smiled at him. 'Please, let me say a few words to my boys?'

The police officers stepped away, relieved for even a momentary respite.

Eileen nodded her thanks and then touched her youngest son on the cheek. 'Luke, I want you to look after Patricia and little Caty for me. And Scrap, he'll be needing his walk when you get home. Will you do that?'

Luke could barely speak. 'Course, I will, Mum.'

'And keep an eye on the father here as well. You know why. And I want you to promise me you'll take care of yourself.'

This time Luke's tears got the better of him. He could do no more than nod. She took his face in her hands, reached up and kissed him gently on the forehead.

Brendan grabbed his mother's hand away from his brother. 'How about me?'

Eileen sighed long and loudly, and looked her other son steadily in the eye. 'Why would I worry about you, Brendan? You can look after yourself. Just like your father.'

'But he's—'

'Dead? That's right. He is. And I killed him. So maybe he wasn't such a big tough man after all. And maybe there's a lesson for you.'

She lifted her chin, turned, and held out her hands to the policemen.

'I'm ready now,' she said.